J.S. Law started in the Royal Navy as an apprentice engineer and worked his way up through the ranks. He has worked on helicopters, ships and, towards the end of his naval career, submarines. He is a passionate advocate for education and now works providing nuclear training and education to the defence and civil sectors. James lives in Hampshire with his partner and his two children. *Tenacity* is his debut novel and the first in the Lieutenant Danielle Lewis series.

Follow J.S. Law on Twitter @JS

Praise for *Tenacity*:

'J.S. Law's taut crime novel **oozes authenticity**. I read this in a day and can't wait for the next in what will undoubtedly be an **explosive** series' Clare Mackintosh

'An **impressive debut**. . . Law knows what he's writing about, and it shows. The sexist antagonism of the men coupled with the cramped conditions make for **gripping**, entertaining reading' *The Times*

'J.S. Law is a **powerful new voice**, and his heroine Dan Lewis lives up to the title, *Tenacity*. She is fearless and doesn't quit in the faces of all odds. The murky world of submarines and murder make *Tenacity* **addictively readable**, and memories of it linger like dreams' Patricia Cornwell

'If Law manages to hold his course into nuclear noir, this series could go for as long as the **atom-powered** *Tenacity*' *The Sun*

'Tense, claustrophobic, and **totally absorbing**, this book should be on every thriller reader's radar – or should that be sonar? Absolutely **superb**' Matt Hilton

'A **gripping** read. . . I don't remember being this captivated by a debut novel since Lee Child published *Killing Floor*. . . A stand out read' www.grabthisbook.net

TENACITY

J.S. LAW

headline

First published in 2015 by
HEADLINE PUBLISHING GROUP

First published in paperback in 2016 by
HEADLINE PUBLISHING GROUP

1

Cataloguing in Publication Data is available from the British Library

ISBN 978 1 4722 2791 1

Typeset in Meridien by Palimpsest Book Production Ltd, Falkirk, Stirlingshire

Printed and bound in Great Britain by Clays Ltd, St Ives plc

MIX
Paper from
responsible sources
FSC® C104740

Headline's policy is to use papers that are natural, renewable and recyclable
products and made from wood grown in well-managed forests and other
controlled sources. The logging and manufacturing processes are expected to
conform to the environmental regulations of the country of origin.

HEADLINE PUBLISHING GROUP
An Hachette UK Company
Carmelite House
50 Victoria Embankment
London EC4Y 0DZ

www.headline.co.uk
www.hachette.co.uk

To my family and friends who supported me on this journey – thank you.

Acknowledgements

Thanks to Elizabeth, Sammy and Elaine for your patience and support.

Thanks to my mum, dad, Vicky, Alan and Carol, who I know are always on my side.

Thanks to my friends Steph B, Steph R, Martin & Mary, Sara and Matt for reading and critiquing, in the nicest possible way, until *Tenacity* was ship shape, and to Matt Seldon for all his creative endeavours.

To Jonny Geller and Kirsten Foster at Curtis Brown, to Vicki Mellor, Sara Adams, Darcy Nicholson, Tom Noble, Sarah Bance, Frankie Edwards, Yeti Lambregts and Sarah Badhan at Headline, I thank you all for your help and support, it is very much appreciated.

And finally. . .

To all my brothers and sisters in the Armed Forces who are deployed away from their loved ones around the globe – be safe, look out for each other, and remember, never let the truth get in the way of a good story!

HMS *Tenacity*

1. FWD ESCAPE PLATFORM
2. FWD BUNKSPACE
3. TORPEDO RAM SPACE
4. CONTROL ROOM
5. 2-DECK (SEE DIAGRAM)
6. BOMBSHOP (WEAPONS STOWAGE)
7. SHIPS OFFICE
8. OLD MAN'S CABIN
9. MAIN ACCESS HATCH
10. TUNNEL

11. REACTOR COMPARTMENT
12. MANOEUVRING ROOM + FLAT
13. SWITCHBOARD ROOM
14. DIESEL ROOM
15. AFT ESCAPE PLATFORM
16. FREON FLAT
17. ENGINE ROOM - LOWER LEVEL
18. DOG KENNEL
19. MAIN ENGINES + GEARBOX
20. ENGINE ROOM HATCH

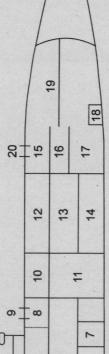

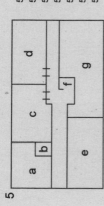

5a. HEADS AND BATHROOMS
5b. ACCESS HATCH - BOMBSHOP
5c. SENIOR RATES MESS
5d. JUNIOR RATES MESS
5e. OTHER COMPARTMENTS
5f. WARDROOM PANTRY
5g. WARDROOM

Image credit © @MattSheldon

Prologue

Tuesday Evening – 2nd November 2010

'How did you know?'

Dan froze and then swallowed as she heard his voice, but she didn't turn around. She placed him as being some way away from her, across the dusty, grey-stone garage floor, next to the door, the only door. She knew that she had some time; this wouldn't be quick.

'Answer me please, Dan,' he said, his voice calm, without any real trace of menace, even though it echoed in the open space.

Dan turned to face him, slowly. The nausea she'd felt on hearing him speak hadn't yet diminished and it needed to be under control when he saw her face.

'So?' he said, his head cocked slightly to the side as he watched her.

Christopher Hamilton's Royal Navy uniform was neat, his shoes polished, and the toecaps bulled to a dark sheen. His white shirt was immaculately pressed and it contrasted perfectly with the black and gold of the Lieutenant epaulettes he wore on each of his shoulders. He was clean-shaven and

1

his hair was cropped short, neatly gelled in place. His eyes didn't bore into her as she might have expected, they weren't reminiscent of a cat watching its prey; they were cool and blue, inquisitive. He looked so calm, was speaking as though he had all the time in the world.

Looking at him and seeing that, seeing the relaxed smile on his face and the way his hands were loosely thrust into his pockets, was, to Dan, the most terrifying thing she'd ever witnessed.

He raised both eyebrows.

'It's a civil enough question, Dan. I just want to know why I've had to come home and find you interfering with my belongings, snooping around in my garage?'

Out of the corner of Dan's eye she could still see the blue-grey skin of Amanda Waller's forearm poking out from beneath a dirty green tarpaulin. The forearm was bent back on itself at a repellent angle, both the ulna and radius clearly snapped and pushing hard against the mottled skin.

Dan had pulled back the tarpaulin, had seen the three women beneath it, their bodies marbled with bruising. The life had long since been drained from them, but the marks gave an insight into the suffering they had endured prior to their violent deaths.

She looked at the door, her eyes involuntarily flicking that way for just a moment.

'Locked,' he said. 'The whole house is locked now. Seems like you just can't be too careful these days; never know who might come calling.'

He reached towards a workbench that ran along the wall next to the door. The tools looked old and dirty, unused in a long time, and they were laid so randomly across the bench that Dan wondered if they'd been arranged that way, as though he might have taken time to try and create the appearance of chaos.

She tensed, watching to see what he would pick up, her eyes scanning and spotting a hammer and a hatchet among the mess.

He smiled, seeming to sense her discomfort as he dragged an old stool towards him.

The sound of the metal legs grating against the bare floor made Dan shiver. It was loud, highlighting how silent all else was around them, how alone Dan was in this house set in the countryside away from disturbances and traffic noise, away from dog walkers and cyclists, away from any realistic chance of help.

She felt cold, frozen, and she knew that feeling this way, feeling frightened, could only lead to defeat; she had to keep going, to find a way to move forward. She looked again at the tarpaulin and felt her stomach lurch for the girls beneath it. The shape of their bodies, dumped in the corner like next winter's firewood, was imprinted on her vision, slipping across her eyes like bright shapes that had been flashed at her in the dark.

'Dan,' he said, easing himself up onto the old metal stool. 'Come on now. I'm being friendly and you aren't.'

'It doesn't matter how I knew, Chris. It only matters now that I do know,' she said, glad the words had come out strong and clear, but struggling to swallow as her throat seemed to stick to itself whenever she tried. 'And I'm not the only one that knows.'

He smiled and shook his head.

'You knowing doesn't matter at all,' he said, and looked at her in such a charming way that Dan was sure he must have practised it.

She could imagine him rehearsing the way he tilted his head and how far he opened his mouth; everything he did now seemed, to her, to be a carefully practised movement, all designed, developed and delivered to hide what it was that propelled him underneath.

'Let's not pretend anyone else knows you're here,' he continued. 'John Granger would be standing at your heel, panting and awaiting his mistress's orders if he even had an inkling of what you're doing.'

Hamilton tilted his head again; a look between friends that said Dan must know he was right.

'And Roger Blackett would hardly send his golden girl into the breach so poorly prepared. I think even he would realise that you versus me is a fairly obvious inequality of arms. Don't you think?'

Dan managed to swallow.

'Come now, Dan, we don't send investigators out alone to scrutinise their colleagues; we don't let them break into their colleagues' homes and search through their colleagues' personal waste. We certainly don't send little girls out on their own to catch the bad men, not with the sheer number of poor young things that have gone missing this past thirty years or so.'

He smiled at her as though they were sharing an inside joke.

'So I know you're freelancing here, and you do too. So, I'll ask again, how did you know?'

He was watching her so closely that Dan was frightened to look away from him, knowing that he could follow her eyes wherever they went, but she needed to know her surroundings, needed to look around and form a plan. She needed a weapon. She would have to fight for her life.

Hamilton was a big man, gristly, not bulky.

Dan knew he spent a great deal of his time compulsively training for triathlons that he rarely did, and disappearing alone onto the moors fell running and camping.

He was physically superior and his manner said he knew it.

Standing in his garage with the sour smell of slowly rotting flesh assaulting her nostrils, Dan realised that she barely recognised this man, the same man that she'd worked with on and off for almost ten years.

'Don't let your mind wander, Dan,' he said, 'just answer my question, because I really and genuinely want to know – you might say that, at some point in the future, my freedom could depend on it.'

'How many did you kill?' Dan asked, using the question as permission to turn away from him, to look in the direction of the tarpaulin and the bodies beneath it, to let her eyes dart around and catalogue everything that was near to her. There was a spade leaning against the wall a few metres to her left. It looked big and heavy and used, albeit some time ago. There were large clumps of dry mud stuck to the surface of the dull metal blade. There was space around her, enough space to swing it, and the only other potential weapon was a pair of hedge shears leaning against the wall only a foot or so closer to her than the spade.

She looked back to him and knew that he'd seen her looking, had read her intent.

'I just want to say now, Dan, that, for the record, I decided several years back not to take you; oh, but how we come to regret these decisions,' he said, chuckling and shaking his head. 'I don't want you to feel bad about that, that I didn't want you; I just thought that you might like to know that you could have lived your life out in safety, from me at least.'

Dan looked at him, unsure of what she could possibly say in response.

'A stunned silence?' Hamilton said. 'Or a stunned gratitude, perhaps? But don't be shy, Dan, tell me how you knew and I'll promise you that you'll be glad you did.'

Dan looked around the garage, then at Hamilton, calm and smiling; she needed time.

'The team at Operation Poacher had suspected it was someone from the armed forces, and probably the navy, for some time,' she said. 'But you know this stuff. It was the pattern of disappearances, the sudden series after long gaps without any.'

'Without any being detected,' he corrected.

'Of course,' said Dan. 'I started to suspect it was someone who had some – but not always complete – knowledge of the investigation; a police officer, crime scene technician, or one of us.'

He nodded, made to ask a question, then seemed to decide against.

Dan waited.

'Why?' he finally blurted the question out, seeming agitated as though he couldn't wait a second longer, as though he might forget what he wanted to know if he didn't ask right away, like a child.

'Changing patterns,' said Dan, taking a small step further away from him to her left. 'I wanted to look at the investigation from a different angle. So, I looked right back over the whole case and I began to map, as best I could, when the various pieces of information were released, and how quickly after that the next event occurred.'

Hamilton frowned at her.

'You not keeping up?' Dan asked, taking another small step away from him and towards the spade.

'Carry on please, Dan,' he said, his eyes narrowed as he focused on her.

'Well, when I looked back it was clear that whenever the Operation Poacher team worked up a victim profile and it became any kind of knowledge within the investigation, the killer would change something, or an event would occur to throw the team off again, to put doubt back in their minds.'

She nodded towards Hamilton, trying to appear as though

it were grudging admiration. 'I'll give you your due; you were good. Some of the subtleties you used to keep them guessing – the spate of young men around Aldershot, the children in Plymouth and later around the Clyde area. You had them believing there were more important cases to look at, that there were other killers operating that they might actually be able to catch.'

He smiled again and nodded appreciatively. 'You made that link. Very good, Danielle, very good indeed.'

'Thank you,' she said, sliding her foot slowly along the floor and taking another step. 'I just started to focus on the investigation, trying to imagine that everything else that could affect or influence the investigation team was done deliberately with that aim in mind.'

'All very interesting, Dan; sounds like the genesis of one of your fascinating papers, which I'm sure would have been widely published, but, in truth, almost impossible to put together. So how did you really know?' He paused and looked at her. 'And be quick now. I'm getting bored and you're easing yourself further away from me all the time, despite knowing you're locked in here with me, which seems a little daft.'

Dan swallowed and stopped her foot from sliding across the floor again.

'I'm telling you,' she said, trying not to let fear creep into her voice and finding it easy to do. 'I started mapping, and yes, I did think it would be a worthwhile paper, to compare the time at which information was released against any incident that then caused that information to be called into question. I specifically looked at the time between the two data points.'

Hamilton was frowning again. He looked upwards as he thought about what she was saying, and Dan took another small step.

'It became clear that there were times when the delay

between information release and some subsequent act that decried it was relatively short, too short. That for the killer to react to what had been released meant that he had to have had the information earlier, and that meant an insider. You were too jumpy.'

Dan tried to make the last comment sound conspiratorial, gently chiding.

He snorted at her last remark and shook his head.

'There were times when you were reacting so quickly that you almost confused the Operation Poacher team by pre-empting what they were going to release.'

Hamilton smiled again and nodded. 'It was a lot of fun.'

'Yeah, I can see that,' said Dan. 'But I'm stunned that I was the first to see it. The last few years you lost your subtlety, got sloppy. You really weren't that smart, but then, me being here proves you're not all that smart.'

He continued to watch her, a long, steady stare. 'You walking out of here would prove that I'm not all that smart,' he said. 'Now keep your feet still.'

Dan registered the first real sounds of stress in his voice, the first cracks that told her she might be unsettling him, and she stepped again despite his order.

'So, everyone else was looking at the bodies we found and trying to decide why you seemed to torture the blondes more than the dark-haired girls.'

He laughed again, but it was different this time, more forced.

'They were wondering whether your mum was blonde, or your sister, or your wife. You know the sort of thing, right? You've been involved in these investigations before; hell, you worked on Operation Poacher twice, hunting for yourself.'

He nodded and snorted again. 'As I say, a lot of fun.'

'You did seem to be having fun,' said Dan, and she took another small step, the shovel and shears now six feet away.

8

'Full of shit, the lot of them,' he began, his eyes leaving her as he looked around the garage. His hands started to fidget as he thought about what she was saying. 'Morons. Always trying to figure out why this and why that, why blondes and why strangulation, why signs of violence pre- and post-mortem. As though knowing that makes any difference at all.'

'Yeah, exactly, all that stuff,' said Dan, hoping desperately to keep him talking. 'Trying to figure out why you do it.'

She pursed her lips and let her eyes flick in the direction of the shovel; he saw her do it, but he didn't approach.

'Do you know why I do it, then?' he asked, smiling, less fidgety, as though he were back on home turf. 'Surely the amazing Girl Wonder has a theory on this – something for one of your lauded papers. Some shit that'd fit on the back page of an equally shitty journal? Do I need to go and clean up at your house? Delete some waffling paragraphs of you dispensing wisdom about why I do these things?'

Dan didn't speak.

'Because I can tell you,' he continued. 'Not that it'll help you very much, but I can tell you why I do it. I can also answer all the little questions like, "why predominantly blondes?" and all that jazz if you want me to.'

Dan shrugged, flexing her fingers to warm them up for a fight that she knew she couldn't win by force alone.

'Educate me,' she said.

'I just like screwing blondes, Dan,' he said, and mimicked her shrug. 'Given a choice between blonde and any other hair colour, I'd stick my cock in a blonde any day of the week. But, I'm just a normal bloke, right? So if there's no blondes, well, I'll fuck a brunette, black hair, ginger, what-ever.'

He stood up, took a step towards her, but just one.

Dan felt her stomach go hollow as she saw him move

towards her. She spaced her feet shoulder width apart, trying to carefully work the soles of her shoes against the dusty floor to ensure they would grip when they needed to.

'Do you know why I choose women?'

Dan shook her head. 'Because you hated your mummy?' she said, watching him, hoping he would look away for just a second to give her an advantage, any advantage.

'Because I'm straight. See, I don't really like screwing men, although any hole's a goal and all that, but women are soft and smooth and weak and small. They're easy to grab, easy to control. You're trusting, honestly, stupidly trusting; your whole gender just cries out "victim", and, well frankly, your whole gender are just disappointingly dumb.'

He was watching Dan carefully now and he seemed to have regained his calm. His hands were firm and he looked ready. 'I think that's your problem, Dan; you think you're smarter than everyone else around you, but you're not.'

'I found you without too much trouble,' she said.

'And then came here by yourself to try and prove it; I think that's one for the prosecution.'

'Chess puzzles,' said Dan, forcing a smile that she hoped he wouldn't like. 'There were some other things that gave you away, but chess puzzles was one of the most hilarious.'

His breathing started to quicken, his hands moving again, flexing and balling, as the agitation visibly built inside him.

'You love to try and talk as though you're some kind of genius, as though you're very, very intelligent and can predict what people will do, as though you're thinking umpteen moves ahead of everyone else, but I watched you with those chess puzzles you try to dazzle us all with, and I know you can't do them; you use a computer programme on your phone to solve them and then pretend you can just see it through natural talent.'

She laughed, a deliberately challenging laugh, as though he might join her in realising how ridiculous she found him.

He was moving more, his face no longer calm, his eyes tracking her.

'That's why I brought in that puzzle from home a few weeks ago, because I knew you wouldn't be able to do it. But what I found really interesting, is that you hadn't even considered that someone might do that to you; you hadn't thought ahead, hadn't calculated what you'd do if someone openly challenged your intellect.'

Dan slid her foot towards the spade, watching him all the time; she was certain that he couldn't attack her until he'd heard what she had to say.

'You just floundered and tried to make excuses before you walked away. Once you were gone, we were all laughing so hard. Not just me, either – all of the other investigators, and especially the admin girls, we were laughing our asses off behind your back.'

'And yet I seemed to be able to outthink you, Dan,' he said, his voice low. 'I seemed to be able to calculate that you'd come here and that you'd be alone, that you'd tell no one else, that you'd save the glory for yourself.' He raised his hand to his ear. 'Still no sirens, Dan, still no help arriving for you.'

She glanced at the spade, letting her eyes linger on it for a few seconds before she looked back at him.

He was watching her, had seen her eyes moving.

'Time,' he said, and moved forward.

His arms seemed to vibrate by his side as he tensed up, as though readying himself for action. The veins on his neck were standing proud and his fingers started to flex again and again as he watched her, the blacks of his eyes seeming to expand like a predator focusing on its chosen prey.

He started to move again, not towards her, but off to the

side, towards the spade. His eyes seemed to have a physicality of their own, as though she could feel them pushing against her, sharp and hard. His mouth was set, but she watched his hands and saw them ball into fists as the rage built up inside him and manifested itself there.

He was closing the distance between them; maybe twelve feet of open space remained.

Dan forced another laugh, bending her knees slightly as she did and readying herself.

He stepped closer again, the spade now equidistant between them.

'You're going to die horribly,' he whispered.

Dan stepped forward. She made a sudden lunge towards the spade, and was sure she saw a slight smile cross his face, as though he had watched her and predicted what she would do. But Dan didn't hesitate. She faked for the spade, turning and lunging for the shears instead. She had them in her hand in a second, light and easy to manoeuvre, and swung them at Hamilton as he was still reaching down to grab the wooden shaft of the heavier spade.

The tip of the blades scraped down past his ear, drawing blood, and Dan made sure not to over reach as she watched him grasp the spade and swing it in one hand, aiming for her head, the fingers of his other hand clasped against his torn and bloodied ear.

Dan, smaller and more agile, ducked below the spade and grasped the shears properly, opening them and driving up towards him as she pressed them shut on impact. The blades bit into him, tearing across the cotton of his white shirt, and penetrating deep into the flesh beneath it.

He dropped the shovel but brought his blood-covered hand from his ear down in a hard arc, landing solidly on Dan's shoulder and sending her to the ground, the force of the blow taking the wind from her.

Hamilton was bigger and much stronger, and even though he was now wounded, Dan knew that the longer this fight went on, the smaller her chances of survival became.

He swung a kick and it landed against her hip, almost lifting her from the ground with its ferocity, the pain excruciating.

She gritted her teeth, fighting to hold onto the shears, even as she saw him ready himself to kick again.

In the instant of him drawing back his foot again, Dan remembered her father speaking to her outside of school as she sat with a bloody knee and a fat lip, sobbing quietly.

The last few children who had watched the altercation had drifted away and she remembered her father's philosophy on life, imparted to her and her sister in fleeting visits between the military operations that so often took him away from them. 'Fights aren't won by the bigger man, Danny. Fights are won by the man willing to escalate the violence the furthest, the fastest. If you're not willing to go the distance, to go further and harder than your opponent will and to do it faster than they're able to, then you've already accepted defeat.'

Dan braced herself for the kick to come and knew that she had to be willing to kill Chris Hamilton if she were to have any chance at all of escaping from this place, of not joining the corpses under the dirty green tarpaulin.

'Please,' she shouted, tensing as the boot hit her and bolts of pain shot throughout her body. 'Please, Chris, I'm sorry, you're right,' she yelled.

He looked down at her, paused for just a second, and then spat on her. He looked as though he was faltering, trying to think of something to say.

It was then that she kicked out, aiming for his ankle and drawing his eyes towards her foot as he easily dodged the kick. Dan immediately drove the shears with all her strength into the already open wound on the side of his abdomen.

His mouth opened wider than Dan could ever have thought possible as she leaned up and pushed the double blades into him as far as she could.

He doubled over, as though trying to close the wound like he might a door, and took a step away from her.

Dan rolled away, moving to her knees and grabbing the spade. In what felt to her like a single movement, she stood up, raised the spade to shoulder height and swung it as hard as she was able to, into Christopher Hamilton's face.

He went down hard.

Dan heard a loud crack and saw a theatrical spatter of blood land across the dusty concrete.

The shears fell out of Hamilton's wound and dropped onto the floor, lying still, as though they'd given up trying to run away from the growing pool of blood that crept across the concrete to catch them.

Dan stood back, watching as Hamilton's chest jerked and spasmed, listening as his breathing crackled and stalled. Then she stepped towards him, put the blade of the spade against his neck and placed her foot on the shoulder, as though she were about to break soil.

'How many?' she said. 'How many are there?'

He said nothing, made no effort to answer.

'You'll bleed out within minutes if I don't get help, so tell me, how many?'

This time she heard a rasping sound and she leaned slightly forward so that she could hear him.

'Lots,' he whispered, just before a cough racked his body, blood gurgling out of his mouth like bubbles from a blocked sink. 'Lots and lots.'

'Where?' she asked, pushing her foot onto the shoulder of the spade. 'Tell me where they are.'

He was starting to go limp, his breathing becoming shallower.

'Tell me where!' she shouted, putting pressure onto the spade and seeing his body react to it.

'Don't know,' he said.

'What?' said Dan, taking the pressure back off the spade. 'I said where are the other women? Where are their bodies?'

He was dying as Dan watched. He was bleeding out, starting to shiver, the gaps between activity and peace seeming to extend with each cycle.

'Do you want to die here?' she shouted. 'Tell me where they are! Where were you going to take these women? Where?'

He laughed, blood coming out of his mouth like a Halloween zombie mask, but the rasping unmistakable. 'Don't know,' he whispered.

'Then you're going to die here in the same place they did,' said Dan, taking her foot off the spade.

It clattered as she tossed it to the floor several feet away, the noise of metal striking concrete drowning out Chris Hamilton's dying breaths as it echoed around the garage.

Looking down at him, Dan knew he deserved to die. Felt nothing for him as she watched him creep slowly towards his end. But the information he had, the women he'd hurt and the closure he could bring to their families if he talked . . .

'If you want me to call for help, then tell me where you hid those women's bodies. Tell me how many there are. Or I swear I'll watch you bleed until you die, just to be sure you do.'

He laughed again, the sound like sandpaper on rough wood. 'I don't know where they are,' he said, each word taking longer than the last. 'And you haven't got it in you.'

Chapter 1

Thursday Afternoon – 25th September 2014

'Ma'am?'

Dan looked up at the young naval policeman who was leaning around her office door as though he might lose balance and topple in if he didn't deliver his message and be on his way soon enough.

He was young, bursting with confidence, and a little over-familiarity, but his navy uniform was immaculate and the shirt so white that it took on a bluish tint in the dull glow that came in through the window, and Dan could work with that; he had attention to detail.

'Head of Kill's here to see you,' he said, using the slang term for the Crimes Involving Loss of Life division which never failed to grate on Dan's nerves. 'Commander Blackett. He's downstairs signing in now.'

Dan watched him and said nothing, the silence drawing out between them and the young man's position leaning on the door becoming tenuous.

He waited, watching her for an acknowledgement, and

when none came he eventually released the door frame and stepped properly into the office, free-standing.

'Thank you,' said Dan. 'Could you turn the lights on and show him up, please.'

'Ah, he asked if you would go down and go for a walk with him,' he said, trying for a smile. 'The Commander said,' the young policeman paused, hesitated. 'He said the fluorescent lights make you grumpy.'

Dan smiled and watched the young man relax a little. She was new here, had taken over the Portsmouth unit only a day ago and had been away from the Special Investigation Branch for a good while before that. Many of the younger police didn't know her, but they would get to, in time.

'In that case, you better leave the lights off,' Dan said. 'Thank you, I'll go down now.'

He nodded and was gone as Dan stood and grabbed her issue waterproof jacket and tricorn hat.

Commander Blackett was waiting for her outside, across the car park near to her car. His hand was moving in slow cycles from his mouth to his side and back again, the smoke signals rising after each one confirming that little had likely changed with Roger Blackett.

He took a long, deep draw on his cigarette as she approached, and smiled broadly.

'You look good, Danny,' he said, reaching out to shake her hand though it was clear he would have embraced her had they not been in uniform. 'In fact, you look great.'

Dan shook her head and ignored him.

'You still torturing yourself for miles upon miles every day?' he asked.

Dan nodded.

'Too bloody vigorous, Danny. I'm sure it can't be good

18

for you, you know, putting your body through that, but if it keeps you healthy and happy . . .'

She watched him, one eyebrow raised, as he drew on his cigarette with the intensity of an asthmatic drawing on an inhaler.

He smiled. 'Don't you lecture me, Danielle Lewis. I'm a lost cause, and anyway, I'm giving up.'

'You've been giving up for twenty years.'

'Ah well, life's for living,' he said, 'all about pushing boundaries and seeing what you can get away with.' He tossed his stub into a large, wet pile of others on the ground next to a bin.

'How come you're out and about in Portsmouth?' she asked. 'I heard you liked being tucked up safe and warm in your office these days.'

'I came to see you,' he said, as though that were sufficient reason for the head of her branch to drive for four hours and turn up unannounced at her office, asking to go for a walk. 'Can we walk for a short while then?'

Dan shrugged and waited for him to lead the way.

They walked steadily through the dockyard, Blackett talking as they went, catching her up on promotions and news from the navy police and its Special Investigation Branch, as well as gossip from a circle of mutual friends that Dan hadn't seen or heard about for years. He was talking, but not really saying anything.

They passed the carrier berths, and HMS *Illustrious*, the newly decommissioned British aircraft carrier. She had seen from a distance that the flat, grey flight deck was free of aircraft. It looked as smooth and empty as a Sunday morning car park in the dull light. Now that she was closer, she was no longer able to see the flight deck, just the sailors that were bustling around the ship beneath it.

Roger began to tell her about his time on board *Illustrious* as the Master at Arms, the senior policeman on the floating town that held upwards of a thousand sailors when it deployed. He spoke quickly as Dan watched the sailors working on the grey passageways that looked down onto the concrete jetty, or unpacking stores and supplies on dry land, near to one of the gangways.

Dan fixed her eyes dead ahead. She felt their gazes fall on her like the shadow cast by the twenty-thousand-ton hulk. Some glanced surreptitiously sideways, others simply stood up and motioned to their friends. It was as though their eyes, and the darkness cast onto the ground by the ship, possessed actual weight.

Roger talked on, oblivious, as they moved towards the rising masts of HMS *Victory*.

Portsmouth Dockyard had changed since she had last been here. It had grown and modernised. There were more cars and fewer people, but the layout was the same, and she relaxed again as they headed towards the cobbles of the Historic Dockyard, passing visitors and tourists on their way to the *Mary Rose*, or HMS *Warrior*; all hoping to see some history only a few hundred feet away from the modern warships that still had a hand in shaping it.

'I was hoping to speak to you last night,' he said, a change in tone alerting Dan that she needed to listen. 'I tried your mobile, thought we might be able to grab a drink.'

They walked along towards the waterfront. Several sailors saluted Blackett as they passed, Dan aware of their eyes flicking towards her after they did so.

They stopped at the water's edge, and Roger lit another cigarette. 'I thought, at first, you might've changed your number, but your dad and sister said they haven't spoken to you either.'

'What's up, Roger?' she asked.

She wrapped her arms around herself.

'I'm glad you've started to let your hair grow back,' he said.

The words sounded odd and random, irritating.

'It's a long drive from Plymouth to Portsmouth to tell me to call home,' she said.

'Your dad's worried, we all are.'

'I'll call them.'

He nodded, seeming to accept he wouldn't push it any further.

'That's not the only reason I'm here,' he said. 'Do you remember a sailor called Stewart Walker?'

Dan shrugged again. 'Not from recently; I knew a Stewart Walker when I was in basic training.'

'That's him. You joined up together. Then you both joined HMS *Manchester* straight after you passed out of Raleigh.'

Dan nodded, her features unchanged. 'Yeah, "Whisky" Walker, I remember him. I haven't heard from him in years.'

'He died the day before yesterday. Hanged by the neck on board HMS *Tenacity*, one of the nuclear hunter-killer submarines that run out of Devonport. It's believed he committed suicide.'

Dan turned to look at Blackett for the first time since their conversation had started.

'Believed?'

He nodded. 'This is a nasty one, Danny. I know you've only just arrived back with Kill, and I won't hide the fact that I didn't want this one for you, but I need an investigator to come and work out of Devonport Dockyard for a few weeks.'

He turned and looked out across the water.

He was hesitating; she could see it in the way he looked away from her. The way he focused out to sea as if engrossed by the nothingness between them and the Gosport Peninsula, which looked back at him from barely a mile away. She could still recognise all his mannerisms even though she hadn't seen him in well over a year; he was a constant.

He reached for his cigarettes; half pulled one out, and then thought better of it. His tongue poked out from between his pursed lips as he took a few moments to thread it back into the nearly new pack.

'And?' she prompted, waiting for the rest.

'And . . .' he reached for his cigarettes again and pulled the same one back out, lighting it with his back to the wind. 'And, I need to know how you are. I know you've only just taken over the Portsmouth unit, so I know that you're back, but I need to know that you're really ready to come back.'

'What?' asked Dan, her voice sharp, incredulous. 'What does that even mean?'

'It means you had a tough time, a really tough time, and that affects people.'

'And I dealt with it.'

'Some of it.'

She turned on him, faced up to him.

They weren't at work any more, they weren't in uniform; they were friends of over twenty years, and Dan was fearless in that knowledge.

'I dealt with it,' she said, her eyes boring into him and her teeth gritted.

He looked back at her, not angry as he might well have been, just patiently, waiting.

She turned away and looked out to sea in the same direction that he'd been looking.

A small white boat was being tossed around by the swell a few hundred yards from land. It was completely at the mercy of the waves around it, only held in place by a taut anchor rope that could break at any second.

The wind picked up and was topping the waves, forcing

the crests down into small white mounds, like the backs of kneeling worshippers.

Together, the elements battered the hull of the small craft and tested the anchor's resolve.

'The Hamilton case took a lot out of all of us,' he said, his voice low and thoughtful. 'None of us saw that coming and no one paid the price you did. No one could have predicted it was one of our own—'

'I'm fine,' she said, cutting him off. 'Tell me about Walker.'

'The way you were treated by the press. The sheer scale of what Hamilton did.' Blackett seemed to be speaking to himself now, not really looking at Dan, as though he were seeing it all again, reading out the highlights as it played through in his mind.

'Do we have a timeline for Walker?' asked Dan. 'And have interviews begun? Or can I get down there before they do?'

'What happened afterwards . . .' his words trailed off.

Dan stopped and looked at him. He was the one she had turned to after it had happened, the one she had trusted to help her.

They looked at one another and neither spoke for a long time.

'I'm OK, Roger,' Dan said. 'Really I am, and I want this. I'm ready for it.'

Chapter 2

Thursday Evening – 25th September 2014

Returning to the house felt odd. The colours were no longer of her choosing, and her tenants had laid laminate flooring in the hallway but had taken the rug that had covered most of it, leaving grime lines that ran like flower borders a foot from each wall. In the living room, where there was carpet, it looked worn and dusty, with depressed patches dotted around the floor in all the wrong places. Her own house now reminded her of one of the many married quarters that she'd moved into as a child, as she and her sister had followed their dad around the country from military base to married patch. The cheap housing provided by the armed forces always had an air of not being home, but she and her big sister Charlie would still dash inside, ignoring the magnolia walls, worn carpets and mismatched cupboard doors in the kitchen, as they tried to bagsy the best bedroom.

Dan's furniture and belongings had been delivered a few days before and most were still stacked neatly in the centre of the living room. She placed her workbag in the hallway, outside of the open archway that led to the small kitchen, and looked at what she owned. It was barely recognisable to her after more than eighteen months in storage.

The doorbell rang and Dan turned and paused. She let the time tick by, listening for receding footsteps that would signal that the caller had moved away. Then it rang again and through the frosted glass she saw a small figure waiting, motionless and patient.

The figure stood as still as Dan for a long moment, and then bent forward before small, white and veiny fingers groped to lift up the letter box. Dan knew that she was discovered.

She walked quickly to the door and opened it, taking care not to skin the fingers as she did so.

'Danielle,' said the old woman, giving Dan a broad smile as she straightened up. 'I knew I'd seen you go in there. It's good to have you back. You'll have to come around for a barbecue as soon as you're settled in. Derek can do his special Frikadella that you like; you know the weather doesn't bother him. We can sit inside and drink warm wine while he freezes and cooks our dinner.'

Dan smiled.

'Hey, Martha, I'm going away again already, down to Plymouth this time. I'm actually right in the middle of packing now, though, so I really need to get on – sorry. I'll call in when I'm back, though, and a barbecue, even in September, sounds great.' She began to slowly shut the door.

'That's OK,' Martha continued unperturbed as she strained to look past Dan and along the hallway into the house.

'OK then,' said Dan, inching the door closed a little bit more. 'Thanks for popping round and send my love to Derek.'

'Don't forget this,' Martha handed over a red plastic Royal Mail bag, full to bursting with redirected mail. 'Postie delivered it today while you were out, all from your old address in Scotland.'

Dan took the package, having to release the door and use both hands as she did. The markings showed the address of the Faslane naval base where she had worked for the past eight months or so, since returning from her sabbatical.

'Thank you,' she said.

She stood for a moment looking at the package which contained several smaller bags – weeks of mail that had managed to catch up with her in one go. She smiled and thanked Martha again, pushing the door slowly closed, like she had as a young navy policewoman clearing back rubber-neckers from a fresh crime scene. The door finally shut, she sighed and tossed the redirected mail onto the floor next to her rucksack; there was nothing that needed to be opened now.

She turned and headed slowly up the stairs, past the clean patches on the walls where pictures had protected the paint-work.

Her black, navy issue holdall was open on the floor next to her bed. It looked like a disembowelled slug. Clothes were spilling out, their arms and legs entwined, and her laptop was resting against it on one side.

The phone began to ring.

She waited, frozen again, as if the caller might be able to slip their fingers through the handset and see her hiding. It rang and rang as Dan pondered that she had no food in the house, no furniture she could really use, save the bed, no clothes beyond those clawing their way out of her holdall, but she did have a working phone and broadband internet; the priorities of the modern world.

The answering machine took the call.

Dan waited.

'Hey, Sister-bear. It's me with my one-way monthly check-up call. Roger told Dad you're back down in Portsmouth and I feel like we haven't spoken for way too long. I also have some *very* exciting news to tell you. A few of us are heading out for a few drinks next Saturday, nothing special, just a girly night, but it would be really great if you would come home for it. Dad and Mimmy Jean would really love that too,' there was a pause and maybe a little sigh before Charlie continued. 'We all really miss you. Dad thinks he's done something wrong, but I told him you're just taking some time—' The machine beeped and cut her sister off.

Dan waited in silence, looking at the wall and making sure that any tears that had formed in her eyes were fully clear, and until she was sure that her sister wouldn't call back to finish the message. Then she sat down on her bed, the only piece of furniture that was in a usable state, and listened to the message again, twice.

On the bedside table she looked at the photograph she always kept there. She and Charlie, and their stepmother 'Mimmy' Jean, were gathered around her dad, Taz Lewis, in the centre of the shot. They were at an armed forces family sports day and Charlie had just won a prize, a cartoon character Tasmanian devil that was the genesis of her father's nickname. He was a force of nature, unstoppable and wild, and Team Lewis were unbeatable, simply because the girls believed that having Taz Lewis on your side meant you were halfway to victory already. There was no 'just enjoy yourself, honey' for the Lewis girls; second place was the first placed loser, and anything short of victory just meant trying harder, working harder and pushing forward, always pushing forward.

'If you always aim for the stars, then you might just hit them,' he would say as he held their hands.

'But what if you miss?' Dan had once asked.

'If you try hard enough, really give it everything you've got again and again, then you won't miss.'

'But what if you do miss?' she had pressed.

'Then you'll have spent your whole life looking at the stars, and I'll be there to give you a push,' he had replied.

Dan's fingers played across the handset's buttons until she began to dial her sister's number. She was quick at typing it, one of the few she bothered to remember these days; all others just anonymous access codes stored on her mobile. All that was left to do now was push the green button, listen to the ringing for a few seconds, and then lie to her sister.

Time passed as she stared down at the digits displayed on the illuminated screen. Then, not sure why, she pushed the red button, cleared away the number and lay down, resting her head against her pillows.

'It's all about control, Danny.'

She sat bolt upright, her pillow twisted, contorted into submission and gripped tight in her clenched fists. Her arm flailed for the bedside lamp, groping along the cable and searching for the switch, but not finding it. The lamp crashed to the floor and she leaped out of her bed, heading for the door. Her shaking hand found the main bedroom switch and light filled the room instantly, allowing her to look around and take in the markers, the things around her that she recognised, that told her she was safe; it was just the dream.

Her back was pressed against the door so tight she could have been lying down on it. Her breathing was laboured, she was panting, drawing in breaths as though she had just finished another run, one that was harder, more demanding than any before. It was a few moments before she sat back on the bed, letting her breathing settle and looking around at the chaos.

Her eyes were heavy and her mouth dry as she glanced at the clock: 4:54 a.m. There would be no more sleep tonight.

The house was silent and not even the murmur of a neighbour's television, or the scavenging of a hungry fox outside, permeated the walls as she started to pack. It wouldn't take long; she hadn't really unpacked.

Dan hesitated. She became aware of her own breathing. It was the only thing she could hear and it was getting louder and faster again. The urge to speak, to shatter the silence, grew inside her like a tumour. She thought of calling her sister, to hear Charlie's voice if nothing else, but to say what? Dan could hide what happened to her from almost everybody; she could function daily and deal with it, as long as nobody knew. But any of the people in the photograph – Charlie, Jean, her dad – would see it as clearly as if she were still covered in the blood and bruises, as if her clothes were still torn and her back still raw.

Dan reached for the handset, ran her fingers over the keypad as though she were admiring jewellery she knew she couldn't afford.

It was late now, though, too late, and Dan checked the clock and put the phone back on its stand. She knelt down, reaching underneath the bed and pulling out a portable document safe. It was heavy and she needed both hands to get it onto the bed and place it next to where she wanted to sit. She used her thumb to make sure that the four combination dials were thoroughly mixed up. But instead of dialling random numbers, Dan looked down and saw that she had set the combination perfectly, had unlocked the safe.

The lid opened without a sound and she looked at the picture on top, the one she always kept there, stared at it, her vision narrowing as though blinkers had appeared suddenly either side of her eyes, cutting out all else around her. She shook her head and shut the safe quickly, spinning the dials properly this time, as though, if she did it quickly enough, she might forget the combination and be unable to open it ever again.

'Not today,' she said quietly.

She stood and carried the document safe and her holdall down the stairs, loaded all of her gear into her car, and padlocked the safe to the vehicle security point.

The red package of redirected mail caught her eye as she began to pull the door to. She stopped and leaned in to collect it, before drawing the door tight shut behind her. She tossed the package into the boot, before shutting that too and preparing for the early morning drive down to Devonport.

Chapter 3

Dan showed her warrant card to the armed guards at the entrance to the Royal Dockyard, Devonport, the Devon naval base that was home to the Royal Navy's 'hunter-killer' nuclear submarines.

They cradled their Heckler and Koch MP7s in their arms as they watched her drive past.

The view out to sea looked unfamiliar and it took a few seconds for Dan to realise that it was the absence of grey warships, which only a few years ago would have dominated every seaward glance, that jarred against her recollection as she drove towards the submarine squadron building.

The interior of the drab, grey-stone submarine complex still featured the dull blue linoleum and filthy magnolia paint that had been there the last time she'd entered. The pictures on the walls that escorted her up the stairs – similar-looking photographs of indistinguishable submarines in varying colours of choppy water – looked brand new, though, and she glanced at each one, guessing at its location as she climbed the stairs towards Roger Blackett's new office.

A large lady, her long flowery skirt flowing out behind her like Batman's cape, was skipping down the stairs at a rapid rate of knots. Her cheerful humming sounded the alarm too late and she ploughed into Dan, knocking her and immediately catching her again by the arm only a second before Dan would have tumbled back down the stairs.

'I am so, so sorry,' the woman yelled, steadying Dan and dusting her down. 'It was my fault, I always take the stairs.' She pointed at a small gadget on the belt of her dress. 'It's for the step count.' The woman smiled and waited.

'It's fine, honestly,' said Dan, trying to take a step back to create some space between them. 'I'm fine.'

'Lieutenant Lewis?' the woman asked.

'Yes.' Dan couldn't help but raise an eyebrow.

The woman replied with an even bigger smile. 'Good. Commander Blackett said you'd be here shortly. He's got someone in with him right now but said he wouldn't be long. Grab a seat upstairs in the outer office and I'll let him know you're here as soon as I get back. I'm just going to collect the mail, and bag a hundred steps on the way.'

Dan nodded and tried to smile as she navigated around the woman, unable to suppress the thought that she was unlikely to be quite so chirpy as she bagged her steps on the way back up the four flights.

Dan saw herself enter Blackett's outer office, her reflection matching her actions in a long mirror that hung on the wall facing the door. She looked tired, she looked drawn and then she looked away and took a seat.

'She's been on the bench for too bloody long, Roger,' sounded an unfamiliar voice through Blackett's office door. The voice was raised but not shouting, its upper-class accent suggesting that Blackett's companion was almost certainly an officer at least as senior as Blackett himself. 'You packed her up and let her swan off on sabbatical, and none of us were sad to see her go, but she's back now, she draws her wages, and she needs to be put to use.'

Dan checked that she was still alone and moved to a seat that was closer to the door. She picked up a copy of the *Navy News*, or 'Dockyard Dandy' as it was known around the fleet, and opened it to roughly halfway.

'There is no reason at all that she should not pursue this, none at all. It works for everyone and we can soon see if she's even half as good as you say,' continued the unknown voice.

'And if it goes public? After Hamilton?' Roger Blackett's words carried less clearly through his office door. He didn't normally raise his voice, not outside of a bar anyway, and both he and the person who had replied to him had paused, silenced; even four years later, Hamilton could still hush all who remembered him.

Dan strained towards the door, waiting for the silence to be broken.

'It's outside of your control, Roger. The decision has been made; live with it.'

'She'll be down here today,' Roger replied, his tone seeming to acknowledge that there would be no further discussion.

Footsteps sounded on the linoleum, turning to soft pads as the woman she had passed on the stairs entered the carpeted office and gathered some final steps.

Dan concentrated on the article in front of her, slowly straightening herself up as she became aware how much she had leaned towards the door when eavesdropping.

'Thank you for waiting, ma'am,' said the assistant, still smiling from rosy cheek to rosy cheek, but obviously trying not to sound out of breath as she shuffled into the room with the post under her arm. 'I'll let him know you're here.'

Twenty minutes later, without a further raised voice, Blackett's door finally opened.

He held it wide and gestured with one arm for his guest to pass through. The man was senior to Blackett, marked as a naval captain by the four gold bands on each epaulette. He was tall and gaunt, with black hair that was slicked back from an eerily high forehead, like a throwback from an East End gangster movie. His long, pale fingers clutched the white cloth of his formal cap and stretched so far across it that they looked as though he needed an extra knuckle.

Dan had to look away as he changed his grip, his fingers looking even whiter against the gold braid that covered the black peak of his cap, confirming his seniority.

He placed the cap neatly onto his head and looked down his narrow nose at her, pausing and waiting until she made eye contact.

Dan met his cold, grey stare before he nodded, like a boxer might acknowledge a future opponent, and made his way out towards the stairs.

'Danny, come in, please,' boomed Blackett, a broad smile etched across his face as he held open the door.

His enthusiasm sounded false and he looked tired.

Dan walked into the office and stood in front of one of the wing-backed leather chairs that faced Blackett's desk, but she didn't sit down; not yet.

'Who was that?' she asked, aware that it was none of her business.

Blackett frowned as he shut the door behind him and then sighed.

'Captain David Harrow-Brown, new Head of the Joint-Chiefs Investigative and Intelligence at GCHQ,' he said. He seemed to drop the fake smile and let his shoulders slump forward as he shut the door. 'Our new boss.'

His office was a large square on the corner of the building, with dual aspect windows looking out, on one side, past the grey buildings that hid Frigate Alley, and on the other to a wide road that separated the submarine complex from a series of fenced areas, like small compounds, that Dan knew were the secure berths for the navy's nuclear submarines. High fences blocked access on three sides, with the water providing the final boundary.

Berthed in one of these 'exclusion zones' was the smooth, black floating mass of one of the remaining Trafalgar-class nuclear submarines, HMS *Tenacity*. It was identifiable to Dan by the name and ship's crest printed onto the side screens running alongside both gangways, like the advertising boards beneath the handrails in the London Underground. The submarine looked small, what could be seen of it, but Dan knew that, like an iceberg, there was much more of it submerged below the murky waters.

Blackett sat down behind his desk, slumping slightly, and gestured for her to be seated.

She said nothing as she waited for him to begin.

'Danny,' he said quietly. 'It's not out yet, hasn't made the press, but there's more to what we discussed yesterday than just Walker's suicide. A few days ago, on the Sunday evening that HMS *Tenacity* docked back into Devonport, Walker was the Duty Technical Senior Rate on board the submarine. That evening, while he was here assisting with the shutdown of the nuclear power plant, his wife, Cheryl Walker, was beaten, raped and murdered. Her body was left near to a remote car park up on the moor. As I say, so far no details have made it into the press, but it won't be long, because this one was really horrible.'

'Was she killed there? Do we know *why* she was there?'

Dan became suddenly aware of herself, heard herself ask the questions in short, clipped sentences, and felt the uncomfortable stiffness in her legs – a hangover from her run yesterday and the long drive this morning – begin to subside. It was as though her blood was now pumping properly, clearing away toxins and restoring life. Blackett's question from yesterday flashed into her mind again: 'I need to know if you're really ready to come back?' he had asked, and she knew that she was.

'I think the Devon and Cornwall police suspect that she may have been meeting someone, and that she was attacked and killed near to where her body was found,' Blackett said.

He paused.

Dan looked up at him, their eyes meeting.

'She was in the early stages of pregnancy,' he said. 'Left behind two other children, ages three and seven. They were staying with Cheryl's mum, a few miles away from the family home, not far outside the city. That's where they'll live now, for the foreseeable future at least.'

'Is the unborn child Walker's?' asked Dan.

'It's possible. He had some time off the boat and would've been home within a timescale that would allow it, but the lab'll confirm it.'

'So Walker's informed of his wife's murder, when?'

'Early on Monday morning. The commanding officer released him immediately and we arranged for the Church of England Bish to meet him at the family home. The commanding officer and the ship's company were told it was a serious compassionate issue, but nothing more.'

'Walker goes home, and then what?'

'We're not completely sure,' said Blackett honestly, but with obvious embarrassment. 'He spoke to his wife's parents by phone and asked them to keep the kids for a few more hours. The Bish, a Reverend Brian Markton, had apparently been working with Walker on and off for several months. He knew the family well and had spoken with Cheryl several times too. He offered to stay with Walker and also to go round to Cheryl's parents with him, to inform them. Walker told him that he needed some time and would call him later. He also asked the police Family Liaison Officer to leave, which they reluctantly did. Then he dropped off the grid.'

'Seems a little slack,' said Dan, watching Blackett carefully.

'I agree,' he said, with no trace of defensiveness. 'But we'd spoken with *Tenacity*'s coxswain and confirmed that Walker was on board and on duty at the time of her death. So, he wasn't a suspect and you can't force someone to take help.'

Dan's mind was gaining momentum as it began to run through the maze of options, each possible route throwing up more questions, more uncertainties and more challenges.

'Then . . .' she prompted, urging Blackett to continue feeding her the information.

'You can read the reports for the details, but on Monday evening the Bish went back round to the house and couldn't raise a reply. The police forced entry.' Blackett took a deep breath. 'And he'd gone. The next time he surfaced is when, on Tuesday evening, he was found hanging by the neck above the lower level ladder in HMS *Tenacity*'s engine rooms.'

Dan was thinking hard, her lips tight together and her tongue moving back and forth behind them like a lion in captivity.

'How much did *Tenacity*'s crew really know about what happened to Cheryl Walker?' she asked.

Blackett was watching her carefully now. 'The Devon and Cornwall police requested a complete media and information blackout, so *Tenacity* were aware he was leaving on compassionate grounds, but not why; they'd have guessed it was very serious, though.'

'And a murder in a relatively small community . . .' said Dan, more to herself than to Blackett. 'Whispers must have been spreading.'

'I'm sure they are,' said Blackett.

'How did he get onto the submarine?' Dan asked after a pause. 'They must have been watching for him.'

'You're right, and we don't know. We think he drove back to the dockyard late on, but we've yet to find any CCTV to confirm it. The submarine would've been quiet after the reactor was shut down. So, apart from a small forward duty watch and the nuclear watch-keepers aft, everyone else would've left the boat. Nobody saw him.'

Blackett leaned forward and pointed to a tiny Portakabin just inside the exclusion zone. Dan had to stand up so that she could follow his gesture as he explained the possible route.

'In the dark, we think he sneaked past the health physicist, who mans that small Portakabin for a period after shutdown. Then he would have crossed on that aft gangway and climbed down into the engine rooms through one of the aft hatches.'

Dan shook her head slowly. 'You've lost me.'

Blackett leaned back in his chair and reached for a pen, but seemed to think better of it. 'Think of it this way,' he said, using his hands to form a long shape, his fingers touching at the tips. 'The nuclear reactor is roughly in the middle of the submarine.'

He pulled his hands slightly apart.

'In the front half, forward of the reactor compartment, are the living spaces, the submarine control room and other compartments.' He nodded towards the other hand; the one that Dan was supposed to imagine was the back of the boat. 'Everything aft of the reactor compartment is engineering: the manoeuvring room, where they control the reactor, and the engine rooms. Walker would have known these spaces like the back of his hand; pardon the pun. He must have climbed down into the submarine behind the reactor compartment, straight into the engine rooms and then . . .' Blackett shrugged, not wanting to say it again.

Dan looked down at the submarine again and walked through what she understood of the route in her mind.

'And our anaemic friend from GCHQ?' she asked, gesturing towards the door, as though Captain David Harrow-Brown had left a pale but indelible stain on it as he had passed through.

'He wants an investigation conducted that deals purely with the suicide, but that also, concurrently and covertly, establishes the whereabouts of every member of HMS *Tenacity*'s ship's company on Sunday night when Cheryl Walker was murdered.'

Dan sat back down and leaned against the leather. She looked at her thighs and screwed up her face as she thought.

Blackett seemed to sense her next question. He didn't wait for her to speak.

'*Tenacity* sails on patrol again in four days and the powers that be desperately want that to happen. We need to understand the circumstances surrounding Whisky Walker's suicide and make sure we have anything we need, any answers or information, from *Tenacity*'s crew that might support the investigation into Cheryl Walker's death.'

He leaned back and swivelled his chair as he turned so that he could see the dockyard outside the window.

Dan could see his shoulders rise and fall as he breathed. She knew he wasn't done, knew there was more to come. This was classic Blackett, going around the houses to get to where he wanted to be.

'What is it, Roger?' she finally asked.

He still didn't turn.

She saw him exhale and reach for a cigarette, holding it in his fingers but not lighting it.

'We've known each other a long time, Danny. Been friends since you joined the navy, what, almost twenty years ago?'

'Eighteen,' said Dan.

'Eighteen years, and I've known you longer than that, knew you when you were a little girl, known Taz since I was in my early twenties.'

She didn't speak.

'I haven't really changed,' he mused, worrying at the unlit cigarette. 'I still smoke, still drink, still expect Scotland to win every game of rugby and I'm still disappointed when they don't.' He turned to look at her and half smiled before turning away again, as though he couldn't look her in the eye as he said whatever he had to say.

Dan felt as though a single droplet of freezing water had been placed onto the nape of her neck and was slowly running down her spine as she looked at his profile, saw his tired eyes, his slumped shoulders; he looked older now than she had ever seen him.

'But you've changed, Danny. How could you not have after all that happened? I watched you after you got Hamilton; everyone loved you, a young, talented, ambitious, pretty female investigator bringing down the most wanted serial killer in the country . . .' His voice trailed off and they sat in silence for a moment. 'I also watched, and hopefully supported you, when they turned on you, when your theories were leaked about the possibility of Hamilton not being alone . . .'

When it must have been clear that Dan wasn't going to speak, Blackett nodded, snapping out of his trance as though the words had just been deleted and the subject never broached.

'*Tenacity*'s Commanding Officer, Commander Melvin Bradshaw, wants the preliminary investigation into the suicide done quick-sharp,' Blackett said, with renewed vigour. 'He wants it done efficiently, to minimise disruption and to get the men moving on from it and ready for patrol. It's a brotherhood, Danny. These men are part of a very tight-knit community and they take the loss of one of their own very hard. Also,' he turned away from her again and looked out of the window. 'Something isn't right here, Danny; something stinks.'

'You mean, why me?' asked Dan, her jaw clenching as she remembered Harrow-Brown's insistence that she be the one to carry out the investigation.

'Danny,' he turned to face her. 'You know better than to think I mean it like that. But I know the Commanding Officer of *Tenacity*, I know Melvin very well. Do you?'

Dan shook her head. 'The name's familiar, but I doubt we've ever met.'

'Well, before GCHQ became involved and I appointed you to this task, Bradshaw had already contacted me and asked for you, by name.'

Blackett paused again.

'Well, it's obvious where he could have heard my name before,' said Dan. 'The newspapers didn't spare me.'

'And neither did Fleet HQ,' Blackett added for her. 'Your name was mud up there for a long time and it's still a shade of brown if we're honest; people have memories.'

Dan nodded, saying nothing again as she remembered waking up to a ringing phone, Roger telling her to turn on the news, and the news channel coming into view. Messages were scrolling along the bottom edge of the screen, but the headline led with 'Navy Expert, Danielle Lewis – Hamilton Did Not Work Alone'. Dan had puked, literally been sick in the toilet, as extracts from one of her draft research papers were read out to the world, and commentators wondered at how many killers there were operating under the cover of our armed forces, how many men we were training to take innocent life as clinically as they carried out a military operation, and how many more women had died in other countries, their deaths enabled by the Royal Navy providing transport and anonymity to the killer, Christopher Hamilton. The fallout from the leaked paper had hit her life like a tsunami.

They were both silent as Blackett placed the unlit cigarette down on his desk. Leaning forward he pulled open his bottom desk drawer, reached inside and pulled out a bottle of twenty-one-year-old Royal Salute and a crystal tumbler. He poured a measure, without offering any to Dan, and took several sips of the whisky.

Dan raised an eyebrow as she saw the distinctive porcelain flagon. 'Someone's gone up in the world,' she said. 'I remember when it was a half-bottle of Grouse berthed in your bottom drawer.'

He took another sip, sniffed loudly and smiled at her. 'Melvin Bradshaw is the longest serving submariner still on an operational submarine,' he said, savouring the smell of his drink and ignoring Dan's comment. The story, or the whisky, seemed to breathe some life and animation back into him; Blackett loved to tell a story. 'He joined *Tenacity* before she commissioned, as a young stoker.'

Dan's eyebrows rose.

'A marine engineer, down in the engine rooms; dirty, smelly work. They cover everything from the toilets to the nuclear power plant and all the engineering that falls in between, but the point is that Melvin started at the bottom.'

Dan almost interrupted him. She had known full well what a stoker was; her surprise had come from the fact that one of them was now the Commanding Officer of a nuclear submarine.

'Melvin's guys adore him, or they just don't last. He's always been a popular Commanding Officer and that he worked up through the ranks, as we did, buys enormous credibility in the submarine environment. But anyone who knows Melvin would describe him as "old school". You know what I mean?'

Dan nodded. She knew. 'So you want to know why he requested that a woman be assigned to the investigation?'

She watched, waiting for Blackett to shake his head or protest at what she had implied. He didn't.

'It's not unusual to ask for a Kill Team officer from outside the home port, you know that. With cuts driving everyone towards joint operations, there are less than half a dozen qualified Kill investigators still in dark blue, and it's not a huge leap to see why they wanted navy for this one. It's always better to have someone who knows the navy, but has no meaningful connection to the ship's company. I'm just saying . . .'

He paused again and Dan started to get frustrated with how long it was taking him to say what he was thinking. It wasn't like him to flounder this much.

'I'm just saying,' he repeated, 'that I want you to be careful.'

Dan shrugged. 'Of course.'

'I've already appointed an assisting investigator to the suicide. You'll join him, take over as lead, and liaise with Devon and Cornwall police to offer assistance if they need it.'

Dan eyed him, immediately suspicious.

'Who?'

He turned away from her, swivelling his chair to look back out the window as he took another sip of whisky.

'John Granger,' he said.

'Smart move,' Dan said, her voice beginning to rise. 'Really smart. When the press do get involved, and they will, they'll *never* notice that you've reunited the team from the Hamilton investigation, and if they do, I'm just certain they won't make a big deal of it.'

'I trust Master at Arms Granger,' he said, and spun around to face her, some of his whisky swirling out of the glass and landing on his desk as his voice rose to meet hers. 'You chose not to and it nearly cost you your life. I hope that's a mistake you won't be looking to repeat.'

Blackett was banging the desk now, punctuating each point he made with a heavy thud of his yellowed fingers.

'He's a former submariner, he knows boats and he knows these waters, he's swum them before, and you need to get back into a team.'

'Back into a team?' Dan asked the question as much to check that she had heard him correctly as to confirm what he meant.

Blackett stood up, his palms pressed down against his desk as though he was holding it there, and by doing so, preventing himself from ripping it aside and bodily shaking her.

Dan didn't flinch. She met his stare, unblinking.

'What?' she said.

'You know? I should tell you "what", because I am your friend, pretty much the only one you have, and somebody needs to bloody tell you.'

Dan shook her head and raised a palm to stop him. 'I'd better get going then,' she said, and stood up quickly, making to leave. 'I assume John knows where to find me?'

'Danny,' said Blackett, his voice softened and the word drawn out so that it was more than a name, it was a question, a request to stay, and maybe even a grudging apology all rolled into one.

Dan stood straight, looking ahead, and waited.

Blackett sighed. 'I just . . .' he paused.

Dan could feel him looking at her, knew that he would be searching for some words to make amends. She heard him sigh again.

'Tomorrow, they're expecting you at *Tenacity*. Miranda has the case files for you to collect on your way out.'

Dan turned her back and opened the door.

'One more thing,' he said, stopping her.

He held up an envelope, clean and white. 'Your dad sent this for you. He asked me to place it into your hand so he'd know you got it.'

Dan stepped back and took the envelope, then turned and left the room.

As she left Blackett's office, Dan couldn't be sure as to why she had reacted so badly to the news that John would be assisting her. She'd known that he was based here, that she might bump into him, but now they'd be working together – closely together – maybe for several days or weeks, just like they had four years ago when they were hunting Hamilton, and Dan had no idea at all how that made her feel. The mention of his name had been like a blow to the abdomen, like she'd run as quickly as she could and gone a long, long way, only to glance over her shoulder and see the past jogging up behind her, fresh and ready to carry on following her wherever she went.

Standing outside the office, the door shut behind her, with the letter from her dad clutched in one hand, Dan's head began to feel like the static on a late night television screen.

Chapter 4

Friday Morning – 26th September 2014

It was a short drive from the submarine squadron building up to the Wardroom in HMS Drake, where Dan would be accommodated with the other commissioned officers that lived in the naval base.

The Wardroom building was an imposing sight. A long, three-story structure, built in the 1800s from Plymouth lime-stone, it looked splendid, intimidating and dramatic as it gazed out over the Hamoaze estuary.

Dan parked up behind one of the new-style accommodation blocks that sprouted out from the original building like an unsightly growth.

Another officer, who Dan didn't recognise, parked up nearby and smiled at her as he locked his car and then walked briskly inside, twice glancing back over his shoulder to look at her again as she followed him in.

It only took moments for Dan to check in with the hall porter and get her room number and key, before finding her room on the third floor. The door to Dan's room was only differentiated from the others by a small name tally that stated her name, date of arrival and date of departure, and it struck her as totally reasonable that in a place like this they were planning for her to leave before she'd even arrived. The room reminded her of modern university accommodation. A few good-sized wardrobes, a desk and chair and a bedside cabinet were all present and correct. The bed was neither double nor single, but something in between; a size that would be comfortable and spacious for one person, but was unlikely to be much fun for two, not that that would be an issue. The curtains were wide open, but they looked thin and flimsy anyway, incapable of blocking much light.

She slipped off her shoes and opened the door to the small en suite wet room, rinsing out a watermarked glass under the cold tap and half-filling it. The water was cold and tasted earthy, and she took a small sip, and then finished the rest off in a long gulp. Filling the glass again, she carried it back through to the sleeping area and placed it on the desk. She put the case file next to the chipped desk lamp, pulled out the wooden chair, upholstered with garish red cushions that almost matched the over-laundered duvet cover, and sat down to read.

The letter from her dad had slipped down inside one of the files and she felt it for a moment, turning it over in her hands. The envelope was plain white, simple, as would be the paper inside it, but opening it wasn't.

Dan placed it to one side, unopened, and began to leaf through the files.

Walker's service records were all that she expected from her distant memories of him. A good spread of experience, strong reports and a few misdemeanours in his early years; nothing serious, just the mark of a bit of character.

'Nothing unusual about our boy,' she said out loud, her voice echoing in the bare space around her. Looking over at a radio-alarm clock on the bedside table, Dan considered some background noise, but was drawn back into the files before she could decide if she really wanted the disturbance.

She turned to the initial report of the suicide. The first picture was labelled 'Engine Room' and it looked to Dan like the inside of a 1950s, tractor-driven spacecraft. A dark area with large pipes running in all directions and metal objects jutting out from all surfaces, as though the picture was the inside of an enormous car engine taken from under the bonnet. The flash had been used and, outside of the immediate area, the rest of the compartment just looked empty, lifeless and dark.

Dan shivered. She leaned over to the radiator beneath the window and placed her hand on it. It felt like it was cooling down from its morning shift, and the tick, tick, tick of the contracting metal broke her concentration to confirm this. It wouldn't work again now until it prepared for the accommodation populace to return at the end of the working day.

There were more shots of the engine room in the files, particularly the site where Walker had been found hanged. In one shot it was possible to see that that part of the engine room was accessed down a very long vertical ladder; the picture was entitled 'Access to Engine Room – Lower Level' and an inserted arrow showed the pipework to which Walker would have secured the noose before stepping out into space.

'What a cold, godforsaken place to die,' said Dan, finally standing up and walking over to the bed again. She was restless, unsettled. She managed to get the radio-alarm clock to play some music with relative ease and then sat back down, looking around the room again, scanning its bare walls and empty shelves, before forcing her mind back to the job in hand.

She recognised John Granger's handwriting on some of

the pages. It hadn't changed. It was still neat and steady, each letter formed so that it could be reliably read again. The ink was even around the letters, not lighter in some areas as you would expect of a person in a rush – a doctor or nurse scribbling quickly – but uniform, someone who took the time to get things right.

She placed Walker's Naval Service Record to one side and picked up the Devon and Cornwall police's initial sharing on the murder of Mrs Cheryl Walker.

It felt heavy, much heavier than any files she'd had from the civilian police in previous investigations. Dan wondered whether she'd been sent a full case file by mistake as she undid the string tag that was wound around two metal pins to hold the information safely inside. She pulled out the preliminary report and spread the rest of the folder contents out on the desk. She noted a list of names – no doubt those people that the police had, or would, look to interview – and scanned it quickly, then placed it aside, looking at the pictures first. There were a lot, more than she had seen in any previous sharing for a murder investigation. She flipped past images of the victim's house, her car, the car park where she had been found, stopping when she found some images of the victim.

The first picture showed a woman's face, bloodied and marked, but without the swelling around the eyes and cheeks that you would expect to see from an assault where punches were thrown. Her hair was matted, and the early pictures showed it covering her face, sticking to her skin. Further on, the pictures changed to show Mrs Walker's face with the mask of hair cleared away, revealing a grisly view of a badly broken nose. Her hair had been cut roughly from behind, and a separate shot showed that some of the hair smeared across her face in previous pictures was no longer attached to her head, but had been clinging there only by virtue of the dried blood.

Dan felt her eyes start to dart across the pictures, speeding up as her heart beat faster. The next picture showed the back of the woman's head and Dan could see more clearly where the hair had been hacked from her scalp. It looked like a child's doll after a pair of scissors had been secreted away and used in the silence of a four-year-old's bedroom.

Dan's breathing became shallow. It looked as though whoever had done this had tried to scalp the woman.

The next picture was a shot of the victim's naked back and buttocks.

Dan looked at the picture and felt the room begin to spin. She blinked several times, but it seemed as though this shot was grainy where the others were crisp and clear. She forced a deep breath and wiped at the cold sweat that had formed on her brow. Blinking twice more, she looked towards the window.

'Jesus,' she breathed and stood up, turning to walk somewhere and then realising there was nowhere to go. Her hand caught the remainder of the glass of water and it spilled onto the rough carpeted floor, spreading out steadily to find its own shape, dark against the light brown carpet. Dan stepped in it on her short journey to the toilet. She just made it in time. The vomit landed in the pan before dry heaves ripped through her, tensing her abdomen until it felt like the muscles would rip away from her bones.

'Shit,' she said quietly.

Her head lolled back against the cool tiles as she looked at the ceiling for a long time, letting her heart rate fall and her breathing recover. Then she stood up and walked, unsteadily at first, out of the en suite and grabbed her car keys from the bed. She walked quickly through the block, down the stairs and back out to her car. The wind ambushed her as soon as she stepped outside and she noticed that it had begun to rain. The elements seemed to drive at her, the wind chilling the raindrops the instant that they landed on her thin white shirt. It felt as though she was drugged with a local anaesthetic, like she was aware of the biting cold but could feel no discomfort, as she hurried across the car park and opened her boot. The portable document safe was immediately inside and she fumbled with her keys as she unlocked the metal wire that secured it to the car. Her hands were shaking and the box felt heavier than normal, but she hoisted it out.

The red Royal Mail package was there too, next to her safe, the colour drawing her eyes. She grabbed it, tucked it under her arm, and slammed the boot shut.

Back in her room, she tossed the red bag of mail onto the bedside table and placed the safe down on her bed. She dialled in her code, her shaking fingers twice selecting the wrong numbers as she tried to access the contents.

The picture was on top, where it always was, and she lifted it out and looked at it before placing it down on the bed and turning back to shuffle through more of the papers. She put aside missing persons posters and dubiously obtained police reports, some in foreign languages and marked with translation notes, each with matching newspaper clippings detailing the stories of missing girls. Her handwritten notes and annotations covered them, or there were sheets of foolscap stapled to their backs. Dan burrowed down further into the box until she managed to scoop her fingers below the very last file. She levered it out and opened it. There were pictures of a victim, beaten and bruised, and she flicked through them until she found the one she was looking for, the picture of the victim's back.

Dan took this picture back to her desk, sat back down, and looked again at the photograph of Cheryl Walker.

Cheryl's hair had been cut deepest on the left side of her head, indicating that whoever had inflicted the wounds to her back would likely have been right-handed, using his left hand to control the woman by her hair, while he beat her with his right. He would then have reached across her with his right hand and drawn the knife from left to right as he cut her hair, freeing his hand as he did so.

It was Cheryl's pale, naked back that really drew Dan's eyes. It looked like a dirty, discarded bird feather, her spine the central shaft. There were deep welts running along the length of her back and ribs on both sides, peeling away from her spine like barbs running parallel to each other, getting smaller as they neared her thin and bloodied neck.

Dan ran her finger across the picture, tracing the lines of bruising. Then she laid the other picture, the one from her safe, next to it.

'Oh God,' she said.

The markings on both pictures were more than similar; they were the same. The scars to the back of each woman's neck, where the hair had been slashed, matched like a signature repeated. The marks feathered down each victim's back were inflicted with a different weapon, sure; the later ones with something thin and hard, the earlier ones with something thicker, a leather belt. But the pattern was unmistakable, like someone had beaten the woman as though he were a jockey and she an animal that needed to be submitted and broken.

Dan used her finger to trace the injuries on both pictures again; they could have been sketches drawn by the same artist. The cutting of the hair, the scars across the back of the neck, the nature of the beating, it was all too similar, too much of a coincidence.

Chapter 5

Dan recognised some of the places that she passed on her way to the Walkers' home, but not many. Like most of the navy folk who came down here for short trips or professional courses, she was transient, living within the dockyard, only really leaving it to enjoy the delights of the Plymouth nightlife – and she had a scar on her right upper arm to remind her of that.

The content of the police files flashed in front of her eyes like a fighter pilot's head-up display as she drove. She needed to see the family home, to see where Cheryl Walker had lived and shared space with her husband. After that she'd go and look at the place where the body had been found and any other locations of interest. Reverend Brian Markton was high on her list of people to see and Dan was hoping she'd be able to fit him in today, in case his previous meetings with either of the Walkers could throw some light on their mind-set in the weeks and months running up to the end. She'd spent a large portion of the late morning and early afternoon making her meticulous notes and now she needed to do something active, something that meant she was moving, hopefully forward.

The Devon and Cornwall police's lead investigator – he'd answered the phone only as 'Cornish' – had been welcoming, used to working with a military liaison on cases involving members of the armed services. He said he would contact her when he needed her help and expertise, had already spoken with a Master at Arms Granger and had all he needed for now; the investigation into Cheryl Walker's murder was proceeding, but from his tone, it was proceeding very slowly.

Dan recognised that Whisky's suicide likely didn't register on Cornish's sonar at the moment. He would have the press chomping at the bit to release details about Cheryl, and his boss, and their bosses, breathing down his neck for something they could offer the public when pictures began to be released of the photogenic murder victim.

He assured her there would be someone at the house to meet her when she arrived and apologised that he didn't have time to meet her himself.

Dan suspected that she wouldn't hear a lot from Cornish for the time being, but when she did it would be a relentless chain of interviewing sailor after sailor, establishing their whereabouts and relationships with the Walkers, ferreting out any possible motive for involvement.

Blackett had been clear that she was on board to investigate Walker's suicide, but he'd ordered her to eliminate as many sailors as possible from involvement in Cheryl Walker's murder.

It bothered Dan, as she drove towards the Walkers' home, that the priority for this investigation seemed to be to ensure *Tenacity* sailed unhindered, not to find Cheryl's killer.

Driving down partially finished roadways in the brand-new housing estate, Dan saw the panda car parked at the end of a driveway and knew she had found the house she was looking for.

It was a broad house with a wide driveway leading to a large, brilliant-white double garage door. From the front windows alone, Dan guessed that there must be at least four good-sized bedrooms. The garden was immaculate; no flowers, no gnomes or a sundial, no signs of a personal touch, just plain, beautifully green grass and a hedgerow which both looked as though they had been trimmed using scissors and a spirit-level.

Dan pulled up and parked, then crossed to the house.

'Help you, ma'am?'

The young police officer approached her from the side of the house, appearing from a pathway that ran behind some trees alongside the garage, probably to the back garden.

As he moved closer, Dan could smell the thick stench of fresh tobacco; no need to guess what he had been doing.

'Dan Lewis, Special Investigation Branch.' She held up her warrant card. 'I spoke with the lead investigator, Cornish, this morning and arranged to come and take a look around.'

The young man was nodding the whole time she spoke. 'Yup,' he said cheerfully, looking pleased to be actually doing something. 'You're on my list, Miss Lewis, please go right in. Forensics are done, so no need for suits, just wipe your feet and don't move anything. Gloves are on the side, just in case.'

He smiled broadly as he delivered his spiel, as though proud at how quickly and efficiently he could dispense it without a single error, slip of the tongue or hesitation.

Dan resisted the urge to pat him on the head and tickle him under the chin; instead she lifted the corners of her mouth for him and nodded appreciation.

He looked her up and down, and then smiled before turning and walking back towards the side of the garage, pulling another cigarette out of his packet as he went.

Dan started to head for the front door.

'One last thing, ma'am,' he called quickly.

She turned.

'There's one other person inside. Just so you know.'

Dan nodded and turned away again. She felt her shoulders slump a little; maybe John Granger had received her message after all.

The young policeman's eyes followed her as she walked into the house.

Dan could feel him watching her as she moved, was aware of her navy-issue trousers tightening around her legs and bum as she took the steps up to the front door. She was torn between conflicting urges: either to enter as quietly as possible, so as to sneak in without immediately having to deal with John, or to rush through the door just to escape the feeling of being 'checked out', or, more accurately, 'examined'. A third option was the one she chose. She turned to look at the young policeman, watching and waiting.

It took a moment.

He looked up at her face, saw her expression, and then immediately looked down to his boots, turning away and stepping out of view behind the corner of the house.

The heavy wooden door opened quickly, but with only the slightest sound as it brushed over the large fitted doormat. Dan shut it slowly and took a pair of gloves from the box just inside. There were only medium size left and they dangled from her fingers and gaped around her wrists. She took them off again and shoved them in her pocket.

The hallway was wide and tastefully furnished in a minimalist style. The centrepiece, dominating the hallway from one wall, was a large picture of the Walkers.

Whisky's face had hardly changed in the years since she'd known him, his smile still broad and genuine. He was lying on the floor facing the camera, and alongside him on one side was a pretty woman with beautifully long red hair, Cheryl Walker. On the other side was a young boy, his mother's double.

The three of them were resting their chins on clenched fists while the second child, the eldest, jumped over the three of them, the shot catching him in mid-air.

Walker was flinching slightly as if the boy might land on him.

All of them seemed to be genuinely smiling or laughing.

It was a snapshot, a moment in time that captured a happy family. The picture was printed onto canvas and had a brilliant white background that blended into the light paintwork of the wall behind it.

Dan looked at the picture closely and wondered where it would hang in the future, if at all.

It was hard to see that this woman could be the same as the one in the pictures she'd looked at just a short time ago, but it was her; the same pale complexion and long hair.

'Happy,' whispered Dan, already lost in her thoughts. She turned to walk further down the hall.

The house looked like a show home, laminate floors and tasteful pastels on the walls, but, so far, none of the mess and chaos that Dan had expected to find in a household with two boisterous young children; a house, not a home; not unlike the building that Dan had returned to yesterday.

She wandered around the ground floor for a while longer, noting more evidence of the 'happy family', but none that indicated that they actually lived here. Eventually Dan walked to the foot of the stairs and looked up. Taking each step slowly, she stopped to look at more pictures of the family as she passed: a collage from a holiday, recent-ish, and the wedding shots that she assumed were obligatory on a wall like this one. She paused and looked more closely at some of them; one in particular caught her eye, a close-up of

Cheryl and another woman, a bridesmaid maybe, familiar. Their faces were pushed close together, cheek to cheek, and their arms were visible, wrapped around each other's necks like best friends who'd never let go.

'Were you really happy?' said Dan, moving slowly from one picture to the next.

'I'm so pleased that I'm not the only one.'

Dan jumped and turned towards the top of the stairs. She lost her balance momentarily and grabbed at the bannister to steady herself.

'Sorry, sorry,' said the woman, taking a step down and clutching Dan's arm. 'That was bloody stupid, surprising you on the stairs like that. I'm really sorry.'

'It's fine, really,' said Dan. 'Stairs just seem to have been a dangerous place for me today.'

The woman, standing a step further up, towered over Dan and seemed to realise this. She apologised again and climbed the step back up onto the landing, moving away to give Dan some space.

Dan followed.

Even on the landing the woman was much taller than her, maybe even a full foot taller, she guessed, but, unlike a lot of tall women who seemed to stoop to try and hide their height, this woman was upright and tall, proud looking, maybe a little stern, like a strict headmistress from a private girls' school.

'Dan Lewis, SIB,' said Dan, offering her hand up to the woman.

'I know who you are,' she said, shaking hands. 'I'm Felicity Green, the Voodoo Lady.' Felicity's eyes went wide and she held her hands out like a child's mock Halloween monster as she introduced herself and gave Dan a broad smile. 'Short for Danielle?' she added.

Dan nodded.

'Man's name for a man's world?' Felicity said, squinting at Dan. She had a similar expression to the one that Dan's granddad used to give her when she questioned his made-up stories about his time in Africa fighting the Zulus, playful and warm.

'We just like to shorten things in the navy, it works well enough.'

'Ah yes. I was reliably informed once that my nickname, if I were to have joined the navy, would have been "Theresa". I won't lie, Dan, I never really understood that.'

Dan smiled, genuinely. 'So why is there a voodoo lady here?' she asked.

The woman drew in a deep breath and looked around the landing. 'Just getting a feel for it really, trying to fathom what kind of family they were. Much the same as you seem to be doing. I'm one of the criminal psychologists in the UK National Crime Agency.' Felicity paused, still looking at Dan with a half-smile that, in another time and place, could have passed for mischievous. 'And I would be lying if I didn't say that I was intrigued at the opportunity to come and meet you. I read the papers you wrote in the aftermath of Operation Poacher and Hamilton's arrest. I thought your work was outstanding. Your paper examining the failings of the investigation's processes and procedures did lead to changes, you know. And your other paper, regarding Hamilton's motivations and experiences, your theory that he may not have been working alone, was ground-breaking. I thought you were very unfairly treated.'

'So, you're working up a profile?' asked Dan, trying for nonchalant and ignoring the compliment, which could only lead to a discussion about Hamilton. 'I didn't realise that they profiled every murder now.'

Felicity smiled and nodded, seeming to acknowledge Dan's reluctance and tacitly agreeing that she wouldn't push any further. 'No, well, this one is unusual.' She paused, her eyes never leaving Dan's. 'Sustained, fractured and violent,' she added. 'We offered to come and take a look.'

Dan said nothing, waiting for the woman to look away. She didn't.

'And because it isn't the first time he's done it, is it?' said Dan, watching Felicity's face carefully for her reaction.

The woman smiled and looked at Dan for what seemed like a long time. 'I think you'll provide real value here. I gather you've only spoken very briefly to DI Branok Cornish, but I told him I thought as much, and I think he'll be keen to hear your thoughts. I'm aware, and he reminded me, that your role is liaison and that you'll be focused on the husband's suicide, but I also asked that you be given a full case file, so you should have seen as much as we have on Cheryl Walker. Tell me, though, what makes you think he's a repeat attacker?' she finally asked. 'Surely not just because I showed up?'

Dan paused before answering. She looked at Felicity and liked her. Liked the way her expressions changed as she spoke, the way she leaned in to say some things, as though you were part of a conspiracy that no one should be allowed to know about, and then suddenly smiled as though the whole idea of a secret was preposterous and juvenile. She liked the way Felicity seemed to speak with her hands, animated like an excited child, yet not to be conscious of it, confident enough to act any way she pleased. She liked the way Felicity spoke, not afraid or embarrassed to be educated and well spoken, but not making it feel like a barrier that she hid behind either. Dan felt that she wanted to talk to this woman, to tell her what she knew – some of it, anyway.

The question lingered in her mind as she thought back to her cabin in the dockyard, to the lockbox that was in there, and the images trapped inside it that resembled so closely the crime scene pictures of Cheryl Walker; impossible to share that secret, though, not now, not with anyone.

Before Dan had to speak, the front door opened and they both instinctively looked down towards it.

The hallway glowed lighter for a moment and then darkened again as a large frame filled the doorway and the familiar form of John Granger came into view.

He looked around, not seeming to notice them at first, and grabbed a pair of gloves from the box next to the door. He pushed his hand into the first one, ripping the latex as it failed to stretch over his thick fingers and wrist. He tried again, and ripped another, and then he picked up two more and shoved all of them into his pocket.

Felicity leaned in and whispered into Dan's ear. 'You know what they say, big hands . . .'

Dan pulled away and looked wide-eyed at the criminal psychologist.

'Big gloves,' said Felicity, making a face as if she was unsure what Dan may have thought she meant. 'Just a professional observation.'

Dan was smiling again, despite herself, turning back towards the stairs as John Granger looked up and their eyes met.

He didn't smile back at her.

'What are you ladies laughing about?' he asked, as he began to climb towards them.

Dan watched as he approached them, the smile drifting off her face.

'John Granger, Master at Arms for the SIB,' he said, holding his hand out to Felicity.

She smiled and shook it, introducing herself as she did so.

'We were just about to walk around up here,' said Dan. 'Why don't you take downstairs and we'll compare notes?'

His eyes lingered on hers until Dan looked away.

'I'll just stick with you guys. Two pairs of eyes are better than one.'

'And three are better than two,' added Felicity, with a broad, energetic smile, as though she was only moments away from shouting 'One for all . . .'

'Lead the way, Doctor,' said John, as though this was a fun family outing and they were all going on a treasure hunt.

Dan's jaw clenched tight.

'There's only one really interesting room up here,' said Felicity, talking back over her shoulder as she walked. 'Although you should, of course, check out all of the others too.'

John stepped back and extended his arm, gesturing for Dan to go next.

She did.

They followed Felicity to a small room at the front of the house. It was furnished as a study, and a space-age computer system stood on a dark solid-wood desk. A large all-in-one printer and photocopier rested on a matching wood filing cabinet next to it. At one side of the room, tucked away against the wall, were several plastic crates. The lids were off and Dan could see that one of them was filled with pictures, all of them framed with the same black, modern-looking painted wood.

There were small nail marks dotted around the wall.

'So these pictures were up and have since been taken down?' asked Dan.

Felicity nodded. 'It's interesting, really. We have absolutely no idea at all why they were taken off the wall. They were packed neatly into the box, as though this was deliberate and unrushed. The room looks too recently painted for it to have been done for an impending redecoration. Also, all of the pictures are from his career: pictures of him with friends, gifts and keepsakes from different places he worked. None are of Mrs Walker or the children.'

'Are they all accounted for?' asked Dan.

Felicity smiled, impressed. 'You're good,' she joked. 'The investigators counted the nails and there is a single picture missing. We have no clue as to what it contained. The investigating team took pictures of them in different sequences on the wall and then showed them to the eldest child, but he wasn't able to help.'

Dan nodded as she listened.

'We have a rough idea of the size, as some of the pictures marked the wall and so we can tell roughly where we think the missing picture was hanging.'

'Why take them down?' asked John.

'Were they going to move house? Or maybe they were separating and only he was leaving?' asked Dan, aiming the question at Felicity.

'We really aren't sure. There is a suspicion that she may have been, and I do mean may have been, having an affair. We have no proof of this, but there were extra requests for her parents to babysit and she was staying out later and dressing more provocatively, according to her parents, at least. That behaviour isn't completely unprecedented from what I gather; navy folk are away so much I think any weakness in a relationship could be quickly exposed. I understand that submariners are away and out of contact for particularly long spells, but I'm sure you two know more about these pressures.'

She looked at Dan and then at John, who nodded and said nothing.

Felicity moved across to the desk and sat down on the plush leather chair.

'I do think that they may have been packing to leave and

then been interrupted,' she said. 'There is nothing to confirm that either way, of course; nothing says that they were going and nothing really shouts out that they were staying. If someone were to be leaving, then I'd suggest they were doing so in secret. The only other thing we are relatively sure is missing, is a secure container.' She opened the top desk-drawer and showed them the space. 'The friction markings on the wood where it was taken in and out fairly regularly have given us a rough size, and the eldest child confirmed that Daddy had a special black box that no one was allowed to touch.'

John moved over to look at the drawer, but Dan knelt down by the crate and pulled on her gloves.

She started pulling out the pictures one by one. There were shots of Walker at various stages of his career. Some were formal, some less so. She paused as she pulled out one that she recognised. She was there, standing alongside 'Whisky' Walker and a handful of others.

They were outside the submarine museum in Gosport, fourteen of them from her basic training intake at HMS Raleigh, lined up alongside a huge chain that led to an anchor which towered over Dan's tiny frame.

The boys were bending their backs, facing each other in teams of six and seven, as though they were going to pick the chain up and have a game of tug-of-war.

Dan was standing in the middle, the only girl; she would be the referee.

They were all smiling; it was a long time ago.

'You knew him?' asked Felicity, her face a frown.

'A very long time ago,' replied Dan, putting the picture back.

She pulled out another one. Walker again, with a small group of men she didn't recognise. Below the picture, mounted onto the frame, was a short piece of black tubing.

'To Whisky – From the Forward ME section – HMS TORBAY' read the message engraved onto a small piece of polished brass.

'What's that?' Dan asked John, holding the picture up without looking at him.

He walked across and leaned over her, looking carefully, feeling close.

'Emergency breathing system air hose. The Chief Stoker's in charge of all the air systems on board.'

'Why would they mount it like that?' asked Dan.

'Can be the bane of your life if it goes wrong. He probably had a hard time with a defect at some point and they gave him this as a leaving gift as a kind of joke.'

John shrugged and turned away, looking around the room.

Dan placed the picture back and looked into the other crate. It was full of boxing trophies, medals, certificates for coaching and awards.

'I'd forgotten he was a boxer,' she said.

'Never understood the attraction, myself,' said Felicity. 'But judging by those medals and trophies . . .' She paused, stood up and crossed the room. Leaning over Dan, she reached into the box, flicking through the pictures like cards in a Rolodex until she found the one she was looking for. 'And with his physique,' she added, showing Dan a picture of Walker in what looked like Diego Garcia.

His overalls were half removed and tied by the sleeves around his waist, his torso revealed, lean and muscular.

'I'd say he would be a very difficult man to overpower,' Felicity concluded.

'He wasn't overpowered,' said John quickly. 'He committed suicide.'

Felicity put the picture back and stood up. 'Of course, I didn't mean that that wasn't the case.'

Dan watched the woman over her shoulder. Their eyes

met and they held the look for a few seconds until Felicity broke off and walked out of the room and slowly down the stairs.

Felicity walked to the front door with them, lingering behind Dan by a few paces and stopping to look at the pictures on the walls and the few other ornaments that were dotted around on the dustless shelves.

'I'm going to nip round the side and speak to that young copper,' said John, as he reached the door.

'I thought you quit?' asked Dan.

He shrugged. 'I got dropped off,' he added, looking at her. 'Blackett thought we could get up to speed in the car.'

He smiled at her and went outside.

She knew he would approach the young policeman, smile, make a joke and be friends with the man in the time it would take a normal person to make a formal introduction; that was John Granger.

'Something isn't right here, is it?' said Felicity, as though she had been waiting for John to leave them.

Dan wasn't sure if it was a direct question to her or if the woman was just thinking out loud.

'No, it isn't,' she said.

'Can you place a finger on it?' Felicity asked.

Dan had a strange feeling that she was being tested.

The Felicity from upstairs with her infectious smile and gleaming eyes seemed to have gone for the moment. Dan felt that now she was meeting Doctor Green, Criminal Psychologist.

'I can put my finger on quite a few things,' she said slowly.

Dr Green tipped her head slightly, saying nothing and waiting for Dan to speak.

'The house just seems too clean and ordered, especially considering that he was away and she was alone with two kids.'

'Definitely,' said Felicity with a smile. 'You don't have children, do you?'

Dan was taken aback by the sudden change of subject. 'No,' she flustered.

'John does, though, I think,' said Felicity, as though her mind were leaping about at tangents.

'Yes, he does.'

'Look at the walls,' Felicity continued, changing tack again as though Dan hadn't spoken. 'They're immaculate, no marks, no scuffs.'

Dan ran her hand across the paint at about waist height. 'Could they have been cleaning and decorating with a view to putting it on the market perhaps?' she asked.

Felicity pursed her lips. 'Maybe. We did find some receipts for work done amongst the others for expensive shoes and fashion boutiques. Mrs Walker had had the hallway painted only a few weeks ago; we thought it could explain the pictures having been taken down in the study, but the painters say they were finished and that they were only contracted for the hallway and lounge. The Walkers also had a cleaner, three days a week.'

Dan nodded. 'I thought that too.'

'What? That they had a cleaner?' asked Felicity, with an eyebrow raised and a wicked smile. She was teasing and Dan knew it.

'No, that there was way too much money here.'

Felicity nodded.

'Far too much,' she agreed. 'I understand that nuclear submariners are paid more than other sailors of similar rank, quite a lot more in some cases. I had one patient, many years ago when I was training, who was continually getting into fights for flicking pound coins at the "skimmers",' she said, making inverted commas with her fingers as she used the slang term for sailors who embarked on ships instead of submarines. 'But not this much more money, and not with a wife that didn't work, so far as we can tell, anyway, and who had a personal trainer at the local gym twice a week.'

Dan nodded again. 'Your guys will be investigating that, though.'

'We will,' said Felicity. 'But, Dan, I can tell you one or two things I'm as certain of as I can be. The man that killed this woman knew her and he hated her, whether he feels he had a reason to specifically hate her, or whether he simply hates all women, I don't yet know. But, she knew him too and he had been here before, in this house, and he knew the husband. I'm certain of it. The brutality of it, the way he marked her, the sustained nature of the attack—'

'You've mentioned that twice now,' interrupted Dan. 'The fact that the attack was sustained.'

Felicity was thinking, clicking her tongue against the roof of her mouth. 'Yes, it's very strange. We may never know why for sure, but Cheryl Walker was badly beaten first and then there seems to have been a break in the attack. We believe that the sexual assault, and a number of other injuries including the strangulation that led to her death, happened some time afterwards.'

'What about interrogation?' asked Dan. 'Could they have been trying to get some information from her? That could explain a break in the attack.'

'Possibly. We really don't know, but then there's also the remote location up on the edge of Dartmoor; there are no indications that anyone else drove her car. We're fairly sure she went there of her own free will, and that leads me to believe that this was someone that Cheryl knew *very* well and that she trusted; this was a friend, maybe more than a friend.'

'And she went to meet him on the same night her

husband's submarine returned – a break-up gone bad?' asked Dan.

'We're not sure that an affair was even happening,' said Felicity. 'But we'd be fools not to consider it.'

'These types of relationships usually start within a close circle of friends, though, don't they?'

Felicity nodded. 'Yes, usually.'

'And the majority of their friends are navy, aren't they?' asked Dan, knowing the answer.

'Yes, we think that the vast majority are. And the vast majority of that vast majority, we think, are submariners.'

'I'm sure you're right,' said Dan, looking back at the big picture of the family that looked into the downstairs hallway. 'But in that case, why aren't you investigating on board *Tenacity* yet? He went there to die, that must mean something.'

Felicity seemed to sigh and Dan was unsure what to read from it. 'The truth is, Dan, we really do believe she may well have been involved with someone in some, as yet undefined, way and that it had to have been going on for several months. An attack like this would seem to have brewed over a period of time, built up and festered over multiple periods of contact with Cheryl, whether that be knowingly on her part or imagined on his. *Tenacity* has been away, and so at this time, we believe that our efforts are better placed searching for someone who could have been in contact with Cheryl in the months leading up to this attack – the guys on *Tenacity* have a watertight alibi for that period.'

'I don't know,' said Dan. 'I think there's more to it than that. Walker was clearly serious about dying, so then why go to *Tenacity*? It wasn't a cry for help; if he'd wanted that, he could have taken pills and waited for the police to kick the doors in and rescue him.'

Felicity was watching her closely now, visibly tuned in to everything she was saying.

'But he risked accessing the naval base and sneaking on board the submarine, exposing himself to several opportunities to be noticed and stopped, to finally do it on board *Tenacity*; there has to be a reason for that.'

'Maybe you're right,' offered Felicity, pursing her lips as she thought it through. 'But you are right about something else too,' she said, coming over and standing next to Dan to look at the picture. 'I don't believe that this is the first time Cheryl Walker's attacker has committed a crime like this one, not the first time at all, but we can't find any other instances to link to this attack.'

The two women were both looking at the family picture as though an answer might appear to them, coming into focus if they waited and watched for long enough.

Dan was biting her lip. 'There was a message in this attack, Felicity,' she said finally, knowing that Felicity was looking at her now. 'I just don't see it as an affair gone wrong, I really don't. I think it was done so that Walker would know who did it and why.'

Felicity was silent and the pair studied the family portrait for a few moments more, before Dan spoke again. 'I'd really like to speak to some of the people that knew them, to help me get a feel for Cheryl and her relationship with Whisky.'

Felicity looked serious. 'I wanted you to see the files, Dan. I believe that you might have some great insights into a complicated case and I'm really interested to hear them, and to ensure that you're listened to. But Branok Cornish is a down-the-line type of detective and he won't want you crossing any boundaries. Your role as Naval Liaison will be one he can live with, although I think if he finds out that you knew Walker at all, even years ago, he'd try to red-card you—'

'We'd never investigate anything if you took that approach; the navy isn't that big.'

'I know, and I agree,' said Felicity.

The door opened behind them, and Felicity lowered her voice instinctively as John started to bustle inside.

'I'm just warning you, one friend to another, how Branok will be. If you start trying to actively pursue his case, he'll shut you down, no doubt about it. So, for the sake of peace, I'd suggest not speaking to any of them without his permission, which he won't give.'

Dan nodded, she had suspected as much.

'I'm sure you're right,' she acknowledged.

Chapter 6

Friday Afternoon – 26th September 2014

Dan moved her bag onto the back seat as John opened the passenger door. She looked at him as he got into the car.

He had lost none of his physique in the years since she had last seen him, looking trim around the middle, his arms still well muscled. He always reminded Dan of a bouncer, or a bodyguard, someone whose job it was to protect.

John Granger was the type of person Dan would normally go to some lengths to avoid. He was loud and had a personality that barely fitted through the main dockyard gate. But working with him on Operation Poacher, tracking down and eventually catching Hamilton, she'd come to really like him and consider him a friend. They'd trained occasionally at lunchtimes, going for runs around the dockyard or Plymouth, or around the streets in London if they were on-site with the Operation Poacher Task Force. They'd often ended up eating together in the evenings when away, even catching an occasional movie and once a show at the theatre, a production that John had barely managed to pretend he enjoyed.

However, when it came down to it, when she had gone to Hamilton's house almost four years earlier, looking for the proof she needed to convince herself that it was Hamilton who was responsible for several decades of missing girls and grisly murders, she hadn't trusted John to come with her.

There was more to it than that; wasn't there always? She hadn't wanted him to be at risk in the early part of her investigation, particularly as she began to look at the whole team, John included. Then, as the lie grew and she became more embroiled, it began to feel impossible to involve him; too much was at stake. Dan would risk herself and her own career, but not her friend's; John never saw it that way.

His face, as he saw her being helped from Hamilton's house, had stayed with her as one of those moments in time in which she could accurately pinpoint having made a big mistake. First, his features were etched with worry, borderline panic, as he looked for her. Then there was relief, verging on bliss, as he'd seen her battered, but safe and alive. Then she'd watched his face change for the final time in their friendship. She was sitting in the back of an ambulance, a medic fussing around her, and he was standing with Roger Blackett, who explained to John what had happened, what Dan had done, what she had done without him.

She stole another look as he slid into the car and then immediately lowered the window on his side, tweaking the air freshener to give off more fragrance.

'Still hate those that smoke the evil weed, eh?' he asked, raising his eyebrows and looking out of the partially open window. 'There's none so judgemental as a poacher turned.'

'When can I speak to the ship's company?' she asked, ignoring his comment. 'I'd like to do it as soon as possible.'

He lowered the window further on his own side and rested his elbow against the door frame.

It was cold, but Dan said nothing.

'She's been out today. Been day-running, pre-operations tests and training. She'll be alongside later,' he said.

'I thought she'd be made to stay alongside?'

He shook his head. 'She's getting ready to sail in a few days and they have to prepare.'

'I assume if *Tenacity*'s just out and back in UK waters, then we won't have to wait for customs or anything? We can just get straight on board?'

'Submarines don't ever deal with customs,' said John. He wasn't looking at her, wasn't making eye contact in the way he normally did when he spoke with people. 'Customs don't have the security clearance, and getting them dogs down the main access hatch ladder, well, that would be a real trial.'

She knew he would be smiling at his own humour and resisted the urge to join him.

'So we can get straight on board then?'

He shook his head, still without looking at her; she could feel it.

'They'll want to shut down the reactor plant and that'll take a few hours, but after that we should be able to get on board. *Tenacity*'s had a rough time lately, a lot of operational running, long periods away from families. I spoke to the Coxswain yesterday – three marriages failed during their last running period; that's three more wedding bands on the collection line.'

He still wasn't looking at her, and Dan kept her eyes to the front, watching the road and checking the rear-view mirror at unusually regular intervals.

She wanted to remain silent, but when John didn't continue she felt compelled to speak. 'So what are you saying, John? This isn't the first suicide investigation I've managed.'

'I'm saying that I heard what Doctor Green was saying

to you at the end there. I'm saying there's already a lot of stress on board. I know the Coxswain and he's been on *Tenacity* forever, so I know what those boys have already been going through. I'm saying that I'm keen that we keep focused on the suicide. We do our jobs and we do them properly. We're not directly involved in the murder investigation, that's for the civvy police, Branok and his team. We've just to gather information, see where people were and confirm that they were where they say. We're in an assisting role, providing information. This won't be glamorous and we won't be single-handedly taking down killers this time out.'

He stopped and let his words hang in the cold air.

Dan watched the road with the intensity of a teenage gamer watching their screen. It felt like a cheap shot coming from him and yet she had little ammunition to throw back. She had gone off-brief when hunting Hamilton – she had been in an assisting role then too – but it was never about the recognition, that was unfair. Dan honestly couldn't have cared less who did or didn't know what part she'd played. It was about justice. It was about the right people, the victims, having the right priority. She heard what John was saying, and maybe he was right, but it was what he wasn't saying, what was implied, that was burrowing under her skin like a parasite.

She swallowed and weighed her response. 'I understand,' she said. 'And we are focused on Walker's suicide. But that'll involve interviewing the whole crew and we're also briefed with ascertaining their whereabouts in the days running up to Walker's suicide and during . . .' She paused, thinking about how she could phrase it, what name she could use that would make her sound objective, as though she wasn't already more invested with Cheryl Walker than she should be. 'Mrs Walker's death,' she finished.

She was aware that he nodded, seemingly appeased.

'But John, if *Tenacity*'s due to sail in three days, then I—' She almost kicked herself. '*We*, still need to get on board as soon as possible.'

He had stopped nodding and they finished the journey in silence.

Dan's mind was clouding as she queued to enter the dockyard gate. She reached up and rubbed her eyes. The long drive and a bad night's sleep had left her feeling worn out.

'Where will *Tenacity* be berthed?' she asked as they drove towards the squadron building.

'Eight Wharf South again, but you've a few hours before she gets back alongside.'

'OK, I'll drop you off. I'm going back to the Wardroom to get some sleep.'

'If in doubt, rack out,' he said, turning to look out of the window.

Dan could tell he was trying hard to suppress his loud and jokey manner as he turned back to face the front.

'You look tired,' he said quietly.

She picked up on a tiny hint of his long dissolved Irish accent.

'I am,' she said, after a moment.

She stopped the car at the bottom of the parade ground and waited for him to get out.

'I'll call you before she gets in?' he said, and then walked away.

Sleep felt like such a good idea, but Dan knew that her head was going to have none of it, as ideas and thoughts, memories and feelings, churned around and mixed together, blurring like running colours in the wash. She parked up behind the Wardroom and stretched as she stepped out of the car.

The leaves from the surrounding trees seemed to be falling at an alarming rate. The ground around her was carpeted in them and, after mixing with the rain, they had created a soft layer of mulch that made navigating the inclined pathway to the entrance quite deadly.

'For God's sake,' said Dan out loud, as she slipped on a patch of damp leaves for the third time. She stopped and thought about it for a second, decided against continuing. She knew where she was going to go.

Reverend Brian Markton was sitting and reading quietly in a small anteroom at the back of the dockyard church.

Dan knew that she hadn't made a sound on the thick carpets as she had approached, and yet he didn't seem surprised when he looked up over the top of his reading glasses to see her standing at the door.

'Hello, young lady,' he said, his voice the epitome of a true West Country accent. 'How can I help you?'

Dan tried not to let his comment bother her. It seemed to be a right of privilege to men of the cloth that they could refer to everyone around them as though they were younger, less experienced in life, and in some way less wizened. She showed him her warrant card, again eliciting no reaction.

'I'm investigating the death of Stewart Walker,' she said.

His brow furrowed and his head nodded slowly. 'Of course, you must be *the* Danielle Lewis from the Special Investigation Branch, Loss of Life division. Come in, grab a pew, I'm pleased to meet you.'

He pointed to a comfortable-looking armchair, one of a matching pair that sat next to each other at a forty-five-degree angle.

Dan sat down, sinking too far back into the soft cushions and noticing that he had tactfully avoided using the nickname normally associated with her team. She thought about shuffling forward and perching on the edge, but Reverend Markton had moved across and taken the seat next to her. Moving further forward now would have brought them uncomfortably close.

He seemed relaxed, his legs crossed, palms down on his thighs, looking at her patiently.

'So what would you like to talk about?' he asked good-naturedly, and Dan felt that she had lost the lead in this interview.

'I understand that Stewart Walker was talking to you in the months leading up to his death, that you had several meetings with him and also Cheryl Walker?'

He nodded.

Dan looked at him closely. He was stout, not fat, but a well-built man getting older. His stomach muscles had begun to surrender slightly and yet his thick forearms and powerful hands gave a hint that he had laboured and would likely still be strong and capable. He had a drinker's nose, marked with red blood vessels and bent from an untreated break, likely many years before. His black clerical shirt and white collar looked impeccably clean and pressed. The only object that drew Dan's eyes was the small set of gold submarine dolphins that were pinned neatly over his left breast.

'He did speak to me, and yes, several times,' Reverend Markton said quietly. 'As did Cheryl; the whole situation is just wretched.'

'What situation?' asked Dan.

He looked at her more cautiously now, as though he had taken offence to the question and might think carefully about future answers. 'The situation that led to a young man taking his own life,' he said.

Dan could sit back no longer and used the arms of the chair to pull herself forward so that she was perching on the hard lip at the very edge of the deep cushion.

He was smiling. A knowing look passed over his face as if he had understood exactly why she had moved forward, had figured her all out in just a few minutes.

'What did he talk to you about when he came to see you?'

'We discussed a number of things that were on his mind,' offered Reverend Markton.

'Can you tell me what sort of things?'

'Not in great detail, no. There was talk about his family life, Cheryl, the kids . . .'

Dan looked into his unwavering eyes.

'Did he talk to you at all about moving home, or leaving the area, perhaps?'

'That wasn't something we spoke about, no.'

'Did he tell you anything at all that might help me to understand what may have led to him taking his life?' She waited, seeing his lips move, but no words came out.

His face became a mask of intense and personal pain. It was as though inside him, his conscience and his sense of duty were physically duking it out and each blow landed by either side meant only anguish for him.

'The loss of Cheryl would have been a clear and obvious blow,' Reverend Markton said, with an air of understanding so thick that Dan could have choked on it. 'They were a very close and loving couple, but I really don't know what I can say to help. We just talked, like many people do with me. That's what I'm here to do.'

'He wasn't religious, though, from what I can gather. Why do you think he'd talk to you as much as he did, as opposed to his friends or relatives?'

'Look, Danielle, I've already spoken to John Granger and Branok Cornish and I'll tell you what I told them.'

She bristled at the mention of John being here and the fact that he hadn't mentioned it to her.

'I'll help you in any way possible. If there was anything at all that I believed would be of use to you then I'd tell you, but I can't just disclose everything that Stewart discussed with me.'

Dan shook her head and stood up to leave. She was edgy and tired, too tired for this shit.

'Wait, Danielle, wait,' he said. 'I'm bound and protected by clergy-penitent privilege.' He also stood up. 'But I can say that I would never, in all conscience, withhold information that might aid your investigation. I, more than anyone, would desperately like to know why Stewart chose the path he did; even in the face of such overwhelming grief. He had his brothers around him, he had options.'

'You've been very helpful,' said Dan, already walking away.

He reached out for her, his fingers brushing her arm.

'If you do want to talk, anytime, day or night, then you only need to come here,' he said quietly.

Dan shook her head and began to walk away.

Passing through the church she looked up at the shape of Jesus on the cross. It had been a long time since they'd seen each other.

Chapter 7

Friday Afternoon – 26th September 2014

Her cabin was cold and there was nowhere in it where she felt comfortable. Dan needed to get out and do something, to make some progress, to prove that she was doing the right thing, or if not, at least doing the wrong thing for the right reasons.

The letter from her dad was on her periphery, but she didn't look at it, couldn't deal with it when she felt her position was already so weak.

Reverend Markton had been no use at all, obstructive even, and the police suspected that Cheryl's attacker had done this before, but they couldn't establish a link to a previous attack; Dan could.

She knew she had information that she should share, which would aid the police in their investigation, but she couldn't explain to them the origins of it, wouldn't be able to come clean about what she knew and how she knew it. In her mind now, she hated herself for this. It was weakness that stopped her from telling them, from telling anybody about the files in her secure box, the pictures and information gathered from a sabbatical year that commenced exactly one year and one day after Chris Hamilton was sentenced to life imprisonment without hope of parole.

She was still hyper-aware of the letter but she had to move forward; there was no time to deal with these thoughts now. If she couldn't share the information, then she had to turn it to her advantage, use it to make amends with the investigation.

Felicity seemed sold on the angle that Cheryl had been murdered by a lover or someone in a relationship, that the motive for murder lay somewhere inside Cheryl's life, tangled up with children and a husband that was rarely home.

But Dan couldn't believe it. It just didn't work. Not because of how Cheryl had died, but because of how and where Walker had, and she couldn't shake that thought from her head.

The Walkers' home was still fresh in her mind and she thought back through all that she had seen and done, considering every moment again, trying to see something that might offer an insight to her, a glimpse of a way forward. Then she let her mind replay the conversation with Felicity, even the warning about how DI Branok Cornish might deal with her if she tried to interfere beyond her remit.

One of the photographs on the stairs came back to Dan, the two fast friends hugging cheek to cheek, the familiarity of the faces. She stood up and crossed to her desk, sorting through the papers until she found the list of names that had come with the case files. She scanned it quickly, then more slowly, reading each name in turn.

The second woman's face, the friend, was in the forefront of Dan's mind, not someone she knew well, but a face she'd seen before. She focused on the female names, none of them hitting the mark, until near the bottom, she saw it: Gemma Rockwell.

'Lieutenant Gemma Rockwell,' said Dan out loud.

She smiled and felt as though she could have punched the air. The navy was a smallish place and she remembered Gemma from an event or social in one of the Wardrooms, though she couldn't place the exact time.

The warning from Felicity played again in her mind, that she shouldn't probe outside her liaison role, but Gemma Rockwell was navy. She was armed forces, uniformed personnel and, as such, was fair game.

Now, Dan just needed to find Gemma and hope she wasn't away at sea.

It was the end of the working day when Dan made her way up the gangway of HMS *Lancaster* and stepped onto the flight deck. She'd had to wait at the bottom for several minutes as sailors walked down the ramp, heading home for the night and leaving the ship behind in the hands of the duty watch.

Gemma Rockwell was dressed in her No.1 uniform, a neatly fitted black suit, with white shirt and tie and two gold bands around the cuff of each sleeve showing her rank, which was equal to Dan's. She was placing her tricorn hat on as she hurried out onto the flight deck looking flustered. She was the Officer of the Day and as the rest of the crew exited, her hassles were just beginning.

Dan extended her hand and shook Gemma's by way of greeting.

'I don't have a lot of time,' said Gemma before Dan could speak. 'The Captain's living on board at the moment; it's a nightmare.'

'That's fine. I won't take much of your time. I'm surprised you're here. I thought you'd be at home, to be honest.'

Gemma nodded and Dan noticed how red and blotchy her face was and how her eyes never quite settled on Dan's; this was someone who was hurting.

'The mob doesn't recognise friends as compassionate cases,'

Gemma replied. 'I'd rather be here anyway. We're low on qualified Officers of the Day and if someone drops out it just gets crapper for everyone else.'

'Keeps the mind off it too?' asked Dan.

Gemma nodded and checked her watch.

'I just wanted to talk to you a little bit about Stewart and Cheryl Walker,' began Dan. 'I understand you and Cheryl were close friends?'

Gemma looked at Dan and seemed to think hard about her reply.

'That policeman with the funny name said I shouldn't say anything about anything to anyone else. He made it clear that if I breathed a word of it I'd be in trouble. He seemed to think he could keep what happened a secret.'

'Well, I'm with his team,' said Dan, making sure she held eye contact and pulling out her warrant card. 'So I'm going to ask you to do exactly the same things as DI Branok Cornish did.'

'That's him, Branok Cornish,' said Gemma, seeming to relax at Dan knowing his name.

'But I do want you to talk to me about how Cheryl was in the days and weeks leading up to her attack. I'd also like to ask you about her relationship with Stewart Walker.'

Gemma nodded, but not in a positive way. She was nodding to say she was frustrated, that she had said this before and that she didn't want to say it again. 'That's what he asked,' she said. 'Was Cheryl seeing someone? Was she having an affair? Did she tell me who she was hanging out with? Did I think she'd lie to me?'

The nod had changed to a slow shake of the head now and Gemma's eyes were filling with tears.

'I'll tell you what I told them,' she said. 'I don't *know* anything. She was my friend, for years now, my best friend. We talked every day, except when I'm on here, because the signal's pants. She was up and down, but when Stewart was away she always was. Two kids on her own, months without any messages, news or emails.'

Dan just watched and waited, letting Gemma talk.

'She was just Cheryl, you know, just normal. I don't know anything to help, I really don't.'

'Ma'am.' A voice rose from off to Dan's left, near to the hangar that bound the forward side of the small flight deck.

Gemma and Dan both turned to look.

'Captain's looking for you,' said a young able seaman. 'He's in his cabin.'

Gemma nodded. 'I'll be right up.' She turned back to Dan. 'Look, I have to go. When the policeman came he made an appointment and I spoke to him at the regulating office. If you'd do that, then I'd have more time.'

'It's fine,' said Dan. 'I'm almost done, I promise, but I just want you to do one thing for me. I'll be quick.'

Gemma looked impatient.

'I don't want you to tell me what you *know* – I understand that you feel you don't know anything that will help – but I want you to tell me what you think, what you feel.'

'I'm not feeling very much at the moment.'

'I know,' said Dan, 'I can only imagine. But do you think that Cheryl was having an affair? Do you feel that she would have a relationship while Stewart was away? Even something fun and casual, something harmless?'

Gemma looked nervously in the direction of the ship's superstructure and the space where the young sailor had called her from. Then she looked back, making eye contact with Dan and holding it.

'No,' she said, shaking her head. 'I really don't think she would. You know, Cheryl was gorgeous, funny, loud. She loved to be the centre of attention, she bought shoes and clothes she couldn't afford, she sometimes flirted just for fun, but she loved her family and I really don't think she would do the dirty on Stewart. If she did, I really do think she'd have told me.'

'I believe you,' said Dan, 'and I believe she would have confided in you, but I just want to ask one more thing—'

'Ma'am?' It was the young sailor again.

'I'm coming,' said Gemma. 'Look, I really have to go.'

'I know, but please, it's important, one last thing. Forget about knowing things, just concentrate on what you feel and tell me, how do you think Cheryl felt about *Tenacity* coming back this time?'

Gemma looked off in the direction of the submarine berths, as though she might see *Tenacity* watching her as she spoke about it. She seemed to think about it hard, pursing her lips and shaking her head again, as though she couldn't reconcile what she was thinking and what she was about to say.

'Gemma, I don't need any proof, or any evidence, I just want to know what you feel, no more than that,' Dan said.

Gemma looked back and sighed. 'I think she could have been frightened.'

'Why could that be?' asked Dan. 'Why would you pick up on that, do you think?'

'I really don't know. She never said anything or did anything, but there was something different this time.'

'Did you ask her about it?'

'It wasn't like that, it was just . . .' Gemma paused again. 'I really don't know, I'm sorry.'

'It's fine,' said Dan. 'Honestly, just one last question.'

'I really have to go now,' Gemma said.

'I know, but very quickly, why frightened, why not nervous or anxious; why did you say frightened?'

Gemma started to walk away, stopping a few yards from Dan and turning back. 'I don't know,' she said. 'You asked me how I felt and that's what I felt. It wasn't an anxious excitement, it wasn't pre-return nerves. I don't know what it was, but you asked me to tell you what I thought, and I have. If I had to give it a name, I'd say it was fear.'

Chapter 8

Friday Evening – 26th September 2014

Dan's mind hadn't stopped. For hours, images from the investigation flicked through it like a never-ending slide-show, the animation effects spinning the pictures away, or dragging them in close as they scrolled through. They were interspersed with memories of John Granger after the Hamilton case, his face when he realised she had gone to Hamilton's house without him, had carried out an entire investigation without including him, that she didn't trust him. Then there was Blackett, first on the scene, furious, yet relieved to see her alive. Her sister Charlie, her dad and the Tasmanian Devil toy, all looking at her, followed by more images from the pictures inside her secure box. Felicity Green's face morphed into the Reverend Brian Markton shaking his head in sorrowful apology, then Roger Blackett again, saying 'I will tell you what'. Then there were other recollections that began to appear, probing at her defences; ones that she knew must never again break through.

When John called, it gave her a reason to open her eyes

and escape the memories; something that she felt would have been too much like cowardice before then.

On the walk down from the Wardroom, she had stopped and looked out to sea. The amphibious assault ship, HMS *Ocean*, was alongside in a maintenance period and dominated the skyline. Behind it and to the left, gliding slowly along the Hamoaze, she saw the black lines of a surfaced submarine as it drifted towards its berth. She could clearly see the conning tower and masts, and knew that it must be *Tenacity* stealing her way back towards home.

Dan stopped and watched until the submarine finally drifted from sight, first dwarfed, and then swallowed behind HMS *Ocean*.

She met John near to the Senior Rates Mess and he fell in beside her as she walked past him.

'Why don't you bring me up to speed on what you've done?' she said. 'I gather you've already spoken with Reverend Markton. I would have thought that worthy of mention?'

She felt him sigh next to her, but he didn't reply.

'Well?'

'Well, I spoke to him, not interviewed, just spoke to him, and he said pretty much nothing,' John said. 'I wouldn't go and interview anyone alone. As you know, that's not how we do business in the SIB. I can arrange for us to go and speak to him later on today if you want to, together?'

They walked on in silence for a while.

'Can we get straight on to the ship now? I'm sure I just saw her coming back in.'

'Boat,' John said.

'Sorry?'

'Submarines are boats, not ships.'

'Thank you, I'll bear that in mind,' she said with an almost imperceptible shake of her head.

She turned towards him, not stopping. 'You know, John, I feel like you have an issue with me and I do wonder if it would have been better if you had declined this assignment.'

'Planned to,' replied John. 'Tried to.' His voice was matter-of-fact. He watched the pavement directly ahead and made no move to face her. 'Commander Blackett called me directly, would have me and only me.'

Dan turned to look at him as she walked. 'He asked you before me, knowing I was going to be the lead? Told you it would be me?'

John nodded.

Dan pursed her lips and felt her cheeks go red. 'And?' she questioned.

'And he's a Commander and I'm a Master at Arms. He said I had to do it and so I had to do it; that's how it works in the Royal Navy. It's a very hierarchical environment.'

Dan shook her head again, making no attempt to hide it this time. She just felt powerless to fire. A comment about how he might adhere more closely to the hierarchy and show a little more formality jumped to mind, but she knew full well that he was a professional investigator in his own right. He had been trained and nurtured to operate in a strict rank structure, but to think for himself, to recognise and respect other people's views, opinions and skills. Pulling rank on a senior Master at Arms would do little more than set him against her more firmly.

A young female sailor was walking towards them and Dan accepted her salute, returning it.

'Phone away, young lady,' boomed John, ever the policeman.

The sailor looked sheepish and slipped the phone that had been carefully concealed in her left hand into her pocket.

'I don't want to see that again, please,' he added. 'The call can wait until you're in your cabin. Understood?'

'Yes, Master,' said the girl, and turned, almost marching now as she carried on up to her accommodation.

Dan swallowed as they walked on, annoyed at John for this and not really sure why. It was his job to maintain discipline and order and his authority as a Master at Arms stretched across all naval real estate.

Ahead of them now, illuminated by street lighting around the exclusion zone, the conning tower of HMS *Tenacity* began to rise into view.

Dan knew it had to be *Tenacity*, the only Trafalgar-class submarine currently alongside, the other six elsewhere or decommissioned to make way for the new Astute-class submarines that would shortly be in service.

'Who's on board?' she asked, as they neared the submarine exclusion area.

John stopped and held out a hand for her to do the same.

'That's the exclusion zone,' he said, not looking at her and obviously refusing to acknowledge her tone. 'Like a security perimeter. We need to wait here and be signed in.'

He walked over and showed his ID card to the Health Physics Monitor.

They spoke for a few moments before he returned.

'The Commanding Officer is on board, Commander Melvin Bradshaw,' he said. 'He's going to meet you. He has the Marine Engineering Officer with him too, and the Coxswain is bound to be there somewhere. The engineers should finish off shutting down the plant soon, but the boat will still be busy, so we might have to wait a while.'

Tenacity's tall black conning tower was the only clearly visible part of the boat. It was rocking gently with the ebbing tide, the remainder of the submarine hidden below the dock-side wall.

Dan knew enough about submarines to know that the masts sticking out of the tower were likely to be communications masts, tall enough to penetrate the surface whilst the submarine remained dived and out of sight. A smaller mast at the back looked as though it was shooting out a pressurised jet of steam.

'What's that?' she asked, gesturing to John, conscious not to sound too sharp.

'Diesel exhaust mast. Sometimes they run diesel generators to give extra electrical supplies when the reactor's shutting down. They should have shore-side electrical power,' he said, looking at his watch. 'Must be a problem with the shore supply for it to be taking this long.' He pointed to three thick black electrical cables that ran across the jetty and disappeared over the side.

He stepped forward into the exclusion area and nodded to the Health Physics Monitor, assuring him that they wouldn't go too far.

Dan followed.

A cluster of hats came into view towards the back end of the submarine. Around them, people were moving about on the submarine's casing, out of sight from those outside the exclusion zone.

To Dan's left and past the conning tower, a number of sailors appeared near to the forward gangway. Dan watched them line up atop the black casing.

'Do you know what they're going to do?' John asked, still without looking at her.

Dan pursed her lips and shook her head. 'Strange bunch, all of them,' she said.

He chuckled, sounding genuine, and nodded. 'They are that. I'm one.' He pointed to the set of gold dolphins that were pinned to his shirt above the left pocket.

All of the submariners wore them on their white shirts or dress uniform. The submarine insignia: a gold badge showing two dolphins facing each other with their snouts meeting below a crown. Submariners wore it on their belt buckles and their lanyards, it was on T-shirts and even watches. To a man, they seemed to covet this badge and wish for everyone around them to know they'd earned it.

'Something needs to be a little bit different about someone who spends months locked away in one of them. No daylight, no news, no contact with families or loved ones,' John was saying. He paused as he watched the men on the casing quickly arrange themselves into a straight line.

A voice command, barely audible in the wind, brought them to attention as a short, fat man, the Commanding Officer, Commander Melvin Bradshaw, judging by the gold braid on the peak of his uniform cap, climbed up the ladder that led from within the submarine and stepped onto the casing. A tall, wiry Senior Rate with a slight limp followed him as he walked towards the line of young sailors.

'They're getting their dolphins today,' said John, and smiled.

Dan looked at him out of the corner of her eye. It was late in the day and she could see his thick black stubble shadowing across his face. She knew he would continue to talk to her now; she'd received many of his friendly monologues in the three years they had worked together, before she'd caught Hamilton. John was always willing to share knowledge and experience, and was unable to sustain any kind of hostility towards anyone for long, a man that thrived off the team around him.

'The Old Man – that's what they call the Commanding Officer of a submarine – he'll give them a speech about what it means to be a submariner. Then the Coxswain gives them each a measure of rum. Their dolphins are at the bottom of the glass. They have to down the rum in one and catch the dolphins in their teeth. Then they're in.'

'They're in?' she asked.

He turned to look at her. 'They're in,' he agreed.

'Drink rum and catch a badge in your teeth and you're in. All sounds reasonable,' she said, slowly, sarcastically.

Dan watched the men on the casing. She saw the Old Man talking to them, but wasn't able to make out what he was saying. Then she saw the rum being poured, the gold pin that bore the dolphins being dropped into each glass, and one being handed to each of the young sailors in turn.

In a single coordinated movement, they threw back their heads and downed the rum.

Dan stood in silence, waiting.

A chuckle escaped from John's lips, raspy from smoking.

One of the young sailors fell to his knees, clutching at a hastily provided bucket.

John's laughter grew louder as the sound of the sailor vomiting rose above the noise of the wind.

'Will he still get to keep the dolphins?' asked Dan.

She watched Granger laugh for a second more and shake his head, not saying no, just enjoying being part of it again, even from a distance.

'He'll get to keep them,' he said, and then cupped his hands around his mouth. 'Well done, Deeps,' he bellowed.

The Commanding Officer and the Coxswain turned to see who had shouted. They seemed to recognise John, the Coxswain raising his hand in greeting, before both turned away quickly, shaking hands with all of the sailors.

Then, the ceremony over, the Coxswain climbed back down into the darkness of the submarine while the Old Man walked along the casing, heading aft. He disappeared from view, skirting around the base of the conning tower.

'I wouldn't have thought you'd be allowed to go round the side of the conning tower,' Dan commented. 'It looks pretty narrow.'

'There's a handrail and enough space for your feet,' John said.

'And if you fall in?'

'Then either you, or someone else that sees you fall in, calls Man Overboard. Then all hell breaks loose. The Queen's Harbour Master gets called in, butts get kicked and names get taken and hopefully someone drags you out before you drown,' said John. 'So it's just best if you don't.'

Dan frowned. Then she looked around and walked closer to the submarine.

'Dan,' said John, surprised. 'Ma'am,' he corrected quickly, conscious of people around them.

'It's ma'am like jam, not ma'am like smarm,' said Dan, flashing a smile, and then she turned away, walking towards the edge of the jetty.

On the casing a number of sailors, mostly in blue overalls and black berets, appeared to be pulling at the black cables and shouting instructions down into the submarine through another open hatch.

Standing off to the side, a few feet from the conning tower, was a cluster of three men. One of them was dressed in blue overalls, as the many sailors around him were, but his sleeves were rolled up and his beret was in his pocket. Next to him was a face that Dan recognised, but couldn't immediately place. The man was dressed in filthy white overalls and had also removed his beret; he looked as though he was in deep conversation with the Commanding Officer.

'Hello, ma'am. Hello, Master.'

The voice came from behind and Dan turned to see that John Granger had followed her, albeit at a distance.

A few yards away from them both she saw a short, slightly overweight young sailor standing with a dishtowel in one hand. He used the towel to finish drying his hands and then offered Dan a relaxed salute.

'I'm Able Seaman Ben Roach, ma'am,' the sailor continued in a flowing cockney accent. 'I'm the Old Man's steward.

Met you before, I think, Master?' he said, gesturing towards John, but not pausing. 'The Old Man is expecting you, asked me to take you down into the wardroom and get you a nice cup of tea.'

'I think I'll just go over and introduce myself first,' replied Dan, already starting towards the aft gangway.

'With respect, ma'am, the Old Man said to take you straight down.'

Dan ignored Ben and continued to walk towards the aft gangway that would take her from the jetty across to the submarine casing and allow her access to Commander Bradshaw. As she approached, she could see that the Old Man was on the phone. She began to hear his booming voice as it carried above the sound of the wind and waves.

'I don't care how short of dockyard workers we are; I don't care who's on strike or who's not paying for overtime. I want my shore supply working and my boys out of here and in the bar by twenty-one hundred, is that absolutely clear?'

She could see that all of the men who were working on the cables were also half listening, smirks apparent on a few of their dirty faces.

Bradshaw used his free hand to firmly end the call and turned to the mass of blue overalls.

'You finish this up, men. There'll be a team down from inboard to sort their side out within the hour.'

He smiled, his particularly bushy eyebrows rising into a large 'M' as he did so.

There was a small cheer from some of the men as they carried on about their work.

Dan continued to approach, paused to step up onto the gangway, and watched the eyebrows drop into a furrowed frown as she did so.

'Steward Roach, I asked you to take our guests to the wardroom,' shouted the Old Man, completely ignoring Dan.

'I did try to do just that, sir,' replied the steward. 'But ma'am was intent on meeting yourself right away, sir.'

Commander Bradshaw glowered at his steward.

Dan shouted into the wind. 'I'm Lieutenant Lewis, SIB. Thank you for offering to support us while we're here.'

The Old Man didn't even look at her.

'I asked Steward Roach to take you below and for you to wait in the wardroom,' he said. 'I will see you down there when I'm ready.'

With that he turned back to the small group of men again and began talking.

'Dan,' whispered John Granger from next to her left shoulder. 'Let's just go.'

'Actually, sir, I understand that this investigation is time sensitive and so I'd like to get going straight away. Perhaps we could discuss an interview location and one of your crew could help me to draw up a list of who's on board now. It would also be very useful if the crew—'

The Old Man spun around and glared at Dan. He took several paces across the small gangway, stopping a few feet away from her.

'Ship's company, Lieutenant Lewis; fishing trawlers have a *crew*. Her Majesty's Submarines have a *ship's company*.'

Dan could see that the men who had overheard the phone call a few moments ago were now listening to this exchange. She paused for just a moment, feeling like a scolded child.

'Yes, sir, I'm—'

'And my men have spent months at sea. We've had only this week in base-port in over four months and it hasn't gone very well. Have you ever been on a submarine, Lieutenant Lewis?'

The Old Man didn't wait for an answer.

'No, I thought not. My men need to go home, or go to a bar, have a well-deserved shower, a beer and some food.

Then, when they have done that, you will be able to book some time with them to ask what questions you need to ask. Is that clear?'

Dan became aware that the men on the submarine casing were no longer just listening; all work had stopped and all of the faces, most with smears of black, like soot or dark grease, were turned towards her, watching the exchange.

Her hands began to tremble with fury and her jaw, the barometer of her emotions, clamped tight shut. She looked around at the men, noting that none of them turned away from her, and took a deep breath.

'I'll wait for you, sir,' she said, in a calm voice. She stepped back, saluted, and without waiting for the salute to be returned, turned away.

Steward Roach signed them in quickly and they began to walk towards the forward gangway.

Dan could see that this gangway was larger than the one at the aft end of the submarine. It led across from the jetty to the casing and touched down forward of a small blue hut that looked as though someone had mistakenly placed it on the submarine's hull, the flat blue sides and square form-factor clashing with *Tenacity*'s black curves and smooth lines. Dan hadn't seen one before, but knew that it was a bullet-proof security box that was placed over the main access hatch, the main entry point to the submarine.

Steward Roach jogged a few paces to get in front of them and began to lead the way, talking immediately.

'First time on a submarine then, ma'am? No problem. We don't use the aft gangway very much; it's only there in case we have an emergency on the nuclear plant, so that people can get off from either end without having to pass above the reactor compartment.' He held out the dishtowel and pointed towards the boat. 'Those red marks there,' he said, turning to look at Dan and pointing to some red lines painted

98

onto the submarine's casing. 'They're the marks that show you where the reactor compartment is, see?'

He led her across the gangway, seemingly unaware that she wasn't really taking part in his impromptu tour. He entered the blue security box, which sat over the hatch to the submarine like a small shelter over a deep well.

The ladder that led down from the main access hatch was vertical and made of polished silver steel. An extension was fitted to the top of the ladder, allowing it to protrude up above the level of the casing, so that personnel could easily step onto the top rung and climb down into the belly of the submarine.

'You'll have to leave your laptop and phone up here, please, ma'am,' said the steward, pointing at Dan's bag and the obvious laptop compartment within it. 'The Upper Deck Trot will keep an eye on it,' he added, pointing to a sailor in green combats with a naval provost armband wrapped around his right wrist. 'Just stick it in the corner of the Trot-Box – like a bulletproof Tardis, these things, and with your very own armed guard,' he said jokingly, this time pointing to the other sentry, who was cradling an SA-80 rifle across his chest. 'Can't get no safer than that, I don't reckon.'

Dan nodded and pulled the laptop out of her bag, her eyes never leaving the hole that led down into the submarine. She placed the laptop in the corner of the 'Trot-Box', peering into the boat as though looking down over a sheer cliff face.

'Ready?' asked John.

She turned to him quickly when he spoke, startled out of her thoughts.

'Should we grab an office up in the squadron building to do this?' she asked. 'It'd be easier to be out of everyone's way.'

John looked confused. 'We'd be waiting hours for them to get off the boat; the Coxswain and the MEO might be here all night. If you want to get going, then it has to be here.' He shrugged as if everything he had said was painfully obvious.

Dan nodded and looked down again. The space below looked brightly lit now that she could look straight down past the lip of the hatch, and she could see Steward Roach waiting for her below.

The entrance to the submarine was small and the ladder felt slippery, such that Dan had to pass her rucksack to John and have him hold it for her as she scaled the long ladder. Once inside, she reached up and took back her bag from him and then stopped to look around. The area was fitted with a short-pile, institutional carpet similar to that fitted throughout the accommodation blocks. As Dan turned she saw a large white airlock door, with red fluid drips running down from near the hinges and spreading out, like a badly considered map over the dirty white paint.

'That's fifty-nine watertight bulkhead, ma'am,' said the steward, continuing his constant flow of commentary. 'That leads back through the Tunnel and into the engine rooms.'

'The Tunnel?'

'That whole section between the two watertight bulkheads is the reactor compartment, ma'am, remember the red paint marks? The Tunnel goes through it so when the reactor's operating we can still get from forward, where you are now with all the accommodation and the control room and stuff, to the engine rooms that are aft. If you go through the airlock doors and take a few paces, you'll literally be stood directly over the top of a nuclear reactor.'

Dan smiled, trying to look unimpressed.

'That's the Old Man's cabin in there,' he said, tapping his hand against a polished wood sliding door that was half open.

Dan peered inside quickly and pulled her head back out. The spaces around her were confined, but not as dark and dingy as her imagination had decided they might be.

'It's tiny,' she said, her unease starting to subside as her interest in this new environment was kindled. 'My couch is bigger than that room.'

Steward Roach pulled a face of mock hurt. 'Ma'am, that's the most grandest cabin on the whole submarine. It all gets smaller and sparser from thereon in.'

She smiled, unable to stop herself, and moved away from the ladder as she heard a call of 'Below! Clear the ladder, one down.'

She looked up to see John Granger's backside descending towards her.

'Come on, ma'am,' piped up the steward. 'I'll get you a brew before Master Granger crushes us all.'

She followed Ben down a short inclined ladder, almost a stairway, and along a narrow passageway until they finally entered a small room with benches lining one bulkhead and a wall-mounted, flat-screen television opposite them. The two tables in front of the seats looked as though each could seat four people in relative comfort. There was no need to ask the question, though.

'About twenty of us in here when we're at sea, ma'am,' said the steward. 'We eat in two sittings and it's used as an office the rest of the time, except on Friday, when the Old Man likes to put on a movie and have popcorn. Tea?'

Dan looked around as she heard a knock at the wardroom door. It was John Granger.

'In you come, Master,' said the steward quickly. 'Old Man said for you both to come and wait in here.'

John stepped through the door, blocking it completely as he turned slightly and ducked his head to pass through.

'Tea?' Ben Roach repeated.

'I'm OK, thank you,' said Dan. 'I only really drink green tea.'

'Might have some fag-bags in the pantry, ma'am,' he said. 'And you, Master?'

'NATO standard,' said John. 'Gash-bag brown.'

'A strong white tea with two sugars and a green tea coming right up,' said Steward Roach without missing a beat. 'Take a seat then and I'll bring it through.'

The area around her was small; it wouldn't even be considered a good-sized lounge in a family home. She had known there would be no windows – this wasn't Nemo's *Nautilus* – but now, knowing how far into the boat she had come, understanding how far light would have to travel to get there, she felt herself swallow, suddenly, though reluctantly, glad of John's presence.

A loud wave of raucous laughter shot through the enclosed area like a thunderclap.

Dan jumped, immediately looking around to see if anyone had noticed her do so.

There was another surge of laughter and some muffled swearing.

John stood up and walked across the wardroom to a second door that led through to a small pantry.

Dan followed, interested, but also having no wish to be alone if John carried on further.

'What's happening?' he asked Ben, who was standing back, his cheery face now stony, in complete contrast to all the other sailors who were laughing and cheering.

Dan peered around John.

Directly across from the wardroom pantry, beyond a narrow passageway, was another room. Inside, through gaps in other onlookers' legs, she could see something on the floor but wasn't able to make out what it was.

'They got Ryan with a Neil Robertson bite,' said Ben,

through gritted teeth. 'They're whipping him with an EBS hose.'

John looked back and caught Dan's frown. He moved aside and gestured for her to come and take a look.

'The stretcher they use for casualties in hard-to-reach places,' he whispered. 'It completely immobilises the person; they can't move their arms, legs, head, nothing. It's horrible.' He chuckled. 'Happened to me at sea on my eighteenth birthday,' he added with a smile.

Dan was able to see more now. The young sailor was lying on his back with his arms and legs perfectly straight, as though he was standing to attention. His head was held firmly facing the front by a strap across his forehead and all along the side of his body were long straight lengths of wood, like splints, that were strapped tightly together. He was completely immobile and she could see that his face was bright red as he winced.

Ben Roach stepped forward. 'Enough!' he shouted. 'Let him up.'

No one listened to him and the jeering continued without pause. Ben looked agitated, stepping from foot to foot, his fists balled.

'John, we can't watch this,' Dan said quietly into his ear. He nodded his agreement.

'All right,' he said, his voice carrying above the din. 'Enough. Let him out.' The crowd quietened immediately as John's voice split through the noise.

Sailors turned to look at him, some recognising him, others recognising the brassard he wore on his right wrist, the laurel leaves supporting a crown denoting his position and authority.

In the new quiet, Dan could hear for the first time a 'thwack, thwack' sound coming from the room. The sailor's face went redder still and he cried out as Dan heard the sound again.

'Enough,' said John, louder this time.

People began to disperse, heads down, sensing that trouble might follow.

'Thwack,' the sound came again and Dan was sure that she could see a tear form in the sailor's eye as he lay helpless on the floor.

John braced up at being disobeyed and made to cross the pantry.

Dan followed him.

He crossed the two-deck passageway, the corridor that ran from the forward end of the submarine all the way along the second level. It was narrow, one and a half people wide at best, and in a few paces John had left the pantry, crossed the gap and entered the Senior Rates Mess where the sailor was bound.

Dan peered around the door and saw a sailor in blue overalls, his sleeves rolled up, his head closely shaven; he had been one of the two men on the casing that she had seen speaking with the Old Man just a few minutes before, his beret still folded flat and tucked into one pocket.

The man brought a long piece of black hose down hard onto the helpless sailor's torso.

'Chief,' John's voice was fully raised. The room echoed with his shout and the man with the hose stopped and looked up.

'Help you, Master?' he asked, his face a picture of exertion that he seemed to easily turn into boredom.

'Enough,' said John, his voice firm.

The two men stared at each other.

Dan could see a sneer on the other man's face, but he stopped and threw the length of black hose onto the floor.

'We're just having a bit of fun, Master,' he said, almost spitting the final word.

John ignored the comment. He turned to Ben. 'Steward Roach, get him out of there.'

The young steward knelt down quickly to comply.

'You all right, son?' said John, looking down at the sailor as he was released from the stretcher.

'I'm all right, Master, thank you. It was just a bit of fun,' said the boy, his voice almost a whisper. His face was red and flustered and he was blinking back tears. He tried to smile at John but seemed to actively avoid looking at Dan at all.

Ben Roach helped the sailor up and reached across to touch him, using his thumb to wipe one of the tears away. 'You OK, Ryan?' Ben was saying quietly. 'They're fucking wankers, the lot of them.'

Dan turned and began to walk back through to the wardroom. As she did, Ben gently lifted a small flap of Ryan's shirt, exposing the pale flesh of his stomach and a long, angry welt that stood proud from his skin. Stopping and turning back into the room, she looked at the mark.

'Master Granger.'

John turned to face her.

'I'd like to keep that piece of hose, please.'

The chief who had been using it shook his head and picked it back up. 'No can do, ma'am.'

'Yes can do, chief,' said John, holding out his hand.

The chief seemed to weigh up his options, deliberately taking time to consider what he should do. Then he smiled sweetly and dropped the hose back onto the floor. He walked towards John who was blocking his route of egress.

The two men came face to face.

John towered over the chief. His back tensed, the muscles on his hands and forearms twitching beneath thick, dark hairs that he swore were a gift of his Irish descent.

The chief, smaller, finer made, looked sinewy by comparison to John's bulk, every strand of muscle visible on his naked forearms, the muscles in his jaw apparent as they tensed and released when he spoke.

'Excuse me,' he said, and waited, his eyes locked on John's.

Dan looked on, as John stayed put, not moving, not backing away.

The two men faced off in silence.

'Please,' said the chief after a long moment.

John nodded and stepped backwards, allowing him to pass.

As soon as the chief had disappeared from view, John bent down, picked up the hose and spoke to Steward Roach. 'Who's that, Ben?' he said quietly. 'I've not seen him before.'

'That's the old Chief Stoker, Master. He left for a while when Whisky took over, but he's come back now that Whisky is . . .' Ben paused. 'Gone.'

Chapter 9

Friday Evening – 26th September 2014

The cup was almost empty, part of the tea bag sitting in the remnants of green tea that remained at the very bottom. The residue looked like oily swamp water and the section of the bag above the waterline had begun to dry out around the edges, slowly turning a muddy brown. The brown was also travelling steadily up the little length of white string that ran from the bag, out of the cup, and around the handle; it was looking more and more like neglected rigging.

Across from her, seemingly content to wait, John was leafing through a large stack of newspapers and magazines that had been brought on board for the duty submariners.

Ben Roach stuck his head around the door from the adjacent pantry, a room about the size of a portable toilet, and made to speak. He had an iPad tucked under his arm, encased in a plush leather case.

'I'm OK, thank you, Steward Roach,' said Dan, before he could offer her another cup of green tea, apparently from the Old Man's 'very own' stash.

He nodded and went back to whatever it was that he had

been watching, humming badly the tune of a song that would have been number one in the charts months ago, around the time that *Tenacity* had left on patrol.

'This is ridiculous,' said Dan, letting out a long sigh.

John looked up from yesterday's newspaper and smiled. 'He's a busy man. Boat just got alongside. Lots to do.'

Dan ignored him. The waiting had reminded her of how tired she was and her eyes felt grainy and sore. The time that she had been made to wait had also allowed her to replay the scene on the casing several times over in her mind. There were so many things that she had thought of now that she wished she had said at the time, things she could have done differently as the Old Man dressed her down in front of a number of subordinates. If her interest in Steward Roach's tour had distracted her somewhat from the embarrassment of that, then the time that she had waited since had only served to rekindle her anger. Every minute was like a gentle puff of wind, feeding oxygen to the fire and ensuring it burned.

'Two hours,' she said under her breath. 'I've got to get out of here. I'm going to find him.'

She edged out from behind one of the small dining tables and started towards the door.

'Hey, Dan,' came a voice from behind her.

It was the Marine Engineering Officer, the face that she had recognised from the group on the submarine casing. He was standing by the small entrance from the pantry, still wearing the same filthy white overalls.

'Is the Commanding Officer coming down?' she snapped.

The MEO smiled. 'Still impatient,' he said, stepping further into the wardroom. 'He's on his way. Sorry it's taken a while, but we've had a few problems with the shore supply and the Old Man's the hands-on type.'

Dan stood in the centre of the wardroom. Seeing the

MEO duck as he entered reminded her that, even given her slight build, she could touch all of the walls in just a few strides and the ceiling without going onto tiptoes. She tried to ignore these thoughts and looked back at him, her mind working hard trying to place his face.

'Aaron Coles,' he said, helping her out. 'We joined HMS Raleigh in the same intake back in 1996.'

Dan smiled. 'Of course,' she said. 'I knew your face as soon as I saw you.'

'I was in Nelson Division. I think you were in Collingwood Division with Whisky.'

'That's right,' she answered. 'I remember.'

'It's easier for me to remember you – two hundred guys and what, seven girls?'

'There weren't many of us back then, that's true.'

John Granger suddenly stood up and Dan whirled round to see the Old Man briskly enter the wardroom.

'Relax, Master,' said the Old Man quickly and gestured for Dan to also sit down. 'Aaron, I want you in on this, please. The Coxswain can't make it, he's working on the Souls On Board return.'

Aaron must have caught a question in Dan's expression. 'It's how the Coxswain officially records who's on board the boat when she's at sea and who isn't,' he said, taking a seat at the second table. 'Has to be submitted as soon as we get back alongside.'

'So, Lieutenant Lewis, I understand you're to assist in the investigation of Chief Walker's suicide. I know some of what's going on, but I'd like to understand what you know already and how you intend to approach this investigation, and what impact it'll have on my ship's company. It'll have to be quick, too; I have to call on the Commodore tonight before he leaves for London.'

'What I know already, sir?'

'Yes, Lieutenant Lewis, I'm the Commanding Officer, I'll require a full brief.'

Dan hesitated.

'Well, sir, Master at Arms Granger,' she gestured to John, 'will be assisting me in investigating the circumstances surrounding the suspected suicide of Chief Petty Officer Stewart Walker on board *Tenacity* three days ago. I'm also here to establish the whereabouts of you and your cre—' she stopped and corrected herself, 'ship's company, during the period since *Tenacity* arrived back from operations. I simply plan to speak to all who were on board at that time and eliminate them—'

'And how long will each interview take?'

Dan paused and felt her jaw clench. Her deep fatigue was being pushed aside by the adrenaline of this challenging conversation, but she couldn't shake it entirely, and she could feel her temper also jostling forward.

'I expect each interview to take no longer than about thirty—'

'And where do you intend to hold these interviews?'

He was staring at her, not blinking, his eyebrows meeting like two hairy caterpillars trading secrets.

'I'll book a room in the squadron building and conduct them there—'

'No. Out of the question.'

'With respect, sir—'

'With respect nothing, Lieutenant Lewis. *Tenacity* is my boat and these are my men. This is our first stop since we left home port several months ago and, after a very short turnaround, will be our last before we embark on a third consecutive patrol. A patrol that will, sadly, be my last as the Commanding Officer of this submarine, and one that will test my men's resolve to its limit.'

He leaned back in his seat, relaxed, the type of man who

enjoyed delivering long, uninterrupted speeches and was used to being indulged when he did so.

'If your plan is to take each of over one hundred and thirty men off *Tenacity* to interview them, then, allowing for watch-keeping handovers, waiting and transit time as they move from *Tenacity* to the squadron building and back again, the time burden will simply be unsustainable. Particularly during this short turnaround. You will need to find some space on board *Tenacity*. I'll leave you to arrange that with the Coxswain. It will reduce the unwelcome impact on the men and the maintenance schedule. My men have had precious few days, since they got back alongside, where there haven't been police and regulators crawling around and watching them. As such, I would prefer you to keep your profile as low as possible and stay out of the way as best as you can.'

Dan slapped her hand on the table, making the Old Man lean back slightly and his eyebrows arch up like two cats spoiling for a fight.

'This is a serious investigation, sir, two people have lost their lives—'

'Two?'

Dan's face reddened.

'Two?' he repeated. He seemed to think back to what she had previously said. 'Suspected suicide? You're operating outside the brief that I've been given, Lieutenant Lewis.'

Her eyes were locked with his.

Around them, John and Aaron sat silent, frozen still.

The sound of Ben's humming had also stopped from the pantry. Only the overpowering rush of the seemingly ever-present ventilation system continued on.

If Dan could have kicked herself under the table, she would have. Her mind was already working through her excuses: she had made a slip, a stupid error, because she was exhausted, because she had let this prehistoric buffoon get under her skin, because she *was* operating outside her brief, because in her mind she could see the pictures of Cheryl Walker and everything about them screamed to Dan that Cheryl knew her killer, that Whisky knew her killer too, and because this woman was more important to Dan than a submarine and its operations. There was no time for beating herself up now, though; it was out, had been said, and Dan needed to move forward from it.

'I was briefed that this was a relatively simple investigation to ascertain the facts surrounding Walker's tragic suicide, nothing more,' the Old Man said, too quietly.

'I can't discuss this with you any further, sir. I will require—'

'You will *require*?' His eyes were wide and his voice incredulous. 'You will *request*, Lieutenant Lewis, you do not *require*.'

'I will REQUIRE access to all members of your ship's company,' said Dan, raising her voice and cutting the Old Man off. 'And I will arrange a room in the squadron complex in which to conduct my interviews.'

'*Require*?' The Old Man was blinking now, as though this was all beyond his comprehension.

'*And* I will require your full cooperation.' Dan waited, glaring at him. 'Sir,' she added after a pause.

It took her a moment to realise that she was standing up, leaning over the Old Man, whose face was now purple with rage.

'Lieutenant Lewis,' he spat. 'I will see you in my cabin.'

He stood up so quickly that his chair fell over, crashing into the pile of magazines that John had been leafing through, and causing them to avalanche off the shelf and slide to the floor. The curtain that was pulled across the doorway was flung aside as he stormed out of the wardroom, his padded middle touching the door frame on both sides as he barged his way through.

'Nice,' whispered John under his breath. 'Very nicely done.'

Dan tried to glare at him, willing him to meet her eyes, but he wouldn't.

'Go easy there, Dan,' said Aaron quietly. 'He's a good man, but you'll get a lot further with kind words than you will trying to use a gun.'

She sighed, looked down at her hands and stretched her neck before turning and following the Old Man out of the room.

It took Dan a few moments to get her bearings, even on the short route from the wardroom back to the foot of the control room ladder.

The submarine decor was like a huge contradiction. It changed seamlessly from a varnished, wood-veneer bulkhead, complete with framed parchment declaring *Tenacity*'s Freedom of the City of Plymouth, to pipework and machinery with flaking paint and oily smears. Edges jutted out randomly, as though the person who had designed them had just made everything slightly too big to comfortably fit. The whole place was too small, too narrow, too dim and too murky, and if Dan felt that way at five feet and two inches tall, she shuddered at how it must feel to others.

Fortunately, the size of the submarine had one advantage, in that it was impossible to really get lost between where she was and where she was going. She found, and climbed, the ladder that she had been escorted down by Steward Roach, and stepped into the control room, crossing it quickly to knock on the Old Man's cabin door. The long main access hatch ladder that she and John had used to enter the submarine was just behind her, a tempting escape point with a pillar of light pointing into the free air above.

'Come,' called the Old Man.

Dan stepped into the tiny cabin.

'It seems that we got off on the wrong foot,' he said, as

soon as Dan was inside and had pulled the curtain behind her.

His demeanour had completely changed in the few moments since he had ordered her to attend him, and Dan couldn't help but raise an eyebrow at the marked difference. The blood had drained from his face and he smiled at her, like an affable uncle, as he gestured for her to sit.

His single bed folded up to form a soft bench that ran along one wall of the cabin. Next to the bench, crammed against the front wall, was a small desk and a folding chair that looked like it might collapse at any second under the Old Man's short, rotund frame.

'I apologise if it seemed like I wasn't taking your investigation seriously. It appears that I have been misinformed and, as such, misjudged the full extent of it.'

Dan nodded, not able to drop her guard, as she watched his jowls wobble when he spoke. Her neck felt stiff and sore, and she tried to let her shoulders drop forward slightly to relax the muscles, resisting the urge to stretch her neck and pull her collar a bit to loosen her black uniform tie.

'Perhaps if you could fill me in on the basics of what is suspected, then I may be able to help, if possible, in a more productive way.' His face looked open and his tone was calm as he spoke. Even his eyebrows, which seemed to have a life of their own, appeared to be calmer now, lying flat and still.

'Sir, I apologise—'

'Don't apologise, please, Lieutenant Lewis. Dan, may I call you Dan?'

She nodded.

'In truth, I rather enjoyed the ferocity of your argument.' He smiled, showing Dan a mouthful of stained teeth.

'Sir, I really can't divulge anything to you at this stage, except to say that the investigation is as you were briefed.

I misspoke; I apologise. I just need to speak to your men and ascertain their movements and location during the short time in question and ask standard questions about their relationship and interactions with Stewart Walker. I will take no more time than is absolutely necessary.'

The chair creaked as he rocked back and forth slightly, his eyes to the floor as he thought.

'But you said "two people" had lost their lives and, as the Commanding Officer, I need to be supremely confident about the safety and wellbeing of my ship's company. You also called it a "suspected suicide", a term no one else has used when talking about this unfortunate incident. If you suspect either foul play, or that any members of my ship's company might be involved in this, or any other incident, you need to tell me. I have a duty of care to these boys. I need to know what you suspect.'

'Sir, I misspoke, and I'm sorry. My only interest is in the suicide of Chief Petty Officer Walker. I really can't say any more than—'

'Lieutenant Lewis.' He stopped.

Dan could see that his breathing was getting heavier again, his nostrils starting to flare on his short, flat nose, and his eyebrows twitching like a boxer's pectorals before a fight.

They sat in silence, looking at each other.

'You may leave now, Lieutenant Lewis,' he said after a long wait. 'You may begin your interviews in the morning. We will cooperate fully. But,' he paused and looked at her for an awkwardly long moment. 'I will have the Coxswain arrange for you to use a compartment on board *Tenacity* for your interviews. This is not negotiable, Lieutenant Lewis, and I will ensure that Roger Blackett is aware of that. It will be much better for us all if you conduct your business here, where my ship's company and I can support you more fully.'

Chapter 10

Friday Night – 26th September 2014

'So what do you think?' asked John as they walked out past the exclusion zone.

'I think he's an asshole. You?' said Dan, trying not to make it obvious how much better she felt to be up in the open space and breathing the fresh sea air, even as the light was fading around her.

John nodded his head and checked behind him. He had a habit of doing that, as though someone might be following him specifically to listen in to what he was saying. 'He's an asshole all right. His guys love him, though, and you can see why.'

They walked on in silence for a while before John, who had been flexing his hands between bouts of wringing them together, finally turned to look at her. 'I think we should clear the air.'

'There's something not right,' she said, ignoring him. 'Surely we'll be more in the way on board that bloody thing.'

'You're right in what you said before. I do have an issue working with you and I think we should just get it out and said.'

'Why was he so adamant that he wanted me on board the submarine, and did you know he asked for me by name?'

'Danny.'

She turned to look at him. 'What?'

He shook his head a few times and then looked along the long, straight road that would take Dan back to the Wardroom and him to his mess.

She paused, thinking. 'I think you're right. We should talk and clear the air, but later. I want to focus on this now.'

She looked around her at the reducing shadows.

'Would you walk back with me?' she asked, not looking at him.

'Sure,' he said, and they fell in together, walking in silence.

Back in her room, she pulled open her laptop and arranged Cheryl Walker's case file on the bed in front of her. She began scanning through the notes she'd made so far, pulling pictures out of their folders and spreading them across the bed, trying to arrange them into some kind of order: chronological, physical, geographical. Nothing worked; nothing seemed to allow her to sense the order in what was, on the surface, an utterly brutal and frenzied attack.

Felicity's confusion about the length of the attack, or whether there had been a break, a respite, before the violence had resumed and persisted through to death had now transferred itself to Dan and she looked again and again to try and fathom what could have driven this behaviour, but found nothing. She thought again of Gemma Rockwell and her suggestion that Cheryl Walker may have been frightened, but why? And was that recollection even real, or was Gemma allowing what she knew to have happened to influence her memories of the past, superimposing an emotion onto her friend that possibly wasn't there?

Felicity had been wrong about one thing, though; there

was some evidence. It came from another, very similar attack, albeit almost two years ago; a separate attack on another woman that was very likely perpetrated by the same person. But Dan hadn't shared this, not with Felicity, not with anyone.

The pictures were in front of her again, and next to the one of Mrs Walker's back, she laid the piece of air hose she had taken from *Tenacity*.

Her mobile phone rang and she looked at it, trying not to feel angry. It would have been easy to blame the call for distracting her just as she was on the verge of something, some thought or idea that would bring this investigation into focus, but Dan knew that this limbo state, the balancing between ignorance and understanding, could last for days, weeks, months or years. She felt close, felt like she should be able to see the web that held all of this together, but it wasn't going to come tonight.

'Lewis,' she said into the mobile as she held it to her ear. The number hadn't been stored in her memory and her first thought was that the caller might have been John.

'Hello, Danielle, it's Felicity Green here. We met earlier today.' Felicity waited.

'Hey,' said Dan, surprised at how pleased she was to hear Felicity's voice. 'What can I do for you?' she added, sitting down on the bed.

'Well,' Felicity began, seeming more nervous on the phone than she had been in person. 'First, I wanted to apologise for pouncing on you today about your previous work. We had only just met and I shouldn't have done that; I'm sorry.'

'That's fine, honestly. Hamilton just seems a long time ago now,' said Dan, looking at the papers and case files packed into her personal document safe, each one of them proving her a liar.

'Yes, I understand, but I also wanted to talk to you about

something else that you said today. You said that Cheryl Walker's attack was a message, that Walker was supposed to have known exactly who had done it.'

Dan closed her eyes. 'I did.'

'Well, I had also considered that angle; given the overt brutality of the attack, it felt like a warning, but death is so final, not so much a warning as the final sanction. That's what made me reconsider. But you seemed to say it as though it were more than just a passing theory, as though you felt you really knew. I just wondered if you could help me along by telling me what it is that made you so sure?'

Darkness had come to the window without Dan really noticing. Her room was well lit – the main light, the desk lamp and the light in the en suite all burned brightly – but it seemed like only a few minutes ago that she had walked back from *Tenacity*, the evening dull, but not yet fully dark. Now it was night and she felt lost in time. The pictures were on the bed all around her, all of them still in the wrong order, and they had been the whole time. She was aware that she needed to speak, to answer the question that had been asked, but her mind was motoring as to how she would deal with the questions that would undoubtedly follow. She saw the letter from her father sitting clean and unopened on the bedside table, just outside the perimeter of her case notes, waiting its turn.

'Danielle?' said Felicity.

'I'm here,' said Dan quietly.

'If now isn't a good time to talk . . .' Felicity offered.

It felt odd to hear that, to have someone suggest by implication that there was ever a good time to talk. Talking was something that Dan desperately wanted to do and maybe Felicity was the right person.

'I can't really explain it,' Dan began, 'but when you said to me that this wasn't the killer's first time, I already thought that. But I think that the reason I'm sure that this was a message isn't anything to do with the attack specifically, although it was very distinctive; it was that they found a body at all.'

There was silence on the end of the line and Dan could sense that Felicity wanted to ask more questions but was holding back, and this restraint made Dan like her and trust her all the more.

'I see,' said Felicity.

Dan sat up and looked around her at the detritus from the crime. A crime that she felt compelled to pursue. Two people were dead, but Cheryl Walker had been murdered in a manner that Dan couldn't ignore. The 'why' was the key: why was Cheryl Walker dead? Why had Dan been drawn into an investigation that struck such a personal chord? Could it simply be coincidence? Was Dan just making the whole thing up, linking clues that weren't really there, inventing a personal crusade? Going way too far outside of her briefing, as she had doubtless done with Hamilton.

'Bollocks,' she finally said.

'Sorry?' Felicity sounded taken aback.

'Sorry,' Dan apologised. 'It's just so frustrating. Look, if you want to, we could get together tomorrow and talk about this some more.'

'That would be great, thank you,' said Felicity, sounding genuinely pleased.

'And,' Dan paused and considered the files in her document safe. 'If you wanted to, when we have some time, I'll also chat through the papers I wrote after the Hamilton case, both of them, off the record.'

'Danielle, I would really appreciate that and I will absolutely assure you your privacy. Thank you very much.'

'I'll text some timings through to this number tomorrow morning, once I know what times I'll be free.'

Dan ended the call then sat looking out the window into the darkness as she thought about what she had just offered to do. The lights from the main Wardroom building reflected onto her window. Some were mounted into the stone walls, illuminating the architecture; others shone upward from the ground like torches, making it look as though the building were about to tell a scary story.

On the other side was the sea view, the horizon filled with small, blinking lights of various vessels. Some were navigation lights, vessels on the move; others were just the domestic lighting on the walkways and waists of various ships.

She looked in the direction of *Tenacity*'s berth, knowing that she wouldn't be able to see the boat from here, but she still didn't move any closer to the window, as it held back the night. She was standing away from it like a wary child watching a zoo lion through the glass wall of the enclosure, not quite certain that the barrier would hold if tested.

She grabbed a cereal bar from her bag and took a bite.

The red post office bag loaded with mail, still unopened, caught her eye. She picked it up, tore open the thin plastic and began to leaf through the envelopes, separating the junk from the journals, and adding the bills that would need to be paid to a separate 'to do' pile, her father's letter at the bottom, forming the foundation of it. A brown jiffy bag was the only interesting item, the only one that she couldn't identify from the outside. The name and address were handwritten, neat and legible, but not recognisable to her. She received little in the way of personal mail and she looked at it as she dropped the junk mail into the bin under the desk. Using a pen to tear the padded envelope open, she shook it gently, turning it upside down, and watched as a metal badge fell onto the desk. It was a set of gold-coloured submarine dolphins, the same gold badge that the submariners all wore on their shirts. There were two sharp pins protruding from the rear, used to hold the dolphins in place on the left breast of the uniform. The blunt clasps that should have covered the pins were missing and both of the pins were covered in an unmistakable, dark red substance, like tiny flakes of rusty iron.

Dan stared at the dolphins and then picked up the jiffy bag and examined it slowly, turning it over in her hands. The bag had been sent from a small post office near to Devonport Dockyard. It was stamped first class and had been addressed to Dan's workplace in Faslane, the naval base she had worked at in Scotland for the previous nine months before being returned to Kill duties in Portsmouth. The post-mark showed that it had been sent, and redirected, first thing on Monday morning, the Monday morning that Walker had been informed of his wife's death.

Dan put the bag down quickly and reached for her coat, found the gloves that she had taken from Walker's house earlier in the day and slipped them on. She was no longer concerned that they were ill fitting and she pulled open the jiffy bag further to look inside. Still inside the bag, stuck to the bubble-wrap lining, was a slip of paper, bloody finger-prints obvious on the white surface.

She placed the jiffy bag down again and rummaged in her holdall for her washbag. In the side pocket she found her tweezers and used them to carefully grip a tiny part of the edge of the paper, pulling it out of the bag. There was only minute resistance as some dried blood struggled to let go of the plastic bubble-wrap. Dan turned it over slowly and looked at the prints before reading the message, written in the same neat handwriting.

TENACITY

On the strength of one link in the cable,
Dependeth the might of the chain.
Who knows when thou may'st be tested?
So live that thou bearest the strain!
Tenacity *must break!*

Dan read the verse three times; she didn't recognise it. She slipped off the gloves, grabbed her phone and turned on her personal hotspot, reaching out to place the phone on the windowsill where the mobile signal was strongest. Then she pulled her laptop in front of her and connected it. She typed in the first line of the note.

The first four lines formed a verse of a poem that had been written at the turn of the century by a Royal Navy captain. It was said to be hardly known outside of English-speaking naval circles and was called *The Laws of the Navy* by R.A. Hopwood.

Dan read the information on a few different sites, but they were all similar.

She searched the envelope again, but there was nothing more to find, and then read the final line again, the cadence of her inner narrative governed by the beating of her heart.

Tenacity *must break.*

Her hands were shaking and she realised her breathing had grown shallow and quick. She stood up, removed the gloves and ran her hands through her hair as she paced, trying to think. It had been years since she had known Whisky Walker and she had barely, in fact never, seen him since she had accepted her commission more than ten years ago. She certainly didn't know him well enough to recognise his handwriting, but she knew, for whatever reason, that this was genuine, that he had reached out to her, that these lines were for her.

She reached for her phone and began to search through

her contacts list for the duty police officer at Devonport. She would need forensics to analyse the envelope and to use it, if possible, to ascertain Walker's whereabouts and state of mind on the Monday. There would be CCTV footage at the post office and likely on surrounding cameras, depending on how long they held the data. The 'blood' would need to be checked too, to confirm what it was and if it did belong to Walker. She would need to see his autopsy to check for the puncture marks, or to understand how the dolphins came to be covered in blood. Then there would be questions from both the naval and civilian police about the poem, what it meant, why it was sent to Dan. The potential for her personal involvement, the fact that she had known Walker previously and was in a photograph with him at his house, coupled with the fact that he had now written to her, sent evidence directly to her, this would certainly rule her out of the case, rule her out of the hunt for the man who inflicted those marks on Cheryl Walker's back . . .

She stopped searching and put the phone back down.

The hunger pangs she'd felt earlier were now gone and she dropped the remainder of the cereal bar into the bin, her mouth too dry to chew.

Did he know he was going to die when he sent it? Was this a suicide note? And why send it to her, after all these years? Why go to *Tenacity* to die – why there?

The coincidences were mounting up, and more and more *Tenacity*'s dark shape grew in her mind.

Dan knew she was a good investigator. After the Hamilton investigation there had been requests for her to be seconded onto the UK's National Crime Agency, an opportunity that she would have seized, had her superiors not blocked it in the aftermath of her leaked paper. Could it simply be that Walker had seen her pictures splashed across the national press and decided that she was the one he wanted? But they all wanted her here – Harrow-Brown, the Old Man, and Whisky. All except Roger Blackett, who said he didn't.

The images from the case files came back to her again, the similarities, the pictures of the backs of two women, feathered with bruising. Those marks were not the precursor to death. They were a warning, a punishment, a visual reminder and a deterrent. They were a sign of domination and humiliation. Those marks were a message to Cheryl Walker, or to someone that loved her, that they were subordinate to a superior power.

Inflicting these marks on the night that *Tenacity* returned made more sense when you looked at them in that context. The beating was something that could be survived, the marks hidden from all but those closest to you. Had Whisky returned home, he would have found his wife branded with these marks. This would be a clear message, a reminder that he couldn't be there all the time, that there were others that could be touched, his wife, his children.

'But why do it and then kill you, Cheryl?' Dan asked out loud.

Felicity was right that death wasn't a warning; it was the final sanction. So why commit murder?

Dan sat down and dropped her head into her hands. There were too many questions.

Death brought police and attention, it brought scrutiny and the SIB. These weren't things you wanted if you were delivering a warning.

Also timing would have to be considered. Submariners were often out of contact with their families and friends for long periods of time. Their programmes changed frequently and without notice, and Dan knew of instances when wives had flown out to foreign ports to meet their men, only to be told on arrival that the submarine wasn't going to be arriving at all.

The attacker had to be sure that Walker would actually see the warning. The attack would have less effect if he didn't feel the full impact of what had been done to Cheryl. That was why it had to be then. That was why it had to be that first night back while Whisky Walker was made Duty, unable to return home for one last night while the message was being delivered.

Dan looked up as she thought about all she knew and all she still didn't. She thought about what Gemma Rockwell had said, the piece of hose that was used to whip the sailor earlier in the day, and the letter from Whisky Walker. Then another thought occurred to her. Another reason why the attack had to happen on that first night back, because the person committing the attack, or the person ordering it, also had no access to communications, or perhaps to Cheryl Walker, because they were also on board *Tenacity*.

The feeling of suspicion and dread towards *Tenacity* was impossible to ignore.

She'd had this feeling before, that all wasn't as it seemed, the same feeling that only she had had when faced with Hamilton. Then, she'd also had hunches and evidence that she couldn't or wouldn't share, but then she'd also chosen not to trust those around her.

She thought about Felicity Green. She may not be able to share the evidence with Felicity, not yet, but if she could meet with her tomorrow and convince her that the police needed to turn their attention towards the submarine, then Dan could continue to be involved in the investigation, could be there when Cheryl's attacker was brought to justice.

She looked at her phone again and picked it up. She texted the number that Felicity had called her from and asked what times might suit for a meeting the following day; Dan was now available as early as Felicity was able. Then she slipped the phone into her pocket and picked up her car keys. There was a supermarket a few miles away. She could buy some bags to preserve the evidence for the time being, then keep it safe in her cabin until she was ready to hand it over.

The phone beeped – a reply from Felicity Green – she was available from three o'clock the following afternoon. Dan acknowledged the text, suggested meeting at the Walker house again, and pocketed it.

She would meet with Felicity and convince her that they needed to turn the investigation towards *Tenacity* as soon as possible.

As Dan pulled her door closed behind her, she knew that the step she was taking, the line that she was crossing in withholding this material, could likely end her career, but only if she was wrong.

Chapter 11

Saturday Morning – 27th September 2014

The knock at the door was almost certainly John and she shouted that she would be ready in a minute and would meet him out front.

She towelled her hair dry and was just picking up her toothbrush when her door was battered by a salvo of short raps, more urgent than before.

'Yes?'

'It's me.' His voice sounded urgent. 'We need to talk, now.'

She wrapped her towel around her, tucking it tight under one arm, and cursed herself for not bothering to bring a robe. She walked to the door, stopping for only the slightest moment to look in the mirror, before she unlocked it and pulled it open just a crack.

'I said I'd be down in a minute.'

He looked at her. '*Tenacity*'s under sailing orders; the boys were recalled last night. They're packing up and securing for sea. She sails on the next tide.'

* * *

'How could you not have known, John?'

He was walking beside her as they marched briskly down the main drag towards the submarine berths.

Dan felt as though she had to jog to stay in front, as he strode along taking two long paces to every three of hers.

'How could I have known?' he asked.

They flashed their IDs and Dan tried to quickly pass through the exclusion zone checkpoint.

John touched her arm and she spun to face him.

'Relax. It'll happen quicker if you follow the procedure,' he said, his arms raised in defence. 'Ma'am like jam,' he added, but Dan was too worked up to smile.

The process of signing in seemed to take an age as Dan impatiently signed the paperwork and the attendant took his sweet time to issue them with some dosimetry.

As soon as they were through, Dan started towards the gangway. The Upper Deck Trot, with his provost armband, was the same one that she had seen on duty yesterday. Dan paced across the gangway, stopping only for a split second to salute before she stepped over the brow. As she placed a foot on the rough black surface of *Tenacity*'s casing, the Upper Deck Trot stepped into her path.

He saluted, but didn't move. 'Can I ask you where you're going, please, ma'am?'

Dan looked past him. 'The submarine,' she said, letting sarcasm slip into her voice.

The trot's face remained unchanged. 'Can I ask whereabouts, and to see whom, please, ma'am?'

'I need to speak with your Commanding Officer.'

The trot turned to another rating, the armed 'gun trot', who was standing a few yards away watching closely, his rifle, usually loaded with a magazine of at least twenty rounds, cradled in his arms.

'Keep an eye, Soapy,' said the trot, and walked over towards the main access hatch.

The whole area was bare now; the bulletproof Trot-Box must have been craned off earlier in the day and Dan, looking around as she waited, spotted it stored away just outside the exclusion zone.

The trot picked up a temporary phone that was lying on the casing and dialled. He spoke for a few moments and then hung up the phone and walked back. 'Sorry, ma'am, boat's under sailing orders and the Old Man is in a navigation briefing. He won't be out for a while. Says he'll try his best to see you when he gets out, but doesn't know how long that'll be.'

'I need to see him now,' said Dan. 'Call him back and tell him that the SIB are here to speak with him.'

'That's just not possible, ma'am.'

'Step aside,' she leaned in and looked at the trot's name-badge. 'Able Seaman Grant.'

Dan produced her warrant card and held it up for the Able Seaman to look at.

His eyes never left hers and he made no attempt to look at the card nor to move aside so that she could pass.

'I said step aside, AB Grant, last chance.'

The trot smiled. It was a shallow smile and he leaned forward towards Dan, as though he was going to say something very personal. 'Sorry, ma'am, but what the Old Man says, goes around here,' he whispered.

Dan paused, thinking and letting her temper subside. 'What time do you sail?' she asked.

The trot thought about it and then shrugged. 'We're going out on the midday tide, ma'am.'

Dan nodded and turned away. She walked back along the gangway, almost bumping into the Chief Stoker.

He was dressed in the same blue overalls he had been

wearing when he had beaten the young sailor with a hose the day before. His sleeves were still rolled up and black marks covered his hands and forearms; his beret was, as seemed the norm for him, rolled up in his pocket instead of neatly on his head where it should have been. He nodded, a slight smirk obvious on his face.

'Don't you salute naval officers, chief?' said John, over Dan's shoulder.

The Chief Stoker nodded and reached for his beret. He placed it on his head using both hands to smooth it against his close-cropped scalp and then stood bolt upright. He saluted in a crisp manner, snatching his hand up to his temple and holding it there like a lead-forged guardsman until Dan returned his salute. Then he smartly chopped his arm down and remained at attention.

'Permission to carry on, ma'am?' he barked like a 1950s sergeant major.

Dan stared at him, never looking away from his narrowed eyes.

'Carry on, chief,' she said quietly.

She heard the sniggers and chuckles from behind her as she walked off the gangway, but she didn't look back.

Passing the exclusion zone boundary, Dan tossed her dosimeter at the sentry and walked out towards the main drag. She had walked for a minute or so when she heard John jog up behind her, the hard rubber soles of his service shoes slapping on the tarmac. She spun to face him.

'What was that?' she asked.

'I'm a Master at Arms, it's my job.'

'You didn't think I could have done it myself if I felt it necessary?'

John looked away and shook his head. 'Look, I'm sorry that the Royal Navy doesn't rotate around Lieutenant Danielle Lewis. There's a structure, a team, and we all play our part in it. What I just did, that's my part. This whole organisation doesn't move at your pace and in your direction, doesn't flex and change to suit your requirements.'

'What has that got to do with—'

'It's got everything to do with everything, and you know it,' he interrupted her, raising his voice and then quickly looking around to check that no one had heard him. 'You're doing it again. Going it alone and pushing everyone out of the way, trying to bend everyone and everything around you to your will. You can't win that way.'

'Jesus Christ, John, this isn't a game. It isn't about winning anything, this is potentially going to be a murder investigation and you're saying . . .' She hesitated. 'What? What are you saying?'

He looked back over to the submarine. People were watching them, but no one was close enough to hear, and he turned back slowly to face her.

'I'm saying that you got away with the Lone Ranger stuff with Hamilton, and I mean *got away* with it. You barely escaped with your life and everyone hailed you as a success.' John paused and shook his head, the pace of his outburst slowing down. 'It wasn't a success, it was a seat of the pants almost-failure, because you wouldn't work with others, within the rules, trust others to help you.'

'You mean I didn't trust you?'

Their eyes met and they held the look for a long moment.

He shook his head again and she remembered it as another of his consistent little traits, the shaking of the head, meaning a thousand different things, from disbelief, to humour, to annoyance.

'Look, John, I made some calls last night and I spoke to the civvy police, to Felicity Green with the National Crime Agency. I'm telling you now, there's a lot more to this suicide than we can see. The link to the murder of Cheryl Walker is more than just Walker's grief. I'm certain of it. And as I'm trying to investigate it, I'm being stonewalled.'

'*We* need to work together then,' he said. 'Not have me standing around watching the Danielle Lewis Show.'

'Yes, you're right, and *we* need to talk to the crew of that bloody submarine,' she said, turning back to look at it as though she could plan a route to charge on board right now and corral them into an interview room.

'If what you're saying's right, then the old bill would have enough to have the sailing order revoked.'

Dan was shaking her head. 'No. They'd need a suspect, an individual, more evidence to convince them to concentrate their efforts in that direction. Even if they had a suspect, they'd just pull that guy off the boat and pier-head jump someone new into his place. They need time to investigate this properly and I'm supposed to be meeting Felicity Green later today to discuss it.'

She looked down at her feet, could feel that she was grinding her teeth again as she thought hard. 'We need to talk to some of the people on that submarine, John.'

'How are you so certain?' John seemed to be thinking back, processing what she had said. 'Who did you talk to at Devon and Cornwall? I know all the coppers there.'

Dan thought quickly, about what she knew and what she wouldn't tell. 'I'll fill you in on all of it as soon as we figure out what we're going to do,' she said.

'Don't do something stupid, Danny,' he said, but she was already walking away.

Chapter 12

Saturday Afternoon – 27th September 2014

When Dan returned to *Tenacity* the Old Man was waiting at the gangway to meet her. She calmly registered with the Health Physics Sentry, withdrew some dosimetry and walked past the auxiliary machinery and bustling sailors, before stopping to salute as she crossed the gangway and stepped down onto *Tenacity*'s hard black casing. She saluted again as she faced him.

He was chewing gum, his jaw slowly working at it and his eyebrows responding like waves lapping against a shore-line. Silently, he stared at her for several seconds as she stood and waited.

'So, Lieutenant Lewis, I gather you made some phone calls.'

Dan didn't answer.

John had followed her across the gangway and was standing behind her holding his naval issue grip, a large, heavy-duty holdall that matched the black of *Tenacity*'s surface.

Around them, sailors were going about their business,

but making little attempt to hide their interest in whatever had drawn the Old Man onto the casing this close to the submarine's departure.

Dan placed her holdall on the deck.

'Well, Danny.' The Old Man said her name softly, as though he were addressing a niece that he was especially fond of. 'I have also spoken with Fleet HQ and while it seems that I cannot completely stop the lunacy, I was able to temper it a little.'

Dan refused to react and show her confusion. She forced her face to stay neutral.

'There is only a single available berth to sail with us today, one and only one. One of you may board and the other must stay.'

Dan felt as though she had been punched in the stomach.

'That wasn't my brief, sir,' she said.

'Well, now it is. Make whatever calls you wish, but whichever of you is sailing with us needs to be down below in five minutes. No laptops and no phones.' He smiled. 'I look forward to welcoming one of you on board.'

He turned away and began to climb down the ladder back into the submarine.

The hole that he was climbing into seemed even darker than it had the day before, maybe because he seemed to fill it almost completely.

Dan looked towards the access and remembered how little the light had penetrated down inside the submarine. She'd convinced herself, though she would never have voiced it, that she could climb back down inside *Tenacity* if John was with her. Now the idea of re-entering *Tenacity* alone, of climbing down into the windowless interior, seemed impossible.

'Look, Danny,' John whispered. 'It's only six days' transit to the patrol area and there's three days of exercises and work-up, so it'll be manic. I'll go. I've deployed on submarines loads of times. I'll do the interviews.'

Dan was about to answer him when the Old Man's voice cut her off.

'Listen to your Master, Danielle,' he said, and Dan was sure that he had knowingly phrased his words in that way. 'If you do, at least some common sense will prevail today.'

It felt as though everyone around her was watching and waiting for what she might do, but despite them, Dan wasn't about to go down there alone because of a barbed remark from a misogynistic prick. She looked at John. He was already squatting down and making sure his gear was ready. It seemed like everyone knew the outcome even before the decision had been made.

The Old Man was gone now, his minions maintaining a surreptitious vigil in his absence, and Dan's mind was once again in tumult. John would, and could, do the job, of that there was no doubt, but there was another job that needed to be done, one he didn't know about, with evidence that he didn't know about, and one he might not complete even if he did.

As she looked at the black hole into the boat, she questioned herself again. How sure was she that Cheryl Walker's killer dwelt within *Tenacity*, and how desperate was she to speak to them all and see if she could hunt him out, unmask him as she had with Hamilton? What did she actually know? The note from Walker wasn't conclusive, far from it. The location of his suicide could mean nothing at all. The piece of hose that she had taken from *Tenacity* the day before could have matched the wounds on Cheryl's back, but it was by no means a certainty and the hose was likely used on all of the submarines. Gemma Rockwell was grieving for the loss of a close friend; her feelings and memories could reasonably be clouded by that. Felicity's hypothesis that

Cheryl's killer knew her and Stewart Walker made it likely that it was a fellow submariner, but it confirmed nothing.

Dan felt her resolve wilting.

'Can you start clearing your gear off the casing please, ma'am, we're readying to sail now,' said the trot, his eyes as blank and cold as they had been a few hours before.

'Readying to sail,' she whispered, barely audible, only to herself. They were readying to sail less than twenty-four hours after her slip about a second death. They were moving out of her reach. All the loose strands that ran like rigging through her mind, they all seemed to lead to *Tenacity*, and *Tenacity* was sailing.

'No,' said Dan. 'I'll be embarking. Master Granger will remain behind.'

She sensed a change around her, but couldn't put her finger on what exactly it was.

John frowned as he looked up at her from next to his bag.

She handed over her laptop and phone to him. She had known that the computer wouldn't be allowed but had hoped to chance her hand. In preparation, and to John's protests, she had spent much of the previous hours printing out over two hundred pages of additional investigative notes and photocopying the rest of her case files for just this eventuality.

He handed over the thick folder of case-related papers that he had been carrying and she placed it on top of her bag.

'Put that in your bag, quick,' he said, handing her phone back to her. 'Everyone does it, you can't get a signal anyway, and you'll have some music at least. Do you have headphones?'

Dan shook her head, starting to feel numb, looking at the hatch and feeling her resolve weaken like ice under flowing water.

He knelt down and pulled some headphones out of a side pouch on his bag and handed them to her. Then he rummaged inside the bag and pulled out two packets of baby wipes that he showed to her and then forced into a side pocket of her holdall. 'I'm worried, Danny. I don't like this.'

'I'll be fine,' she said, and heard how hollow her own words sounded.

She had made the calls earlier with so much confidence, focused and absorbed by the knowledge that she had to achieve her aim, had to get on board *Tenacity*. Now that she knew she would be going alone, her growing dread and fear were joined by anger as she saw her small reflection in John's eyes.

'I'll be fine,' she said again.

'Time to clear the casing please, ma'am,' barked the trot from behind her. 'Either go ashore or go below.'

She turned to glare at him.

He stared back, his face a caricature of indifference.

John touched her hand.

She pulled it away – not snatching it so that other people might notice, but quickly, so that he would know it wasn't a welcome gesture.

'You could have trusted me, Danny,' he said, his voice low and urgent. 'I'd have had your back. I'd have followed you to Hamilton's house, you know that?'

He was nodding at her as he spoke, his eyes serious as he looked at her; she knew he was telling the truth and letting something out that had been simmering for a long time.

'I know that now, John, and I'm sorry,' she said.

'I'll be waiting whenever you're done here,' he said, seeming to ignore her reaction.

He looked agitated.

'What are you so worried about?' she asked quietly, looking

at the tension on his face and becoming more anxious about what the answer might be. 'From what I can gather, the hardest part will be getting some peace down there.'

His eyes met hers.

'Don't be fooled, Danny. Submarines are about belonging. If you don't belong, and you don't, they can be the loneliest places on earth.'

She swallowed. It had been a very long time since she had seen him look this preoccupied.

'I'll be OK.' She nodded and tucked the heavy file of paperwork under one arm, picking her holdall up in the other.

The trot stepped back, allowing her access to the ladder.

She held out her holdall to him, shaking her head at John as he moved forward to help.

The trot looked at it, but did nothing else.

'Could you help me, please?'

He snatched the bag from her and tossed it onto the casing next to the hatch.

'And these.' She offered him the papers. 'They're quite heavy, so please be careful.'

'You'll have to clear the casing now please, Master,' said the trot as he snatched the papers from Dan's hands.

Dan looked back once more and watched John walk across the gangway and onto the jetty.

The trot took the pile of papers and looked at Dan dispassionately. 'One down,' he shouted. 'Clear below, one down.'

Dan had climbed down several rungs, her head just dropping below the level of the casing, when she heard, faintly above the roar of the air conditioning and the sound of busy voices, the trot whisper to his colleague. 'I bet it's not the first time she's gone down.'

Dan paused, weighed up a response, and kept on descending as the chuckling faded and the noise of the submarine filled her ears. Once at the bottom, she reached up as far as she could and the smiling trot lowered her holdall down so that, on tiptoes, she could just reach it with her fingertips. Taking the weight, Dan prepared for the trot to let go and managed to bring the bag down to her chest. As she bent down to place it on the floor she heard a loud rustling sound from directly above her. Instinctively she covered her head as her large collection of paperwork burst from the bands that were binding it and flew down from the main access hatch. The main body of the papers clung together for a moment and then separated like giant confetti as they bumped off the polished metal rungs. The majority of the papers missed her head, but, as she allowed herself to look up, she saw that the main access hatch was obscured by page after page of printed words mingling with photo-copies of graphic colour photographs that were all floating down towards her.

'Below!' shouted the trot, the standard naval warning call when something has been dropped from an elevated posi-tion.

As the last pages fluttered to the deck, Dan looked into the long control room and could see faces spaced evenly all the way along the many panels, monitors and equipment that bordered it. On the right-hand side, as she looked, was the chart table, covered with navigational charts, pencils and Post-it notes. The three officers who had been poring over the material, now stood and looked at her, not glared, or even stared, just looked, as she stood, up to her ankles in sheets of paper and pictures of a hanged man and his brutally murdered wife.

She knelt down quickly, snatching at the pictures first and trying to sort them into a pile. They were quickly gath-ered and hidden away as she began to collect the other papers together, scrunching them up as she tried to order them in any way that would allow her to escape from there, to get away from the leering faces that just stood and watched her.

No one made any move to help.

She looked back up at the access hatch.

The trot was staring down at her.

Just for an instant, Dan thought that she should climb back up, catch up with John and head back to the Wardroom. Now felt like a good time to talk, to clear the air and talk about any subject he chose.

'Barely been on board for one minute and already you're making my submarine look untidy, Lieutenant Lewis.'

It was the Old Man. He was leaning against the frame of his cabin door and his boots were resting on some of the sheets of paper. 'Get this mess tidied up immediately. I have a submarine to get to sea.'

He turned away quickly, his feet pivoting on the spot and ripping the pages beneath them as he stepped back into his cabin and pulled the curtain shut.

Dan looked back down and continued to gather the papers. She hated that she could feel tears starting to well in her eyes and she bit down hard, biting until her jaw ached as she tried to control her anger and frustration.

There was a loud hiss as the hydraulically operated airlock door behind her, the one that led to the Tunnel and over the top of the reactor, began to open.

Shuffling out of the way, she looked up as the Marine Engineering Officer, Aaron Coles, stepped through the metal threshold. The way the door was designed, with a rim that went all around it, meant that Aaron had to simultaneously duck his head and lift his foot up as he stepped through.

His foot hovered for a few moments, looking for a place to land, until, eventually, he had to carefully place his dirty black boot down on some of the papers. It took a few seconds for him to close the door and then he turned to her. 'What the hell happened here?' he asked.

'It was an accident, I think,' said Dan, gathering papers furiously.

Aaron looked up towards the access hatch and then back down.

'You,' he said, pointing to a young sailor in the control room. 'Go and grab a gash bag and help tidy this stuff up.'

The sailor returned a few seconds later with a large black plastic bin-bag and knelt, starting to put papers into it.

'Back to your position, Able Seaman Rose,' said the Old Man, appearing back at his cabin door. 'We're getting this boat ready for sea, MEO. AB Rose isn't a babysitter; he's a professional, qualified submariner with a job to do.'

Aaron, also kneeling and collecting papers, looked up at the Old Man, and Dan watched as their eyes met. He took the bag from the young sailor and continued to help Dan pick up the remaining pages as AB Rose returned to his watchkeeping position.

It only took a minute, with both of them working together, before the black bin-bag was full of papers, some crumpled and creased, others dirty from the footprints of passing boots or with smears of hydraulic oil from the watertight airlock door.

The oil was red and made the pages look as though someone had washed their hands in blood and used the documents as paper towels, scrunching up pages indiscriminately.

'I'll take you down to your pit,' said Aaron, reaching for Dan's holdall and easily swinging it over his shoulder. He reached forward again to pick up the black bag of papers.

She looked at his extended hand, dirty with grease, small white scars on strong fingers, the marks of a career engineer. Dan couldn't help but raise an eyebrow at the luminous pink and yellow bracelet that peeped out from beneath the cuff of his filthy white overalls covering his watch.

'From my daughter,' he said, seeming to spot her hesitation. 'It's a friendship bracelet. I said I'd wear it for luck this trip. Me and her mum have split up, so she likes me to wear it, because it glows in the dark; every submariner's nightmare is when all the lights go out.'

Dan nodded, and hoped that every submariner's nightmare didn't happen very often. 'Thank you, but I can manage,' she said, keeping the gash bag and also offering to take back her holdall.

He didn't hand it over and Dan quickly followed him as he turned and walked into the control room and towards the stairs that she had taken with Steward Roach yesterday on their way to the wardroom.

'MEO,' barked the Old Man. 'I need to see you in my cabin, please. Chief Stoker, show Lieutenant Lewis to her pit.'

Aaron looked back at the Old Man and nodded. 'Yes, sir,' he said and then turned towards Dan. 'You'll be all right, the chief will show you where to put your grip. I'll come and check on you in a while and show you around.'

He held Dan's bag out to the Chief Stoker, who had appeared from deeper within the control room.

The Chief Stoker looked at it, but, like the Upper Deck Trot, did nothing, seeming to challenge Aaron in the same way that he had faced John only a day before.

Aaron's face remained calm and still and the Chief Stoker continued to chew lazily on his gum.

'Take this please, chief,' said Aaron, his voice confident.

'You don't get bellboys on submarines, boss,' replied the chief, but he smiled and took the bag anyway, not missing a beat on his gum. He turned and looked Dan up and down slowly, finally meeting her eyes. 'Second thoughts, sir, it'll be my pleasure. Anything for a lady.'

The chief stepped back and gestured for Dan to descend the inclined ladder that led out of the control room and down onto two-deck.

Dan stepped onto it, clutching the low handrail, and made to continue down.

'Stop there please, ma'am,' said the chief, his voice loud, carrying across the control room. 'You should face a ladder when descending it on board a submarine.'

Dan clenched her teeth, fighting not to react, as she turned to face the ladder and continued down. She watched the chief smile at her until she reached the bottom and turned to see a sign that read '2-deck'.

There was a smattering of laughter from above, before the chief descended, quickly and sure-footedly, down the ladder to meet her.

As soon as he was down he handed her holdall back to her.

'Follow me.'

Dan followed him, dragging her holdall in one hand and clutching her black bag full of paperwork in the other.

As they walked along the two-deck passageway, Dan's bags bouncing off the walls and nearly tripping her in the narrow space, the Chief Stoker shouted out names and gestured absently with his hands.

'Junior Rates Mess is in there; galley is in there; Senior Rates Mess is in there; you saw that yesterday as I recall. Wardroom pantry in there, that's where you get all your dinner plated up and served to you all officer-like. Sonar space there, don't ever go in there, you're not cleared.'

He finally stopped a few feet away from another large hydraulic door, similar to the one that was next to the main access hatch, but this one was fully open and a metal clip held it in position.

'This is twenty-nine watertight bulkhead. Forward of

twenty-nine is predominately bunk-space. You'll be wanting to never go through this bulkhead, ever.'

He pointed behind her. 'In there is the senior rates' showers and heads,' he said. 'And down there –' he pointed to a small hatch about the size of a car's sunroof – 'is what we affectionately call the bomb-shop or, more traditionally, the weapons stowage compartment, or WSC for short.' He paused and smiled. 'This is where you'll be sleeping.' He climbed down the short vertical ladder and waited at the bottom.

Dan placed her bags on the deck and climbed halfway down. Then, bracing her back against the hatched entrance, she reached for her bag and lowered it down.

The chief again made no move to help her.

'Please, chief,' she said.

He sighed and took the bag, tossing it onto the floor before repeating the step with the black bag of papers.

As soon as Dan was down he began to talk at her again. 'These are a mixture of Spearfish torpedoes and Tomahawk Land Attack Missiles. One of the bomb-heads will come down and brief you on emergency procedures. They also have to do rounds down here every six hours.'

He gestured to a series of cots that were mounted on what Dan assumed were vacant weapon racks. 'Choose any pit you like,' he continued. 'We're around six bombs light and can usually fit two pits comfortably on one missile rack, so you got twelve luxury pits to choose from.'

Dan looked around.

The ceiling was low and there were bare pipes bearing multi-coloured markings, like coloured bar codes, running over every wall and surface. Down the centre of the room was a raised area that was stacked to waist height with dry foods and tins. Either side of the centreline were large weapon stowages, and on them were mounted row after row of six- or seven-metre-long weapons. The room was cold and every edge was sharp, metallic and unforgiving; it was light, though, the fake, bright glow of numerous bulbs eliminating shadows everywhere.

'The lights never go out down here, but you'll get used to that,' said the Chief Stoker, barely pausing for breath. He pointed to a small area at the back of the compartment, a space the size of a school gym mat. 'That's the only place on board that's big enough for anyone to do a proper workout. We've stowed the weights, though, 'cos no one is allowed down here now, unless it's a duty requirement.'

'What do you mean?'

'Well, ma'am, since you bungled your way on board here, and with us having no proper Wrens' accommodation and all, you now have your own suite. The lads aren't allowed down here except for weapon movements and maintenance, so no workouts on this trip.'

'But I—'

'And, you see them other eleven pits,' he pointed to the empty rows. 'Well, they were going to be filled by trainees, people trying to earn their dolphins, potential submariners; useful folk. But now, seeing as you're here, all those lads are in the bunk-space that I told you about, the one through twenty-nine bulkhead. They're hot bunking, working on opposite watches so that when one finishes work, he wakes up his buddy who vacates the lovely hot bunk for him, and so it goes on. That means that twenty-odd extra guys will now have to share a bed and a tiny locker that wouldn't have had to share if Granger had sailed.' He made a point of staring straight at her. 'You won't know this, but hot bunking fucking sucks.'

He was leaving her in no doubt as to his opinion of her enforced presence on board *Tenacity*.

'One submariner gets out of his pit to go to work,' he repeated, making the fingers of his right hand walk along his left forearm. 'The other submariner finishes work and gets in.' His fingers walked back again. 'No privacy, no stowage space, and the mess-deck forward of twenty-nine gets stinkier and stinkier by the day.'

'But—'

'The senior rates' heads I showed you up top?' he interrupted, and pointed up and out of the entrance hatch, not letting her speak.

She nodded.

'They're yours now, too. So, when you want to take a shower, you put this little sign up.' He picked up a laminated sign from one of the panels and handed it to her. It read 'Ladies Only'. 'And for the duration of your ablutions, you get two showers and two pans all to yourself; the other one hundred and twenty-nine of us living on board *Tenacity* will share the other four showers and four pans between us. My maths isn't great, but someone as educated as yourself could probably work out the ratio.'

'This is ridiculous,' said Dan, finally speaking over the top of the Chief Stoker's monologue.

'Yes, ma'am, you're absolutely right, it is.'

Chapter 13

Saturday Afternoon – 27th September 2014

The Coxswain found Dan almost as soon as the Chief Stoker had left her alone in her new sleeping quarters.

He climbed down the ladder and turned to her, smiling in a good-natured way. 'So what do you think of it then?' he asked, before he had introduced himself. 'I wasn't sure if it was you or big Johnny Boy going to be coming with us, but Lieutenant Commander Coles seemed certain that you'd embark and he was right.'

The Coxswain held out his hand to her. His skin was very tanned, and although he was likely in his early forties, he had the look of a much younger man, someone that spent his time in the outdoors pursuing physical activities whenever he could.

'Jago Maddock,' he said. 'I'm the Coxswain here and I'll be helping you as much as I can with whatever it is you need.'

'Nice to meet you . . .' Dan paused. 'Jago?'

He laughed. 'My parents are old-school Cornish. It means James, but everyone here just calls me Coxswain, or Jay.'

'Danielle Lewis,' said Dan, shaking his hand. 'Most people just call me Dan.'

'I'll be sticking to ma'am for the time being,' he said, his lips pursed. 'Sets the wrong tone if the lads hear you being called by your first name.'

'I'd really like to get going on my interviews, to be honest, Coxswain. I wasn't sure how quickly I might be able to find somewhere to sit and start calling people down.'

The Coxswain was still smiling, but he was also raising his hands as if to slow her down. 'I know you'll be chomping at the bit to get going, but you need to hold your horses. Things work at a set pace down here and nothing will be happening until we're dived. That's just the way things are. You can let me know if you have anyone that you specifically want to speak with soonest and I'll try and get them in early; other than that, I'll put out a list each day of who is down to be interviewed and when, and we'll just work through it.'

Dan nodded her thanks. 'Lieutenant McCrae?' she said hopefully. 'He was Chief Walker's section officer. He's one I'd like to speak with as soon as possible.'

The Coxswain looked very serious. 'Lieutenant McCrae to the front of the queue it is then. Seems about right that he should be near the front too, the men would follow him anywhere.'

Dan raised her eyebrows, impressed that this officer could garner such obvious respect.

'Of course, they'd mainly follow him out of curiosity, you know, to see what he might do.'

Dan couldn't help but laugh.

'Yup, a proper commissioned officer. He's like a puppy, that one; runs around all excited and leaves little messes behind him for others to clean up.' The Coxswain grinned, showing straight white teeth. 'I'll be sure to get him into the schedule early on.'

'And there's no chance I could see him quite soon? Maybe today?'

'None,' said the Coxswain.

'OK,' said Dan, sensing that any argument would be futile. 'Thank you.'

He turned to leave, then stopped. 'Oh, and as for that little toerag that dropped your stuff down the hatch . . .' He watched Dan's reaction carefully. 'Yup, I was thinking as much,' he said, as though her expression had answered some unasked question for him. 'I'll be dealing with him, so don't you be worrying about that. No way to act and he knows it, or at least he will once he's spent a few watches scrubbing out the bilges.'

It was around an hour and a half later when Aaron popped his head down through the hatch, his mop of blond hair hanging down as though he were being electrocuted from above. He called her name.

Dan was sitting on one of the bunks nearest to the centre-line of the bomb-shop and was looking into space. Quickly, she reached for a piece of paper as though she had only been taking a break.

It hadn't taken long after the Coxswain had left for the smile to drop from her face and the reality of her situation to kick back in. She had positioned her holdall at the head end of her bed, or 'rack' as it was known, so that she could lie on her belly and easily reach down into it for her stuff. The black bag of papers was carefully hidden underneath her rack; it would take at least ten seconds for a determined searcher to find it.

She tried to smile at Aaron, but she'd been replaying the Chief Stoker's words in her mind again and again.

Aaron's face changed into an upside-down frown of its own and then disappeared, being replaced with a pair of black 'steaming bats', the leather protective boots worn by submariners and sailors alike. His legs followed and with a small jump he was on the deck and walking towards her.

'You OK?' he asked, seeming genuinely concerned.

'You know,' she said, looking him in the eye. 'The Old Man could well be charged with obstructing my investigation over all the little stunts he's pulling.'

Aaron recoiled at the force of her tone and held up his hands, palms out.

'I think he's watertight, Dan,' he said evenly. 'We don't have girls on submarines and so arranging for you to get your own sleeping area was a reasonable step.'

Dan's eyes narrowed.

'My exclusive use of the heads, while I'm *in* them, is reasonable, but I can do everything possible to use them when the crew aren't. All I need to know is when you guys change over watches and I can stay out of the way and use them when the watchkeepers are sleeping. But he's deliberately acting to turn the crew against me by displacing twenty-three guys to give me the biggest fucking cabin on the submarine.'

'Wow, Dan, relax,' said Aaron.

He was close now, standing over her. Seeming to realise this, he looked around before sitting down on a stack of boxes that were labelled as containing catering-sized tins of baked beans.

'There must be somewhere else I could sleep?'

Aaron shook his head. 'Dan, you kicked up a lot of fuss to get on here. You even went outside of the Submarine Squadron and straight to Fleet HQ. The Old Man has to make sure he does things right. And,' Aaron paused, as though he were about to raise a point he wasn't sure that he wanted to. 'Well, you could have just let John Granger sail in your place. He's a qualified submariner and would have caused minimal disruption. But it was your choice not to do that, and the Old Man said from the beginning that he was certain it's what you'd do . . .'

She shook her head and turned away from him. His hand touched her shoulder and she recoiled.

'Sorry,' he said quickly. 'I was just—'

'It's fine, really. I'm just jumpy and need to get on with the interviews; I feel like time is just passing and being wasted.'

'Well, the Coxswain runs a tight ship, so I'm certain he'll get the interviews started as soon as he can. But first,' Aaron changed tone as he spoke, making his voice sound cheerful, 'I need to give you a quick safety brief. One of my guys will give you a full safety walk-around once we're dived.'

He walked to the back of the compartment and rummaged around in a box, before pulling out a black rubber mask, attached to a very long piece of rubber hose. Holding it up to her, he smiled. 'EBS,' he announced. 'Emergency Breathing System. You need to know how to use this in case there's a problem with the air; fires aren't uncommon on boats and the smoke can spread through the whole boat in seconds. We drill this three to four times a week when we heave.'

Dan raised an eyebrow.

'Heaves are damage control exercises: fires, floods, collision damage and the like. We'll do a lot of them in the next few days as we get worked up ready for patrol. EBS is a crucial, and constant, part of submarine life and you need to be able to use it.'

His voice had changed. He now sounded formal, authoritative, as though he had stopped trying to be her friend and had started into a mentor role, delivering a lesson that he had given many times before. 'It's a totally sealed face mask that allows you to breathe using a stored, pressurised air supply.'

152

When Dan didn't take the mask, Aaron demonstrated it himself.

'You pull the mask over your head, just the same way as you do with a service respirator,' he said, loosening the straps. 'Once on, you can only breathe when the hose is properly locked into one of the EBS couplings.' He pointed up to several small-bore pipes that ran in regular intervals across the deck-head above her. Each tube had a brass connector jutting out at a right angle from it every twelve to eighteen inches. Aaron stood up and forced the connector end of the rubber hose into one of them.

Air began to hiss. 'It's positive pressure,' he said. 'So, if you get a bad face-seal, the air should push out of the mask, not let smoke or contaminants in.'

He pulled the mask on fully and took a deep breath.

Dan could see his eyes and cheeks bunched up through the clear plastic visor. His breathing sounded heavy and he said, 'Come to the dark side, Dan. Feel the power of the force.'

Dan laughed despite herself and shook her head.

'Watch me,' he said, his voice heavily muffled. 'Able to breathe,' he said, then he reached up to where his air hose was plugged in and pulled the end out. 'Not able to breathe,' he said. After he spoke, he took a deep breath in and the face mask sucked tight against his face. He reached up and plugged the hose back into the connector, the mask filled out again and his breathing resumed.

'You see?' he asked, when he had removed the mask.

Dan nodded, the thought of the mask up tight against her skin already seeding a shiver deep in the pit of her stomach.

'So, if you've been told to "don EBS" and you need to move around, you take a deep breath, hold it and unplug the connector.' He showed her again how to plug and then unplug the hose. 'Then hold your breath until you get to where you're going, or are on the way, then plug it back in again and breathe; we call it fleeting. You'll see the lads doing it during exercises; it takes a bit of practice but you'll get there.'

He handed her the mask. 'Put it on and have a go.'

Dan grimaced. 'You going to clean that?'

His laughter rang out, echoing around in the small area. 'You're on a boat now, Dan. We submariners are not universally known for our proactive approach to hygiene. They get disinfected after each exercise, so you'll live.'

Dan took it and wiped the inside with her towel to Aaron's obvious amusement. She felt, as she had so often during her naval service, that she was on the brink of doing something that she really didn't want to, but had no choice. Whether it was jumping into the pool from the five-metre board during the naval swimming test, or climbing down through the hatch that led her on board *Tenacity* in the first place, she knew she could do it. Everyone had fears, but you controlled the fear, the fear didn't control you. She slipped the mask over her head. The rubber straps caught on her hair and she twice had to stop and sweep her fringe back away from the face seal.

Aaron stepped towards her and helped tighten the mask around her face.

'Now breathe normally,' he said. 'It's already plugged in, but I want you, when you're comfortable, to fleet over to there.' He pointed to a spot a few paces away.

The mask felt unbearably tight. Dan could already feel a sheen of sweat forming as the softer parts of it, which formed the seal with her cheeks and chin, were pushed hard against her. The visor was scratched and slightly discoloured too, and Aaron's face became obscured as though she were looking at him through a lightly frosted but dirty window.

She took a few even breaths and then inhaled deeply and held her breath.

Reaching up, she pushed the connector and pulled out the male end of the rubber hose. It was tricky and it took her a few attempts to do it with one hand as Aaron had shown her. Once it was out she moved across the short distance to the next connector.

Her lungs were well developed from running and she was a competent swimmer, happy to hold her breath and swim a length underwater, but this already felt different, hotter, and more claustrophobic. The pressure on her face was contorting her lips and the straps seemed to be tightening on her scalp and were starting to hurt.

She reached up and tried to push the end of the hose into the new connector. She didn't push hard enough and as she let go, the pressurised system spat her connector out and the end of her hose fell to the floor.

'Shit,' she mouthed, her voice sounding muffled and deep.

She picked it up and tried again.

The rubber touching her face was now wet with sweat, which seemed to be made worse by the heat of the submarine.

Dan let out a small amount of breath to ease the growing pressure on her lungs. She pushed the connector again and felt it come loose. The whole thing wasn't helped by the fact that she had to stand on tiptoes just to reach the pipework.

'You have to engage it properly,' she heard Aaron say. 'Make sure you push it in hard. You'll hear a positive click and then the air will flow.'

Dan tried again, also letting out some more breath. As she reached up again, she instinctively tried to breathe in. The mask sucked back onto her face, the rubber caving in as it had with Aaron. She pushed harder on the connector.

'Don't panic,' came Aaron's voice. He sounded calm, measured. 'Just push hard until it clicks.'

Dan tried again, but it wouldn't go. She took another involuntary breath and the black rubber mask sucked tighter onto her face. She tried once again with the connector, but her chest was starting to contract. It felt like someone was sitting on her and pushing down onto her ribcage and abdomen. Her hands were shaking and the sweat between her skin and the rubber seal made it feel as though the mask was a giant leech clinging to her face. All of it was distracting her, ruining her focus. She dropped the hose and reached both hands up towards her mask. She pulled at the rebreather, the lump that the hose was attached to, desperately trying to create a gap to allow some air in; the straps were on too bloody tight. She reached behind her head and tried to loosen them, then felt the surges of blind panic begin to engulf her.

Suddenly there was air.

Aaron stood in front of her and released the straps in a single movement, pulling the mask up and over her head.

Dan gasped, bending double, her mouth wide.

'Jesus,' she said.

'You're OK,' said Aaron. 'You're OK. It takes a bit of getting used to, that's all. We'll practise again.'

'That thing's bloody dangerous,' she said, trying to smile and recover her breath at the same time.

'That thing is the single most important piece of lifesaving equipment on the submarine,' sounded a familiar voice from behind Aaron.

Dan spun around to see the Chief Stoker leaning against the back of one of the missile tubes near the entry hatch. His face looked odd, uneven, as he smirked at her.

'Yes, thank you, chief,' said Dan, standing up and wiping her brow.

Aaron patted her once on the shoulder. 'Practise,' he said. 'It's easy once you get the hang of it. Everyone struggles at first.'

Dan ignored him, instead maintaining eye contact with the Chief Stoker.

'Was there something you wanted, chief?' Aaron asked.

The Chief Stoker shrugged and turned to climb up the ladder. 'The Old Man wants to see ma'am in his cabin before we dive,' he barked, and was gone.

Chapter 14

Saturday Evening – 27th September 2014

Dan stood with Aaron for a moment, saying nothing. She had wiped her face with a baby wipe from one of the two packs that John had shoved into her holdall and was already grateful to him for what had seemed an odd gift.

'We're diving soon,' he said, breaking the silence. 'Don't worry about the EBS thing, OK? Just practise when you're alone. But you best get along to see the Old Man, he's not good when he's kept waiting.'

'There are times when he *is* goo—'

Dan's voice was drowned out.

'DIVING STATIONS.' The order was called over the main broadcast.

It made Dan jump as the general alarm, like an angry klaxon, sounded immediately afterwards, three loud blasts before the main broadcast carried on seamlessly. 'DIVING STATIONS, DIVING STATIONS. OPEN UP FOR DIVING, UNCOTTER FORWARD AND AFT MAIN VENTS. ALL REPORTS TO DCHQ.'

'I need to go,' said Aaron.

He made to climb the ladder, stepping back at the last minute as two submariners rushed down it.

They looked at Dan for only a split second before going about their duties.

One of them grabbed a black handset from near to the hatch and spoke into it.

'DCHQ, WSC.'

The sailor waited until Dan heard an incomprehensible reply laced with static.

'Weapon stowage compartment closed up at diving stations,' the sailor reported.

Dan followed Aaron out of the bomb-shop and walked with him quickly along two-deck.

They parted at the bottom of the ladder that led to the control room and Dan turned and climbed back up towards the Old Man's cabin.

The control room was quiet, only a murmur of functional communication audible. The white lighting had been switched off and only red bulbs gave the room any light, making everyone's eyes seem like black orbs. Dan hesitated and then steeled herself as she entered the darkness.

She could hear orders being passed quietly among the operators, each whisper repeated back, word for word, to confirm it had been received and understood. She took deep breaths, in through the nose and out through the mouth; she was OK and this place was OK.

A long row of screens was manned along one side, some larger than others, with images glowing green against the red ambience.

Seat after seat was filled with sailors wearing headsets, white cotton pads protecting their ears from the earpieces, and dark microphones pressed close to their mouths into which they seemed to whisper constantly.

Nearer to Dan, several officers stood at the navigation

table plotting marks onto the charts with stumpy pencils.

Many of the men stopped and looked at her briefly as she stepped off the ladder onto the carpet and Dan didn't hesitate any longer than she needed to as she turned right and carried on towards the Old Man's cabin at the base of the main access hatch ladder. The pillar of light that had shone in from the hatch the last time was now gone and Dan forced herself not to look up at the heavy hatch that blocked it out. It already seemed like a long time ago that she had been on her knees picking up papers at this very spot.

'ALL COMPARTMENTS CHECK COMMUNICATIONS WITH DCHQ ON THE DC NET,' boomed the next command over the main broadcast; this one sounding odd as she could hear both the main broadcast, and the Ship Control Officer, who she was certain was the Coxswain, speaking the order somewhere close, but out of sight.

Steward Roach stepped out of the Old Man's cabin as Dan reached it, almost bumping into her.

'Steward Roach,' she said, greeting him with a smile.

The steward nodded at her, red-faced, and lowered his eyes as he shuffled past her without a word.

Dan shrugged, although no one could see the gesture, and knocked gently on the door.

'Come.'

The door was partially open with only a thick blue curtain covering the entrance. Pulling it back, Dan leaned in and saw the Old Man sitting on his chair facing his desk.

'Commander Bradshaw,' she said quietly. 'You requested that I come up?'

'No, Lieutenant Lewis,' replied the Old Man without looking up from the screen of the small laptop. 'I *required* that you came up, and so you did. Take a seat.'

'FORWARD MAIN VENTS UNCOTTERED,' announced a

different voice over the main broadcast, this one sounding more tinny as it emanated from a small speaker within the cabin.

'FORWARD MAIN VENTS UNCOTTERED,' repeated the Coxswain, acknowledging the words from his position on Ship Control.

Dan took a deep breath and sat down in the same position on the makeshift couch that she had occupied on her last visit, listening as 'aft main vents' were also reported as 'uncottered'.

They sat in silence for what seemed to Dan to be a very long time. She became aware again of the constant noise of the air conditioning system, which fed powerful blowers, or 'punkah louvers', that continually discharged strong jets of cold air into the warm submarine atmosphere. There was one in the Old Man's cabin, cut into a long piece of square metal trunking, and it was aimed directly at the rotund man as he sat at his desk.

'Is there something I can help you with, sir?' asked Dan, breaking the silence.

He ignored her.

She leaned back against the cushions and crossed her legs casually; that did the trick.

The Old Man turned and looked at her, noting her posture and ensuring that she knew he didn't like it.

'I gather, Lieutenant Lewis, that you are unhappy with your sleeping arrangements?'

Dan thought before she spoke, taking a deep breath and wishing for the first time in a long while that she could have a cigarette, although she had given up several years ago. The extra thinking time it would allow, as she took a long draw, would have given her some time to consider her response.

'Lieutenant Lewis?'

'I didn't realise that so many people would have to be inconvenienced,' she said slowly. 'I had been informed that there were other places I could have slept that would have caused less inconvenience to the ship's company.'

He snorted, making no attempt to hide his contempt for her answer. 'I don't think you gave any consideration to the inconvenience that having you on board would cause.' He stared at her, his small eyes shining below his bushy, unkempt eyebrows. 'Your decision not to allow Master at Arms Granger to embark in your stead was a poor one.'

Dan held his gaze and waited.

He was deliberately waiting; she knew it was a standard, almost childish interrogation technique. He was hoping that she would feel the need to fill the silence. She didn't.

'Lieutenant Lewis,' he said, the irritation clear in his voice. 'I have been forced to accept you on board my submarine. You may think that calling *Tenacity* mine is an overstatement, or maybe a sign of fondness or endearment, but let me assure you that *Tenacity is* mine, and my law, and the laws of the Naval Service through me, are all that apply here.' He paused for breath, seeming to calm. 'I can appreciate your resolve to complete your interviews and see this through. Indeed, I asked for you to lead this investigation after a firm recommendation, but I insist that you now inform me fully of your concerns. I would also like you to detail to me why you felt it was you and not Master Granger that should embark my submarine.'

Dan hesitated. 'Sir—'

'Don't bullshit me!' he shouted suddenly, cutting her off and slamming a hand down onto the surface of his desk. A cup full of pens and pencils tipped over and there was an ominous rattling as a yellow pencil rolled across the desk, each side of its hexagonal shape tapping out its progress towards the floor.

Dan leaned further back, her heart racing as she was caught off guard again by his abrupt change of tone.

He leaned in close to her, the smell of stale sweat and tobacco wafting in her direction. 'Do you think your celebrity status affords you special treatment, Lieutenant Lewis? Do you think that your fifteen minutes of fame in the national press buys you that?'

Dan didn't answer him.

'Well it doesn't, and from what I can gather, and my sources are excellent, your little stunt after the Hamilton enquiry left you with few friends and many, many enemies. So, tell me now, or I will contact Fleet HQ again and inform them that your position on board HMS *Tenacity* is already untenable and that I want immediate clearance to have you boat-transferred off.'

Dan breathed through her mouth, taking a moment to recover herself as she watched him.

He was glowering at her, leaning in towards her to try and crowd her physical space and intimidate her.

She was certain that he knew exactly how his mood swings affected people and that it was a practised manifestation of his nature, something that he would have been unlikely to get away with outside the autonomous power of an armed forces environment. Her jaw clenched not only because he was trying to intimidate her, but because it was working. Her hands clasped together to stop them from giving this away and she leaned forward to meet him.

'If you could have done that, sir, you already would have,' she said, enunciating every word carefully, hoping that delivering her message slowly and deliberately would both demonstrate confidence and hide her true nerves. 'I am not able to communicate any information to you beyond that which you already know,' she finished, leaning away from him as though she were doing so of her own will, because she had said all she was willing to say, and not because being that close to him for even a second longer would have caused her confident façade to crumble like aging stone.

He leaned back into his chair, the plastic creaking as he did so, and smiled. His demeanour changed again in an instant. He made a snuffling sound that was first a laugh, and then became a fit of coughing.

'I like you, Lieutenant Lewis,' he finally said. 'I wish I had a dozen men like you.'

Dan ignored the remark.

'I'll cooperate in any way I can,' he said, shaking his head as though they were old friends enjoying a joke.

'I'll need a room, or office, to carry out my interviews,' said Dan.

She watched as he shook his chubby head.

'This is a submarine, Dan,' he said. 'We don't have space like that. You're welcome to use the bomb-shop, but there aren't many private spaces on board here; you'll find that soon enough.'

Dan looked deliberately around the cabin and then back at him.

He laughed again. 'Not in one million years,' he said. 'Tell me,' he paused, changing the subject. 'Why "Dan"? Why a boy's name? You're pretty enough. A little plain, maybe, hardly masculine, though, so why a boy's name?'

'It's just my name, sir,' she replied.

'Your name is Danielle.'

'Which shortens to Dan,' she said.

'I thought you girls liked things like *Danni*?' he asked, looking as though he were genuinely interested. 'You know, Danni, with an I?'

Dan's eyes had closed and she had sighed before she could stop herself. 'I don't really like Danni with an I,' she said, trying not to sound irritated. 'Not even if you replace the dot above the I with a little love heart.'

He pursed his lips and thought about what she had said as though it were a complicated thing.

'Come,' he said suddenly, standing up and gesturing as if she were a dog that was curled up on the couch and now needed a walk. He stepped out into the control room and Dan fell in, reluctantly, behind him.

'We're diving any minute,' he said over his shoulder. 'Ship Control Officer of the Watch, report?'

'Submarine closed up at Diving Stations, forward and aft main vents uncottered, sir. *Tenacity* is opened up for diving.'

He turned to Dan and smiled again, then pointed to a monitor mounted above the ship control console. 'Watch that,' he said and turned away to pick up a handset.

'Officer of the Watch, Commanding Officer,' he snapped.

'Officer of the Watch,' came a quick reply.

'Clear the bridge, come below, shut and clip the upper lid. I have the submarine.'

The order was repeated back, with the exception that the last line was 'You have the submarine, sir.'

The monitor that the Old Man had directed Dan to watch showed the open water in front of the submarine as viewed by a camera that Dan guessed must have been mounted on the front of the conning tower. It was just light outside and she could still see the whites of the bow wave as the sleek black hull cut through the water, peeling it aside like scissors running through wrapping paper.

The horizon looked clear and grey, with only a few clouds drifting across it.

Her attention was grabbed by movement off to her right as two men, dressed head to toe in red Gore-Tex, climbed down into the control room from an access that Dan had not noticed before.

'Bridge cleared for diving, upper lid shut, two clips, two pins, all personnel checked below, sir.'

Dan noticed two young sailors off to her left.

They were clutching books, each one opened up and folded back to expose the lists of training objectives that they would have to meet in order to gain their submarine qualification.

The Old Man approached her and leaned in towards her ear. He seemed to wait for her to recoil, pausing as if giving her the chance to do it. When she didn't, he whispered to her, 'It's tradition for personnel to witness their first dive from here in the control room. Watch the camera and enjoy the view. Stand with these two, they'll talk you through what they've learned.'

He whispered it all with his lips almost touching her ear. It was as though she could feel them moving and disturbing the air as he formed his words; the warm breath dampening her skin.

Dan refused to back away, despite the tension building in her.

He stepped back. 'Ship Control,' he barked to the Coxswain. 'Dive the submarine.'

'Dive the submarine, sir,' said the Coxswain.

'DIVING NOW, DIVING NOW.'

The order came back over the main broadcast and Dan looked back up to the screen and the outside world only a short distance above her. She swallowed, her mouth dry and resisting the act.

Orders were passed, repeated and obeyed around her as she focused on the screen. She caught some more words, meaningless to her, as she was drawn in deeper to the camera view.

Tenacity seemed to have slowed down, the white wave suppressed as the water now lapped gently against the bow. She became aware of the boat rolling, recognising that it was more pronounced than the ships that she had been on before, because of the submarine's round shape. Then she was aware of the submarine dropping in the water. The deck was changing angle beneath her as the aft end of the submarine dropped a few degrees down.

'It's so that when the front goes down the arse end doesn't breach the water. If it did, then the propeller might stick out and it'd just spin and over-speed, then trip,' whispered one young sailor to the other, his information breaking through in a snippet as Dan watched the sky on the monitor change with *Tenacity*'s movements.

Then the front of the submarine began to drop, the angle of the deck changing again, and Dan reached out and placed a hand on the back of a nearby chair, aware that the sailor using it looked back for only the briefest moment before resuming his duties.

'Bows down, keep safe depth,' ordered the Old Man, now the only voice audible to Dan.

The scene on the screen changed slowly as Dan watched. Her grip on the chair tightened as *Tenacity* leaned forward.

The grey horizon, and the few clouds that had been there, disappeared from view, and the light that the sky had brought began to fall into shadow. Water appeared at the bottom of the monitor, gurgling and splashing against the lens and moving steadily upwards across the screen as the picture grew darker and darker, until suddenly there was only the murky water of the sea rushing towards her, and a few seconds after that, nothing.

She continued to watch the blank screen, aware of orders being passed again and again, aware that the boat changed angle again, and aware when the periscope was manned and she was hustled out of the way as one of the young officers commenced an 'all round look'.

It seemed like she had been watching the blank screen

for a very long time when the main broadcast finally broke her trance. She shivered, unsure how long she had been watching for, unsure as to what had happened around her as she focused on the black screen. The control room felt colder than before and Dan looked slowly around.

The Old Man was looking right at her, watching her.

'FALL OUT FROM DIVING STATIONS, FIRST WATCH, WATCH DIVED, PATROL QUIET STATE, FIRST WATCH.'

As the Ship Controller made the pipe, the Old Man continued to look at her, never once looking away, never blinking.

Dan finally broke the deadlock, looked around, unsure now of what to do or where to go.

Everyone else had a purpose.

The young sailors that had been standing next to her were talking to a panel watchkeeper as he explained what he was doing and asked them questions about submarine systems.

Other submariners seemed to be relaxed in their watch-keeping positions, some chatting quietly, others leaning back in their chairs and just watching their screens.

Everyone had something to do and somewhere to be.

She hadn't seen the Old Man approach her, didn't realise he was beside her until, once again, she felt his lips near to her. Pulling away this time, Dan turned to face him, his eyes like black coal in a snowman's eye sockets, in the dim red lighting.

'You know,' he whispered. 'Some of the young submariners, those who haven't dived many times before, they have coffin dreams when they sleep down here. The mind plays tricks when it knows you're deep in the ocean, away from the light, with only the hatches and your brothers protecting you from the dark water. And there's no way of getting off. I don't think there's anywhere else in the world quite like it.'

He stepped back, a broad smile spreading further across his face, before he turned away and walked back to his cabin.

Chapter 15

Saturday Evening – 27th September 2014

The Coxswain was still sitting in the Ship Control position as Dan left the control room. Without the possibility of visiting him and chasing down some interviewees, she was unsure of where she should go; back to the bomb-shop seemed like her only option, to sit alone and prepare for her investigation to, eventually, begin.

A loud whoosh and a bang made her turn towards the large airlock door that led aft over the reactor towards the engine rooms.

Aaron was making his way forward from the engineering compartments aft of the Tunnel. He smiled and waved for her to come closer to him so that they could talk quietly at the back of the control room.

'Hey,' he said, as she neared him. 'First dive normally makes people a little nervous. How was it?'

Dan shrugged. 'It was interesting,' she said, and then, her eyes still fixed on his, she added, 'final.'

Aaron laughed quietly and nodded. 'You'll see daylight again, don't worry, I'll see to it personally. I'll meet you in the wardroom for a brew in about, fifteen?' He pulled his daughter's friendship bracelet out of the way as he checked his watch. 'That OK? I'll introduce you to all the boys, but I need to do rounds of the forward compartments first.'

Dan nodded and watched as Aaron stepped forward and stuck his head into the Old Man's cabin, speaking with him in the same hushed whisper, before he carried on through the control room, stopping to greet and talk with other sailors as he went.

Dan headed back to the ladder that would take her down towards the wardroom and followed the same route that she had taken the first time she set foot on *Tenacity*. This time she stopped to look at the pictures that were mounted in assorted frames along the wall. She read the full list of battle honours associated with the name 'HMS *Tenacity*', and saw several paintings of different ships that had shared the name over the years. They were all surface ships prior to the current one, the first submarine to bear the name.

The blue curtain, identical to that on the Old Man's door, was closed and as she followed the artwork slowly towards the wardroom entrance, the voices of the officers talking within became slowly audible.

'I'd fuck her,' said one. 'If that's the standard of chicks they're going to put on boats, then "co-ed" gets my vote.'

'She is fit as fuck,' joined a different voice. 'Great ass; it'd have to be from behind.'

'What if she wanted to see your handsome face?'

'I'd throw my photo ID on the pillow and let her feast her eyes on that, the lucky bitch.'

There was raucous laughter and Dan felt the need to turn away and go straight to the bomb-shop, to be alone, away from everyone, but her anger surged and she suddenly felt compelled to stay and listen, to know what they would say.

'Problem is, most of 'em don't stay like that. She's forgotten to draw her Wren's arse from stores, and they only come in one size.'

'Yup, extra-fucking-humongously-fat,' said another.

There was a murmur of agreement and more smothered laughter.

'Bag the gremlin?' suggested one voice.

'She's hardly a gremlin,' argued another.

'He's right,' began a northerner, his accent putting his origins somewhere near to Newcastle. 'I'd crawl naked through three fields of broken glass just to sniff the last cock that fucked her,' he finished.

The response was more loud laughter and some banging on the table, before someone else's voice rose above the noise, 'There's something horribly wrong with you northern monkeys.'

Laughter filled the room.

Dan was standing a few feet away from the curtain, next to the officers' heads and showers, her jaw clenched tight. She had stopped actively listening to the conversation that was going on, but could still hear snippets as unknown voices described how she might enjoy a wardroom gangbang and whether she liked sperm in her mouth or, most likely, across her face.

Her hands shaking, she turned and stepped away from the curtain, following along two-deck on her way back to the bomb-shop.

'Hey,' said Aaron as he walked towards her from the forward end of two-deck. 'I've just done rounds forward of twenty-nine bulkhead; it absolutely stinks in there already. Sixty bodies and next to no ventilation.' He pulled a face as though he could still smell it now. 'You blowing me out? I thought you were coming to meet everyone for a brew.'

Dan drew in a deep breath, her heart pounding. She thought about telling Aaron what she'd heard, taking action against the flock of bleating bastards hidden behind the blue curtain. But, even with the anger that was fizzing within her, she could see clearly how the Old Man would view this; the majority of his loyal wardroom against the word of a single interloper.

'You OK?'

'Yeah, sure,' she lied, forcing a smile. 'I just caught my head on one of the pipes.'

Aaron laughed. 'Yeah, there aren't many submariners who don't have a few scars on their head. You get used to it, though, it's like a sixth sense. Come on, I'll make you some tea.'

He stepped past her.

'No. I'm going to go and get some work done. Thanks. The Coxswain needs some names from me so that he can start arranging interviews as soon as possible.'

He frowned. 'It'll take a few hours for safety checks and stuff and, with the best will in the world, you won't be interviewing anyone until all that's done. This is probably the only chance you'll get to meet most of the wardroom in one go, and the Coxswain's still on Ship Control anyway. Once we get properly into patrol routine half the boat will pretty much always be in bed, or on watch, except mealtimes and heaves.'

Dan was shaking her head faster than she meant to. 'Honestly,' she said. 'I really don't feel like it.'

Aaron stepped close to her and leaned down to speak quietly. 'Dan, what happened?'

Dan said nothing.

'Look, whatever happened or didn't happen, if you don't face them now, crack a few jokes and gain some allies, then your trip on here is going to be more of a nightmare than it's probably already shaping up to be.'

She leaned back to look at his face, but his eyes looked caring, concerned and earnest.

'They're all good guys, a little rough around the edges

maybe. They're excited about this trip too; the Old Man has promised it'll be a good one, a proper send-off for him. They just need to get to know you. Most of them remember you from the newspapers a few years back, so you've a bit of instant kudos to cash in already. Come on, give us a chance.'

He took her arm and gently guided her back the way she'd come.

Dan let him lead her until they reached the curtain, where she jerked her arm free and forced another smile. The noise in the wardroom was loud and continuous, way louder than she imagined a submarine would ever be.

Aaron smiled back at her, opened the curtain and stepped through.

A wave of greetings swelled the noise.

'Enginessssss,' shouted one voice, the leader, and several joined him.

Dan stepped across the threshold behind Aaron and it was as if she had stepped into a soundproof room; the noise stopped instantly.

She waited in the doorway and looked at the long line of faces staring at her from the bench against the wall and from a few chairs dotted around the room. They all wore the same rank badges as she did, or were more senior, and to a man there was a set of gold dolphins on the left breast of every shirt; that felt like the real difference.

She felt herself swallow hard. 'Christ,' she said, trying to laugh. 'Do you submariner types practise that? I've never seen the navy act with such measured precision.'

They just looked at her. No one said a word. All smiles had vanished.

'Fellas,' said Aaron, his voice firm. 'Pack it in, we've got a guest.'

A few of the officers looked across at Dan and then up at Aaron.

'So,' said Dan, swallowing again and taking the initiative. 'How good are you lot? If I step back outside does the noise start up again the instant I cross the threshold?'

Aaron laughed.

'Probably,' said someone from the back of the room.

Dan threw her hands in the air in mock disappointment. 'You blew it,' she said. 'Before you spoke, I thought that I'd finally met the *actual* silent service.'

There were a few titters of laughter.

'Yeah, McCrae, you broke our vow of silence,' said a young-looking officer who was squeezed onto the long seat with too many others.

Standing in front of the gathered wardroom, Dan felt her hands shaking and put them in her pockets.

'Go ahead, Dan,' said Aaron, nodding towards the doorway. 'Step back out and see if he can keep up with the game. He's been our Simon Says champion for nine straight months. You're up for the challenge, aren't you, McCrae?'

The officer was silent, his cheeks reddening as the attention shifted onto him.

He mumbled something under his breath that sounded a lot like 'fuck off'.

'Aw man,' said Dan, again in mock disappointment. 'Simon didn't say "use profanities". You're out already.'

She looked around at the faces watching her, many now with grins as they listened.

'Are you guys absolutely sure he's your Top Gun? Because it seems a bit weak that he's gone down so easily in the first round of play.'

The officer, McCrae, seemed to be formulating a reply, his lips moving without sound, and Dan was certain that any retort would certainly be a play on her use of the term 'go down'. He seemed to be about to speak.

'One, two, three,' said Aaron, as others joined in with

him, their voices rising as they counted McCrae down like referees in a boxing match.

'The three-second wit barrier has been exceeded and your right to reply has been formally revoked!' said an officer that Dan didn't recognise.

The room exploded into laughter and McCrae, his face red, stood up and made to leave.

'And bonnie lad's given up his seat for the lady,' shouted the officer with the northern accent. 'To the victor, the spoils,' he announced, gesturing towards the empty seat as though he were a courtier to the queen.

McCrae stormed out of the room, throwing Dan a snarl as he passed her. Her hands were still in her pockets and she was glad of it. Although she refused to flinch from him, he was a big man and his eyes, piercing into her, made it clear that, for him, this was no joke.

'Grab the seat, quick,' said Aaron, pointing to the gap that McCrae had vacated. 'There's a three-second rule on seats too.'

The gap looked small, too small, and the men either side were already leaning apart to make room for her, so it was as spacious as it was going to get.

She shook her head. 'I'm fine, really.'

Aaron seemed to detect something in her voice. He stopped for a moment, looking at her carefully. 'Yeah, she doesn't want to be squeezed in between you two fat lads,' he said, winking at her.

There was a single chair next to a computer in the corner behind her, the one that John had used while he leafed through magazines the day before.

'I'll move,' said the officer who was sitting there, before he was asked or coaxed.

'No way,' said the guys either side of the space that had been Dan's. 'That's not a fair swap.'

'What will it be, Dan?' Aaron asked. 'Green tea, right?'

'She can't have anything,' piped up the first voice that Dan had heard.

She looked down at a Lieutenant Commander that she guessed must be Craig McAllen, the Executive Officer, and second in command of *Tenacity*. He was looking back at her with the same compassion that a cat has when looking at its prey.

'What you on about, Craig?' asked Aaron, turning towards the man, his eyes narrowing.

'*Tenacity*'s rules are simple and they apply to all ranks and rates, regardless of gender, Aaron,' replied the XO. 'She's not a qualified submariner and hasn't earned the privilege of sitting in here outside of mealtimes.' He turned to Dan now. 'You can eat here, three times a day, but after that you need to leave like every other non-qual; equality should mean just that.'

The wardroom was silent.

Aaron scrunched up his face and looked around them all, finally settling on Craig. 'I think this is a bit different, don't you?' he finally asked.

The XO looked at Dan and then back at Aaron and then, without the slightest change of expression, said, 'No. I really don't.'

'Look, it's fine,' said Dan. 'I should be subject to the same rules as everyone else. I don't have a problem with that. I'll catch up with you all later.' She turned and walked out of the room. She heard Aaron call after her and the curtain being drawn shut. Then some voices were raised and a low murmur of background conversation began to build among other officers.

As she followed along two-deck, she had to pass the entry to the wardroom pantry where she could hear the argument continuing. She tried not to look, but saw Steward Roach leaning against the sink.

He was in a world of his own, his eyes tight shut.

'Excuse me, ma'am,' barked a sailor as he approached her in the narrow passageway.

Dan pushed herself hard against the bulkhead to get out of the sailor's way, but she still felt his chest brush against hers.

Their eyes met, as he seemed to lean into her far more than necessary.

She shivered as he moved away, still leaning back against the bulkhead, her breathing shallow.

The sounds of the argument in the wardroom seemed to fade as Ben Roach popped his head out of the pantry and she looked at him, immediately noticing his bloodshot eyes.

He looked like a different young man to the bright and chirpy wide-boy that had greeted her just a day ago.

Dan looked away first, embarrassed, as though he had caught her in a moment of personal weakness, as though he could see and eavesdrop on her private thoughts and vulnerabilities.

'Sorry,' she mumbled, still looking away, not sure what it was she was being sorry for.

She started to walk away, glimpsing from the corner of her eye the steward lifting a kitchen towel and drying his eyes. She stopped and hesitated. 'Are you OK, Ben?'

Their eyes met for a long time until she watched Ben's shoot off to the side.

He turned away from her in an instant.

Dan looked to see what had drawn his attention.

Leaning against the door to the Senior Rates Mess, his arms folded across his chest, was the Chief Stoker.

He smiled and nodded at her, not moving away or pretending that he was doing anything else. He just watched her, smiling, staring. His sleeves, as always, rolled up, his arms crossed.

Dan walked away. She felt his eyes follow her as she walked along the rest of two-deck. Her hands were still shaking and her grip felt weak as she climbed down the ladder into the bomb-shop. Reaching safety, she shivered and her eyes filled with tears.

'No,' she whispered. 'I will not cry.'

She walked over to the bunk that she had chosen and froze.

Lying across her bunk was a length of black hose, the same type that she had seen used as a whip only a day ago and had taken from the submarine, the type that matched so perfectly to the bruises and welts on the back of the late Cheryl Walker.

It was coiled up like a thin black snake, its head disappearing underneath her pillow.

Dan swallowed and reached for it, her hands still shaking as she lifted the pillow up and revealed the black rubber mask. She caught a glimpse of something yellow across the visor and turned the mask over, pulling out a note.

Thoroughly cleaned and ready for use. Practise! Aaron. :-)

Dan exhaled and let a small sound escape, maybe a laugh of sorts, as she tossed the mask back down on her bunk.

'Getting silly, Danny,' she said to herself quietly. 'Need to focus.'

She sat down and pulled the black gash bag full of papers out from under her bunk. 'Sorting this lot out could be a start.'

Chapter 16

Sunday Morning – 28th September 2014

After spending a portion of the night checking through her investigation papers and trying to put some of them back into order, Dan had remained awake for what seemed like the rest of the night, listening to strange and sudden noises that pierced the constant drone of the air conditioning: pressurised air being vented, hydraulic actuators moving equipment, and all of this intermingled with seemingly random sailors coming in and out of the bomb-shop to complete their duties, or just to stomp around. Sleep had not come easy and she was exhausted.

They didn't pipe 'Call the Hands' to rouse the sailors from their beds, as they did on the surface ships that Dan had embarked on previously, and she was awoken instead by the sound of someone moving and talking near to her. Her eyes opened quickly but they refused to operate correctly despite, or perhaps because of, the comforting bright lights. She blinked repeatedly, clearing them like a dirty windscreen, each blink revealing a little more of her surroundings. She tried to find something she recognised; something familiar that would remind her where she was. Instead she saw a young sailor walking around each of the missiles and torpedoes in turn holding what appeared to be a small handheld hoover.

Behind him, like a line of baby ducklings, other young sailors followed, watching what he did, some taking notes, as he explained the process of 'sniffing'.

She looked at her watch: 08:32. Breakfast was long since done and she remembered that she had also missed the evening meal the night before. Her stomach ached and her mouth felt dry as she swallowed and watched the submariners across the short wall of supplies that ran forward to aft along the centreline of the bomb-shop.

The sailor, his charges in tow, approached her, standing only a foot from her bunk, and seemed only then to realise that she was awake.

He was young, thin and gangly, his face littered with pimples. He seemed to panic at the sight of her, as though he hadn't seen her in there over previous watches when he came down to go about this same duty.

'Sorry, ma'am,' he said, stumbling over the words. 'I have to come down and sniff every six hours. In case the bombs leak.'

Dan opened and closed her eyes a few times, working them to ensure they would stay open as she spoke.

'Thank you,' she finally said. 'I appreciate it.'

She was sure that she did appreciate it too; the thought of sleeping alongside leaky bombs really didn't fill her with a warm fuzzy feeling.

The boy nodded and turned away, finished his job quickly and told the others he would talk more when they were out of the compartment. He quickly headed towards the ladder.

The others exited first and he turned to nod at Dan before starting up the ladder himself.

'Excuse me,' asked Dan. 'Is there a canteen on board? Anywhere I can buy something to eat? Chocolate bars would do, anything really.'

The young sailor turned back and smiled at her.

He was one of the first people to have done so in a fashion that seemed genuine, aside from Aaron, since she had boarded HMS *Tenacity*.

'Sure, ma'am,' he said. 'Go up this ladder onto two-deck, then go forward through twenty-nine bulkhead, that's the big door right up there.' He pointed up through the hatch. 'Keep going forward and climb the ladder that's right in front of you. That'll take you onto the forward escape platform; it's a small compartment with all the escape gear and loads of other systems running through it. You can't really go anywhere else if you keep going forward. Then, look behind you and you'll see two doors side by side. The one on the right, as you look aft, is the Coxswain's store.'

Dan nodded and smiled, thinking that if it came to the worst, she could catch the Coxswain later in the morning. 'Thank you.'

'No worries, ma'am. The Chief Stoker runs a little shop out of there,' the sailor continued. 'Cigarettes and chocolate and stuff. Just ask him and he'll open it up for you.'

Dan's smile faded.

'Thank you,' she repeated, but much more quietly and with a smile that, even by her standards, felt forced.

She waited for the youngster to disappear up the ladder and rolled out of her bed, carefully watching the sharp metal edges and jutting pipes that seemed to make every surface around her a potential hazard. Just moving around the boat felt like climbing through brambles.

The night before, she had paid particular attention to the timings of when the submarine crew had handed over the watch.

The forward submariners did a straight six hours on and then six hours off routine and the watches changed around the key mealtimes.

Dan had written it down in her notebook and decided that she would never use the heads and bathrooms in those crucial hours between twelve and two, or six and eight, when one forward watch was rising, showering and eating prior to going to work, and the other watch, after being relieved at their post by their opposite number, were doing the opposite and preparing for sleep.

She listened carefully; the submarine seemed quiet.

The Coxswain had scheduled her interviews to start just after 10:00, coinciding with Walker's Section Officer finishing his watch on the nuclear plant. It had felt like another delay, but not one worth arguing over, and Dan had pretended to agree grudgingly, to relent to the Coxswain's request, but in truth, she thought she might need the time to settle herself in and sort out her thoughts. She had to conduct the interviews, find out where people were and who they were with before Walker was found hanged, and during the evening of his wife's murder. She had to find out how *Tenacity*'s morale was as she returned from her last patrol, how Walker's morale was, how his marriage was. But, and this was the really tough part, Dan needed to find out why someone might want to attack, and later kill, Cheryl Walker.

First, though, she felt grotty and uncomfortable from the submarine environment. The heat seemed to cause a state of constant perspiration and the atmosphere was made from equal parts oil and stale air that permeated her skin and clothes.

She climbed the ladder up onto two-deck and took the few paces towards the senior rates' heads, knocking and listening; it was as close to silent around her as she imagined the submarine could get. After a second's hesitation, she stepped into the tiny compartment, turning back to place her laminated sign on the door and then closing it behind her.

There were two tiny showers on one wall, and two 'traps' on the other. Across from the traps were two sinks. Apparently around forty sailors shared this facility, which was only marginally more spacious than her own tiny bathroom in her two-bed terraced house in Portsmouth.

She stripped off, her eyes never leaving the door. She had not wanted to undress at all the night before and had tried to sleep almost fully clothed, but the relentless heat had forced her to partially disrobe. Now, she nervously placed her clothes on the hooks behind the door before stepping into the shower cubicle.

The cubicle was small, the shower head only just rising above her head-height and the curtain clinging to her hips and legs as she turned herself around under the stream of water. The shower was, thankfully, warm and she began to relax, closing her eyes as the water fell onto her, but still listening for any sound as she felt it flowing down her body. She was aware of the time, but the flowing water drowned out the air conditioning and it felt refreshing to wash away the grime and rid her body of the constant stench that submariners were often goaded about. When her conditioner was rinsed out, she ruffled her hair to get rid of surplus water and stepped out onto the floor. She dried herself, dressed and then set about the cubicle making sure she had left no trace of hair or mess that could be considered a lapse in communal etiquette. Gathering all her stuff together, she looked around the senior rates' heads and decided that they were in a better condition now than when she had arrived. She turned and opened the door, immediately recoiling at the face that was waiting outside, standing directly in the centre of the doorway.

'Jesus,' she gasped, stepping back.

'One minute, ma'am,' said the Chief Stoker as he pushed past her and entered the heads.

He was naked except for a small towel wrapped around his waist.

Dan swallowed, stepping backwards, but turning to face him.

His torso was completely ripped, not a single ounce of fat visible across his physique. His abdomen was a perfect six pack and his whole body was rippling with lean, lithe muscles.

It was his tattoo that held Dan's attention.

It started on his ribs and seemed to work all the way around to his back and over his shoulder. It was a sequence of hexagons, but like Chinese symbols, each one subtly different from the others, made up of six different individual lines, but all of them in synthesis; it was like no tattoo Dan had ever seen before, resembling how the first concept drawings of a man-made honeycomb might look, and it covered a large portion of his upper body.

'Can I help you, ma'am?'

She shook herself out of her trance and looked up. 'You could wait outside in future, please,' she said, making herself face him while she stood her ground.

The Chief Stoker didn't wait for her to leave. He dropped his towel, fully revealing himself to her, and smiled.

'One minute, ma'am,' he said again. 'Every submariner on board only gets one minute to shower.'

Dan turned her back and walked out of the heads.

'Twenty seconds to get wet,' he was saying loudly as she walked away. 'Then turn it off, soap up and you have forty seconds to rinse.'

He was still talking as she climbed down into the bomb-shop, only becoming too quiet to hear as she walked towards her bunk and began to put her things away.

All traces of the relaxation that she'd felt in the shower drained away like the water that had brought them. Leaning against the chest-height missile mounted above her bunk, she felt herself shudder. She took several deep breaths and then stood upright again. Looking over to the ladder to ensure she was alone, she turned her back to the bunk and slumped down onto her bed, wincing as her shoulder caught on a length of sharp polished steel.

'For fuck's sake,' she said through gritted teeth.

She felt a surge of fury rise up from her stomach and had to clench her fists to stop herself from screaming. Only a few days remained for her to complete her investigation and she hadn't even been able to start interviews due to the submarine's routine. But really, the investigation was currently at the back of her mind. That the ship's company of HMS *Tenacity* felt, almost to a man, that they could do as they pleased, that they were empowered to act towards her in any way they wished without fear of retribution, was at the forefront. Why hadn't she acted? Why hadn't she taken action after the papers were dropped when she came on board? Why hadn't she challenged the officers over their conduct in the wardroom? Why hadn't she immediately charged the sailor who had so obviously rubbed himself against her? And now, the Chief Stoker felt able to reveal himself without consideration for what Dan might do.

Her thoughts were interrupted.

There was some noise from above, the sound of a few sailors up and about, chatting and laughing. She couldn't help but look in their direction, couldn't help but wonder if they were talking, or laughing, about her. Maybe the Chief Stoker was recounting to them what had happened in the heads, what he had done and got away with.

She stood up and walked towards the ladder. She would go now and speak to the Old Man, take action to make sure that his crew understood how they should act. She imagined his face as she told him, imagined how it would look as he processed that each incident was her word against that of another. Would he smile as he assured her that there would be an investigation? Would he chuckle as he informed her that she was now involved in an investigation against members of *Tenacity*'s ship's company and that, as such, she could no longer be part of an investigation involving those against whom her own complaint would be made? Would he tell her quietly that the best course of action, obvious to all from the outset, would have been to let John Granger embark and investigate, avoiding all such problems?

The signal that the Old Man would send to Fleet HQ would make uncomfortable reading.

It would be arranged for Dan to be boat-transferred off the submarine, with not a single interview completed and less than twenty-four hours after she had embarked.

She turned back towards her bed and reached beneath it to pull out the black bag of papers for her investigation. Her anger hadn't subsided, but it had morphed into a festering determination. It was an hour until her first interview and she needed to be ready.

Chapter 17

Sunday Morning – 28th September 2014

'Hey, ma'am.'

Dan looked up at the young sailor, then down at her list.

'Lieutenant McCrae said he's going to be late. He told me to come down first,' he said, approaching her slowly. 'I'm not supposed to be here until later on, after lunch, but he's tied up with a snag back aft.'

The sailor shrugged and waited, as though it was a take it or leave it offer and he really couldn't have cared which way she flopped.

'Name?' said Dan, trying not to sound peeved, but remembering her interaction with McCrae in the wardroom. It didn't surprise her that he might pull something like this, a little slight, an action that said 'I come when I decide, not when you say'.

'Richie Brannon,' he said, smiling now. 'I was supposed to be at two-thirty.'

Dan scanned down the list from the Coxswain and spotted his name, making a note about the changed time.

She had tried to get a couple of folding chairs earlier in

the morning to set up at the end of the bomb-shop, in the space where people worked out, but had been told in no uncertain terms that chairs were like 'rocking horse shit'. In fact it seemed to her that there was nowhere to sit down on board the submarine unless you were at a watchkeeping position or eating your lunch. In the end, she made off with a folding stool that she found tucked under the second desk in the Coxswain's office on three-deck and felt glad that she had.

She arranged the stool in the exercise space, facing forward so that she could perch on the edge of her bed, and readied a sign that stated 'Interview in Progress – No Entry' that the Coxswain had printed off for her, before she'd stolen his stool. Finally, she felt she'd made the best of a bad situation.

'Grab a seat, Richie,' she said, gesturing to the stool and watching him sit down.

He looked determinedly relaxed in the way that people often did when they came for an interview with the Special Investigation Branch, the way that said they were certain they'd done nothing seriously wrong, but a mixture of too many movies and a sailor's guilty conscience meaning that they weren't one-hundred per cent sure that they wouldn't incriminate themselves if they said too much or looked too pensive.

Dan worked quickly through the basics, putting Richie at ease before she started to ask other questions.

'How long have you been on board *Tenacity*?' she asked.

'Not long, ma'am. Only about three months.'

'Did you know Chief Walker quite well?'

'Well, we all kinda know each other, at least a bit,' he said. 'You know, I did some work for him once or twice. Helped him fix the aft hydraulic plant, but that's about it.'

'Did you socialise with him at all?'

'Well, again, ma'am, we all kinda socialise a bit. There's not that many of us and so when we go out, we tend to go together, or bump into each other at some point, you know?'

'But you wouldn't describe yourselves as friends?'

'Not really, ma'am.'

'Where were you on the night that Chief Walker died?' she asked, changing her tone and watching his body language change as she did so.

'I was, errr, at home, ma'am. East London. I flew back early from the stop off in Martinique, a few weeks before the submarine. Took some leave with my missus and kid. I only got recalled after it had happened. Had to leave them both at my mum's 'cos the Coxswain wanted everyone back on board quick-like.'

Dan looked at the young man in front of her, eager to please with an easily provable alibi, his involvement with Walker insignificant. Her sense that told her when something was wrong was silent as a sleeping cat.

'Who were Chief Walker's friends?'

He seemed to consider this. 'He was friends with a lot of people. There's a big group of them used to all go out together; the Coxswain and Whisky used to sort out the watch bill so that they were all off duty at the same time.'

Dan frowned. 'Seems a little unfair?' she asked.

'Nah, it really isn't. They'd do first night in, and no one wants to do that duty; everyone just wants to get off the submarine. So most people were glad of it.'

'Who was in the group that used to do this?'

'I don't really know, ma'am, a load of them,' he said; it sounded like an apology. 'I haven't been here long and I don't know all of the senior rates that well yet.'

Dan smiled to put him at ease. 'It's OK,' she said. 'You've been really helpful.'

He seemed to like that. Sitting up a little and leaning towards her. 'Can I ask you a question, ma'am?' he said. He looked conspiratorial, as though a few minutes' conversation and a smile had made them friends.

'That's not really how this works,' she said, trying not to sound harsh.

He hesitated, unsure whether to push on, and in that moment Dan considered whether talking to him, answering a question or two, might help in future interviews. It couldn't hurt to try and improve the perceptions of her among the crew.

'I won't breathe a word to anyone,' he offered.

'A secret?' said Dan. 'Doesn't it remain a secret as long as you only tell one person at a time?'

He laughed and shrugged. 'How did you know it was Hamilton?' he blurted, as though if he didn't get it out there and then, he knew he wasn't going to.

Dan watched him, deliberately waiting.

'Sorry,' he said, looking as though he meant it. 'I'm doing a degree in Criminal Psychology at the Open University, so I followed the case and read about it afterwards. Some of the guys on here knew him, you know.'

'That's the same course I started with,' said Dan. 'It's really good. If you put a lot into it, you'll get an awful lot more out. Are you still doing it?'

He nodded. 'Yeah, but it's tough. I'm on here a lot; you can see there's nowhere really to study, and then with the little one when I'm home . . .' He seemed to pause and think about what he had said, about his home. 'I want to get the degree, maybe do something different, earn more cash. I was thinking of applying to the police, you know, less time away from home at least, but I've got two more years' study to do yet.'

'Navy police or civilian?' asked Dan.

She could immediately see from his expression his thoughts on the navy police. She knew what sort of stick he'd get from his shipmates for even thinking about becoming a 'crusher' and wondered if it would be worse for him than it was for her, though she had always felt like an outsider and so it had been only a small step further away in her mind.

'You should keep at it,' she said, not forcing him to air his views. 'Don't give up and don't rule out the navy police; we do some really interesting stuff and it's harder than people like to admit.'

He nodded again.

Dan just looked at him, waiting and saying nothing.

'Are we done, ma'am?'

'Yes. Thank you.'

He stood up and walked towards the ladder.

Watching him go, she tried to imagine what it would be like to have so many demands on her time as he did. Work, child, partner, time away from home, and all the while trying to study and better himself and get home to his family. Dan just had her work and felt as though she had been away from any of those other things for too long.

'Richie,' she said quietly.

He turned back but didn't speak.

'You know those novelty shops with the pictures, the really colourful ones, and you have to stare at a point right in the centre of them and then eventually, slowly, you start to see some bits taking shape, and then you recognise elements of it, but not the whole picture? Then, if you keep looking, eventually the whole thing comes into view.'

He nodded. 'Yeah, I know the ones. My missus can't see them no matter how long she stares.'

'Well, honestly and truthfully, I just saw the shapes come together more quickly than some others. I don't know why.'

He looked at her for a few moments, visibly thinking over what she had said, before he smiled. 'Why do you think he hated women so much? And the other things you said, after it was all over, why did you think he wasn't alone—'

'Knock. Knock.'

Richie looked up at the ladder, cut off in mid-sentence, and Dan was glad that he had been.

Some boots appeared on the ladder and Richie stepped back to let Lieutenant McCrae climb down.

McCrae looked at them both, his face changing from an overly authoritative frown at Richie, to an undisguised sneer as he looked at Dan.

Dan thought about asking him to leave again, to tell him that he should wait at the hatch until called, but she suspected he would simply leave and not come back, and the only thing left to talk to Richie Brannon about was the answer to his last question. Even speaking to McCrae seemed like a more attractive option than explaining the events that occurred after the Hamilton investigation.

McCrae walked the length of the bomb-shop, ignoring Richie's mumbled greeting, and slumped down onto the stool.

'Thanks, Richie,' said Dan, watching the young sailor leave before she drew in a deep breath and turned back towards McCrae. Her clipboard was on her bunk and she turned to a new sheet and sat down to face him.

'Another Richard,' she said, trying to smile. 'Do you prefer Richard, or Rich?'

'Just call me McCrae,' he said, raising an eyebrow and then looking around the bomb-shop.

'OK,' she began, summoning her patience to her side. 'Thanks for coming down. I understand that you were Chief Walker's section officer?'

'Yep.'

'How long had you been in that role?'

'One year, give or take.'

'So how often would you see or interact with Walker?'

'Daily.'

'Were you someone he talked to?'

'It would be tough to get work done if we only communicated using the arts of mime and modern dance.'

Dan stopped and looked at him, weighing him up. He wasn't the first asshole she'd ever interviewed and wouldn't be the last, but he had something about him that made his hostility seem more tangible than many before him; it was hard to place.

'So, I understand that Walker had a number of friends on board. Who would you say were his friends, from your knowledge of him?'

'He was friends with everyone.'

'Were you his friend?'

'I was his boss.'

'So he wasn't friends with everyone then?' said Dan. She was watching him carefully now, seeing how he reacted to her retort; he didn't like it.

He rolled his eyes but said nothing.

Dan changed direction again, trying to provoke a reaction and get him talking. She suspected that if she got him started, he would want to continue, to show off, to try and appear knowledgeable and superior.

'Who decides who does duties on which nights?'

'Coxswain forward. A Nuclear Chief-of-the-Watch aft.'

'Did you know that Walker manipulated the watch bill to ensure that he could take leave with his friends?'

'No, but I wouldn't care if he did. Happens on boats everywhere.'

'But if he was friends with everyone,' she began, 'except you, of course, then that would be very difficult to achieve, right? He'd have to take leave with the whole submarine.'

McCrae was staring at her, his right leg starting to jostle up and down, bouncing on his toe. He didn't answer, just carried on staring.

'Except you, Richard, because you're the only one that wasn't his friend.'

'What the fuck are you doing here?' he said, leaning forward, his leg still jostling and his hands coming onto his knee. 'You've taken up a space on the boat to come and talk about this shit?'

'I want to find out about how Walker was, who his friends were, who he talked to, but I can only use what you tell me.'

'Walker was a submariner; he did his fucking job. He had lots of friends, he had been on boats for a long time. He talked to his friends, his wife, people he met in shops, whoever he fucking wanted to speak to—'

'You?' Dan cut in. 'Did he speak to you?'

McCrae stopped.

'Or shall I go out on a limb and guess that someone like Whisky never really bothered with you outside of work?'

'We talked,' McCrae retorted, quickly.

Dan leaned away as casually as she was able, as though just making herself more comfortable. Every ounce of concentration was now being shared equally between continuing to provoke McCrae into speaking, and controlling her own fear at being in this proximity alone with him. His animosity had grown and spittle flew from his mouth with every word.

'Really? Because I'm not seeing that, you and him, heart-to-hearts . . .' she said, letting her words hang.

'We didn't "heart-to-heart", but I was his boss—'

'Yes, you mentioned that, twice.'

McCrae ploughed on, ignoring her, but his body began to tense as he spoke. 'I had to sign for him to take leave, give my permission, so we talked about that. He'd taken quite a bit of his annual leave allowance and had made a big deal about getting some fifth watch time, that's time off the boat when she's still at sea. I thought he might be having problems with his woman, but he said it was all fine.'

'His woman? Do you mean his wife?'

McCrae seemed to calm a little at this, leaning back slightly on the stool. 'Whatever,' he said.

'Did you know her?' asked Dan.

'We'd met,' he answered.

'What was she like?' Dan softened her voice, trying to change the tone of the interview and keep McCrae in his newly relaxed state.

He didn't speak for what seemed like a long time.

'She was just lovely,' he said, the sentiment as fake as his new smile.

'When did you last see Mrs Walker?'

'Don't remember.'

'Where did you see her, at the family home or at a function?'

His smile was sickly now and Dan couldn't stop a small shudder escaping. She moved again, hiding her feelings as she did.

'I wasn't one of them that went to see her at his house, no,' he said, still leering, trying to appear smart as though he were toying with Dan.

'Who did go to the house to see her?' asked Dan, deliberately lowering her voice, trying to sound conspiratorial, to keep McCrae talking.

'I don't know what you mean,' he replied and looked around the bomb-shop again, bored with the conversation.

'But it wasn't you,' she said, bracing herself, but hoping she could get him back.

'No, it wasn't me,' he said. He stood up. 'Right, enough, I got to go.'

'We're not finished,' said Dan.

'Well, you'll have to book me again,' he said, and walked away.

'I'm sorry about that thing in the wardroom yesterday,' she said. 'It was just a bit of harmless fun. I didn't mean to make you look quite so stupid.'

He turned and hesitated, and for a second Dan thought that he might run at her.

'You didn't,' he said. 'You shouldn't even have been in there.'

'Because I'm not a submariner, or because I *am* a woman?'

He looked around the room, as if checking that they were alone. 'Both,' he said. 'Three places for you lot, the bedroom, the kitchen and off my fucking submarine.' His smile was broad as he winked at her and then climbed the ladder out of the bomb-shop.

Chapter 18

Sunday Lunchtime – 28th September 2014

The scent of lunch seemed to have permeated through the ventilation system and as Dan finished up another interview, she imagined that her senses must have been operating at an enhanced level through sheer physical need; her hunger was beginning to make her feel queasy.

Above her, along two-deck, she could hear the chatter of sailors as they queued, waiting for a seat in their tiny mess-decks to become free as they cycled through the constant, monotonous routine of sleep-wake-eat-work-eat-sleep. She climbed out of the bomb-shop and made her way down two-deck towards the wardroom.

The queuing sailors, a mixture of junior and senior rates, were all waiting for access to their own separate messes.

As Dan passed them, some that she had spoken to already nodded a greeting to her while others didn't. Some of them smiled and many others didn't, but they all looked. Conversation seemed to stop ahead of her and start again in muted whispers and unheard comments as she passed, as though she were the epicentre of a verbal Mexican wave.

The two-deck passageway was narrow, and it was impossible to pass down it without touching and brushing against everyone she met.

By the time Dan reached the pantry she was no longer sure if it was only hunger that was making her feel queasy. The silence as she passed, the blank stares, the closeness that prevented her from having any personal space, the way the submarine forced her near to people, their arm or elbow touching here, their back pressed against her there, all of these things drove a numbness through her body.

She almost bumped head-first into Steward Roach as he hustled around preparing for lunch and carrying the officers' food from the galley, across two-deck and into the pantry, where he would carry out final preparations before it was served.

Stepping into the pantry to get out of his way, and away from all the queuing sailors, she immediately heard chatter from inside the wardroom. Some officers were already there, waiting for their lunch.

McCrae's voice was recognisable as the loudest as he talked over all others around him. He was talking about the foreign ports that the Old Man wanted them to go to. How good they would be, how the Old Man was hoping for a quick stop in another UK port before they went back to Devonport after the patrol, how cheap the whoring was in some of the cities under consideration.

Dan's head physically slumped forward; she had hoped to be in and out first, to be gone before anyone else arrived to eat, even if it meant just taking whatever was there.

'You OK, Steward Roach?' she asked quickly, hoping he would reply and not blank her today.

The young man pursed his lips but didn't look at her. His eyes looked sunken and dark.

'Sure, I'm fine, I am, ma'am,' he replied and made to

skirt around her in the tiny pantry. 'You can't really be in here, ma'am. I need to get all the lunches done.'

Dan stepped out of his way and pressed herself against the wall to let him pass. 'Look,' she said, stopping him and gently placing a hand on his arm. 'We're scheduled to meet later this afternoon,' she said. 'For an interview.'

Ben nodded.

'I was wondering,' she looked at the curtain that separated them from the wardroom, an arm's length away across the small pantry. Her lips curled gently under her teeth as she thought about what to say next. 'Is there any way . . .?'

Ben Roach didn't look at her directly, but he managed a small nod.

'I get it,' he said. 'Come back in ten minutes and there'll be some scran just there.' He pointed to a polished stainless steel catering shelf on one side of the pantry work-surface. 'It'll only be a few rolls; I'll wrap 'em in foil for you. You a veggie or anything?'

Dan shook her head and felt like she might cry with gratitude. 'Thank you,' she whispered, and turned away to head back towards the bomb-shop, steeling herself to run the gauntlet of submariners that she would have to pass to get there.

She waited for as long as she could, checking intermittently until the route was almost clear, before she retrieved her 'scran'. She ate it alone, sitting on her bed, and enjoyed every morsel of the plain, home-baked rolls that she had heard the other sailors call 'fat pills'. It was obvious why. The dough was soft and still warm, but much more dense than the bread she was used to from the supermarkets at home.

Ben Roach had done her another favour too, using a selection of the salad that was still available on the first few days of the transit and adding two thick slices of ham to each roll. Certain that this would count as double rations,

Dan devoured them quickly and washed it down with water from a plastic bottle that had been with the food parcel.

Time was tight and she knew she needed to get through the interviews as quickly as possible in the remaining days that she had on board. The Coxswain ran a tight ship, though, and the men, McCrae aside, were arriving as they were supposed to, or at least informing her when other priorities meant that they couldn't. It was non-stop. With one hundred and thirty men in the ship's company and only six days to interview them all, she needed to hit more than twenty interviews a day. Each one was scheduled for ten to twenty minutes, and, so far, some of them had run over and she was already one person behind as she headed into the post-lunch period, with nothing at all to show for it, except the firm knowledge that McCrae was an asshole.

Dan was already feeling fatigued, the dry atmosphere and heat in the submarine making her feel more tired and grimy than she had anticipated. For the submariners, time of day wasn't really an issue. The boat operated twenty-four hours a day and they were up and awake at all sorts of times on their 'six hours on, six hours off' continuous cycle. Now, though, it was already past lunchtime, and as half of the ship's company settled down to sleep, Dan thought that without a watch, it would be easy to get lost in time.

In the bomb-shop, the compartment where she spent almost all of her time, the lights never went off and Dan was trapped in a perpetual, although very welcome, bright faux-daylight.

In all of the other shared sleeping compartments, such as the bunk-space forward of twenty-nine and the other bunk-spaces down on three-deck, it was the opposite; the lights were only turned on for a period of thirty minutes at the very centre of the watch changeover, a routine that made Dan shiver.

The interviews so far had been like dipping her hand into a bag of 'pick and mix'. There had been a selection of dour, uncooperative sailors who wished to say nothing and had nothing to say. Others had been smooth, too smooth, as though they thought there was a real chance that they might get their leg over with the 'police lady' right there in the bomb-shop. None had offered anything of interest concerning Whisky's death and all had easily checkable alibis for the night of Cheryl Walker's murder, mostly with their families or in crowded pubs with groups of friends.

Then there had been McCrae, hostile and angry, his interview unfinished. He had made comments about Cheryl Walker, about people visiting her house, and Dan needed to follow up on these, but carefully. It was apparent that McCrae's misogyny ran deep and the conclusion of his interview was a necessary nightmare lurking in her future.

The only other theme that ran through the submarine was the excitement about being on the Old Man's last patrol.

The younger submariners looked up to the Old Man as some kind of demigod, to be revered and feared in equal measure. Dan suspected that he was considered in a similar light by many of his older crew members, only experience and pride making them tone down and hide these feelings.

The return of the Chief Stoker to replace Whisky was met, fairly universally, with silence.

'Ma'am,' said Steward Roach, snapping Dan out of her thoughts as he climbed down the ladder and approached her.

She turned, smiled and gestured towards the stool. 'Thank you so much for the rolls, Steward Roach; they were very much appreciated.'

'It's OK,' he replied, without looking at her. 'Before I came to *Tenacity*, when the Old Man took me on as his steward, I hated going into the mess-deck too.'

She watched him as he took the seat in front of her, his eyes never leaving the green painted deck.

'How long have you been with,' she paused, 'the Old Man?'

He finally looked at her, picking up on her pause. 'All captains of submarines are called the Old Man,' he explained. 'They're usually the oldest anyway, but it's just what we call them.'

Dan nodded.

'I've been with him for over a year,' he continued. 'We met a few years before that. He had me transferred across from *Trafalgar* to work for him.'

'Is that normal?' asked Dan, genuinely interested.

'Some commanding officers can pick their own crew, not many nowadays, though. He's had the Coxswain here for years. We're so short of qualified submariners that we all bounce around from one boat to another a lot of the time anyway. The Old Man's like a talisman, though, that's why the lads love him so much. Everyone knows that *Tenacity* gets all the good run ashores, stops over in good places and stuff. We do the hard sea-time too, though, but the Old Man always sees us right.'

Dan waited, letting the silence prompt Ben to continue.

'But, yeah, the Old Man gets most of who he asks for and most of us are glad to get on *Tenacity*; she's a good boat.'

Dan nodded again and looked at her clipboard.

'Everyone seems excited about this trip, because it's the Old Man's last one. Why is that?'

Ben shrugged. 'Decent stops, I guess. That's what everyone likes, a good run ashore.'

'So, you were on board during the last trip to Fujairah? Is that right? That was the last stop before you arrived back into Devonport?'

Ben nodded and then looked back down at the deck.

'Was that a good run ashore?' asked Dan, trying to get back to the casual way that they had been conversing a few moments ago, trying to keep the flow going as he had seemed to be opening up and chatting freely.

She could see that his breath was getting deeper, his hands fidgeting.

'Steward Roach,' she said. 'Ben? Are you OK?'

He looked up; his teeth were chattering and Dan leaned back away from him, unsure what he was going to do.

'Ma'am,' he said, his voice shaking. 'Why are you here, as in, why you? Everyone says you're Kill team. Is it true you're here because of a murder?'

Dan tried to hide her anger at hearing the product of the rumour mill – a product for which she had sown the seed – repeated back to her. She clenched her jaw tight as she thought about her careless slip when she had first spoken to the Old Man and how much more difficult her job had likely become because of it.

'Because we all thought that you were just here to talk about Whisky and what happened with him.'

Dan made sure that her voice sounded calm. 'The Kill teams work with all crimes involving loss of life, including suicide, Ben,' she said. 'And we always investigate a suicide until we know exactly what happened and hopefully why. So, yes, I just want to talk about Whisky.'

'But you're a straight-up murder police. Everyone knows who you are. They're not going to send you for just a suicide, right?'

Dan waited, letting the words settle and watching him closely. 'Why would that bother you so much, Ben?'

'Whisky was my friend. It's bad enough that he topped himself . . .'

Ben was silent and Dan let it continue for a short while. 'Ben,' she started, using his name to coax him into eye contact. 'I would like to ask you where you were over the weekend, but it's all routine stuff for when someone commits suicide. We try to figure out where they were and who they were with in the days and hours leading up to it. How they were acting and why they might have done what they did.'

The sailor's hands were shaking now and his eyes were glued to the deck.

'What's the matter, Ben?' she asked, leaning in and trying again to make eye contact. 'Is something bothering you? Is there something you want to tell me?'

He started nodding his head slowly. Then he looked up at her and his face drained of all colour.

'Ben!' said Dan, the difference in his demeanour stark enough to make her recoil from him again.

But he wasn't looking at her.

Dan turned, following his eyes, until she saw a figure standing at the end of the bomb-shop.

'Get out!' she shouted, immediately standing up and striding towards the figure. 'There's a sign forbidding entry to this compartment.'

'Safety rounds have to be conducted as required, ma'am,' said the Chief Stoker. 'The Old Man asked the Coxswain to remind me about it just a few minutes ago.'

'Get out,' she repeated, stopping a short distance away from him.

He looked around the compartment slowly, his eyes pausing when they fell on Steward Roach. 'I guess I can come back and finish up later.'

He climbed the ladder with practised speed, leaving the compartment as silently as he had entered.

Dan turned back towards Steward Roach, who sat hunched on the stool with his head in his hands.

She walked back slowly, giving the steward time to think as she did so.

'So anyway,' she began, trying to make her voice as chirpy as she could. 'Any good dits from that run ashore in Fujairah then? I gather you're pretty much restricted to the hotel complexes out there?'

Ben didn't answer; he just shook his head.

'You can talk to me, Ben,' she said, reaching out to him, but then thinking better of it. 'Anything you say to me goes no further, not on this submarine, not anywhere. Information from this interview is handled in the strictest confidence; I swear it. No one here will ever know what you've said.'

He shook his head again and Dan knew he was lost to her.

She watched as a tear landed on the green painted deck, making a small dark patch.

'Can I go now please, ma'am?' he asked without looking up.

Dan felt her shoulders drop forward and let out a sigh. She considered pushing hard, laying down the line and seeing where that led. But, after a moment's thought, she just said, 'Sure, Ben, I'll need to talk again, though.'

The steward said nothing as he walked towards the ladder. As he reached up to grab a rung, he turned back to her.

'I was bullied on board my last boat,' he said. 'Everyone hated me, until the Old Man brought me here.'

Dan nodded, not sure what to say.

'I'll leave your scran in the same place for tea as I did at lunch,' he said, and was gone.

Chapter 19

Sunday Afternoon – 28th September 2014

After Ben Roach had climbed out of the bomb-shop, Dan counted to ten and then clenched her fists and grabbed a pillow, holding it tight to her face as she screamed, 'Fuuuuuuccccckkkk!' She was sure that the pillow, and the sound of the bloody air conditioning, would hide her frustration. She took the pillow away and looked at the interview chair that was facing the ladder. Then she threw her head back as if to look upwards and beg for strength. As she did, she banged the back of her head hard against a pipe, immediately bringing tears to her eyes. Recoiling forward in pain and clutching both hands to her head, she pressed her arms over her ears, elbows forward, as though she was struggling to do sit-ups. She turned to look at the pipe, rubbing her head at the spot where she had bumped it.

'No, no, no,' she said to herself. 'Fuck, fuck, fuck.'

She kept on saying the words over and over again, desperate to contain her anger. She walked over to the chair and turned it sideways, so that she could see the ladder from the corner of her eye and the interviewee had a less direct view.

'Ma'am?' a shout came from the hatch.

Dan looked at her clipboard; the next interviewee was here.

'Just a moment,' she called back as she grabbed the baby wipes and wiped her face and eyes.

She knew it would look as though she had been crying; her pale skin and auburn hair gave her a complexion that would turn bright red for hours afterwards. Another curse formed on her lips. It would be one more joke when word got round, one more sign of weakness in an environment where she already felt completely stripped of support.

'Fuck 'em,' she whispered quietly, throwing the wipe onto her bunk. There wasn't enough time for any to be wasted; she had to keep moving through the interviews. 'Come down, please,' she shouted, and readied the paperwork on her clipboard.

'Hey, Dan,' said Aaron, as he climbed down through the hatch immediately after the final interviewee of the day had left. 'You coming for dinner?' he asked, not waiting for her reply. 'I thought we could head along for second sitting. We missed Saturday Steak Night yesterday because we had only just sailed, so we're having Saturday a day late this week.'

He smiled as though that made perfect sense and then made a 'nom nom nom' sound.

'A pretend Saturday night at sea, on a Sunday. How can you say no?' he continued. 'And you've gotta know that Steak Night is *the* premier food night. It's a submarine tradition: onion rings in runny batter, partially cooked chips and,' he paused, his eyes wide as though there was even more excitement to come, 'we're opening a brand-new bottle of sweet chilli sauce. It's guaranteed to mask the flavour of even the cheapest and most overcooked pusser's meat.'

He sniffed, inhaling deeply and exaggerating the act as

he closed his eyes. 'You can already whiff the smoke of burned cow-flesh and be fairly sure that the smell will be reported to Ship Control in the very near future.'

As if on cue the main broadcast drowned out his final words.

'ALL COMPARTMENTS. SMELL OF BURNING THROUGH-OUT THE SUBMARINE, ALL COMPARTMENTS CHECK ROUND AND REPORT TO SHIP CONTROL.'

'Idiots,' said Aaron, with a resigned smile. 'They know full bloody well what it is. We only serve steak one way – cremated. Anyway, you coming?'

'ALL COMPARTMENTS. THE SMELL OF BURNING IS COMING FROM THE GALLEY.'

Dan heard a small cheer from the forward bunk-space. 'I'm not all that hungry,' she said.

He paused and stepped towards her, looking at her more closely.

Dan felt herself start to shuffle on the spot and didn't know exactly why.

'What's up?' he asked. 'Don't let that nonsense last night get to you; rise above it. I spoke with the XO and the rest of the wardroom last night and their behaviour was—'

'Aaron,' she cut him off. 'I'm a female in the Royal Navy. I have spent almost eighteen years "rising above it" and "just ignoring it" and "not letting it bother me".'

She waited, thinking before she spoke. 'It's a very different thing to "rise above it" when I make that choice, when I decide that I'm happy to ignore it. This is different. Here I'm just being undermined. I'm being forced to rise above it, because I don't have the support to do anything else.'

'What do you mean? If there's an issue then we'll deal with it. The Old Man has really strict policies on bullying and harassment, and he's a real stickler for the naval rank structure. If you think that someone's not showing you the correct respect, then tell me and I'll speak to the Coxswain; I assure you they'll be taken to task.'

Dan raised her arms in disbelief. 'Were you in the wardroom yesterday?'

'That's different,' he retorted, looking like a petulant child. 'They were treating you no different to any other unqualified person on the submarine, male or female, regardless of rank or rate.' He paused and smiled at her. 'And you gave as good as you got too, right?'

'Aaron, you weren't there when I was waiting outside for you, you didn't hear what I heard. And since then, one member of your ship's company showed me way more than just the proper respect.'

He stepped back, his brow furrowing as a deep frown spread across his face. 'What do you mean? Who? When?'

Dan shook her head. 'Don't worry, I'll "rise above it". It's exactly what I expected from a trip on board a long black tube filled with one hundred and twenty-nine chauvinist bastards, all united under Napoleon the Pig.'

He scratched his head, ruffling his blond hair. 'Napoleon the Pig? Don't think I've seen that film,' he said.

Dan rolled her eyes. 'For the love of God.'

'What? I'm a nuclear engineer,' he protested. 'I know it saves time if everyone just assumes that engineers know everything, but sometimes, in truth, we don't.'

'And they let you take charge of a nuclear reactor?' Dan was shaking her head.

Aaron looked at her in mock hurt. He was good at it too and the exaggerated pouting of his lip brought a reluctant smile to Dan's face.

'See,' he said. 'We're not all bad. Richie Brannon won't hear a word against you,' he continued. 'He's doing a criminology degree, or something like that, and I think he has a crime-crush on our celebrity detective. So, you going to let me take you to dinner?'

She shook her head slowly. 'Honestly, I'm not—'

'You know,' he said, cutting her off. 'This isn't the first time I've tried to feed you and been knocked back.'

Dan frowned.

'You don't remember?' he asked. 'I thought you were just being polite and sparing my feelings. You know, the opposite to what you did outside the burger wagon in Torpoint.'

He was watching her, a thin smile and a raised eyebrow as he waited for her to catch on to his meaning.

'Oh my God,' she said, the penny hitting the deck. 'That was you?'

He nodded, his lips pursed and looking grim. 'Guilty as charged. My acid house hoodie was a write-off.'

Dan's mouth was wide open. 'I remember now. I poured ketchup all down you.'

'You did.'

'Ah, but you were being bad,' she said, the memory still coming back. 'You wouldn't leave me alone and you kept looking at my . . .' she paused.

'Butt,' he finished for her, letting his shoulders sag and a look of terrible shame cross his face.

'Yeah, I do remember you now,' she said, scrutinising his face and trying to match what she saw now with the hazy and slightly drunken memories of so many years before.

'I tried to feed you then too, if you remember,' he offered. 'I tried to buy you a burger, with extra cheese, by way of apology. I was always smooth with the ladies.'

They both laughed, Dan thinking back and cringing inside at what she'd been wearing – how little she'd been wearing – although it was the style at the time.

'So, can I take you to dinner tonight?' he offered. 'Assuming you accept my apology now and don't tell everyone who'll listen that I was once sixteen and couldn't hold the drink that I wasn't even old enough to consume.'

Dan was still laughing, but she shook her head slowly, about to decline.

He cut her off again, his voice a little more serious than before. 'You can't survive without eating, Dan.'

He stepped towards her and put a hand on her shoulder.

Dan tensed beneath it and felt a tingle in her belly as his touch lingered. She knew that her cheeks were turning red, but she liked the feeling of his large hand touching her; it felt warm and soft. She pulled back quickly, looked away and then straight back at him.

He had taken a step back and looked awkward at her response.

'I'm not starving,' she reassured him, forcing a smile. 'I've got an inside man who's slipping me food on the sly.' She winked. 'It's a shady arrangement, black market food changing hands right under the nose of the authorities and all that. I can't say too much about it really.'

'Ah,' said Aaron, nodding his head. 'Made yourself a friend in the galley, always a smart move when joining a submarine, or a prison.'

She nodded and laughed and it felt genuine.

'And how does this black market exchange take place?' he asked with a chuckle.

'A police officer never reveals her sources, Aaron. I'm sorry, but the identity of my informants and dealers must remain utterly confidential.'

They stood and looked at each other for a short while.

'I thought that was just journalists?' he replied, and scratched his head. 'Well, having been a non-qual on board a submarine once or twice myself, I imagine that the exchange takes place in, or around, the pantry area,' he said, his finger and thumb gently resting on his chin in a pose reminiscent of Sherlock Holmes. 'And, as that's on the way to the ward-room, I offer to escort you to the exchange to ensure your food is delivered safely and the dirty deal goes down without incident.'

He finished and stepped back, swinging his arm towards the ladder in a grand gesture and saying, 'Ladies first.'

Sighing, Dan relented and moved past him towards the ladder.

'I promise not to look this time,' he said, as she placed her foot on the first rung. 'Being smothered in tomato sauce taught me my lesson.'

'That would certainly be ungentlemanly,' she said, with a raised eyebrow, and continued to climb. 'Although there isn't any tomato sauce to hand.'

'Don't look, mustn't look,' Aaron began to repeat, his eyes closed in mock concentration. 'Don't look, mustn't look.'

She chuckled, and sighed again. Her legs felt heavy as she climbed the short ladder, her body drained of energy, and yet this moment, feeling relaxed and talking to someone in a way she hadn't done for a long time, was proving to be the high point of an otherwise shitty day.

Aaron continued to repeat the mantra as he climbed up the ladder behind her.

Dan ignored him and stepped out onto two-deck.

He was up the ladder and standing next to her almost immediately. 'Practice,' he mumbled in answer to her shock at seeing him up so quickly.

He gestured for her to go before him, but smiling, she reversed the gesture. 'No, no, after you,' she said.

He set off down two-deck towards the pantry.

'Don't look, mustn't look,' she said quietly.

Aaron laughed. 'In my wildest dreams, maybe,' he said.

It was only a short distance to the pantry; in fact it was only a short distance to pretty much everywhere, the entire submarine being less than one hundred metres long, but Aaron's broad frame in front of her made it difficult to see anything ahead.

As he leaned to the side to let someone pass, she caught a short glimpse of two people talking where the walkway doglegged past the pantry and Senior Rates Mess doors.

The Chief Stoker, still in his blue overalls, was hunched over another man, leaning into him.

Dan recognised the second figure immediately as Steward Roach.

The steward was backed up against the wall, his eyes wide and his face pale.

'What's going on there?' whispered Dan.

'Jesus,' snarled Aaron, catching Dan unawares with the anger in his voice. 'Give me a minute.'

She stood still and watched as he paced towards the two men, placing his hand on the Chief Stoker's shoulder.

The Chief Stoker was the obvious aggressor and spun like lightning, squaring up to Aaron.

In this setting he looked small, smaller than Aaron anyway, narrower across the hip and shoulder, but Dan watched as, even when the chief had recognised who he had turned on, the man held Aaron's glare and refused to back down. He seemed to have no fear of punishment, nothing to lose, and Dan recalled how he had seemed the same when he had squared up to John only a few days before.

Aaron was speaking, his words not audible to Dan.

She watched them, standing in the middle of the passageway, no one trying to pass her or them, as though they could all sense that this scene was best left undisturbed.

Aaron and the chief were whispering, their bodies faced off.

In the background, Ben Roach was standing and staring, completely still, like a terrified animal.

As Dan watched the scene unfold, her eyes were drawn to Ben's.

He was looking at her, his face drained of colour and his mouth slightly open.

Dan felt as though he was trying to communicate with her, trying to pass an important message with his eyes.

A hand appeared from the Senior Rates Mess, tanned and slim, and touched the Chief Stoker's arm. It was the Coxswain, and as the Chief Stoker spun to face him, he stepped forward and whispered into the man's ear.

Dan watched the chief's shoulders relax and the tension drain away.

Finally, the chief stepped back and looked around. He looked dazed for a second, as though unsure of what had led to this. Then he saw Dan and smiled his usual sneering smile. 'Just can't tolerate people who take more than one minute in the shower,' he said to her, as if this was a reasonable explanation for his actions. 'Can't have too many clean-boys taking Hollywoods, can we?' He tipped his head at her, nodded at Aaron. 'Or clean-girls,' he added, before he turned and sauntered away in the direction of the control room.

'On you go,' said Aaron to Steward Roach, loud enough for Dan to hear.

She walked to Aaron's side, the Coxswain smiling broadly as she did so.

'What was all that?' she asked.

'Boys being boys,' said the Coxswain. 'And some boys just won't seem to learn any manners at all. The Chief Stoker has some issues at the moment that he's needing to be working through.'

'I think this is yours,' Aaron said, picking up a warm bundle of tin foil from the pantry worktop. 'Looks like Steward Roach has done you a steak sandwich, although it feels like there might be a portion of chips in there too.' He lifted the foil package up and sniffed at it.

'Jesus, it does smell lovely,' said the Coxswain, reaching out for the package and taking it from Aaron. 'What has he been putting in there? Mind if I take a look?'

Dan shrugged. 'Be my guest,' she said.

She watched as the Coxswain gently started to peel back one of the flaps of foil.

'Feels like a full steak supper,' he joked. 'How did you go about getting Ben to do this?' He peeled back the other side, but was stopped as Steward Roach stepped out of the pantry and closed the foil over with both hands.

'Now, Coxswain,' he said. 'Can't give away all my secrets.'

He took the package and handed it to Dan.

'Cutlery and napkin in there too,' he said, and smiled, his lips moving up at the edge, but his eyes wide, pleading with Dan to take the package and go.

'You're a genius,' said Dan slowly. She looked up at Aaron and then the Coxswain and managed a grin. 'Looks like dinner is served,' she said and headed back to the bomb-shop.

Dan unwrapped the foil slowly, unsure of what she might find. Why did Ben appear so urgent? Had he secreted a message? She checked the package, even peeling apart the two layers of foil and checking between them, but she found nothing. Picking up the whole parcel, she held it high and looked underneath: nothing there either.

She examined the meal. Steward Roach had done her proud again. There was a good-sized lump of well-done steak, far more than she could really eat, and a good sprinkling of what looked like freshly fried chips. Ben had also managed to add some salad again too, just a tomato and some cucumber, but Dan suspected that fresh supplies were rationed to make them last as long as possible.

She picked up the knife and fork that were wrapped, restaurant style, in a rolled up paper napkin and used the fork to jab at a chip. No salt or pepper, no vinegar or tomato sauce, but Dan reckoned it might be the best thing she'd ever tasted.

'Oh,' she said quietly, as a drop of juice ran down her chin. She picked up the napkin, unrolling it and bringing it up towards her face.

Something to show you. No.2 AMS at 02:00 tomorrow night.

Dan felt her hunger disappear in an instant as she read the words. She turned the napkin over to see if there was any more; there wasn't. Then she cursed herself for not checking it first as she read the message again.

Steward Roach had something to say, she'd known as much. She knew she had to meet him, had to speak to him alone, but she had no idea at all *what* No.2 AMS was, let alone *where* it was.

Chapter 20

Monday Morning – 29th September 2014

'You aren't going to try and earn your dolphins, are you?' asked Aaron with a grin. 'The Old Man would shit a mermaid if the first ever submarine-qualified female came from his boat. I can just imagine the Dolphin ceremony now.'

Dan laughed and shook her head. She looked down at the overalls that he'd given her to put on. They were the smallest set of white ones that he'd been able to find in the tiny storeroom and she'd still needed to roll up the legs and arms to make them fit. They hung off her small frame as though she'd inherited an older sibling's clothes ahead of schedule.

'Hardly,' she said. 'The Coxswain's been very efficient in getting the guys down for interview, but I've a few hours now where I can't speak to anyone. And this is a unique experience. I don't want to feel like I've been at sea on a nuclear submarine and not taken the chance to learn anything about it. Plus, I need to see back there anyway.'

She watched him shrug and followed him as he headed along two-deck, leading her towards the Tunnel and the large watertight airlock doors that led over the nuclear reactor and into the engine room spaces.

'Some of the guys mentioned an "AMS"?' she asked as they walked.

'Really?' he asked. 'Why?'

'It just came up and I didn't know what it was. I write down all the acronyms if I don't recognise them, but it's no biggie.' She tried to look as though she'd already moved on and forgotten about her question.

'Well, they're Auxiliary Machinery Spaces,' he said over his shoulder. 'When you go down onto three-deck, next to where you stole the Coxswain's stool from, go left and follow it all the way around. There's two hatches that lead down into separate compartments; that's them. They house machinery and we sometimes put luggage and other stuff down there. Some of the lads go down there to read, I think – it's relatively quiet – but you're not really supposed to do that. They're out of bounds to all personnel at the moment, so you can't go down there anyway.'

'How come they're out of bounds?' she asked, trying for nonchalant.

He seemed to think about that. 'We're storing some chemicals down there that should have been returned to stores before we left,' he replied. 'So we're keeping everyone out for good old health and safety reasons.'

Dan looked back down the ladder and tried to picture the place. She'd rarely strayed from two-deck, except to steal the fold-up stool, but was sure she could get as close to No.2 AMS as she would need to.

'*Steal* seems like a very strong word,' she said, trying not to seem like she was thinking too hard about what he had said.

Aaron laughed. 'I think the Coxswain's forgiven you. He said something about you being a "gutsy bitch" for even contemplating it. Not many people on a boat go out of their way to piss off the Coxswain. It's a high-risk strategy – he's in charge of the duty watch bill, the shitty jobs list – and Jago's been around for a very long time.' He looked back at her as he walked. 'Although, it may have paid off for you; he said you can keep the stool for the time being. But you're not supposed to be snooping around on your own, so don't do it again or the Old Man will find out for sure.'

Dan followed him up towards the control room and then along and underneath the main access hatch. Looking up now it was hard to believe that it was just water above there now, metres and metres of dark, cold water.

'How deep are we?' she asked, not sure she really wanted to know.

'Couple of hundred metres, I think,' he replied, as though that was perfectly normal and nothing to worry about. 'We've found a nice cold layer and we're heading out into deeper water for some checks. We'll stay fast and deep now until we come back up to safe depth for the heave, but we'll head back into the Southern Exercise areas for a little while again, before we start the transit proper.'

Dan looked up at the hatch again, expecting to hear it creak at any moment, or maybe see a small stream of water start to leak through.

'I've only got a little while,' said Aaron as he pulled back on the hydraulic lever that opened the airlock door. 'The reason you don't have any interviews is because we're heaving soon.'

She watched him as he crab-stepped into the airlock, climbing in after him and waiting as he operated the interior lever to close the door before he opened the next identical one.

'In the old days we used to leave these doors open while we were at sea,' he said, with a tinge of sadness. 'It was called "happy doors" – it saved time and cut down on noise.'

Dan nodded and pursed her lips in disappointment, as if she shared his frustration and longing for the 'happy doors'.

He laughed.

'They were the good days, eh?' she added. 'So who knows we're having a heave?'

'Worst kept secret on a submarine,' he chuckled. 'We stage a damage control exercise: a pretend fire, some electrical losses, or a problem with the nuclear plant. Then we drill the crew and see how they react.'

'Ship's company,' Dan corrected with a waggle of her finger. 'Fishing trawlers have a crew, MEO. Her Majesty's submarines have a ship's company.'

'Of course, ship's company, how terribly crass of me,' Aaron agreed. 'Today we're doing a few serials: collision with submerged object, fires forward and aft, culminating in a casualty on the engine room lower level. Come on, I'll show you.'

They passed through the second airlock door and walked through the Tunnel. Dan immediately spotted a large, circular sealed door mounted flush into the bulkhead. She nodded towards it.

'That's the plug,' Aaron said in response.

Dan groaned.

'No, really. That's what we open when we need to access the reactor compartment. It's all sealed when we're at sea.'

As if to prove it, he bent down a few paces further on and lifted a small round trap door in the floor, revealing a round pane of scratched glass. He pointed down into a room filled with shiny metal pipes and huge lumps of equally shiny equipment.

The room looked clean, scarily clean, like it was made predominantly out of steel worktops from a hospital kitchen.

'There,' he said, pointing to a lump of metal, indistinguishable to Dan from all of the others. 'That's the reactor.'

Dan stared down through the viewing window and nodded. There were lumps and bumps, metal jutting out from all sides, and the floor was like the metal grating used in prisons. 'Takes a bit of practice to recognise all the individual bits though, hey?' she said, not really sure what he was pointing at. 'Is that the flux capacitor next to it?'

He laughed. 'Yeah, I suppose it does take some practice and yes, if you want that to be the flux capacitor, then that's what it can be, but we'll just go on calling it a valve, if that's OK?'

'Have it your way,' she said.

They passed through the second airlock, two more heavy, hydraulically operated watertight doors with a small standing space between them, and Aaron led her past some more valves and heavy machinery.

The whole place looked alien, as though someone had installed the systems in no particular order, running pipes and cables wherever they pleased, and Dan began to wonder how any of the sailors ever told one component of the submarine from another.

The temperature began to rise as they walked further aft and Dan saw another watertight bulkhead door, the last of the bulkheads splitting the submarine into four watertight sections. This one was a single door, similar to the one they called twenty-nine watertight bulkhead, not a double airlock type, like the ones either end of the Tunnel. Through it, she could see the engine rooms, a darkened landscape of twisted pipes, more lumps of metal and dirty corrugated decking plates. It was almost recognisable from some of the crime scene pictures that she had seen in the police files.

'Hang on,' said Aaron as he stepped into a room on his left. Turning back, as if it were an afterthought, he said, 'This is the manoeuvring room. This is where we, God's own offspring,' he gestured to himself and then out around the engine room spaces, 'control the nuclear power plant and bestow upon Command the gifts of both propulsion and power.'

He stepped out of sight and she heard him talking to the manoeuvring room team for a moment before he came back out.

'Through here,' he said and stepped through the door.

Dan followed.

The heat hit her like a hammer blow. It was like walking out of her air-conditioned apartment during her holiday in Greece, when the oppressive heat, at the height of the Greek summer, had engulfed her as soon as she crossed the threshold and caused an instant sheen of sweat over her whole body.

'Jesus,' she gasped.

'Yeah,' Aaron agreed, shouting to be heard. 'It gets hotter when we're in shallow waters or, obviously, as the water temperature rises. It can hit fifty degrees back here during heaves.'

He led her onwards.

'When we heave later, the first thing we do is crash-stop ventilation. When that happens the temperature can really fly up and we need to be careful with the lads being in here. Dehydration can be a problem, especially during something like the casualty exercise that's physically really tough. Also, the heat can lead to a higher risk of fires.'

Dan looked at him closely; he wasn't joking.

She ducked as they passed by a huge metallic lump that he pointed out as the 'aft escape tower' and then took her down a short ladder.

'This is called the starting platform,' he shouted. 'You can follow this walkway all the way around the main engines and gearbox. We can control the propulsion system remotely from here.'

He gestured to two large metal steering wheels and then

pointed out the main engines and turbo-generators in turn; Dan forgot each one as quickly as she heard him name it.

'Down there is the lower level.' He pointed to a short ladder behind Dan.

From where she was standing, Dan could see that the ladder he was pointing at ran down to an intermediate platform. She followed him down and turned back on herself. This platform was filled with more equipment. As she turned again, she saw a gap in the equipment and immediately took a step back. In front of her now was a slim ladder that ran straight down to a metal walkway at the bottom. The route was made more tortuous by the jutting pipes and machinery that were present almost continuously on the way down. There was no safety rail to be seen, just rung after rung of metal disappearing into the belly of *Tenacity*.

Dan thought about Walker and how he would have felt, climbing down into this dimly lit, dirty space as he moved towards his death.

'That's where Walker hanged himself, isn't it?' she asked, recognising the place from both the pictures and the name.

Aaron nodded. He pointed to the side of one of the pumps where people had written short messages and memories in black pen, all addressed to Whisky.

'It's odd,' he said, leaning in close to her. 'We all just carry on. We miss him and we're sad, but it's like in our business, we're just used to moving on. We're like sharks, always having to move forward. It's when one of us finally has to stop that the problems seem to catch up.'

He pursed his lips as he moved away from her.

'Did Whisky have problems?' she asked.

Aaron looked around the engine rooms. 'Doesn't everyone have problems?'

'Not everyone takes their own life,' offered Dan, watching him carefully. 'Even after the death of a spouse.'

'Maybe he'd lost control of his problems and they were catching him up. I know he missed her when we were away; he loved Cheryl. She was why he put up with all this.'

'You found him, didn't you?' Dan asked.

This time it was her leaning in close to him, her hand resting on his shoulder as she stood on tiptoes and spoke into his ear.

'Yeah, I did. I gave my statement to Master at Arms Granger and I'll be happy to chat to you when Jago books me in. Not much to say, really. I was doing rounds, came down here and found him.' He pursed his lips again, frowning, and took a deep breath. 'It was horrible. You know, in the films people always get there in time, they grab the guy's legs and hold him up, screaming until help arrives. I couldn't do anything; I couldn't even reach him because he was hanging out so far. I raised the alarm and tried to pull him towards me with a broom handle, but I couldn't get him. I kept on trying until the duty watch arrived, but he was gone.'

They looked at each other for a short time before Aaron shook his head, as though waking from a daydream, and pulled back the sleeve of his overalls to check his watch.

Dan watched as he moved his friendship bracelet out of the way and pressed a button to illuminate his watch face. 'We need to get going,' he said. 'I'm happy to tell you anything else you need to know when we interview. I can bring you down here again too, if you want?'

Dan nodded her agreement.

'That's where we're going to have the casualty exercise today,' Aaron shouted this time, pointing down the long ladder into the darkness below. 'It's a tough evolution for them,' he continued. 'We'll say that the guy is paralysed and put him in a Neil Robertson stretcher – so he won't be able to help them; he'll be completely immobilised. They'll have to pull him up here manually and get him up to the aft escape platform.'

Dan nodded her head and looked all the way down the sheer ladder again. 'Shit,' she whispered under her breath. Looking down there gave her the same feeling of being off balance as looking down from a tall building.

'The Old Man suggested to the Coxswain that we use you as the casualty.'

Dan stepped back and snorted. 'Not *ever*.'

'Don't worry. I said you'd say that. He'll pick someone else.'

Dan took another tentative look down the long drop. Below, she saw a man emerge from a tiny entrance off to the side of the submarine.

He crawled out of the space on his hands and knees and then stood up.

Dan stepped back. 'Why's the Chief Stoker down there?' she said quietly to herself.

'I don't know,' said Aaron, making Dan jump; she hadn't thought he would have heard her.

She looked up at him, his face pensive as he leaned out and watched the chief disappear from sight.

Dan slid her toe tentatively to the very edge and, leaning her weight back away from the drop, also looked down to the machinery space below.

'Can I watch when it happens?' she asked. 'I can't imagine how they'll get a grown man up there in any kind of reasonable time. Is there a pulley system or something?'

Aaron laughed. 'Nope.'

He pointed back up the way they had come. 'I can set you up back there somewhere. There won't be space to watch right here as we'll need all our hands to recover the casualty, as well as the observers who assess the exercise.' He seemed to think about it. 'They'll be doing all of it in EBS too, so you might struggle to see anything interesting from here anyway and you'll likely end up getting in the way.'

'I could watch from down there?' Dan pointed.

Aaron looked at her for a moment and then shook his head.

'You aren't allowed down there, Dan. If you're escorted, maybe, but I won't be able to spare anyone to be with you, so that won't work.'

'Who does go in the stretcher then? If you are all doing the lifting?'

'Jago will pick someone from forward. We try to get all our engineers involved in the drill itself; it's good practice.'

They walked back through the engine rooms and headed back towards the Tunnel.

Dan relished the moment as she passed out of the engine room and into the air-conditioned manoeuvring room flat.

'I'll put you somewhere on the aft escape platform, OK? You should be able to see plenty from there and get a flavour of what we do.'

Dan looked through the watertight door and back into the hot compartment. Then she nodded.

'We've got a few minutes,' said Aaron. 'Come and say hello to the lads. It's a fact of submarine life that the afties are a bit friendlier than those who work forward of the Tunnel,' he said with a proud smile.

'Is that what they call you, then? Afties?' She watched him carefully in case he was having her on a bit, or winding her up.

'It is, ask anyone.'

'What do you call them?'

He laughed. 'Well, we're Afties, because we work back aft. They work in the front, so it's something that rhymes with front, but that I couldn't say to a lady.'

'Really?' said Dan, mouth dropping open in mock shock. 'How rude and yet startlingly accurate.'

'I know,' he agreed. 'We submariners are known for our

vulgarity; we've been putting the naughty in nautical since 1901. Come on, I'll introduce you.'

Dan couldn't help but let the smile that had formed during her time with Aaron slip quickly away from her face as he stepped into the manoeuvring room, where the nuclear operators sat to control the nuclear plant. She took a step closer to the entrance and paused.

'Fuck that,' she heard, seeing a large, balding chief throw his hands in the air in a show of utter despair. 'Ours are miles better.'

Aaron stepped in, making room for Dan, but not introducing her yet. 'Fuck what?' he asked.

The bald chief turned to Aaron, as if relieved he was here. 'Ah, Boss,' he began, rubbing a chubby hand over his slightly sweaty forehead. 'Tell this non-qual imbecile' – he pointed to a young officer who was perched on a narrow bench at the back of the room, his youth and lack of experience as blinding as his perfectly clean, new white overalls – 'this moron, this oxygen thief, where the best baked potatoes on a submarine are made.' He held his hands out towards Aaron, as if the answer given would be unquestionably correct.

Aaron laughed and turned to look at Dan, including her in the conversation. 'Everyone knows that the best baked potatoes on a submarine, nay the planet Earth, are baked on the main engines of HMS *Tenacity*,' he began.

The chief raised his palms to the deck-head and declared, 'Thank you.'

'But,' continued Aaron, 'there are some traditions to be observed. You always bake the potatoes themselves on the ahead throttles, whilst the Bombays, prepared by the donk-shop horse during the dogs, are baked on the cooler, astern throttles.'

Dan looked around the room at the other operators, who were nodding their agreement, and then at Aaron.

'What?' he asked.

Dan laughed. 'I don't really understand anything about what you just said, and I'm not sure if you really do bake potatoes back here, either,' she said.

She smiled nervously, waiting for someone to say or do something that would chase the smile away again.

'Ma'am,' boomed the chief. 'You come back here during the middle watch and I will show you a culinary delight like you have never seen before.'

Dan nodded her head. 'Sure, I'd like that.'

'Boss.'

They all turned as one to look towards the voice; it was the Chief Stoker.

'Casualty's in place,' said the chief.

Aaron nodded without needing another word and walked past Dan, tagging her arm as he went. 'Listen, we're going to start any second,' he warned her, as he led her out of the manoeuvring room and back through the watertight door into the baking hot engine room. 'Stay here.' He positioned her in an alcove between a metallic sink, with a hot water urn mounted above it, and some red cabinets with signs declaring that they contained breathing apparatus in numbered sets. 'You should be able to see a fair bit of what's going on from here, but you won't get in the way. I act as a safety number so, if I can, I'll come and get you before they start bringing the casualty up the lower level ladder, but it depends how it's going. I can't promise, OK?'

Dan nodded, catching the EBS mask that he tossed towards her.

'You'll need to don EBS with everyone else,' he said with a wink. 'You've been practising, right?'

Dan nodded again, surprised at how nervous she felt, despite knowing that it was an exercise and one that she wasn't even involved in. She looked around the spaces, dark, hot, as welcoming as the barren surface of a forbidden planet would be.

She stirred from her thoughts as the Chief Stoker's voice penetrated the noise.

'Enjoy the show,' he said, looking at her, as though making sure she'd heard him before he disappeared down into the engine rooms.

Her mind was racing as she watched him go.

Aaron had said that the No.2 AMS was out of bounds due to the storage of chemicals. If so, what would Ben want to show her down there and why was he so frightened and secretive? There were lots of nooks and crannies on board where people stored stuff, so why there in particular?

Dan knew that she had to meet Ben and see what it was he wanted to tell her, but she also needed to get down into the engine room lower levels and spend some time where Whisky had committed suicide, but that seemed like an impossible task. She looked slowly around the engine room, thinking about Ben's note, and how she might sneak down to No.2 AMS without being seen. She hardly blended in on board *Tenacity*.

The thought of bumping into the Chief Stoker or McCrae helped her to make the decision. She'd contact the Coxswain as soon as the heave was over. She'd grab Jago, tell him what had happened and show him Ben's note; that was the right thing to do. Then she'd have some help to stop whatever was happening in its tracks.

Ben would be angry when he found out she'd told someone else, and Dan knew she would need to break her word, but standing here in the oppressive heat, she was certain it would be for his own good.

This whole thought process was only just fully formed in her mind, when all hell broke loose around her.

Chapter 21

Monday Morning – 29th September 2014

'SHUT BULKHEAD DOORS!'

The words seemed to shake Dan's bones as the voice bellowed out of the main broadcast and, despite herself, despite knowing it was an exercise, Dan felt her body tense up and her breathing quicken as her eyes darted around the engine room.

The general alarm followed the words; three loud bursts on the emergency klaxon.

The person making the broadcast was all but shouting, the urgency palpable.

'EMERGENCY STATIONS – EMERGENCY STATIONS. STAND-BY COLLISION PORT SIDE. SHUT BULKHEAD DOORS. BRACE! BRACE! BRACE!'

It had only been a few seconds since the first pipe had occurred, but already there were several people in the engine rooms with her. The watertight door had been shut, making the room darker than normal, and the ventilation had stopped. Dan hadn't realised how accustomed she had become to the continuous noise it emitted and now, as the

Ship Controller finished his pipe, for a split second the submarine sounded eerily silent.

The men in the compartment around her grabbed onto various parts of the submarine structure with both hands. They bent their legs and raised their heels off the floor, adopting the 'brace' position.

Dan did the same.

She heard a loud thump from somewhere below her and in that moment the silence was shattered.

'EMERGENCY STATIONS – EMERGENCY STATIONS. LOUD BANG HEARD EXTERNAL TO THE SUBMARINE. ALL COMPARTMENTS CARRY OUT PHASE ONE DAMAGE CONTROL CHECKS AND REPORT TO DCHQ.'

The men around her sprang into action, disappearing down the ladder at a rate of knots as Dan stood up properly, aware that her eyes were wide and that she was covered in nervous goose-pimples.

She heard raised voices from further into the engine rooms.

They were shouting, repeating something, each taking up the call as the message worked its way up towards her.

'Casualty – casualty – casualty. Casualty in the engine room lower level!' screamed a sailor in her direction.

'Pass it on, ma'am,' he said, waiting.

Dan hesitated, unsure if she could remember exactly what had been said in the heat of the moment, but there was no need as she heard the words repeated over the broadcast; the message had made it through.

The main broadcast sounded again and Dan wondered what more could possibly be going to happen.

EMERGENCY STATIONS – EMERGENCY STATIONS; FIRE – FIRE – FIRE. FIRE IN THE SHIP'S OFFICE. DON EBS THROUGHOUT THE SUBMARINE.'

The watertight door was opening, not using the hydraulic lever as she had seen Aaron do; it was quicker than that.

A large man in blue overalls bodily pushed it and clipped it open again. The engine room filled with bodies. The submariners who had been asleep were back aft in what seemed to Dan an instant. The constant pipes over the main broadcast and the sound of the general alarm all left her looking around, feeling more than ever that she was out of place and formed no part of this machine that was operating around her.

Bleary-eyed, the sailors ran into the engine rooms, working valves and grabbing for equipment.

The pipes that kept coming over the main broadcast seemed to Dan to make no sense at all, and yet, despite what appeared to be a mixture of shouting and chaos, the men around her worked in a completely cohesive pattern.

'Don EBS, ma'am,' yelled one sailor as he pulled a mask over his face.

She looked around her.

Everyone else was already wearing EBS. They were fleeting quickly around the engine rooms; the movement, which Dan had found so difficult initially, seemed as normal as walking to those around her as they hurried about their duties.

It was now impossible to tell them apart as they all wore the same blue overalls, the same boots, and their faces were completely covered in the black rubber masks, with their hoses plugged into the breathing system connectors, identical to those in the bomb-shop.

Dan gripped the mask in front of her and hooked the straps over her head, pulling the mask out as far as she could and sliding it onto her face. She reached up quickly, forcing the connector into the system, before she pulled the straps tight. The mask felt cumbersome and she realised that she was breathing heavily, the confines of it reminding her again of how hot the engine rooms were, how tight it felt against her face.

'Break out the breathing apparatus,' shouted a man a few feet in front of her.

He stood facing her, waiting expectantly.

She looked around, raised her palms towards him, not knowing what to do. The large sailor, his overalls already darker around the shoulders as the sweat began to soak through, pointed to the red lockers beside her, gesturing that she should open them.

Dan reacted. She felt her breathing quicken even further, just as her hands began to shake. She was fit, ran regularly, but she already felt weak and out of breath as she turned and fumbled with the first latch. Then she had it open and could see an air bottle and face mask, with a yellow fire helmet resting on top. She dragged it out and passed it to the man.

'Good stuff,' he bellowed. 'And the next one, ma'am. Keep them coming.'

Dan turned and repeated what she had done, handing four more heavy sets of apparatus to the large figure who immediately handed them away to others who had formed a chain behind him.

Past him, through the opening of the watertight door, Dan could see a five-man firefighting team readying themselves, dressed in thick woollen fire-retardant suits with heavy breathing bottles on their backs.

One of the warrant officers was shouting at the men, 'Continuous aggressive attack, get in there and maintain a continuous aggressive attack.'

The men nodded as he patted each one on the back and they headed forward, past the manoeuvring room.

The large sailor who had demanded the firefighting equipment from Dan now turned back to her, grabbing her by the arm to get her attention. He put his head close to hers, something she had seen others do to improve communications.

She closed her eyes as she waited for what he would say.

'Good job, ma'am,' he shouted. 'Now, in those lockers next to you, there's some more huggy bears – the big woolly fire suits. I need them too, OK?'

He waited.

Dan opened her eyes, already nodding.

'Good job,' she heard again as he moved away.

She looked up at her hose connector. She would need to move it, to fleet to a different coupling to reach the kit that he wanted. She looked back to the waiting figure and took a deep breath. Reaching up, she unplugged the hose and stepped closer to the lockers, immediately fixing her eyes on the new connector that she would use. She forced herself to be calm. Her breath was short, the noise and heat making her adrenaline flow, the exertion causing her to need the air more quickly than normal.

The connector went in first time as she pushed it extra hard, waiting to hear that reassuring click before she took a breath. It worked. Immediately she was on her hands and knees and emptying the locker, throwing the gear towards the sailor who gratefully caught it and passed it on.

'THE FIRE IS OUT – THE FIRE IS OUT. THE FIRE IN THE SHIP'S OFFICE IS OUT. ALL COMPARTMENTS TAKE ATMOSPHERE READINGS AND REPORT TO DCHQ.'

Dan stood up and looked towards the starting platform and the route that she and Aaron had used to head down towards the engine room lower levels. She could see a mass of bodies, like a rugby scrum, messy, but moving towards her with a common purpose.

The Chief Stoker was leading the way, watching her the instant he had line of sight.

Dan made to take her mask off, as she heard that the fire was out.

'Keep it on,' shouted the Chief Stoker, and Dan was instantly annoyed she had given him the opportunity.

The big sailor that she had helped so far leaned in to speak to her. 'Don't worry,' he said. 'Chief Stoker's a dick. Just keep it on until the atmosphere's been checked in spec. I'll tell you when.'

He gave her the thumbs up sign and Dan couldn't help but smile breathlessly beneath her mask.

A white flash caught her eye and she saw Aaron step through the small gap that led to the starting platform, where he had shown her the manual controls for the engines.

In the commotion she had forgotten that the casualty exercise had even been happening.

People moved aside as Aaron rushed past the Chief Stoker. Neither was wearing an EBS mask and Dan assumed that that must be the norm for 'safety numbers'.

Behind them came another mass of bodies, their overalls literally soaking wet from the exertion. They were carrying the Neil Robertson stretcher, the shape inside it bound so tightly that movement was impossible, as impossible as it had been for Ben Roach's friend on the day that he was whipped as he lay bound in the same restraints.

The stretcher was designed to support people with back injuries and it remained rigidly straight as it was passed along a chain of men, almost as though it were a log being laboriously worked towards the aft escape platform.

She saw the two men at the front of the stretcher step through. Behind them, four more sailors slipped into gaps and crevices between machinery, to help support and carry the stretcher on the final leg of its journey up from the lower level. Each of them had to fleet in EBS, unplugging their air hoses and plugging them back in a few feet ahead every time the stretcher advanced. Often they would pass their hose to a colleague, waiting patiently until it was plugged in again, allowing the air to flow; they all worked together in fluid motion to achieve the collective aim.

The casualty came into view, bound tight in the stretcher. He wore the same blue overalls and the same black mask as all of the other men.

The sailors were shouting to him to 'breathe' and 'hold' as they fleeted on his behalf.

Dan watched as they heaved him onto the platform.

The casualty's head was shaking ever so slightly.

It caught Dan's eye because the head was supported on both sides by the stretcher and the forehead restrained by a thick strap; yet the casualty's head was shaking frantically now, moving within the tiny space allowed by the restraint.

Dan stepped forward, trying to get a closer look.

'Hang back, ma'am,' said the same sailor who had spoken to her before. 'They'll need to come round this way.'

He moved into the gap with her, pushing her further back and blocking her into the small space.

Dan felt a shiver go down her spine. She forgot about how much she was sweating and the fact that her uniform was wet through. She forgot about how deeply she was breathing, or how heavy the mask felt as it clung by a layer of sweaty rubber to her face. She focused on the casualty.

Then the shaking stopped.

Dan pushed forward towards the stretcher, bumping into the large man in front of her. She reached the end of the travel on her breathing hose and her head jolted round quickly, jerking her neck and causing her to cry out in pain. Ripping her mask off, she pointed at Aaron and shouted, her words lost in the noise of the heave, men shouting and grunting, the noise of the submarine absorbing her words like shadows falling into darkness.

He looked at her, his eyebrows furrowed, and then he held up a hand like a teacher saying, 'Now isn't the time.'

Dan pushed harder to get past the figure that was trapping her in, shouting again, urgent, demanding to be heard, and he finally relented. She watched as they put the stretcher down on the platform, the men panting, soaked from their efforts.

'The mask,' she shouted. 'Take off the mask.'

Aaron and the Chief Stoker seemed to turn towards her in unison.

She lunged forward, pushed her way around the large, sweaty shape that she had been working alongside a few moments before, and tore at the casualty's mask, unable to rip it off as it was leeched onto the man's face, caved in around the rubber seal like a collapsed balloon. She wedged a finger under the seal, releasing the vacuum, and watching in slow motion as the mask regained its shape. When the straps finally gave and the mask was removed, she saw the face beneath it, the blue lips and still waxy skin, the saliva and sweat sliding down his cheek like soap bubbles down an enamelled bath.

Time slowed.

The shouts around her sounded like long, low groans as she looked down and recognised Roach's face, waxy and still.

There were panicked faces and bellowed orders and then the main broadcast, once again, snapped her back into the moment.

'SAFEGUARD – SAFEGUARD,' sounded the main broadcast, the signal that this was no longer an exercise. 'CASUALTY – CASUALTY – CASUALTY. CASUALTY ON THE AFT ESCAPE PLATFORM. MEDICAL PARTIES ARE AT THE SCENE. ALL REPORTS TO DCHQ.'

Dan buckled and fell backwards to sit on the hard deck as the medics closed in around Ben Roach. She watched them check his pulse. She watched his blue face and lolling tongue, the froth running down from his cheeks mingled with sweat, as they tried to revive him. She watched them cut him out of the stretcher and work on him, two medics giving him the kiss of life. Then she watched, after fifteen minutes, the two medics look at each other and nod, tears streaming down the face of one of them as they pronounced him dead at the scene. Finally, she watched Aaron's face turn ashen white, his mouth open and his hands clutch at his hair, while the Chief Stoker stood next to him, watching her.

Chapter 22

Monday Afternoon – 29th September 2014

Dan had to concentrate on the corpse in front of her to be certain this wasn't a nightmare. She knew that it made no sense to do it, but she used the hand that was thrust deep into one of her pockets, grabbed a sliver of flesh on her leg and pinched herself; it hurt.

She shivered.

The wardroom felt cold, despite the normally oppressive heat, and the drone of the ventilation made her want to scream as she looked around at the stony faces of the men standing against the wall opposite the two dining tables.

All of them were looking at something, not each other, though, and not the corpse that had been placed on the table, sandwiched between white bed sheets.

Aaron had avoided her eyes and looked close to tears for the last hour or so, his eyes getting redder and more bloodshot and his complexion turning greyer and more clammy as each minute passed. His hands were still visibly shaking, although no one seemed to be concerned.

The Executive Officer hadn't spoken a word, and Dan got

the distinct impression that he was showing the lads a 'stiff upper lip' in the face of this adversity.

The medical staff, a petty officer and a young leading hand, had seemed to deal with the situation expertly at first. They'd carried out actions as they had been trained to do, but, as time wore on and the adrenaline subsided, they'd both started to look tired and lost. It was as though the training they had done hadn't quite taken them this far, hadn't told them exactly how this would feel and what they should do next.

The curtain that hung across the entrance to the wardroom was thrown back and the Old Man stalked in. He looked at no one and stopped directly next to the body, reached down and picked up Ben Roach's left hand from beneath the loose sheet.

The blue-tinged hue of Ben's limp hand was even more disturbing against the Old Man's pale skin and he held on for a short while, his back to Dan so that she was unable to see his face.

After a few moments he gently placed the hand back down, covered it and patted Ben's chest.

Aaron moved restlessly and then spoke. 'The connector on his EBS hose, it must've been crushed as the stretcher was moved. The lads were all fleeting properly, plugging him in and giving him warnings when they moved, but it was crushed. It was engaging into the system but not letting the air through.' He trailed off, shaking his head.

'There'll be a full investigation, Aaron,' replied the Commanding Officer, without looking away from the body. 'Until then I want no blame, no one taking this onto themselves. Until such time as the Coxswain has finished investigating and handed me his report, then this is a horrible accident and these boys still have a job to do.'

The Old Man finally looked up and engaged with his officers. 'This submarine is four full days away from patrol and the men need to refocus and prepare.'

Dan's jaw fell open.

'We cannot just carry on—'

The Old Man turned and barked at her before she could continue. 'Lieutenant Lewis, my cabin. Now,' he said, and waited.

Dan felt as though she was still wearing her EBS mask, as though her clothes were heavy with sweat and her limbs were drained through exhaustion. She forced herself to breathe steadily. Then, trying to muster what control she could, she walked out of the wardroom feeling the glares all around her, knowing that their eyes were shadowing her as she went.

The Old Man didn't follow immediately and Dan didn't hurry. She walked past the battle honours mounted on the passageway wall, memories of when other men had lost their lives on board previous vessels of the same name.

Someone was crying in the Junior Rates Mess, the place where Ben would have taken his meals and relaxed after his duties.

Dan heard it grow louder as she walked towards the entrance.

A single person weeping, their loud sobs unrestrained and inconsolable. Other than that, the submarine was deathly quiet; even the constant hum of the air conditioning seemed to have diminished out of respect for the dead.

The crying faded away as she climbed up the ladder and entered the hushed control room. Moving quickly through, not hearing a single spoken word as she passed within earshot of around twenty silent submariners, Dan walked to the Old Man's cabin. No one looked at her this time; no one looked at anyone.

She stopped outside the Old Man's door for an instant before she shrugged and stepped inside.

His seat was empty and the cabin seemed more spacious as a result.

Dan took a seat on the bench and leaned back, accepting that she would be made to wait.

When the Old Man finally pulled back the curtain to his cabin, his already red face turned a deep purple as he saw her sitting patiently on the makeshift sofa.

'Never enter my cabin without my express permission,' he said quietly, as he turned the folding chair to face her and lowered himself down onto it.

Dan thought about pointing out that he had, in fact, ordered her to enter, but, instead, she waited calmly without apologising.

'We lost another brother today, Lieutenant Lewis,' he said, without looking at her. 'Someone that meant something to many of us on board *Tenacity*. A submariner who knew the risks he took and understood the aims of what we do.'

Dan looked at the wall, focusing on a picture of a much younger Commander Bradshaw, long before he would have been the 'Old Man'.

He was slim, fit looking and was standing with arms crossed next to a group of young men. 'Royal Navy Boxing Team – 1997–1998' read the inscription.

The young men were dressed in vests and long shorts, most of their haircuts dated in a way that would likely make them unrecognisable to anyone but family or close friends after such a length of time.

Dan focused in on Bradshaw's eyebrows; they hadn't changed, or not by much. Then her eyes were drawn to two young men immediately behind the Old Man in the picture, young and lean, their hair marking them out because it was still short, not fully grown back from when it would have been shaved at basic training.

'*Tenacity* is a one-billion-pound asset, Lieutenant Lewis. An entire submerged eco-system, with a purpose,' he continued.

'You may have your secrets, but we have ours too and the reason for this patrol, the information that we will bring back, is bigger than the life of one individual; any individual.'

He stopped and looked at her, waiting for a response.

'Sir,' she began, not looking at him, still focusing on the photograph and trying hard to keep her voice strong. She wanted to lean forward and examine it more closely, to try and decipher her way through the years.

'Lieutenant Lewis!'

Dan turned to face him, noting that his fists were balled like an impatient and temperamental child's as he waited.

As she looked at him, her mind recalled a still image of Ben Roach's face, then another of the spot in the engine rooms where Whisky Walker had hanged himself, and then a grimy, dark photograph of Cheryl Walker's back, the pattern of bruises that had drawn her into this investigation, that had fuelled her need to come on board this submarine.

Her eyes followed the welts that ran up Cheryl's back, each of them a path that led to *Tenacity*. She needed justice for Cheryl Walker and now she needed justice for Ben Roach, but both were gone, dead, and unable to suffer any more. Ben's death, so close to his offer of help, would be reason enough to get the boat recalled, but only if she could get word off the submarine, and she had no authority to do that. But now, as she thought about what she believed had happened, she considered again the submarine sailing from Devonport early, so soon after she had misspoken. Then she thought about the change in Ben Roach's temperament and manner, the indicators of stress, that he had something to share. He was taken from her too, snatched away as *Tenacity* had almost been.

She looked at Bradshaw. Was he the only man who could give the order to sail, or was there a higher authority at work?

In either case, here at sea, there were no other influencers in play. If Ben's death was no accident, as Dan believed, then that killer was here, trapped on board with her. If *Tenacity* was in Devonport then they would have options – people and equipment coming and going, opportunities to remove or hide evidence – but here, now, at sea, they were as contained as she was.

'I'm sorry,' she began. 'It's been a very upsetting day. I'd like to go now and compose my report and observations on what occurred. I'll make it available as soon as possible, as I believe it may impact on the investigation that I'm certain is about to commence.'

'And why would your observations of this terrible accident impact on our investigation, pray tell, Dan? You were, from all I can ascertain, simply watching. What could you have to offer?'

Dan watched him closely, saying nothing.

'More suspicion, Lieutenant Lewis? More secrets?' he whispered to her.

Dan looked back to the picture of the boxing team, only turning back when she heard the Old Man begin to snuffle like a pig, before it grew into a quiet, gruff laugh.

With all that had happened, with a young man lying dead on the wardroom table, he laughed at her. The sound seemed more alien and disgusting than any other Dan could think of.

He turned and shuffled through some papers on his desk.

'Do you know the Laws of the Navy, Lieutenant Lewis?'

Dan ignored the question, refusing to be drawn, refusing to react.

'I don't mean the law as you think of it, I mean the real Laws of the Navy. Those that tell you how the navy actually works, the laws that help you to function as part of our machine.'

She still refused to answer.

'Well, I'm going to do you a favour, Dan. I'm going to help you out before you draft your secret report. I'm going to offer you some advice that I think you might just be smart enough to accept.'

He found what he was looking for and thrust a sheet of paper towards her, holding it out and waiting until Dan reluctantly took it.

'You can read it all when you're alone,' he said quietly, leaning in towards her. 'But just read this one verse out loud for me, if you will.'

He pointed to the verse that he'd circled in red biro.

Dan looked at it but did not read aloud; instead she scanned the words slowly.

> *Dost think, in a moment of anger,*
> *'Tis well with thy seniors to fight?*
> *They prosper, who burn in the morning,*
> *The letters they wrote overnight.*

She was unable to concentrate as the Old Man, seeming to accept that he would not be able to force her to read, recited the words aloud from memory.

His eyes bored into her and his breath warmed the side of her face.

Dan had to fight the urge to shudder.

'These laws were committed to paper by—'

'Admiral R.A. Hopwood, Royal Navy,' said Dan, cutting him off.

He breathed heavily through his mouth and then smiled.

She could hear his breathing and it felt so close that she was sure that any moment she would involuntarily shiver, an overt reaction to his very proximity; he made her skin crawl.

'And they are wise, wise words, Danny.' He accented her name, putting emphasis on the *D* and drawing out the final syllable as though he were her lover whispering into her ear, begging for her attention.

'Nothing leaves this submarine without my signature; you know that. So you'll have plenty of time to think about the words you intend to draft and the ones I have just gifted to you.'

She could bear his proximity no longer. She shivered, her whole body tensing as she stood up and stepped away from him.

He breathed out slowly, as though he had been savouring her scent, and then smiled. Then, his small eyes peering out from beneath his gathered, bushy eyebrows, he spoke again. 'One last thing,' he said with a smile that made her shiver again. 'You need to think long and hard about who you talk to regarding any secret theories, even tight-lipped hints like the one you just offered me. Emotions are raw and people are hurt. Ideas like that, careless, insensitive, destructive ideas, could cause tensions to boil over, control to be lost, and it's all about control on board a submarine.' He paused. 'I can't protect you everywhere.'

Dan stepped quickly past him and through the door, tripping on the raised threshold and cursing as she did. She hurried away, almost breaking into a run as she reached the two-deck ladder.

The crying was still the only sound she could hear. It was the same person, the same voice and the same heartbreak that was coming from the Junior Rates Mess.

She registered it as she moved quickly towards the bombshop. On some level she wanted to look and see who it was, who on board was the only one who seemed to be grieving openly for Ben. But she had to get away and find some space. She felt like she needed to rip off her own skin, to clench her fists and scream. As she climbed down the ladder, she realised that she was still clutching the sheet of paper with the *Laws of the Navy* printed in neat stanzas down the centre, that single verse circled in red.

Chapter 23

> *Dost think, in a moment of anger,*
> *'Tis well with thy seniors to fight?*
> *They prosper, who burn in the morning,*
> *The letters they wrote overnight.*

Dan read the verse again as she perched on the edge of her bunk, her mind racing. Was it a threat? Was it genuine advice? Or was it simply an act of dominance; a calm and collected way of letting her know that she was in a position of complete subordination?

The Old Man had given her a verse from the same, relatively obscure poem that Whisky Walker had sent to her, but what did it mean? Walker had worked for the Old Man, and maybe he'd got the poem from Bradshaw too? Maybe the Old Man tossed it around like confetti, a form of attempted intellectual snobbery or benevolent education?

She looked up towards the ladder, had done at least a dozen times now. It was a habit that had developed into a nervous tic.

Ben had changed after the slip that she'd made in the wardroom, and only a few people had heard her misspeak. He had then made an effort to try and speak to her in private and that effort had been scuppered until he died or, in Dan's estimation, was murdered.

She stood up and paced in the tiny space before sitting down on her interview stool again and placing her head in her hands, massaging her scalp as though she might knead out some ideas.

What did Roach have to tell, or show her? What did he know? Was his information about Walker, or maybe Cheryl? Why was he selected to be the casualty during the exercise and who selected him? Who had access to his EBS mask before the exercise? Why did the Old Man, and Walker, want her involved in this investigation at all?

Her mind was overloaded with questions, all without answers. She rubbed at her eyes; they were grainy and sore. She knew that she needed some proper, restful sleep, or she was going to cease to function effectively. But, as exhausted as she felt, she couldn't sleep now. Her skin felt grimy from dried sweat; she hadn't been able to shower since the heave, nor since the Chief Stoker had met her after her last one. Deodorant wasn't allowed on board due to its effects on the ventilation system, and the submarine seemed to be permeating its way into her skin, as though she would never be able to wash *Tenacity* off her.

One question kept coming, repeating over and over again: Could someone on board one of the Royal Navy's nuclear submarines really plot to kill a fellow sailor and get away with it?

'Hey.'

Dan looked up. Her head jerked around towards the speaker and the first warnings of a possible migraine appeared behind her eyes like tiny dots on a distant horizon.

Aaron walked slowly towards her, his hands hanging loosely by his side. 'Thought I'd pop down to see how you're doing,' he said, and sat down on her bunk, facing her across the small gap.

Dan thought quickly. She was being blocked in every direction in which she tried to move. She needed a friend, needed support; couldn't do this alone. Looking at the grief etched onto Aaron's face, she made her decision.

'I need help,' she said. 'I need *your* help.'

He looked up at her, his bloodshot eyes a clear sign that he'd been crying.

He nodded. 'What?'

'Aaron,' she paused, knowing this was absolutely the wrong thing to do and at absolutely the wrong time, but seeing no other possible way around it. 'Chief Walker's wife was raped and murdered on the night that *Tenacity* docked back into the UK. One of the reasons that I was sent here, alongside investigating Walker's suicide, was to ensure that no members of *Tenacity* could have been involved in that murder.'

Aaron's face had gone slack.

Dan decided to push on; the decision had been made and she desperately needed someone on her side. 'I believe that a member of your crew may have been involved in this and I think that Ben Roach knew, or suspected, something or someone.'

She reached across him to grab her clipboard, aware that he didn't move away as their bodies came into contact. She hated that even now, even with all that was happening, her stomach reacted, flipping at the feeling of his body touching hers. Refusing to linger, she retrieved the board and sat back down. The headache had retreated for a few seconds, but now it started to grow again, warning her that there was a long night ahead.

'Dan—'

She raised a hand and cut him off. Then, flipping over some sheets, she located the napkin. 'This is what Steward Roach sent to me,' she said, holding up the note written on the paper napkin, but pulling back when Aaron tried to reach for it. 'He wanted to meet me where nobody else would be, to show me something or talk to me.'

Aaron shook his head. 'What are you saying? Are you really telling me that you think Ben's death wasn't an accident? I was there, Dan. I was the Lead Safety Officer.'

Dan looked away from him and took a deep breath, but this couldn't wait, there was no time for grief. Turning slowly, she waited for him to make eye contact. 'I really don't know if it was an accident or not, and if I suspected you, I'd hardly be coming to you now. I need to find out.'

Aaron's face contorted. He looked like he would fly into a rage and Dan recoiled, steeling herself for whatever he might do. His chest heaved, but he gradually seemed to bring himself back under control.

'You know,' he said heavily. 'It was me that told the Old Man to ask for you. I know it was years ago, but I always liked you. You've got a reputation for being fair and honest, if dogged, stubborn and annoying.'

They both chuckled, a strange and guilty sound in the quiet of the bomb-shop.

'I think you're wrong about this. Ben was one of us, he was one of the brotherhood; no one on board *Tenacity* would harm him. But I'll help, if only to prove to you how wrong you are.'

He was shaking his head slowly.

'We're not what you think, you know, Dan. Some of the lads haven't treated you well, but you forced your way on here. You're an occupying force and these guys will resist you. They'll do that and they'll follow the Old Man, and he'll resist you too. But these men give up their families for long months, to live here, amongst this.' He gestured around the bomb-shop. 'It isn't hand-to-hand fighting, Dan. We don't fix bayonets and charge down enemy trenches, but we give up all luxuries and put ourselves in one of nature's most dangerous environments, out of a sense of duty and to protect the people we love, and the ones we don't. Those men that are fighting and dying in Afghanistan, they aren't fighting for the Government, or the Queen; they fight for each other, to make sure that everyone comes home together.' He paused. 'We're no different down here. We work for each other, so that we can all come home together. It's that simple when you break it down. I don't believe that any submariner would do this to Ben, or that any one of them would hurt Cheryl, but if you do, I'll help you to be sure.'

'Thank you,' said Dan.

She wanted to smile, to stand up and embrace him as the ally she'd so desperately needed.

'But Dan, you haven't told anyone else, right? About Walker's wife or what you think about Ben Roach? About that napkin?'

He looked hard at her.

'No, no one knows about the message on the napkin except you, but the Old Man thinks that I suspect foul play and he didn't like it.'

He breathed out and closed his eyes. 'Dan, I have to tell the Coxswain and the Old Man about the napkin, I'm duty bound to. You know that, right?'

Dan nodded, she had known.

'But I won't say a word about Cheryl Walker. I'm going to pretend you didn't either. There's been rumours kicking around since you came on board, but I don't think confirming them would be good for anyone.'

'I agree,' said Dan.

'Just don't say anything to anyone else, OK? Submarines are a fragile eco-system and emotions are high. Ben's body's going into the freezer in a while and the lads don't need to hear any of this; submariners are good at keeping secrets, but not from each other.'

Dan nodded and smiled. 'Thank you,' she repeated.

He leaned across towards her, reaching out and touching her hand. 'Can I ask, how did Cheryl Walker die?'

Dan looked at him carefully, letting him know that she couldn't say too much. 'She was attacked and badly beaten,' she began.

'Do the police have any leads at all? Anything to go on?'

'I really can't say, Aaron,' she said more firmly.

'I'm sorry,' he said, seeming to be aware that he had pushed too far. He sighed. 'It's just so sad that it happened at all. I knew her quite well.'

'It's OK. I've just said too much already, but I needed to know I had someone here who would help me if I needed it.'

He looked at her and held her eyes for a long moment before he spoke again. 'When we eventually get back—'

'Let's just see,' said Dan, cutting him off, conscious of his hand on hers.

'So what do you want me to do?' he asked.

Dan thought about it. 'To be honest, Aaron, I just needed to know that I wasn't alone. I will need help, I'll ask when I do, but I needed to know that I had someone to . . .'

He smiled at her, his hand still on hers.

'Boss!'

They spun around towards the hatch, Aaron snatching his hand back like a recoiling viper.

'Old Man wants you,' said McCrae, his head upside down and a few inches below the hatch.

'On my way,' said Aaron, watching until McCrae was gone.

'Could he have heard?' asked Dan.

'No. But submarines have ears, Dan. You need to be really careful.'

Chapter 24

Monday Evening – 29th September 2014

Dan watched Aaron leave and then looked around the bomb-shop slowly. Instantly, she knew that she had to get out of there, if only for a short while.

The lights were bright and constant, and ordinarily this would be a comfort to Dan, even a condition of her life, but now, as a migraine loomed and the six-hourly rounds seemed like speed bumps in every stretch of possible down-time, it was starting to feel like torture. When the migraine took off, she would be trapped here, lying in the omnipresent blaze as she tried to wait out the storm in her head.

Time was ticking down too, in several ways.

Her investigation lacked pace, seeming to stall whenever she made an advance. She had learned little of note about Walker and less about his wife, Cheryl, and instead of solving a murder, she was certain she had witnessed one.

She grabbed a sheaf of papers, ones that she had sorted back into order but had not yet read properly, and headed up the ladder. Standing on two-deck, she looked along it in both directions before heading towards the pantry. Ben Roach wouldn't be there, and there would be no food parcel on the side waiting for her, but she couldn't resist glancing through the doorway.

Ben's iPad was lying on the worktop in a smart leather cover that had 'Submariners go Deeper' embroidered onto it and a set of dolphins mounted below. Dan couldn't help but step inside and pick it up. She opened the leather flap and switched on the device, but was immediately asked to enter a passcode.

'Crap,' she whispered.

She turned it over in her hands; saw the marking on the back, 'Luxury Real Leather Custom Goods'. Dan ran her finger across the indented markings.

'Very nice,' she whispered, as she felt the quality of the leather, lifting it up and smelling it.

Someone spoke in the wardroom, a quiet voice just a short distance away through the pantry curtain.

Not wanting to be seen but desperate not to lose the chance to examine the iPad later, Dan looked around for somewhere to hide it. She pulled open the top drawer, the one where the Old Man's tea bags were kept in neat, boxed rows, and tucked the device at the very back. Closing the drawer, she stepped quietly back into the passageway.

It was like a ghost ship. No one was moving around and no one was there to see her; *Tenacity* was in mourning.

She looked down two-deck and walked towards the ladder that led down towards the ship's office.

Aaron had said that No.2 auxiliary machinery space was down there, the place that Ben had wanted to meet her, where he'd hoped that they'd be able to speak alone and undisturbed. Aaron had also said that sometimes people read down there, to get away from their own bunk-space, but that now it was out of bounds.

Hesitating for only a second, Dan climbed down the

inclined ladder, conscious of every sound her boots made as they touched the metal steps, and looked around.

The ship's office door was closed and marked with a sign stating 'NO ENTRY'.

Dan could hear voices from within, raised voices. One was the Old Man and he was shouting. The other voice, low and steady, was Aaron, sounding as though he was nursing the Old Man back from the edge of control.

Then Dan heard another voice, quieter still. When it started, the other two voices silenced and she recognised Jago Maddock's Cornish accent.

She fought the urge to listen and become embroiled in the conflict any more. There was no way she could risk being caught wandering, no way she could cope with another clash at this moment.

The bomb-shop seemed like the safest option, but as the voices continued, Dan knew she had to go and take a look. She followed the small walkway round to her left and passed two large grey machinery cases, the first clearly marked as 'Battery Breaker 1'. As she rounded it she saw the two hatches that Aaron had described to her, both clearly marked and one with a wooden blank laid across the hatch, completely filling the gap. KEEP OUT was stencilled onto it. She checked that this one was the No.2 AMS, and then looked around, her heart beating so loud that she was sure someone would come running to investigate the constant thump-thump, thump-thump. She had her papers ready, a story about being lost and wanting to read. Thinking fast, she knelt down and lifted the wooden blank as quietly as she was able, slid it to the side and placed it onto the identical hatch to No.1 AMS.

Looking down into the space, she could see that it was a very small compartment, no bigger than her tiny kitchen at home, and it was filled with chunks of grey machinery. The compartment was accessed by a short vertical ladder and was so low that Dan suspected even she wouldn't be able to stand up in there. Still able to hear the voices in the ship's office, she climbed down. As soon as her feet landed on the green painted deck she saw she wasn't alone.

At the other end of the compartment there was a pile of bags and holdalls. On them, asleep, was a submariner. The name badge on his working rig named him as Ryan Taylor.

His face was red and marked with dirty tear tracks. In one hand he was clutching a leather-cased iPad, almost identical to Ben's.

Dan remembered the day that she had first come on board, remembered how Ben had wanted to stop the hazing that had been going on in the Senior Rates Mess as the Chief Stoker whipped a young sailor in the same stretcher that would later play a part in Ben's death. She recognised the sailor in front of her now, Ben's friend Ryan.

The scene came back to her as she looked at the sleeping sailor. She remembered how Ben had reached across as he released Ryan, how he had gently wiped away a tear as it meandered down Ryan's freckled cheek. Dan hesitated, about to turn away and sneak back up the ladder, when Ryan's eyes opened, bloodshot and sunken, and he focused on her.

'You ain't supposed to be down here,' he said quickly.

Dan looked at him. 'Neither are you,' she said.

He sighed, but didn't look embarrassed that she had found him asleep; he just looked up towards the deck-head, a tear forming instantly in his eye before it walked the well-worn track down to his chin.

'You OK?' Dan asked, as quietly as she could whilst still being heard above the hum of the ventilation system.

He said nothing and Dan thought about climbing back out right away, maybe admitting to Aaron that she'd been down here, despite his warning that it was out of bounds.

There wouldn't be another chance to come back, not once they found out she'd tried to come down here already.

'Can I ask you a question?' she asked, crouching down to face Ryan from across the compartment.

He nodded; his whole demeanour told her that it didn't matter one way or another now.

'How long were you and Ben together?'

He looked at her, his body language changing; it was the first time that he'd really moved since he'd opened his eyes. At first he seemed defiant, angry maybe, and then he looked down at her boots.

'The boys don't like fags,' he said. 'Ben never wanted 'em to know.'

Dan nodded back. 'I think I understand, now more than ever, what it's like to be an outsider.' She tried to smile. 'If it wasn't for Ben, I'd have starved to death by now.'

Ryan smiled as he thought about this, shaking his head. 'He told me what they done,' he said. 'Told me he was feeding you. Some of 'em hated him on his last boat 'cos they said he was bent. Never knew why, though, he was careful as to be paranoid, but he was proper determined not to get tagged here.'

'But you all know each other,' said Dan, more of a question than a statement. 'The submarine service is so small.'

'But here he had the Old Man, didn't he? The Old Man saw him box at a show ages back, only submariner on the card. He liked what he saw, liked the way that Ben banged, so he brought him to *Tenacity* and looked after him. I ain't saying the Old Man likes fags, he probably don't, but he likes loyalty, and he liked Ben.'

'What do you mean?'

'I mean everyone knew Ben had the Old Man's ear, so no one messed with him.'

Dan's legs were starting to hurt from squatting, so she sat

down on the deck and leaned back against a warm metal cabinet.

'How long were you guys together?'

'Couple of years.'

'Did the Old Man know?'

'I think so. Ben told him most things. We used to joke about how we was like two sweets what got stuck together in the packet – you know, when you take one, but it's stuck with another, so you get two? Well, that was Ben and me.'

Above them, the Old Man's voice could be heard, suddenly loud as the ship's office door was opened.

Ryan stopped.

They both sat in silence, waiting.

When the voice died away again, Dan spoke. 'Ryan, was Ben any different these past few weeks? Did anything change?'

She watched as Ryan stiffened at the way the topic had changed so quickly. She'd made it too obvious that she was asking him a question for her investigation, not for her own interest.

'Why d'you wanna know?'

'I really liked Ben. I just wanted to know how he'd been.'

Ryan eyed her suspiciously but seemed to lack the will to meet her gaze for more than a few seconds. 'He'd been a bit awkward the past few days,' he said slowly. 'But who hasn't since you came along? Ben said you was investigating a killing and the boys are nervous about it. We all know you rozzers are experts at fitting people up.'

Dan smiled, ignoring the vehemence of the comment. 'I'm here to find out why Whisky killed himself, a suicide, nothing else,' she said, trying to skirt around his statement. 'The exact opposite of "fitting you up".'

'But you're looking into a killing too, aren't you?'

He was watching her carefully, trying to read her reaction. 'It's just a rumour,' she said, lying with a smile. 'I've heard better ones started in the Naafi queue, if I'm honest. Why do you ask, though? Did it upset Ben when he heard that?'

Ryan sighed. 'I don't know. Everything's been shit this trip, 'specially since you turned up.'

Dan caught the edge to the remark as clearly as if Ryan had directly told her to pack up her gear and leave. Despite this civil conversation, when it came down to it, it was clear that there was no one who wanted Dan to remain on board *Tenacity*; from the Old Man down to the sailor that worked in the communications office, they all wanted her to leave. But that hadn't always been the case.

'I've got to go to the comms shack. Got a periscope run in a bit and I need to prep the signals and get ready for the broadcast.'

He got up and picked up his iPad, his finger catching the screen, which came to life showing a picture of Ben smiling and raising a half-full glass of beer towards the camera.

'Where did you get that?' asked Dan, looking at the expensive leather case and the device within it as Ryan powered it off.

'Ben,' he replied. 'He's got one like it, but brown. This one's blue, for a blue-eyed boy; looks black, though, don't it?'

'It's just really nice. I'd love one. I bet they cost a fortune, though – you submariners and all your extra cash,' said Dan, trying to pass the comment as a joke.

'I don't think they was that much,' mumbled Ryan, and stepped over Dan to get to the ladder.

'Ryan,' Dan paused. 'I'm sorry for your loss. I liked Ben, I really did.'

'Thanks,' he said. 'You got to get out now. You shouldn't be down here.'

'Maybe I could just stay for a little while?' she asked. 'Just to take some time to think.'

He shook his head; there was no doubt that she was going to have to leave.

'Why is it out of bounds anyway?' she asked as innocently as she was able.

'We store secret files from ops in the lock box at the end.' He pointed to a long metal trunk that was partially hidden by the bags he'd been lying on. It was sealed with an old-style safe combination. 'So we keep people out to make it a secure compartment, but we can't actually lock it because of the fire risk.'

'You think it will stay a secret?' she asked, looking at the exposed metal of the trunk. 'That I was down here? I was only looking for somewhere quiet to read and be alone, like you were.'

He nodded but didn't reply, and climbed up the ladder and out of the AMS. 'I'll help you put the stuff back that you moved,' he half-whispered, as he turned and waited for her to climb out.

Chapter 25

Tuesday Morning (Early Hours) – 30th September 2014

There would be no interviews for the rest of the day, no value in speaking to people so soon after Ben Roach's death, and Dan knew that she would need the time. She settled back on her bed for a while, took some painkillers, and readied herself for the migraine to arrive. When it did, after shielding her eyes with the sleeve of a shirt for a few hours, she relented to the overwhelming heat and climbed into bed properly. She was exhausted, nauseous and hating every minute of being trapped in the continuous luminosity of the bomb-shop's ever-present fluorescent lighting. Pulling the white sheet over herself, she draped a clean, damp sock over her eyes and tried to drift off to sleep.

'Danny . . .'

The lights were off.

That was what caused her eyes to open so suddenly; the lights were never switched off in the bomb-shop.

She was breathing hard, her skin greasy with a sheen of sweat, and she had no idea what time it was or how long she'd slept for. The headache had retreated a bit, leaving only a shallow footprint of where it had once been.

Dan blinked and tried to focus. She couldn't. She tried to turn over, to roll off the bunk so she could find the light. She couldn't move.

That was when her eyes really opened, wide.

Her body tensed in panic, like pressure building up beneath a crack in the earth's crust.

'It's the nightmare, it's just the nightmare,' she began whispering under her breath. 'Take back control. It's all about control.'

She stopped trying to move and forced herself to relax back, her heart pounding as she tried to control her breathing, to stop herself from shaking, and let her mind drift out of the dream.

'This is a nightmare,' she whispered again, trying to reconcile that it was her own mind doing this to her, in the same way that it had done many times before.

This felt real though, immediate.

In the pitch darkness she became aware of the confines of the submarine, as though the walls were creeping forward, unseen, pressed inwards by the sea, fitting in close around her like a tailored coffin.

Her head was still able to move a small amount as she tried to look around. She began to turn from side to side, but with the lights out, this compartment, deep below the surface of the sea, was in a state of darkness, the likes of which she had not felt for a very long time.

Dan felt a surge of terror rise within her, powered by the sure knowledge that she was about to lose control, but she needed that control, needed to force her mind to free her, to let her wake up. It was then, as that thought passed through her mind, that she realised the truth.

She was awake.

Her mouth opened and she drew in air, ready to scream. Her body tensed for a fight, but the pain hit her like a sharp hammer blow to the ribs. The air was exorcised from her, making a noise, not unlike the venting of the high-pressure systems on board, as the content of her lungs was forced out.

She tried to double over, gasping for breath, but couldn't, as she felt bonds pull tight around her wrists and ankles. The pain made her feel sick, tears instantly blooming in her eyes, and her body convulsed. She tried to recover from the blow, tried to suck in some air despite the excruciating pain in her ribs. Her mouth opened and closed repeatedly, like a fish out of water, as she tried, and failed, to draw in some oxygen.

She thought that she could see him. It could have been her eyes adjusting to the blackness, or her mind filling in the blanks, but she could make out a shape near to her, a shadow cast without light, silhouetted against the dark.

A breath entered her lungs as suddenly as the strike had ejected it. It was as though her throat had been blocked and was suddenly free and, in that instant, Dan knew she had to fight again. Her arms were stretched out above her head and she tried to pull them down towards her chest, to cover herself with them, but couldn't. Arching her back up and off the mattress, she slammed her body down and tried to rip her hands free, as though she were swinging an axe with all her might.

She couldn't do it, couldn't free herself; the bonds were too strong and tight, and her wrists burned as they reached their limit of travel.

A small red light, on one of the many control panels mounted at the end of the bomb-shop, cycled on. This tiny light source, a candle in a cavern, allowed her to see his outline.

He was there, crouched over next to her bunk. A dark shape, touching her legs, his hands moving slowly in circles leaving a sickening warmth everywhere they travelled, slithering over her legs, moving up past her thighs, but not touching her there.

She dry-retched as his hands paused on her abdomen. She needed to scream, but her throat was constricting and she wasn't sure she could. She tried again to fight off whatever was holding her. Gritting her teeth and in abject terror, she wrenched her body upwards again, arching her back first and then forcing her bum down into the mattress and drawing her knees up towards her chest. She heard a ripping sound; something had given way, a bond was coming free.

It gave her hope and she prepared to jerk her body once more.

He hit her again, the one that was touching her, delivering two sharp, hard blows to the bottom of her ribcage in painfully quick repetition, like an urgent visitor demanding her attention.

Dan collapsed down onto the bed, her throat blocked again and her eyes blinking as she tried desperately not to pass out. Lights flashed and stars drifted across her vision as she fought for breath. She knew she was going to black out; either the pain would do it, or the lack of oxygen.

'Don't do that again.'

The voice was muffled, deep and rasping; she recognised the sound of someone speaking to her while wearing an EBS mask.

Blind panic had fully taken over now and her body was unable to gather the breath that it needed. Every time she tried to breathe in, her chest would convulse, her abdomen would tighten and the pain in her ribs would sear throughout her body. She was shutting down, she could feel it, wanted it. Her mind was going to take her away from this and protect her.

The shape climbed on top of her, straddling her close in

the restricted space between her mattress and the missiles that were stowed above it. The weight of his body pressed onto her thighs, controlling her legs, and his hands touched her again, finding the small dents next to her hipbones, investigating them with his fingers. His touch moved slowly up her body, only the thin cotton sheet separating his flesh from hers as his fingers followed the lines of her ribcage and paused near to her breasts.

'Are they hard?' he asked, his fingers starting to trace around the outside of her nipples, but not touching them.

His touch lingered and then began to move up towards her chin.

Dan threw her head back and then forward again, initially not fighting to escape, just to breathe, but when she realised that she could, that the movement was free, she did it again, this time trying to head-butt the bastard, maybe to get close enough to his hands or face to bite.

Her head was dragged backwards, a hard tube across her throat pulling back at an impossible angle, dragging her back onto the mattress and controlling her, like a choke chain on a dog.

The figure that was straddling her reached towards her throat and allowed each hand to spread in a separate direction across the bottom of her face like a blooming butterfly. Only his thumbs lingered on the centre of her throat, lightly teasing her windpipe.

Dan convulsed again. It felt like her body could breathe out, releasing the precious air, but couldn't take any in, as though she was wearing an invisible EBS mask of her own.

'Relax,' breathed the voice, extending the word as though he were singing it to her. 'Just relax.' He reached a finger beneath the rubber hose that had been pulled tight around her neck and pulled at it, persuading it to loosen until there was enough slack for air to pass.

Suddenly Dan was able to take in a huge gasp of air and she filled her lungs, the relief tangible.

As she did, as the air entered her lungs, his hands tightened around her neck, the thumbs pushing slowly into the centre of her throat and the fingers tightening to trap it there.

The pressure of his grip increased slowly until Dan felt her eyes go wide and begin to bulge. She felt as though her chest, cheeks and eyes might explode. Her jaw opened so wide that it might dislocate. Then the stars came back, drifting across her vision, and, without warning, she began to relax.

'You're causing problems,' said the voice, muffled and deep through the mask. 'You're alone and causing problems somewhere you don't understand. You're not part of this world and you're not welcome.'

The hands were moving again, away from her neck, the hose seeming to pull a little tighter to take up the slack as he touched her chin, moving his fingers around her jaw and neck. Then they roamed away, back down towards her chest.

Dan felt her whole body tense as he cupped her breasts, lifting the sheet and sliding his hand under her bra. 'Come on, Dan, get hard for me,' he said. 'I'm getting hard for you.'

The beginning of a scream left Dan's mouth and the figure let go with one hand and slapped her across the face to silence her.

'Who do you think is going to come?'

He slapped her again and Dan saw the lightning as, once again, consciousness started to drift away.

Her eyes closed.

'Oh no,' said the voice. 'You can't sleep yet, we're not done.'

She felt her face being gently slapped as he coaxed her back to full consciousness.

Another voice spoke up, higher pitched, almost incoherent, hers. 'Please?'

He laughed at her, the sound grating like static through the mask.

'Tomorrow you're going to tell everyone that you want to get off this submarine. You're going to explain that there's nothing to investigate and that you want to leave as soon as possible. It's bad luck having women at sea. Did you know that?'

Dan felt like she was flitting between conscious terror and peaceful sleep.

'Answer me,' he said. 'I want you to answer me.'

She felt another slap, lighter than the others, controlled.

'OK,' she whispered.

He shuffled down the bed, more pain shooting through her body as he leaned hard against her knees, pushing against them the wrong way.

She could see him moving and suddenly felt no weight at all; he had climbed off her, but was still there.

'Shhhh,' he whispered, his face close to hers, the hard rubber of the mask pressing into her cheek. 'You're alone here, but you won't be for much longer.'

Dan couldn't answer; her thoughts flitted between precious air and precious sleep.

'Do you see? I can do anything to you,' he said, speaking more quickly now, pushing his mask harder and harder against her face with every word.

'Your rank won't protect you; your warrant card won't protect you,' he continued, the rate and pressure of his speech building like a train gathering speed. 'You're completely exposed and I can come see you any time I want to, here, or when we're home.'

Dan screamed.

This time, there was no slap to stop it. Instead, she felt

something cover her face, press against it, fit and form around it.

'I told you not to scream. I told you to be quiet.'

Dan recognised the form of an EBS mask as it was forced against her face. She recognised the feeling of the rubber, framing her cheekbones and cupping underneath her chin as she tried to breathe. The mask was pushed against her. She could see his fingers in the dim glow, gloved fingers, like a spider on the visor as he thrust the mask onto her face and held it there.

'You're alone,' she heard him say as she neared suffocation. 'You know that nasty things happen to stuck-up whores; you've seen, haven't you? If you try to share what happened on our date tonight, or if you're still here on *Tenacity* in twenty-four hours, then there's going to be another horrible extermination.'

Dan felt the panic again. The mask was sucking tighter and tighter to her face as it allowed air out but permitted none to enter. She heard the figure chuckle, snorting through his own mask.

'You're alone and I can get to you anywhere you try to go.' They were the last words that she heard.

Chapter 26

Friday Evening – 21st December 2012

Dan could hear her dad shouting in the background and her stepmum trying to hush him.

'He says he misses you,' said her sister, pausing to listen some more. 'And you should've just come home tonight; he says he'd have come and collected you from the airport.'

Charlie covered the mouthpiece. 'All right, Dad, why don't you just come talk to her yourself?'

Dan laughed. 'Charlie, Charlie!' she shouted, trying to draw her sister back.

'Sorry,' said Charlie. 'He's trying to get me to say some joke-insult thing to you about the navy, you know how he does.'

Dan laughed again. 'Tell him I'll sit and listen to some of his stories of Royal Marine heroics and valour when I'm back tomorrow,' she said. 'And once you've said that, just make sure there'll be plenty of wine for me; God knows I'll need it.'

'Dad, I'm not saying any more. Leave me be to talk to Dan.'

There were some protests, but they faded and Dan knew her sister was walking into a different room.

'I swear he's getting worse, you know,' Charlie said as the background noise disappeared completely. 'He made Simon listen to about three hours of the Cockleshell Heroes the other day.'

'My God,' said Dan. 'Were Simon's ears actually bleeding?'

'Pretty much,' said Charlie.

Dan imagined her sister's husband trapped at the kitchen table, being force-fed real ales and being too frightened to just end the conversation and leave.

Charlie would have been heckling her father, telling him he was boring and to leave Simon alone, but Simon, now a sergeant in the Royal Marines and stationed at the Clyde naval base, Faslane, would have sat motionless, interested or feigning it, as her dad, known to all in the Corps as 'Taz' Lewis, waxed lyrical.

'Retirement isn't suiting Dad at all,' Charlie continued. 'He talks about the marines now more than he ever did, and Simon's frightened to pop round with me in case he gets dragged into a whole evening of reminiscing.'

'I'll talk to him when I get home,' said Dan. 'He just needs another interest.'

'Yeah, he does. Anyway, what were you doing?'

Dan sighed and looked in through the window of the tiny pub.

A loud roar of laughter penetrated the glass and she saw the group she was with, a mixture of navy police and support workers, some with their partners and some without, getting in another round of drinks.

'Work social,' said Dan.

'Do you mean work anti-social?' asked her sister.

Singing started inside the pub. Some of them were singing the naval sea shanty 'Hearts of Oak' in harsh, bawdy voices.

The window shook violently as a gust of wind hammered against it.

'Yeah,' said Dan.

'Fuck 'em, Danny,' said Charlie, her uncharacteristic swearing catching Danny out, as it always did on the rare occasions she heard her sister use such language.

Dan sighed.

'Is it the same ones?' asked Charlie.

Dan nodded, aware that Charlie couldn't see that response, but knowing that her sister was pausing for breath, not an answer.

'It's not a problem,' said Dan, cutting in before Charlie could continue.

'They're just jealous of you, Danny. That's all it is.'

Charlie carried on, detailing her thoughts on why the majority of the Royal Navy Special Investigation Branch barely spoke to Dan, if at all.

Inside the pub, Dan could see John Granger seated at one end of the table.

'Roger also told Dad that he was investigating the leak personally,' said Charlie. 'So there's a great chance they'll find someone soon.'

It'd been more than four months now since Dan's papers had been leaked.

Her scathing assessment of current police procedures during long-duration, major investigations had only whetted the appetite of the news agencies. Her theory that Hamilton had not always worked alone, that there was an accomplice still at large, was what made headlines.

Then, with only the shortest break to draw breath, the news channels discovered a later conclusion buried in Dan's draft paper.

Dan had written that it was possible that Hamilton had used his position on board navy warships to travel to foreign countries and kill, undetected and unchecked.

This story – and afterwards Dan herself – was devoured

by a hungry media. The greatest achievement of Dan's life had turned into a genuine nightmare and Charlie had been on the phone or by her side throughout it all.

'It's exactly a year today that he was sentenced, isn't it?' asked Charlie.

Dan jolted at the silence when she realised she was required to reply.

'Yup, a year today,' she said. 'Thirty years' minimum sentence, before they'll even consider parole, and a drop in the ocean compared to what he should have been given.'

'But you got him, Danny, and even if he is ever released, he'll be an old man and can't ever hurt anyone else.' Charlie paused. 'Speaking of old men, is Roger out tonight?'

'No,' said Dan. 'He's not been well, but I'll probably pop in to see him on my way home now. See how he's doing.'

Charlie was silent for a long time before she spoke. 'You know, Danny, we're all super-proud of you, you know, Dad especially. What you did, what you can do—'

'I know, Charley-pants. Thanks,' said Dan, using the child-hood nickname for her big sister, knowing it would stop that line of conversation in its tracks.

'I'm just saying that once you get home, then it won't matter what they think. Team Lewis will be reunited. Agreed?'

'If I agree, do I have to do that daft handshake thing that Dad made us do when we were little?'

'Ha,' said Charlie. 'He didn't make us do it when we were little; back then we loved the Team Lewis handshake. It was when we hit our teens, that's when he *made* us do it, or tried!'

Dan laughed. 'OK, I'll be home tomorrow afternoon. My flight's at two, so get Daddy Taz to meet me at the airport. And tell him I called him that, he'll love it.'

They said goodbye and Dan looked back into the pub,

deciding that she wouldn't go back in. Roger would still be up, it wasn't late, and she could pop in to say Happy Christmas before heading home to pack for her trip north.

Through the window she could see the partygoers reaching for drinks and laughing at unheard jokes, the party in full swing. It would remain that way for several hours to come and would be followed by a Christmas Eve spent with some enormous hangovers.

She turned away, walking across the dark car park and up the short hill towards the overflow area where she'd had to park after arriving late. It was dark, rough ground, surrounded by trees that loomed like a semi-sentient wall dancing in time to the wind; hardly welcoming.

As she reached the top of the small slope and turned in the direction of her car, the wind, shielded by the trees, stopped.

She looked around. She was alone. Her car was parked against some trees a few metres away and she walked towards it quickly and then turned.

There was a sound behind her.

She looked around again. Nothing.

'Sod this,' Dan whispered and started to jog to her car. She was there quickly, too quickly, and she had to fumble with her keys, trying to find the fob that would remotely unlock the doors.

She heard the sound again, behind her and near to the treeline.

She turned and looked around the empty space, trying to stare into the impenetrable darkness that sealed in the gaps between the trees like mortar between bricks. Anger was growing with every beat of her heart, anger at the fear she felt and the weakness it implied. Again, Dan scanned around the car park, as though proving to herself that she wasn't, wouldn't be, afraid.

She considered running back to the pub, joining her colleagues for one more drink, maybe hanging around until others came to their cars, although the vast majority were in the main car park below. She could sit with John, try to make peace and then see if he would walk out with her.

He would do it; without doubt he would. He would walk with her in silence and his confidence and presence might well make her feel better; he was nothing if not loyal and protective of his team. But Dan wouldn't go back and she knew it.

The car doors unlocked with a recognisable thud and the interior lights came on. She yanked the door open and stopped.

A sound again, somewhere in the darkness, a spoken word this time, low and calm.

Her night vision was gone and the light from the car's interior spilled out onto the rough, stony surface, leaving black clouds drifting across her vision. Dan dropped into the car, pulling the door behind her.

A hand grabbed at the door, pulling it, stopping her from sitting down and closing it.

She turned fast, confused that she hadn't seen anyone approach, hadn't heard their footsteps on the rough ground. 'Get off,' she shouted, gripping the door harder and pulling it towards her as she leaned back inside.

She heard quiet laughter from close by, and the door was moving away from her again, opening wider and wider.

A second voice was barely audible on the periphery of her hearing, away from the laughter, away from whoever was dragging the door open. This voice was speaking low, the one she had heard before, providing a kind of commentary.

The car door was fully open now and Dan could see a man's body as he reached in for her, his grip on her arm

274

tightening, starting to hurt, his head and face remaining out of view.

She swung a slap with her free arm, aiming for his hand where he held her, and dug her nails in as hard as she could. As soon as she felt his grip weaken, Dan turned in her seat and kicked out hard, aiming for his groin. Her foot landed with a deft thud that she was sure punctuated the end of the laughter. Then she turned and grabbed for the door again, pulling hard and trying to slam it closed behind her, almost succeeding.

It wouldn't shut.

She could feel someone holding it; see fingers at the top of the frame. Leaning back, both hands on the handle, Dan pulled with all her weight, hearing a yelp as she trapped fleshy fingers between metal pincers.

Her phone rang and she couldn't help but glance at it; it was her dad.

Then the door was dragged away from her in a quick, powerful movement that nearly pulled her bodily from the car. Dan was clinging desperately to the handle, but released it at the last moment, reaching instead for the ignition and the keys that weren't there. Her hand went to the seat, the spot between her legs where she'd dropped them, but she couldn't find them. Suddenly, the seat seemed to be getting further away. Her hair was being stretched too, her long hair, pulling her through the door.

A scream escaped from her lips, but not just fear, anger too. She pushed off the door frame with her feet as she passed through it, driving herself towards the man who had her and taking him to the ground. Her hands were claws, scratching at him, scavenging for his eyes. Her teeth were bared, biting anything that came near; Dan was going to fight and she was on top.

Stars filled her eyes and she felt as though her brain had

exploded like a firework inside her skull. Her hearing stopped, replaced by a constant, high-pitched ringing, a long monotone that emanated from the centre of her head. A wave of nausea followed and she fell off him, but not to the ground; someone else had her now. Through the haze she could feel someone wrapping her long hair around their hand as though it were the reins of a powerful, unbroken horse. Her eyes closed.

No. Stay awake. Fight.

She drew in a deep breath and screamed again, digging her nails into the hand that was now firmly secured to her hair.

He cursed, definitely a man. Then he hit her again, same side of the head, and she felt the life drain out of her.

She was moved around, manhandled, and now looked down at her car bonnet, felt her features contort and her lips and nose spread out as she was bent over and her face was slammed against it.

She felt her nose start to bleed, even thought it might be broken, as one man used his grip on her hair to slam her face against the paintwork again. She edged her face slightly to the side to try and ease the pressure. Now her cheek was crushed up against the bonnet, blood running down from her nose and into her mouth, flowing out like spilled ink onto the silver paintwork.

There was more low laughter from behind her.

She couldn't tell how many were there, but definitely two, maybe even more than three.

Her hair was taut across the back of her neck as one of them held her face down and when she felt another pressure, thin and cold, touching down onto the skin of her neck, burning, as only steel can, she knew he was holding a knife against her.

The commentary was low and quiet, reaching her ears

from beneath the other sounds, as though the commentator was standing slightly away from the attack, in the treeline maybe, watching and talking. 'Control her head,' the commentator said. 'Control her.'

She was moving again, her body being tossed around as though she were in a stormy sea, as they grabbed her waist, taking off her black leather belt.

The movement, as they pulled her around, caused tiny little increases in freedom as the knife, hovering over her hair, cut into it, releasing her strand by strand from his grip.

Dan moved her head slightly, feeling more of her hair let go as it met with the cutting edge of the knife.

The one that was holding her hair moved around to the side of the car, the knife moving and pressing down, more hair breaking free like the berthing lines of a departing ship.

'Now,' said the commentator from his vantage point. 'Now.'

There was a pause. And then she felt the blade disappear for a moment, before the cold air licked her back as her shirt was cut open, exposing her skin and her spine to the night.

'Now!' the commentator repeated, and she felt a pain cut across her back, her whole body tensing up in response, more hair being freed by the blade as it returned to subdue her.

The sound was odd, familiar, but he had hurt her again by the time she realised that he was flogging her with her own belt.

'Thirty,' said the commentator, his voice louder, more excited, but no closer.

She felt the one with the belt stand close behind her, pressing against her as the blows sped up, became harder, alternating from side to side as though he were thrashing a horse at full gallop.

Exhausted breaths.

The blows slowed and she heard him panting.

'That's half,' said the commentator. 'Change over.'

Her attacker paused, she could hear his breathing, hear him unwrapping the belt from around his hand again, getting it ready to pass over to a second attacker who would finish.

Each moment he waited in silence, the grip on her hair became lighter and the knife worked soundlessly, cutting her a pathway to possible freedom.

The commentator's voice was there again and she could hear him speaking in a low, continuous stream but couldn't make out what he was saying. The man holding her was half turning to listen, his grip light as he began to speak back to the commentator or his other accomplice in a hushed, and rushed, tone.

He turned further, the knife moved away from the remaining ropes of Dan's hair, and then it appeared next to her on the bonnet, a thick wood-handled hunting knife, gripped in a leather-clad hand as the man turned further away, leaning on the car as he spoke.

Dan could move her head a bit. It felt as though half of her hair was free and the other half still joined to his other hand.

They were still talking, the words quiet and continuous, but shrouded from her by her own concentration.

It was then that she did it.

Dan reached for his hand, only a few inches from her face, and grabbed it, using the small amount of head movement she had to bring his covered flesh to her teeth. She felt leather tear and maybe a bone crack, but she needed the knife and that was her focus.

He released it, shouting in pain, and Dan was waiting.

She felt her head jerk back as he pulled on the remaining hair to control her, but as he did, as he pulled it taut, she slipped her hand around the heavy carved wooden handle, and ran the blade across the back of her own neck, cutting the last strands of hair and freeing herself from him.

She rolled over on the bonnet, turning to face them.

The man had staggered back, clutching his injured hand to his chest, her hair still dangling down from between his fingers.

There were three of them.

Their faces weren't visible to her, but she saw three shapes, two standing close to her, one of them clutching his injured hand, and behind them, barely visible against the dark tree-line, she saw the final one, the commentator, and she knew he was looking at her, his speech broken.

In that moment, she rolled again, off the side of the car bonnet and onto the stony ground.

One of them stepped forward, the one with the injured hand, reaching out for her, grabbing at her with his good, gloved hand, her severed hair hanging from it like tassels.

Dan slashed with the knife, feeling it strike home and dig in, feeling minimal resistance as it parted his skin.

He recoiled.

She ran.

They were standing between her and the slope that led back to the pub, and so Dan made for the trees that moments before had seemed like a boundary wall, impermeable, impassable, but was now her only route to safety.

She clutched her torn clothes to her chest, oddly aware again of the freezing air touching her as she ran at full pace. She didn't know if she heard the commentator order the men after her, or if her mind had added that to give further speed to her escape, but behind her, she heard the sound of shoes on stone as she was pursued.

A hand gripped her shoulder, pulled her back, turning her away from the safety of the trees.

Dan allowed it, allowed herself to be turned, but only for

a moment. She thrust the knife into him, pushing until it would go no further, and left it in there as she turned again to run on. She broke the treeline as though it were the ribbon at the end of a race, but someone else was coming.

She could hear him behind her, and was now sure that the low voice was near to her too, whispering to her, but she didn't stop.

The trees tore at her loosened clothing, ripping at it as she ran, wooden fingers reaching out for her bare flesh and trying to slow her down, to restrain her, but she never broke stride.

The thick branch jutted out at eye level, an invisible blockade in the darkness, as though this tree were holding out its arms to stop her. The blow to her face was hard, her own momentum providing the force, and her body and legs continued forward where her head couldn't.

Stars and lightning, swirling shapes and patterns, and she was on her back on the freezing ground, unsure of how long she had been like this. She blinked. Her hand went to her face and felt a liquid that she couldn't see. There was no pain, though; she was numb to that.

Consciousness was now a question and as her arm flopped back down to the ground beside her, she could no longer tell if her eyes were open or shut, if she was awake or asleep.

The voice was still there, though, penetrating the haze. 'Control,' it whispered, deep and low. 'It's all about control.'

She had to go, had to stay awake, the voice was right, she had to regain control and get away from there, but she couldn't move.

Dan thought of her dad and of Charlie and their stepmum, of Team Lewis and the need to keep going, to fight on, to never stop, to succeed.

Her head spun as she lay looking up into the darkness,

trying desperately to search for the sky through the branches of the trees that she knew were above her.

The black night had crept in around her, like thick, black oil being poured carefully over a mould, finding every gap, every crease, cut and cranny.

The voices had gone and she could hear no sounds in the woods around her. After a time between wakefulness and sleep that was long enough for her to start shivering with the cold, Dan heard footsteps on the distant stones and a car's engine start shortly after. She heard her colleagues leave the pub sometime later, could hear them shouting, could have called out to them, but didn't.

It wasn't just dark where she lay, it was the very absence of light, and every sound, every rustle, every breath of wind that she heard in the absolute darkness, was the commentator's whisper, sometimes offering her reassurance and guidance, telling her she would be OK, and then, as suddenly as a gunshot, he would promise terrible things, and then describe to her the black, unseen terrors that gambolled on the periphery of her mind.

Chapter 27

Tuesday Morning – 30th September 2014

'Ma'am.'

She heard the word, but it was far away, being spoken by someone else to someone else. It was an echo, dream-like, not for her, nothing to do with her at all.

'Ma'am.'

There it was again, but closer, too close this time, closer than it should have been.

Dan's eyes opened in an instant. She immediately flinched and then blinked, her hands grabbing for her face, scratching at her skin when there was no mask there to be cleared away.

She closed her eyes again, squeezed them tight as the memories of that assault, buried so deep and for so long in her past, now resurfaced. She was breathless, tired and weak when her memory of the previous night also began to flood into her mind, darkness and panic coursing through her body. She was unable to filter the events that were old from those that were new.

The lights in the compartment were back on and burning

and she fought to overcome the brightness that ruthlessly attacked her eyes.

She sat bolt upright and banged her head against the missile above her cot. The blow was hard and Dan thought she might lose consciousness as her hand went up to the small wound. Instinctively she recoiled from the impact, cried out, and then scrabbled backwards, away from the figure that was leaning towards her. She almost fell off the end of her bed, one hand slipping off the edge and down onto her holdall.

She watched, stunned and recoiling again, as the figure before her seemed to mirror her actions.

He stepped back, eyes wide in terror, arms flailing as he stumbled over something on the centreline of the bomb-shop and fell backwards.

'Shit, ma'am,' said the figure, coming into focus. 'Fuck's sake.'

The voice was familiar and it sounded panicked and annoyed.

Dan's eyes were still adjusting to the light as she looked around, taking in the compartment, looking for the markers. It looked the same, but she wasn't the same.

She remembered where she was, remembered what had happened. Finally, she saw Ryan Taylor on the floor a few feet away from her.

He had fallen over a large stack of tinned food and was sprawled on his backside, rubbing his arm as a small trickle of blood ran down it.

'You OK, ma'am?' he asked. He sounded frightened now. 'I didn't mean to . . .' He paused, visibly unsure of what he had done that he didn't mean to do. Then he picked up a foil package that was lying next to him on the deck and held it up in his good hand. 'I brought you some fat pills to eat, that's all. They've got me covering Ben's duties now.'

He looked worried as he waited for her response, holding out the foil-wrapped rolls like a peace offering.

Dan realised that her hands were shaking, that her breathing was shallow and choppy, that her eyes were wide and glaring; she was going to cry.

'Thank you,' she whispered. 'I really appreciate it, but would you mind leaving me alone, please? I'm . . .' She paused. 'Tired.'

Ryan nodded repeatedly. He looked as though nothing she could have said would have given him greater pleasure than leaving her alone. 'Yeah,' he said, climbing to his feet. 'Yeah, sure.'

He looked back at her as he walked towards the ladder, not taking his eyes from her for even a second, as though he thought she might spring out of bed and attack him from behind at any moment.

As he reached the ladder he stopped. 'Coxswain says he's got your interview list for today. It's in the ship's office.'

Dan felt a stab of panic. There was no way she could face up to leaving the bomb-shop, let alone carrying out any interviews.

'Can you . . . can you tell him that I'm not feeling well enough to do them today, Ryan?'

He nodded and turned to climb the ladder.

As his boots vanished through the hatch, Dan felt her body take a huge involuntary breath. It sounded loud, as though it was coupled with a deep moan, and she filled her lungs until she thought they might pop. The breath held firm inside her and Dan was unable to let it out. It was as though her body was unsure of what to do next, as though it might never let the air go free. Her mouth was wide and tears started to run down her cheeks as a low wail escaped from her and the air slowly leaked out. She turned and thrust her face into the pillow, not allowing any further sound to escape as the sobs came one after the other.

When she finally pulled away, there was a small smear of blood on the dirty grey pillowcase. Her head was bleeding, not much, just a small weep where she had banged it against the cold, hard metal that formed the body of the missile above her bed. Dabbing at the wound with her two fingers, Dan felt a small lump and winced. She sat up slowly this time; not really knowing how long her face had been in the pillow or how much time had passed since Ryan Taylor had left her with the food.

She turned quickly, her eyes snapping towards the hatch; there was no one there. Then she turned her body, wincing as the movement brought shocks of pain, and placed her feet onto the floor. Immediately she lifted her foot back up again as she felt it touch something hard. Without looking, she knew it was the hose, the one attached to the mask that was the last thing she could remember. She looked down and her eyes followed along the length of it until it disappeared beneath her bunk.

Her ankle caught her eye, red from where she had been bound, the skin not broken, but raw and angry from where she had fought. She reached down and pulled at the hose until the mask came into view.

She felt her breathing start to shorten again, felt it get easier to breathe in than out.

'No,' she stammered. 'No.'

She clenched her teeth until her jaw hurt and gripped hard at the mask, squeezing the tough rubber out of shape until she felt the panic pass.

Slowly, as control returned, she placed her foot onto the deck again and stood up. She was aching all over, her muscles sore from exertion, but it was the pain in her ribs that felt the worst.

Each attack had been accurate and powerful, deliberate and designed to cause maximum pain.

Her hands explored her ribs gently as she tried to assess what damage had been done, the pain from the lightest touch making her wince as the words of the warning came back to her, beginning to loop continuously like an unwanted sound bite in her mind.

'You're alone and I can get to you anywhere you try to go.'

Chapter 28

Tuesday Afternoon – 30th September 2014

The rolls that Ryan Taylor had brought her were plain. Just a simple piece of fatty, tinned ham placed in the centre of a lightly buttered, homemade roll, but it didn't matter; Dan retched before she even got one near to her mouth. She wrapped it back up in the foil, the logical part of her knowing she should keep it for later, but the smell meaning that she had to get the food away from her, out of sight. She hid the foil package inside her bag at the head of her bed, rummaging around to force it deep towards the bottom.

Since hiding the food, she had also found somewhere new to sit.

There was a narrow alleyway at the back of the bomb-shop that ran athwart-ships, across the width of the submarine, allowing access between the bulkhead that marked the aft limit of the bomb-shop and the ends of the missiles and torpedoes that ran in the forward to aft direction. Down this alley, and after climbing over bags and stores, in the very back corner of the bomb-shop, Dan felt safe.

The alley was so tight that even Dan had had to take time to climb carefully along to her spot and then to lower herself down backwards into a sitting position. From here she could look across the deck of the bomb-shop, underneath the missiles and her own bunk, and see the moment anyone entered the compartment.

Her refuge was hard to get to, small and cramped, with only one way in and one way out. Her pillow helped to ease the discomfort, as did wearing the loose-fitting pair of overalls that Aaron had found for her.

She had broken another rule before climbing in here. She had turned on her phone inside the bomb-shop, using the built-in camera to take pictures of her ankles, wrists and ribs. After that she had turned the phone off again, the missiles and torpedoes remaining unexploded, and had carefully pulled on the baggy overalls.

The paracetamol that she'd packed seemed to be buried deep inside her bag. For the first few days she'd simply left the bag wide open and had been able to lean over the end of her bunk to rummage for what she needed, the bag perfectly placed in reach like a pillow that had flopped off the end of the bed. This time she couldn't tolerate her back being to the entrance hatch and she had knelt down, her eyes checking the hatch like a learner driver checks the rear-view mirror, and searched the pockets of the black holdall.

Now she tried to read, sitting in her private space with a relatively clear view across the deck, including the area below the hatch, her papers scattered all around her.

There was no hurry and Dan was taking a long time with each sheet as she repeatedly glanced up to check there was no one there. She was mumbling, constantly mumbling, could hear herself doing it, but it beat grinding her teeth, and she carried on saying out loud segments of what she was reading and thinking.

'It was a mistake,' she said, flicking through the piles of evidence and then dwelling on a single sheet until she had read it. It was taking ages; she would read a paragraph and then instantly forget what it had said. She would write a note and instantly be unable to read her writing. Some of the papers were sorted back into order, but many, many more were still disorganised, random and crumpled, from where they had been thrown down the main access hatch.

'It was a *big* mistake. Silly, stupid.'

She found the pieces of paper that she was looking for and nodded her head.

'Yes,' she said, quite loud this time. 'I wasn't sure before, I couldn't possibly have been.'

She opened the report, most of it held together in one corner by a green treasury tag while the other bits were easily identified by checking for tears in the corners from where they had ripped away from the main body. The pages were crumpled and dirty, some with footprints on them and others with smears of hydraulic oil, but she could clearly make out the title, *Early Hypothesis of Offender Profile – Doctor F. Green*.

Dan made careful notes as she scrutinised the profile, going carefully now, page by page, writing so slowly and meticulously that she was certain she would be able to re-read her writing when the time came. She checked that each sheet was numbered and in the correct order, and when she located a gap, she pulled the gash bag towards her and rummaged until she found and inserted the missing page. Then more reading and more notes, losing herself in the document. She tried to manually cross-reference details, flicking back to other reports as she pieced together a picture of how, where and why this offender operated. The certainty that he was on board the submarine at this very moment drove her onwards, the memories of what he had done to

289

her lurking at the back of her mind. They tried to surface from time to time, tried to distract her from what she was doing, to cloud her mind and distort her focus, to make her look up towards the hatch and check for feet and ankles approaching her den, but she fought to keep them in check.

It kept coming, though, the feeling of him in the restricted space, the sensation of her head being dragged backwards whilst he was atop her in the dark.

Her whole body jerked suddenly and the files that were open on her lap slipped off, their pages scattering as far as they could and some slipping down underneath the torpedoes to join the debris and dust that lay there undisturbed and almost inaccessible.

A scream rose up from her stomach and she clenched her teeth and scrunched her eyes closed as tight as possible. Her whole body was taut and she closed her fists so forcefully that she felt one of her nails start to pierce the skin on her palm. Frustration rushed over her like a storm pounding rocks and she knew that behind her eyelids tears were gathering in number, each one ready to run down her face as soon as she allowed the floodgates to open.

She was certain she had a rapist, a probable killer, on board the submarine, knew it in her heart. But sitting there, frightened in a way that she had promised herself she would never be again, Dan began to feel that it was hopeless, as hopeless as fighting back when you're completely outnumbered, as hopeless as taking on a whole team when you're on a team of one. She opened her eyes and started to gather the papers back up again. She had to roll slowly and painfully onto her belly and reach into the empty space beneath the weapon mounts to retrieve the pages that had slipped away from her. Once she had them, once her breathing had slowed down again and the thoughts had been pushed back into their compartment, the hatch firmly shut and clipped, she forced herself to return to laboriously cross-referencing the facts and collating her evidence. She searched for another document that had been on her lap, eventually seeing it on the floor more than an arm's length away below the end of one weapon. Dan looked at it and then back at her notes. She knew that without a computer, alone, without brainstorming and discussion, trying to bring the strands of the investigation together was near to impossible.

She leaned her head back against the bulkhead. Words came flooding back to her, and her tightly shut eyes allowed the face of Roger Blackett, her good friend and mentor, to form in her mind. He was in his office, standing behind his desk, glaring at her. 'I should tell you "what", because I am your friend, pretty much the only one you have, and somebody needs to.' He had turned towards her as he had spoken the words, and then, his voice not even raised, 'You need to get back into a team.'

Eyes still shut tight, she drew her head forward slowly, lifting her hands up and cradling it gently, allowing it to rest and the tears to fall straight down onto the grey-white pillowcase that she was sitting on.

Now John's face appeared, a face she should have trusted. 'We need to work together,' he said, with a familiar expression.

Her breathing began to slow and Dan felt as though she were regaining control of herself again. A final thought entered her mind. She saw the paper come into focus and then the black font that made up the words take shape after it.

> *On the strength of one link in the cable,*
> *Dependeth the might of the chain.*
> *Who knows when thou may'st be tested?*
> *So live that thou bearest the strain!*

'Teamwork,' she said out loud, the words echoing and sounding odd from her sore, dry throat. 'It's not just one of them; it wasn't just one of them last night and there must have been more than one all along. Is that what you were telling me, Whisky? There's more than one of them? There has to be.'

The realisation was obvious; she had known it all along but hadn't voiced it, not to herself, not in plain, understandable English.

Walker was a strong man and an experienced boxer. It was unlikely that a single man could have hung him without signs of a struggle.

Felicity had virtually said as much too.

As Dan forced herself to remember what had happened to her, to make sense of it, she knew that a single person did not restrain her last night. She was tied down, but as she considered it, trying to look at what happened through the eyes of a police officer, cold and emotionless, she knew that there had to have been a second person present. When she had tried to lash out with her head, she had been pulled backwards, a tube around her throat to control her, the angle making it impossible for the man atop her to have done it. Then she remembered his fingers loosening the noose, how it had tightened slightly as his hands moved away from her face, moved down towards . . .

Dan gasped and shivered, looking up at the bomb-shop entrance and taking a moment to recover herself. She had to put herself through this, had to face what had happened and learn what she could from it.

There had to be a second person at the head of her bed, kneeling or sitting on her holdall behind her, pulling her backwards by the neck, choking her.

Dan knew that now, no longer thought it, was certain; there were two men there last night. Two men willing to attack her, two men willing to keep that secret.

Her mind jumped to Cheryl Walker now, the nature of the attack against her, sustained and violent. Could it be the work of two men, encouraging each other, guaranteeing that each had done enough evil to ensure their silence, that each was fully committed to both the crime and the secret? Could they have stopped midway to talk and plan, for one to coerce the other if doubts arose?

Murderers working in pairs were rare, but it wasn't the first time Dan had seen it, or at least suspected it. She had been as certain as she could be, without hard evidence, that Hamilton had not always worked alone, that he'd had help to manage his killing undetected for so long. This was a theory that had been sensationalised by the press and emphatically condemned by both the police and her superiors in the Ministry of Defence after her papers were leaked.

She thought of the marks on Cheryl Walker's back and then the matching ones that had been left on her own back in an attack that had taken place one year, to the day, after Chris Hamilton was sentenced to thirty years' imprisonment. Dan's assault had been a punishment, a warning and a humiliation in one.

It had been designed to make her feel powerless and vulnerable, to break her confidence and suppress her will, and it was most certainly not carried out by the imprisoned Hamilton.

Her mind again began to refocus on the events of that night – the knowledge that they must have been waiting for her, watching her, patiently standing by for when the opportunity presented itself.

'Not now,' she whispered, driving those thoughts to the back of her mind.

She picked up her pad again and began to scribble.

'Hey.'

Dan recoiled from the word, feeling her eyes widen as she looked around quickly to see who was there.

'Dan, you OK?' asked Aaron. 'Why are you sitting behind there?'

She collected her papers, closed her notepad quickly and tried to hide what she had been doing.

'Jesus,' said Aaron.

He began to climb towards her, stepping over pipes and equipment like a sure-footed goat in its natural environment. 'Dan, what's the matter? You look awful.'

As he approached, Dan leaned backwards, away from him. She cursed under her breath, hating her own reaction and at the same time pushing her papers further away from his line of sight.

He knelt before her, reached out to place his hand on hers, but she whipped her arm away.

'Dan, tell me what's wrong.'

She looked away, too embarrassed to make eye contact.

'Tell me what's happened,' he said, more urgently.

'I'm just,' Dan started. Her words broke. 'I'm just exhausted.'

'Jesus. You look like shit and we've treated you appallingly,' he said, not making eye contact and nodding at his own realisation. 'I spoke to the Old Man again last night. We sat in his cabin for hours, most of the night, and really had it out. It's fucking shameful and he knows it.' Aaron was shaking his head now. 'I'm ashamed of myself,' he said. 'I had a duty to step up a long time ago. I'm sorry, Dan, I'm sorry I didn't support you.'

Dan heard the words and tried to think of somewhere else, somewhere where meeting Aaron would be a positive experience, where she wouldn't want to writhe and slither away from him.

He looked at her and their eyes seemed to catch, locking

together. Then he leaned in towards her, his face moving close, his hand reaching for her cheek and his eyes fixed on hers.

'I can't,' she said, turning her face away.

He seemed to come out of a trance. 'Of course, I—'

'It's fine,' said Dan, leaning back against the wall again and sorting her pillow out beneath her. She looked at his face and saw him reddening around the neck.

'Dan, I'm so sorry, I just,' he paused. 'There's no excuse.' She held up a hand to stop him.

'I just can't,' she said again. 'Not here, not now, but not never.' Her voice sounded normal to her again, recovered, if a little cold.

'Of course,' he said, showing his teeth in a silly grin. 'That was awkward,' he said, flashing a hopeful smile.

Dan laughed. It sounded, to her, as fake as it was, but she could see that it made Aaron feel better and he leaned back against some of the bags and tried to look relaxed.

'So what's up? You do look awful, and the Coxswain said you called him and cancelled all of your interviews today. He said you've only done about a quarter of the ship's company, although there's been a lot going on to hold you back, I guess.'

'I'm just going through some of my notes. Background stuff, really, it'll take me a few hours, but needs to be done.'

'Anything I can do to help?'

'No.' Dan tried not to make the word sound too harsh, or too urgent. 'Not yet.'

Aaron seemed to notice her tone. He paused and looked at her, as though he was going to probe further, but didn't. 'I thought you might like to know that Ryan Taylor's covering Ben Roach's duties.'

Dan nodded.

'He told me about your agreement with Ben. You know,

the black market food trafficking? I told Ryan to keep it up. That way we can at least see to it that you don't starve to death, although I'd much prefer you to come to the wardroom and eat a proper meal. I won't lie, Dan, you look really unwell.'

His eyebrow was raised, questioning her.

'You sure know how to charm the ladies,' she replied, trying to make it sound good-humoured, maybe succeeding, but she was reaching the end of her ability to keep this going. 'I just prefer to keep my distance. Is it OK if I just be alone for a little while?'

Aaron looked hurt, his cheeks reddening again. 'Of course,' he replied and stood up to leave. 'Two more rolls here for you,' he said, as he stepped over her holdall, 'and we had a nutty issue, chocolate bars, so I got you one too. It's all on your bunk.'

He turned back to face her.

'Nutty is—'

'I know what nutty is, Aaron,' she said. 'First time on a submarine, not first time in the navy.'

He made a mock scared face. 'Well, I better go. It's lunch in . . .' he looked at his watch. 'Now.'

She watched him walk to the ladder and climb silently up and out of the compartment.

As soon as he was gone, she rubbed her eyes with the heels of her hands and leaned her head backwards against the bulkhead again.

The task was enormous and she looked at the pages and pages of notes. The certainty that there was more than one person working against her, coupled with the submarine environment where she was a clear outsider, played on her mind. She was alone, that was the message that had been sent last night, but she didn't need to be.

Dan sat up and looked around the compartment, the alien

pipes and equipment seeming to accentuate her feeling of being out of her zone, an intruder in this established space. She needed help, needed to get this boat alongside the wall, needed a search team inside No.2 AMS. She needed some support, to have Roger Blackett with her, and John Granger too, and she needed some proper sleep somewhere she knew she'd be safe.

There was only one way to get those things and that was to get a message off *Tenacity*. It would be a huge risk; she knew that. It also meant giving her attackers exactly what they wanted, but it was a step that needed to be taken and that she was sure would contribute to their ultimate undoing. She picked up some documents and pulled out the list of cancelled interviews. Running her finger down it until it hovered above one name.

Chapter 29

Wednesday Morning – 1st October 2014

The shouts reached her long before she heard his footsteps on the deck above her.

He was screaming her name, nothing else, no rank or title, just her surname, 'LEWIS!'

She was, she assumed, to go up there and present herself to him, but Dan didn't like assumptions and, instead, remained seated on her bunk steeling herself for his arrival.

'Lewis,' he screamed again. 'Here, now.' He barked the order as though he were an angry owner calling back his dog.

Raising her eyebrows and clenching her jaw, she smoothed the material of her trousers down across her thighs and continued to wait.

After a few moments she saw his boots, then his wide calves and wider waist that touched all sides of the hatch as it slithered through.

Then he was down, his boots on the deck. His face was a ruddy purple, like a fresh bruise, and his eyebrows seemed to have merged into a single dark line that rose up at each end; he looked like a snarling bull set to charge.

'When I call you, you come,' he seethed, spittle flying out in visible droplets as he addressed her.

Dan swallowed hard and tried to smile. 'Sorry, sir, I didn't hear you call.'

A shudder passed over him, a visible rage that started low down, near to his well-padded middle, and travelled up his shirt, quivering his fat flesh as it advanced.

Dan watched its progress, seeing it travel past his shoulders, down his arms and only being prevented from leaking out of his fingers by his tightly clenched fists.

'I know what you did.' He let the words hang in the air.

Dan continued to watch him, observing his body as it manifested his rage.

When she said nothing, he continued, more spittle flying across the space between them as he spoke. 'Taylor, who will now be charged for Direct Disobedience, confessed.'

'Taylor knew nothing,' said Dan slowly. 'He has nothing to confess. I faked your signature and lied to him about the signal; he did nothing wrong.'

'So you admit it.' He was pointing at her now, his finger uncomfortably close to her bruised forehead.

'Of course.' Dan stood up, moving quickly around his outstretched arm, and handed him a piece of paper. 'Here's a statement of what I did and, of course, the reasons why I took the steps I did. I've been denied access to a computer and it's handwritten. There's only one copy, so be careful.'

The Old Man smiled. His exterior seemed to offer no buffer between his mood and the appearance that matched it. He took the paper, looked down at it and read silently. His hands were both unclenched now and his smile remained.

'You know,' he began, leaning back against the ladder and looking at Dan.

He licked his lips before continuing.

'I've rather enjoyed having you on board. You have a

drive to achieve your aims and I admire that.' He looked around the bomb-shop and moved towards a bench seat covered in a dirty blue canvas that doubled, when the seat cover was tipped backwards, as a toolbox. Sitting down he gestured for Dan to sit opposite him.

She didn't move.

'What you've done here will end your career, Danny,' he said softly. 'I'm going to see to that. But I want you to know that in another time and another place, I think you would have served me well. I think we would even have been fast friends.'

He sighed and shook his head, glancing down at the letter she had given him and scanning it again.

'What I would do to have someone like you in my brotherhood,' he said, looking up at her again.

'When will I be leaving?' asked Dan, hating how close her voice was to breaking.

'You requested immediate removal. I am expecting to surface in a few hours and to meet your boat transfer in the early hours of tomorrow morning. You may think us very callous, but we were heading back towards land so that we could get Steward Roach's body ashore for his family. *Tenacity* will meet you back in Devonport two days hence.'

He stood up and walked the few paces back to the ladder. 'Will you join me tonight for dinner in the wardroom?' he asked, turning his head slowly towards her and locking eyes. 'I don't want your last memories of your time here on board *Tenacity* to be dark ones.'

Dan refused to look away, but didn't speak.

He waited a few moments before he shrugged and lumbered up the ladder, like a cyclist who hadn't forgotten what to do, but who had lost the proficiency and smoothness of motion that came with constant practice.

Dan sat back down on her bunk, looking up immediately as someone else approached.

Aaron stepped off the ladder and turned towards her with a grim smile.

'I hope you know what you're doing,' he said, shaking his head. 'A submarine being called off operations is a Prime Ministerial level briefing. We're supposed to be operating as part of an international task force; this is gonna cause more than ripples, Dan.'

'This is going to cause great big waves,' she replied.

She looked down at her hands; they were pale. One more night, she thought, just one more night and I'll have some back-up. John and Roger will come; they won't be able to stop themselves.

'The Old Man's after your blood, Dan, don't be fooled by the pep talk. He's been around a long time and he knows how to play this game,' said Aaron, through pursed lips.

Chapter 30

Thursday Night – 2nd October 2014

The roar of high-pressure air being blown into the ballast tanks was deafening, drowning out all other sounds on board the submarine, but was a welcome jolt as Dan sat and waited in the bomb-shop, fighting sleep like a toddler at bedtime.

The world moved beneath her, like an elevator powering her upwards, as *Tenacity* was propelled to the surface.

The sound of the air stopped suddenly and *Tenacity* began to roll, tumbling in the choppy sea. The movement seemed worse than any of the ships Dan had been on previously in her career, the submarine's rounded hull seeming to allow *Tenacity* to lean and roll at will, but each movement was a blessing for Dan as it drew her closer to departure.

No one had come to speak to her for hours, save Richie Brannon, who had been sent to brief her by the Coxswain.

Dan wondered if this was because Richie was the only member of *Tenacity*'s crew that he could guarantee would be civil.

Richie told her that a transfer boat from Devonport would meet her and take her the few hours back to land. He told her that it would be bitterly cold 'on the roof' and she should put on as many layers of clothes as she was able to fit beneath the small, hazardous duties life jacket that he handed to her.

And so she waited in silence, dressed in most of her clothes, her bag packed and ready.

'You need to be coming up now please, ma'am,' shouted a voice from above, the Coxswain.

She climbed the short ladder, pushing her bags ahead of her, surprised when Jago grabbed them with unexpected ease and carried them along two-deck for her.

'Well,' he said as he prepared to leave her at the bottom of the control room ladder, 'I'm not sure you enjoyed your stay with us, if you don't mind me saying so, but it was good to meet you and I wish you luck in the future.'

He held out his hand and Dan shook it.

Word had spread that they were heading home and the submarine was silent as she paused at the bottom of the two-deck ladder and looked up.

The control room was in darkness, only red lights illuminating the essential equipment. The men worked in silence, their eyes like black orbs in the burlesque glow, and everywhere shadows lurked and waited for the dim lights to force them onward to another place.

Dan would never have willingly climbed those steps, but she knew she'd pass through almost anywhere to get off *Tenacity*.

'What you waiting for?'

She turned and saw McCrae standing a few yards away from her. He must have come out from the wardroom and she wondered how long he had been watching her, how long she'd been looking up and hesitating.

'Off you pop then,' he continued. 'I did say, though, didn't I? The bedroom, kitchen or off my submarine. Looks like it'll be number three for you, for now.' He grinned at her. 'I should have said bedroom, kitchen or out the navy, but it looks like that last one'll be happening now too.'

Dan swallowed, waited, made sure she was focused before she spoke so that her words wouldn't fail her. 'I think we'll see each other again soon, McCrae,' she said, sounding calm.

'I'm sure of it,' he replied. 'But we should have given you more of a send-off. What's today's toast?' he asked, as if thinking out loud. Then he raised an invisible glass to her, 'A bloody whore with a sickly lesion,' he said, bastardising the traditional Thursday toast with a grin that Dan was sure was supposed to be maniacal and intimidating, but just looked stupid.

'It's "A bloody *war* or a sickly season",' said Dan. 'It means you want people to die so that you can get promotion. I can see why you'd remember that one, because I can't think of any other reason a dickhead like you would get promoted.'

She didn't wait for a response, nor to see his reaction, but simply used this exchange as the final motivation she needed to walk quickly up into the darkened control room.

No one spoke to her at all in her final moments on board. Not even Aaron was around to say goodbye as she climbed up the ladder to the main access hatch and was helped onto the casing.

Sea spray caught her face and the cold wind bit her cheeks as she waited briefly in the dark, icy night. It felt odd to be so close to the sea, only a few metres above the waves, and yet to see no hint of land in any direction.

The sailors performed their duty expertly, talking to the men on the small boat that was holding firm alongside *Tenacity*, and Dan was helped onto a rope ladder with thick wooden treads that was slung down over the curved side of the submarine, pinched at the bottom between the two hulls.

Firm hands grasped her as she neared the bottom and she was hauled unceremoniously onto a small fishing vessel.

There was more noise, more shouting, and then someone else appeared at the entrance. It was Ryan Taylor. He sat down across from her, not looking or speaking, the worry lines like deep waves across his forehead.

She watched as the small boat separated from *Tenacity*, her vision grainy with tiredness and her eyes watery with relief. After a while, she was unsure as to whether she'd watched the submarine until it had disappeared into the horizon, or whether the dark had simply taken it first. Either way, as soon as it was gone from view, with her holdall clutched tight to her chest, she lay back against a tattered bench and surrendered the fight to keep her eyes open.

Chapter 31

Friday Morning – 3rd October 2014

The first thing she saw as she opened her eyes was John's bare shoulder in front of her.

An old and faded tattoo of a burlesque dancer looked back at her. She recalled him showing it to her one evening and telling her he'd had it done in Gibraltar when he was seventeen, only a year after he joined the navy and on his way to his first proper deployment.

She felt as though she was close enough to see the blurring black lines that made up the boundary of the picture and seemed to be desperately trying to contain the fading spread of the dancer's red corset. Dan couldn't see all of the detail, though, as it was a good five feet from the bed to where he was lying asleep on the couch.

When they had docked early that morning, and the stranger had shaken her gently, Dan had jerked away from him, almost lashing out with one hand while the other searched her face for any obstruction.

The man had stepped away, as so many people seemed to do, and the bright, natural daylight had stung her eyes as she looked past him to the land outside the boat.

Ryan Taylor was nowhere to be seen when John had stepped on board, taken her bag and offered her a lift to the Wardroom.

They'd driven together in silence, until she quietly asked him to wait while she collected some stuff from her room and then to drive her to a hotel, anywhere decent.

He'd done as she'd asked without question, fending off phone calls from Roger Blackett and barely heard orders for her to immediately attend the sickbay at HMS Drake. He'd carried her bags to reception, and then up to her room, and then, when Dan hadn't asked him to leave, he had stayed the night, sleeping on the sofa. In the whole time, they had barely exchanged a dozen words.

Twice he'd made to speak. Twice he'd known better.

Dan had needed someone she trusted to be with her while she slept, just for a while.

The people she trusted most in her life were far away from here, unsure of what they'd done to be so quickly omitted from her life, but John had stayed without question.

He stirred, his head moving on the pillow and his shoulders flexing, making the burlesque lady dance like a fading mirage.

'You OK?' he asked, without rolling over.

'How did you know I was awake?'

'You fidget in your sleep and you're not fidgeting now.'

He rolled over onto his back. His broad shoulders were too wide for the narrow couch and he turned again, shifting on the spot so that he faced her.

'Will you be getting up today?' he asked. '*Tenacity*'s being held at the buoy; she comes alongside tomorrow morning. We'll have something from Steward Roach's preliminary autopsy sooner than that, and we've to get your statement.'

He looked tired.

'I didn't even register that they'd taken Ben off. I didn't see him,' she paused. 'His body, being moved.'

'He was on a different boat, Danny. There were several boat transfers last night.'

Dan thought about that for a moment, trying to recollect seeing any other navigation lights on the water around her, but she couldn't. She'd been exhausted and confused, her mind as tumultuous as the sea around her, any focus she had simply aimed at functioning until she got off *Tenacity*. 'John.' She paused again.

'Don't worry,' he said, rolling off the couch and sitting on the edge with his blanket pulled around his waist. 'I'll get going whenever you want me to.'

He stood up.

'But you have to tell me what happened on *Tenacity*, all of it, and on record,' he said. Then added, 'No secrets.'

Dan nodded. 'I will. And John . . .' She paused, letting the silence draw out. 'I am sorry.'

He turned to look at her, trying to look confused, but failing; he knew what she meant.

Dan turned away from him, facing the window. The curtains were only partially drawn, but they were so thin that the light was still streaming in as though they weren't there at all. She could tell that he was still watching her, not moving, waiting.

'I already told you,' he began. 'I would've had your back. I'd have come with you, to his house. You didn't have to go alone.'

'I know that now,' she sighed. 'I think I knew it then too. I won't make excuses about being worried that you knew Hamilton, because I know that you'd have done the right thing. Maybe that's why I didn't, or couldn't, tell you, because I was doing the wrong things to try and prove myself right.'

He was watching her closely.

'I didn't want to risk you being drawn into what I was doing,' she continued. 'If I'd been wrong, or even been discovered before I was proven right, there'd have been consequences.'

'I thought we were friends,' said John. 'We take risks for each other, face consequences together; that's what friends do.'

The words were heart-breaking, sounding like a hurt little boy's words coming from a fully grown man's mouth.

Dan turned to face him.

'We were, are, well, you were.' The words and thoughts were jumbled. 'I think I'm just a bit of a shitty friend to have,' she said. 'I think that might be why I don't really have very many of them.'

John raised an eyebrow and tipped his head, but he didn't disagree.

'I do currently have a vacancy for one, though,' she offered. 'And because I know you, I'd be prepared to let you skip formal interview and go straight to a probationary period.'

He laughed out loud; it was the first time she had heard him laugh around her in several years. It sounded good, full, genuine, and Dan actually smiled as she listened to him.

'OK,' John said, still grinning. 'I'm game for the role, but I'll need an advance on wages. I need to know what you know, what happened, all of it.'

'OK, but I only want to tell it once. Would you call Roger and tell him I'm coming in to give a statement?'

John nodded, and picked up his phone.

Chapter 32

Friday Morning – 3rd October 2014

When John pressed the stop button on the interview recorder his hands were shaking and his mouth was set into a line as hard and straight as the dockyard wall. He didn't look at Blackett, who was also sitting silently and examining the table.

John's fair skin contrasted with his dark hair and hinted at his Irish descent, but Dan could see that it was his inherited Irish temper that was being tenuously kept in check.

Blackett started to speak, opened his mouth to do so, but stopped and said nothing.

'Danny,' said John, then stopped and fell back into silence.

'How much proof do you have of what happened on board *Tenacity*?' asked Blackett. 'Do you have any proof? Any evidence at all?' He paused and looked at John before continuing. 'A lot of this is your word against someone else's, Danny, but there's areas where you could have gathered evidence.' He paused and looked away again before adding, 'We're going to need to get you examined, Danny.'

'Do you think I'm lying?'

'No,' said John.

'Of course not,' agreed Roger. 'But whether I believe you or not won't count for anything in court.'

'Well, there isn't any proof left, aside from the pictures I showed you and the bruising on my ribs.'

'So it's your word against,' Blackett paused. 'Whose?'

'I don't know, for sure.'

'But you suspect the Chief Stoker, Chief Campbell, as having some role in all of this?' Roger asked. 'But not alone, with someone?'

'Yes. That's what I think, but I can't prove it.'

'Do you believe the threats made against you?' he asked.

'I don't know,' said Dan, more quietly this time, watching John's hands close into fists.

A knock at the door made all three of them turn.

A young naval policeman walked in holding a sealed envelope.

Dan spotted the security stamps on every seam. It had to be the preliminary autopsy report on Steward Roach; she had requested its immediate delivery.

'You can't be part of this investigation any more, Danny,' said Blackett, looking away from her. 'You know that. What you've just told us means you'll have to sit it out, you're a victim.'

Dan leaned over the table, slowly and deliberately, moving her face closer to his. 'Fuck. Off,' she said, and then sat back, waiting.

He was shaking his head again before he tossed the report onto the table and stood up. 'John, I need a team up to search Lieutenant Lewis's cabin immediately and to pick up the length of air-hose. It'll need to go straight to the lab, along with the note and the dolphins. Then get on to Branok Cornish and tell him what's happened.'

He stopped to look at Dan.

'Branok will want your blood for this,' he said. He turned back to John. 'If we're lucky they might still be able to get footage from the post office the package was sent from. We'll also need to reinterview Lieutenant Gemma Rockwell. Have her brought in and let Branok know you're doing it; he'll likely want to have someone sit in.' Roger turned back to Dan. 'If there's anything else, Danny, now's definitely the time.'

'There's nothing,' she said, glad that her security box was back in her car, somewhere they were unlikely to look.

She reached for the report, opened it and pulled out the few thin sheets of paper. The initial presentation was standard stuff; the body was a few days old and some evidence may have been lost, although the correct procedures were followed on board *Tenacity*. Dan scanned through it, not knowing what she was looking for and not expecting to find it. She knew how he'd died; she'd been there, unable to stop it.

The autopsy report contained nothing at all – nothing that she could use – and she had known that that would be the case. What could there be? He had been killed in front of twenty witnesses; what else could the report possibly have found?

She threw the papers onto the table towards John, who was still sitting motionless, looking at the table top. 'There's nothing there,' she said.

'What did you expect, Danny?' said Roger. 'By your own admission he died exactly as *Tenacity*'s investigation team said he did. You think someone deliberately let him suffocate, but an autopsy can't reveal that.'

She stood up and walked away from the table.

'We've next to no proof or provable motive for any of this, Danny. Walker's death will shortly be ruled a suicide; I've seen the coroner's report. We've only your word about a note from Ben Roach and, because we have no proof—'

'They must have taken it,' Dan protested.

Roger ignored her, continuing on. 'Because we have no proof, we have no motive for an attack on Ben either. We have nothing at all to move forward with. In fact, the only person that we have the proof to bring any charges against in all of this, is you, Danny, for withholding evidence and interfering in the course of a criminal investigation.' His voice trailed off at the end, his temper running out of steam and slowing to a guilty sigh.

'I have to go,' she said.

'You can't,' said Blackett, seeming to refocus back onto her.

'I can,' she replied.

'No,' he said, his voice the one that was used to being obeyed. 'You need to be medically examined and, Danny, if you've something you know, something about this investigation, then you need to tell me right now.' He paused. 'I can't protect you if you don't.'

Dan opened the door, pausing before she left. 'And just a moment ago you were telling me that I was the victim.'

Chapter 33

Friday Evening – 3rd October 2014

The house looked different this time. Even though insufficient time had passed for decay to really set into the property, the place now looked deserted, uncared for. It wasn't just the too long grass, or the upstairs curtains that were still open this late in the evening. It was the way the house seemed to be in mourning, like the windows were eyes, big, dark and sorrowful, and the doorway was the mouth, fixed forever in a shocked expression.

Dan pulled up and waited in her car. She wondered how to deal with her removal from the investigation, what would happen if she was found to have come here knowing she shouldn't have.

Five minutes passed, and then ten, before she picked up her mobile and dialled.

'Sorry,' came the immediate reply. 'I'm inside already. I didn't hear you pull up.'

Dan frowned and looked at the house. There were no lights on inside.

The pathway looked dark and unwelcoming until, suddenly,

it brightened and the house yawned as a light was turned on and Felicity Green pulled open the front door.

The woman's tall silhouette beckoned to her and Dan grabbed her bag and walked down the pathway and into the house without a second's hesitation.

'No lights?' she asked by way of greeting.

Felicity shook her head. Her auburn hair was tied back in a neat ponytail and it swished from side to side.

'It's weird, I know, but sometimes I just like to sit somewhere in complete darkness, lights off, eyes closed, and think without visual distractions. It really helps me to focus and compile all the facts, to get my mind inside what's gone on. You should try it.'

'Not likely,' said Dan.

If she had been unsure about Felicity before, then the feeling that she now had at meeting the woman again, standing with her and seeing the cool intellect in her eyes, dispelled any concerns. She knew she could trust this woman and knew she would.

'So what's up?' asked Felicity, the casual question seeming odd in the eerie silence.

Felicity was watching and waiting.

'I want,' Dan stopped, '*need* to talk to someone.'

'You can talk to me.'

Dan nodded and her eyes flitted to the lounge door.

'Any reason why here?' asked Felicity, gesturing to the Walkers' home around her.

'Kind of,' said Dan, moving towards the lounge. 'Yes, but I need to talk to you first and then I'll explain.'

They sat down on the settee, at either end of the pale three-seater.

'I can't tell you it in chronological order,' began Dan. 'It doesn't work that way for me.'

'That's fine,' said Felicity, sitting back as Dan began to speak.

She recounted her experiences on board *Tenacity*; she left nothing out as Felicity listened without interrupting.

'Oh, Dan,' said Felicity when she was finished. 'Have you reported all of this?'

'I made a statement today. But there's more; I have to make you understand why I went on board *Tenacity*.'

'Good luck, Dan, because I can't think of a single reason that could get me to go onto a submarine,' said Felicity without any trace of humour in her voice.

Dan rummaged in her backpack and fished out some files. She had dispensed with the lock box tonight and had everything she needed loose in her bag. She placed pictures of Cheryl Walker's bruised back onto the settee between them, and then pulled out pictures of a second woman, pictures that were almost identical.

'Look at the similarities in these two pictures,' Dan began. 'Not just the obvious bruising from the beating, but the way the victim was controlled, the way her hair was used and then cut, the position she must have been in when this attack took place. I think these two separate attacks were perpetrated by the same person; it's more than just coincidence, it's a pattern.'

Felicity's lips were pursed tight as she looked at the pictures.

'This woman was attacked in a car park in Portsmouth two years ago,' said Dan, pointing to the pictures of the new victim. 'She escaped during the attack, but I don't think she was going to be murdered.'

Felicity examined the pictures, turning them over one after the other. 'These aren't police pictures,' she remarked.

'She was dragged from her car by a group of males who beat her and whipped her over the bonnet. One of the men . . .' Dan searched for a word, ignoring Felicity's comment as she tried to get this story out while she still had the courage, 'inflicted these marks with the victim's belt.' Dan traced the welts down the woman's ribcage. 'Look at the shape of them, the way they were delivered.'

Felicity was nodding but said nothing, her eyes hard and her mouth set into a grim straight line.

'Do you agree they could be the same attacker?' asked Dan.

Felicity sighed. 'Maybe. It's certainly possible that this could be the same perpetrator that attacked Cheryl Walker. There are a number of striking similarities just by casual inspection. The brutality of the attack, the whipping from side to side of the ribcage, the hair being severed . . .'

Dan was leaning in towards the police psychologist, hanging on her every word.

Felicity picked up the second picture and examined it closely. 'Who else knows this happened to you, Dan?'

Felicity's question was like a hard slap in the face and Dan took a sharp breath. She waited, unsure of what to say. She had known that she would need to tell Felicity the truth, that the pictures were of herself, that these pictures documented a turning point in her life, that this humiliating attack had eclipsed or erased every other event and relationship that came either before or after it.

'Only one person,' Dan answered, her voice different, as she became the subject of the conversation, as she became the victim in her picture. 'An old and very dear friend.'

'And they let you keep this a secret?' Felicity looked grave as she asked. 'Because I would argue that if a person did that, then they aren't much of a friend at all.'

'He did as I asked him to do.'

Felicity drummed her fingers on the file, clearly thinking. It seemed like a long time before she spoke.

'I don't know what you want me to do here, Dan, I don't understand. I want to help you, but you need to give a statement to the police and hand these pictures over as evidence. This may or may not support the theory that this attacker has committed previous crimes, but having this information could have helped, and not having it may well have hindered the investigation.'

Dan shook her head. 'I can't do that. Not yet.'

'Well, if you won't help yourself, Dan, then I can't help you either.'

'No,' she repeated. 'I will get help. I'll talk to you about it, but at the moment I need to focus on Cheryl Walker. I need to figure this out and I can't do it alone.'

'And you can't ask anyone else, can you? Because you won't tell anyone about your assault, so no one else knows the whole story. For that reason they'd be of no help to you anyway.'

Dan nodded in reluctant agreement.

'And John? You said that you trust him?'

'No. I mean yes, I do, but not with this, not yet.'

'You need to talk about this, Dan. Secrets like this are what destroy us and change us. They drive people away from us and stop us from being who we really are and who we want to be.'

Dan reached out and took Felicity's hand, squeezed it and then gently lowered it away from her. 'I do have some people to talk to and they want to talk to me. I have a sister, a stepmum and a dad who don't know why I don't come home any more, or why I can't talk to them.'

Felicity seemed to think, looking away and giving Dan the time she needed to wipe her eyes and compose herself.

'OK. I'll help you, but I have some conditions,' she said eventually.

'I agree to them.'

'You don't know what they are.'

'Full disclosure, I tell you everything, and I agree to make a formal statement to the police,' said Dan, 'and I seek help once this is done.'

Felicity waited, looking at her for a very long time before she nodded. 'OK, tell me.'

'You've seen the similarities in the attack. But that wasn't the only reason that I had to go onto *Tenacity*, although my intuition still tells me that the link to all of this lies on that submarine.'

'I believe in intuition,' said Felicity. 'I think you can often get a feel for someone very quickly, a subconscious indication of the type of person they are. Following your intuition can be a key part of life, but you also need to train your analytical mind, not to override your intuition, but just to risk assess what you're doing.'

Dan nodded. 'I didn't do that risk assessment.'

'But that doesn't make you responsible for what happened,' said Felicity, 'remember that. The person or persons that attacked you are responsible. You are not.'

'Thank you,' said Dan, and she meant it. 'But there were other factors too. I interviewed, or rather I unofficially spoke to, Cheryl Walker's friend, Gemma Rockwell. She told me that she felt like Cheryl was frightened about *Tenacity* coming back. She couldn't put her finger on why, but she really believed it. I checked that that was what she meant, checked that she really meant fear, and she was sure, Cheryl Walker was afraid.'

'OK,' said Felicity. 'I'm starting to see an indication, but I'm still not climbing down that ladder with you yet.'

Dan nodded. 'But you haven't seen this yet.'

She pulled out her phone and opened up her photographs. She showed Felicity pictures of the note and the dolphins that she believed Walker had sent to her.

'You're right, I haven't seen this evidence,' said Felicity, swiping the touchscreen to re-examine each of the pictures again.

'You will, the next time you go into work. I only handed

it over to the naval police this afternoon. It was sent directly to me almost a week ago.'

'Oh, Dan,' said Felicity, the same words that she had used in response to Dan's treatment on board *Tenacity*, but sounding so different in this context.

Felicity shook her head.

Dan pushed on. 'I think that Walker thought he was leaving me a clue that I would see. Something that he was too frightened, or maybe unable, to tell someone else, something I would recognise that would link them together.'

'Link who? Link what?'

'Link whoever attacked Cheryl Walker to *Tenacity*.'

'Dan, I'm going to be really candid here. I understand that you believe more than one man attacked you on board *Tenacity*; I get that. But even if it were true that these men were working in cahoots to some end, it is a massive step to then apply that back to Cheryl Walker's attack. It's very difficult indeed to share a secret as big as murder. You know as well as I do that killers seldom work together, and when they do, there is normally a very deep relationship or bond that binds them: family, lovers . . .'

'I know, and I can't figure it out either. It's like there's more than one thing happening and the lines are jumbled together. I won't be able to see it until I can separate them.'

Felicity pursed her lips again. 'You really think all of these deaths are the work of two people?'

'Yes. Maybe.' Dan sighed. 'I don't know.'

'But you also hypothesised in your leaked paper that Hamilton was working with a partner, more or less, didn't you? It almost cost you your career by all accounts.'

Dan raised her hands, immediately defensive. 'That was different.'

'Why?'

'There were a lot of pointers that Hamilton wasn't acting alone.'

'No one else saw them,' said Felicity.

'That isn't relevant at the moment,' said Dan, growing impatient.

'I think it might be,' said Felicity. 'I can believe that you were attacked by two people, but if you want me to believe that you have encountered another pair of killers working together, then I need to know that you don't just spot conspiracies everywhere you look.'

Dan sighed. She realised that she would need to discuss this, that she had wandered into another condition of Felicity's help.

'OK, aside from the victims that we found in Hamilton's garage, we also found DNA for several other women on and around Hamilton's belongings and in the house,' she said, speaking quickly, trying to move past this and back to the case in hand.

'Yes. And he confessed to the bodies you found but denied killing anyone else, including instances where there was DNA evidence in his home,' added Felicity.

'But, aside from the ones we found, he never told us where any of the other bodies were, not one,' said Dan.

'That's not unusual,' said Felicity. 'After all, he denies killing them.'

'He also never told us how many people he'd actually killed.'

'Also not unusual,' said Felicity, shaking her head, pushing Dan harder to make her case.

'And yet, we know that he did kill many more, and after killing all those people and getting away clean for all those years, almost thirty years all told, he didn't know how to get rid of the three bodies he had in the garage.'

'Or hadn't managed to get around to it.'

Dan shook her head. 'No, I was there. When I found the

bodies and Hamilton found me. When he was down and bleeding out before Roger arrived and Hamilton knew it was over, he just shrugged, like it was no big deal, and said "I don't know" – said it several times – and I was there, I was asking, and I had a shovel at his throat. Those were his exact words. The life was draining out of him and I'm telling you, intuition or not, he was not lying; he really didn't know.'

'That's tenuous, Dan,' said Felicity, still shaking her head, visibly unconvinced.

Dan held up her hand to stop Felicity. 'OK. Now think about his IQ and think about the evidence that we found,' she said. 'The man was no genius – smart, yes, but not *really* smart. There's no way he managed on his own for so long. The three we found in the garage were the ones that he had done alone. That's why he fucked them up so badly. There was no fixed method, all attacked and mutilated, but in totally different ways and with different tools, in different places, and the amount of evidence for those three crimes was unprecedented. It was like he'd barely bothered to do anything more than wipe down the worktops after he'd massacred them; he was experimenting, playing around, trying to find what else would work for him. I think he was losing control.'

Dan turned over a piece of paper and drew three crosses on the back.

'Even though forensic evidence suggests he'd killed many times before,' she said, drawing a circle around the three crosses. 'These three were him flying solo and we caught him. The other ones . . .'

She began to draw other crosses in a separate group to the original three.

'The ones where we only found tiny traces or trophies – where we still, to this day, haven't discovered any sniff of a body – for those ones he had help. He had help to plan them and to get rid of the bodies afterwards. I don't think he has a clue where those bodies are, not a clue, and I think he was simply waiting for his accomplice to come and help him tidy them away; those women were in short-term storage.'

Felicity seemed to be thinking it over, saying nothing and processing what Dan had said.

'Think about it, Felicity, three bodies on shelves in his garage and the rest disappeared without a trace . . .'

'You're making huge leaps,' said Felicity. 'Killers cooperating is a very unusual phenomenon.'

'I know, you said that and I agree, usually there has to be a deep relationship, but I think there *was* a deep relationship. I think, for Hamilton, it came from the navy.'

Felicity sucked her teeth, the first time Dan had seen her do it, and then clicked her tongue against the bridge of her mouth as she thought about what she was hearing.

'It's not impossible,' said Felicity. 'Hamilton joined the navy at sixteen years old and had no close family outside of an aunt he never saw. He was almost completely disassociated from his parents, who seemed only too happy to sign him away to the navy and forget about him. Someone in the navy could have taken that role, but it would need to be someone that was a constant throughout his career, an individual, a perceived authority figure maybe, and we did look for this type of connection; your paper wasn't ignored just because it was published in the red-tops before it could have made it into any of the professional journals.'

'Or someone who met him several times during his career and maintained a contact that we weren't able to find,' said Dan, unwilling to talk again about how her paper had been leaked. 'Someone in the background, whispering to him from somewhere we couldn't see.'

Felicity stopped as she thought about that, her eyes never leaving Dan's.

'OK,' she said, 'OK. So, say I follow your thought process,

though I don't necessarily agree, but can you make anything like a similar argument for this situation?'

'I was attacked by two men on board *Tenacity*,' said Dan, her voice rising. 'We know there are two, so I don't need to make the case for this one – it's made.'

'No,' said Felicity, holding up a single finger to stop Dan in her tracks. 'It doesn't make the case at all. You were attacked by two men who, by your own account, could have killed you, but didn't. Two men working together to attack and intimidate, that I can believe. You're asking me to consider murder, and that is a separate thing entirely.'

Dan sat back and let her shoulders drop; it was like being scolded by a disappointed tutor.

Felicity let her words hang.

'I don't know if that's what I'm saying,' said Dan. 'Something's stopping me from seeing clearly.'

'Right,' Felicity clapped her hands and made Dan jump. 'So let's remove the act of murder for a moment, remove the deaths from the equation and treat them as irregularities.'

'But it was the murder that drew me into this,' said Dan.

'We'll come back to it. Now, what do we have left?'

'We have a man whose wife was beaten, and who then committed suicide.'

'Yes,' said Felicity, 'and it will shortly be ruled as such by the coroner, so for this exercise, let's leave it as just that, a suicide.'

'OK,' said Dan. 'Well, he had too much money, he worked on board a submarine, he died there, and his death forced an investigation on that submarine. I think he also tried to manipulate it so that I would investigate.'

'Then there was your time on board *Tenacity*,' said Felicity, taking over the narrative. 'The threat by two men, the young steward wanting to speak with you, and his subsequent death.'

Dan dropped back against the soft cushions and let her head rest against them. 'Another death – two irregularities is too many,' she said, throwing her hands up in despair.

Felicity was clicking her tongue against her teeth again. 'No, it isn't,' she said. 'It really isn't. Not if they're both the work of a single attacker.'

'I don't follow,' said Dan.

'You said there was more than one thing going on here, and it was clouding what we could see. Maybe you're right. What if there is a pair working together, but they aren't both involved in all of the decisions?'

'So one member of the couple acting alone, doing things that the other doesn't know about or wouldn't do?' asked Dan. 'Not a pair of killers. A pair of attackers with a single killer.'

Felicity was nodding her head slowly. 'One of them has their own separate agenda and they're prepared to go further than the other,' she agreed. 'Look at Cheryl Walker's murder; we've been puzzling over the timeline, but if you break the attack down, then there are two separate phases to it, a very nasty beating . . .'

'And sometime later, a murder,' finished Dan. 'So, she may have been beaten and intimidated by the pair acting together, but only one of them went back, or stayed back, to kill her.'

'Now a single killer,' said Felicity. 'That I can believe.'

'But how does that answer the question about Ben Roach?' asked Dan. 'Why would a killer expose himself again?'

'Well, for Ben Roach, if we follow your line of thinking, we have a motive and that changes things. He was killed to stop him from telling you something. I think we have to assume he was going to reveal to you who this pair are and what they'd done,' said Felicity, seeming energised, as though she believed they were making progress as much as Dan did. 'But it would still be possible, and indeed very likely, that he was actually killed by a single person.'

'If we find the couple, then we can identify their motive—' said Dan.

'And then identify which of them is willing to commit murder for it,' finished Felicity.

Dan could feel hope building, as though she could begin to see a pathway to follow.

'Walker wanted me to find this link, because he sent me that message. Maybe he knew who they were, maybe he was blackmailing them?'

'It could explain the money and the attack on his wife,' said Felicity, standing up. 'But when we spoke on the first day we met here, and again in the subsequent phone call, you gave me the impression that you had some insight into Cheryl's attack, that it was a message. I can see now that you had information that we didn't, but I think my argument still stands, that death isn't a warning.'

Dan thought about what Felicity was saying, about the attack on Cheryl Walker, about the attack several years ago that had left her life in tatters. 'I think, now, that maybe our theory about two partners with separate agendas may work to solve that too. The beating,' Dan paused and looked away from Felicity. 'My beating,' she continued, 'happened exactly one year to the day that Chris Hamilton was sentenced to thirty years' imprisonment. My attackers were waiting for me. It wasn't random.'

It felt odd for Dan to hear herself talk about this, to hear words that had so far never been spoken aloud, had always been contained within her private thoughts, suddenly out there for someone else to hear.

'During the attack there were three men, but one of them was standing away from the others and he was controlling them verbally, dictating what they should do, teaching them how to do it. When they began to whip me, he said to them that it had to be thirty. I'm absolutely certain of it. He said it had to be exactly thirty.'

Dan managed to look back at Felicity, not in the eye, but in her direction.

Felicity's mouth had dropped open. 'Oh Dan,' she said. 'It was a punishment. He got to you, got someone to get to you even from inside prison.'

'Yes,' said Dan, feeling as though she was drawing strength from speaking out loud about this. 'But it was someone he knew well and trusted, someone who could deliver a very specific punishment, in a very specific way. Not a killer to serve up revenge – a friend who could deliver a measured message.'

'That's why you never told anyone.'

'Yes,' said Dan, 'it was done to humiliate me. So that people would know I had been got to. I believe it was supposed to put me back in my place and teach me a lesson; it was a message. That's why I think that Cheryl Walker's attack was also a message.'

Felicity reached out and touched Dan's face, gently lifting her chin until their eyes met.

'And you've carried this alone since then? Not sharing it with anyone?'

'I couldn't share it,' said Dan, hearing her voice break. 'I could live with the pain, but my dad, Charlie . . .' Dan's words trailed off. 'He wanted them all to know, for us all to be hurt by it.'

'You're a brave, brave woman, Danielle Lewis.'

Dan looked away again and Felicity lowered her hand.

'The pictures were taken by a very old and dear friend, Roger Blackett. I went to his house as soon as I was able to get back to my car. I asked him to take these pictures; I needed to keep some evidence. I asked him to help me to get home and then I asked him to support me in taking a year-long sabbatical. He was my superior at the time, and after the papers had leaked my theories no one particularly wanted me around anyway, so I took the time off and went away to heal.'

'And did you?' asked Felicity.

'No,' said Dan. 'I didn't.'

The two women were silent for a long time, both deep in thought.

'So how do we find the clue that links these men together; how do we find the rotten pair within the submarine's barrel?' asked Felicity, her voice changing in tone and lifting the mood with it.

Dan sat up straighter, glad the topic had changed. 'I don't know. They're just one massive clique and they all seem so bloody inbred. They all know each other. They all know each other's families,' she paused.

'But you suspect this Chief Stoker, right?'

'I do, but I have no evidence to support that.'

'OK. But you want to go right back through the place again, don't you?' asked Felicity. 'You think now that you've had these ideas and suspicions, that if Walker did leave you a clue, now you might recognise it.'

Dan was nodding, standing up. 'I do. You fancy helping?'

'I do,' said Felicity. 'But Dan, you know I can't withhold evidence too. You know I'll have to report everything we've discussed tonight to Branok Cornish when I speak with him first thing tomorrow morning, and I do mean everything, Dan.'

'You should do whatever you have to do,' said Dan.

'I know.' Felicity walked past Dan and headed towards the stairs. 'Shall we start in the study?'

Chapter 34

Saturday Morning – 4th October 2014

The night started with high hopes as Dan and Felicity spent time going back through Walker's house room-by-room, cupboard-by-cupboard, and drawer-by-drawer. A good hour was spent looking through and discussing the pictures from the spare room, desperately trying to fathom some link or order, but there was none. After that, their enthusiasm waned, but they continued through every other nook and cranny in the house. By the time it started getting light outside, both Dan and Felicity were empty-handed and exhausted.

The parting was quiet; they were both tired and talked-out.

Dan fell into her car, immediately noticing the seventeen missed calls on her mobile phone.

They would be from Roger Blackett and John. There was a message too, the small icon illuminated to prove it, but Dan had no stomach to hear it at the moment and she tossed the phone back onto the passenger seat.

The urge to get some sleep was strong and she considered

booking back into another hotel. She had her things in the back of the car and the idea of another night in fresh sheets, with a warm bath, seemed very tempting. But as she pulled out and turned around in the road, she knew she would need to head back to the dockyard.

Her phone rang; this would be missed call number eighteen, Dan decided, and carried on driving.

Her thoughts were continuous and mixed, as though she was trying to do a jigsaw puzzle depicting a scene of waves. There were hundreds of pieces and it was impossible to tell which order they went in, or if any were missing; so many were similar and seemed to fit into multiple places.

Being convinced there was a killer on board *Tenacity* was one thing, but suspecting that this same person had attacked her so many years ago seemed stupid in the cold, hard light of day.

She tried to order her thoughts as the traffic density increased near to the dockyard entrance. She held up her pass, not really looking at the guard and only fully stopping when she realised he had no intention of moving aside to let her car pass.

The man stood in front of her vehicle, looked down at her licence plate and then at the armed police officer who was standing nearby, cradling his Heckler and Koch MP7 across his abdomen.

Dan sat back in her seat and waited. In her mind, she had figured out what it was already; Blackett had placed her name on the gate with orders that she be sent to his office as soon as she showed her face.

The man stopped next to her window and twirled his fingers, gesturing for her to wind down the window.

Dan did.

'You should probably just do a push-button motion these days,' she said, without a smile. 'Nobody actually winds their windows down any more.'

He seemed to sigh before looking at her. 'Do you have any identification please, ma'am?' His voice was absent, as though he was bored, but Dan suspected that he was delighted to be the one to stop her.

'Yes. I just showed it to you.'

'May I see it again please, ma'am?'

Dan handed him her Special Investigation Branch ID and waited as he walked back into the small shack that was set up between traffic lanes for the security supervisor to use.

He picked up a phone, examined the card carefully as he spoke, and then walked, very slowly, oblivious to the ever-growing queue that was forming behind Dan's car, back to her open window.

She had thought about shutting the window again to see if he would do a pushing motion this time, but he didn't look smart enough to be so easily trained and so she thought better of it.

He leaned down and looked inside at her. 'Ma'am, I'm going to have to ask you to—'

'Report immediately to the squadron building and Commander Roger Blackett?' she interrupted.

He looked heartbroken for an instant. His mouth opened but no words came out until he stood back up, looked around at all of the other cars and said, 'Yes.' He handed her ID back and waved her in.

'Moron,' said Dan as she drove away. She hoped he'd heard it, but couldn't be sure.

The thought of disobeying Blackett crossed her mind. She contemplated heading up to the Wardroom and grabbing some sleep, taking a shower and spending some time trying to gather her thoughts, but decided against it. There would be enough questions to answer. Her phone was still on the passenger seat and she looked at the message icon.

'Forewarned is forearmed,' she said, and played the message over the car speakers.

The short message from Roger Blackett was enough to confirm that she wouldn't be taking any detours, and Dan couldn't help but accelerate as she drove towards the squadron buildings.

John met her just inside the door.

'John,' she said, not even looking at him. 'We're missing something, something that we, that I, shouldn't be missing. Grab all of Ben Roach's belongings and bring them into the interview room; I want to go through all of them again, but we need to be really quick.'

John didn't answer, nor did he move out of her way.

She stopped and looked at him.

'What?'

'Blackett's up there waiting for you, Danny. He's not alone. They're waiting for you in Interview Room One.'

Dan frowned.

'I'm sorry. I tried to help as much as I could; as much as you'd let me,' he said, and slipped past her without another word.

She watched him as he pushed open the door, thought about reaching out for him, maybe following, but the door slammed shut before she could do either.

It only took a few seconds for her to get to the landing and a few more to reach Interview Room One, but it felt like a long time. Her stomach was empty and her eyes were sore and she was sure the metallic taste of bile was ebbing at the back of her throat. The early signs of a migraine, probably through lack of sleep, were lapping at the bows of her mind. She blinked hard as she stood outside the door and slapped herself lightly on the back of the neck to jolt some life into her flagging brain. Then she knocked.

Blackett opened the door.

'Hey, Roger,' she said quietly, her heart sinking as she saw the grave look on his normally friendly face.

'Lieutenant Lewis,' he said, his voice stony. 'Come in.'

He stepped back and waved her into the room. 'You remember Captain Harrow-Brown.'

Dan looked down at the Captain as he sat on an interview chair, leaning back with his long legs delicately crossed and his hands, the white fingers laced together, resting on his thighs.

He didn't smile or nod a greeting and even though she was standing and he was seated, he managed to look down his long, thin nose at her.

'Take a seat, Lieutenant Lewis,' said Blackett, as he moved around the table and sat down across from her.

'So, what's going on?' she asked. 'I've an investigation running and I'm making progress, if you—'

The Captain snorted, cutting Dan off and making her turn to look at him.

'If you wanted an update,' she continued.

'There is to be no update from you, Lieutenant Lewis,' said the Captain slowly. He touched the tips of his fingers together and pointed both hands, palms together, towards her. 'There will be no more updates from you at all.'

She looked at Blackett, her oldest friend, a friend of her family and her dad, but he turned his head away and looked out of the window, powerless to help.

The Captain stood up and tossed some papers towards Dan. He did so with a flick of his wrist, in a way that seemed designed to ensure that they scattered as they landed before her.

'This is a report from the Commanding Officer of HMS *Tenacity*, Lieutenant Lewis. A report concerning your behaviour during your short time on board, behaviour that has resulted in a one-billion-pound asset being pulled out of global allied operations. A situation that leads to a briefing at Prime Ministerial level, a briefing that I personally have to deliver, and all because, what? You got claustrophobic?' He sneered as he turned away from her.

'I was attacked, physically and violently. My investigation was blocked at every turn on board that submarine.'

'Really?' The Captain spun around to face her again. It seemed as though he was enjoying it, as though there was an audience watching and he was playing to them. 'And yet no one knows about it? No one at all until you submitted this . . .' He paused, seeming to search for words as he gestured to a piece of paper that was waiting on one side of the interview table. Her handwriting was instantly recognisable and the letter looked as though it had been perfectly preserved since the moment she had handed it over to *Tenacity*'s Commanding Officer. 'Fabrication,' he finished, seemingly happy with his word choice.

'It's the truth,' she said quietly.

'What is truth, Lieutenant Lewis? Because I have various accounts in this report, signed by numerous serving officers and ratings that describe your behaviour on board HMS *Tenacity* in quite some vivid detail.'

She looked at Roger Blackett again, trying to meet his eyes, but he still wouldn't look at her.

'You did not take a single meal the entire time you were on board. Despite the time-sensitive nature of your assignment, you cancelled whole days of interviews. You spread rumours that you were investigating a murder, something you were, in fact, not there to do, and then managed to witness a "murder".'

He used his fingers to make air apostrophes as he spat the word murder towards her like a dart from a blowpipe.

'A "murder" that has since been proven to have been a terrible accident and which your callous actions made far,

far more damaging to the ship's company and their morale. You were then "physically attacked",' he performed more air apostrophes, 'by multiple assailants – a scenario that has previously featured heavily in your career theories, I might add – but chose not to mention this to anyone on board at all, but instead to compromise secure communications to send a message back to Fleet about this alleged murder and assault.'

He paused to look at her, his narrow face making his eyes look as though they were sinking deeper into his head as Dan's vision narrowed.

'And these events, I should duly note, only cover your conduct in the naval investigation. The civil police are also keen to speak with you concerning a whole raft of indiscretions including withholding evidence. Have I missed anything?' he asked, and waited.

'Missed? No,' she said. 'Interpreted in the way that suits you best, yes.'

The Captain's face darkened and she saw his jaw muscles clench tightly. They were over-pronounced against his skinny head, the muscles bunched clearly underneath his skin, which looked as though it were a translucent material that was stretched across bare bone and knotted rope.

'Dan,' cautioned Blackett as he spoke for the first time.

'No, Commander Blackett,' said the Captain, using Roger's rank to remind him of his superiority. 'Let Lieutenant Lewis speak. I doubt she can do any more harm to herself, or others, at this juncture.'

Dan sat back, but maintained eye contact with the hawk-like Captain.

'But let me go on, please, Lieutenant Lewis, if I may?' he said with a sneer of sarcasm. 'You managed to bypass security protocols to send your message, subjecting a young and inexperienced sailor to what will likely be a custodial sentence, and then came back into the arms of your former partner, a subordinate, with whom Commander Blackett saw fit to pair you.'

Dan recoiled, her mouth open.

'Don't try to deny it,' said the Captain slowly. 'We know that Master at Arms Granger spent the night before last in a hotel room with you.'

Dan looked back to Blackett, caught his eye, pleading. But he shook his head slowly and looked away again, this time down at the table.

'So, we are to believe that the ship's company of HMS *Tenacity* sexually harassed you, that someone attacked you during your time on board, and not only did you do nothing, report it to no one, seek no help, refuse to be examined upon your return, but you ran immediately back to the first man you knew to get your leg over? Hardly the actions of a recent victim of sexual harassment and assault; don't you agree, Lieutenant Lewis?'

Dan sprang to her feet, her fists clenched.

'Oh sit down, please, Lieutenant Lewis,' said the Captain, his face a mask of scorn. 'Spare us all your righteous indignation.'

'Roger?' Dan looked to her friend.

He shook his head again, but still said nothing.

'There will be no help for you this time, Lieutenant Lewis,' said the Captain, with what might have passed for a smile. 'You are relieved of duty, subject immediate. You are to return to your home and remain there until court martial proceedings can be brought against you. You are not to contact Master at Arms Granger, nor any member of the ship's company of HMS *Tenacity*; you are no longer part of that investigation, although you may be required to give statements in support of it, and about your conduct during it.'

'I gave my statement to the Commanding Officer of *Tenacity*; you already have it.'

'Yes, and it will be used in the investigation, Lieutenant Lewis, you have my word on that.'

Dan felt the room begin to spin slowly around her.

'You should also know, Lieutenant Lewis, that the job you were sent on board *Tenacity* to complete has been accomplished in less than two days by my officers. All information has been gathered with reference to Chief Walker's unfortunate suicide, and all members of *Tenacity* have been accounted for on the nights in question. This information will be handed to the appropriate civil authorities forthwith.'

'Roger?' she asked again, more quietly this time.

'You are done here, Lieutenant Lewis,' said the Captain. 'This investigation is done and so, I strongly suspect, is your career in Her Majesty's Royal Navy.'

Chapter 35

Saturday Afternoon – 4th October 2014

It seemed like, and probably had been, hours before Dan saw Roger Blackett push open the door to the drab squadron building and walk towards his car.

She was sitting in her car nearby, watching and waiting.

He must have spotted her as soon as she opened her door, immediately looking behind himself, back at the squadron building entrance and then up towards the darkened windows, as if instinctively checking that he wasn't being observed. Then, seeming to weigh it up, he reached into his pocket, pulled out a packet of cigarettes and walked slowly over to a small sheltered alcove between two buildings.

Dan also looked around before she hurried over and joined him.

'You can't be here, Danny,' he said, as soon as she was in earshot. 'I can't talk to you at the moment, you know that.'

She stopped once she was in the alcove and out of view. 'I'm not lying,' she said.

'I know you're no liar, Danny. I'm in no doubt of that. I

338

know John Granger's no liar either. But that won't count for shit at court martial; the evidence is all against you. They've twenty-odd statements about you from *Tenacity* and not one reads well.'

'I was alone, Roger. My word against all of theirs.'

'You chose to be that way, Dan—'

'They wouldn't let John on board,' she cut in, her voice rising.

Blackett shook his head. 'Danny, you chose it a long while ago. I told you to get help the night that you were . . .' He paused and then shook his head, seeming not to know what word to use to describe the night Dan was attacked and flogged. 'I told you to tell people, to trust the folk around you. You should have gone home; I'd have taken you myself. You could have told Charlie and your dad, had people around you that loved you and cared for you. You chose not to and you've been alone ever since.'

'I had you.'

He snorted and nodded. 'And if I were a real friend, Danny, a better friend, I'd have *made* you go to the police that day. At the very least I'd have made you go home, take help. I should never have done what I did. Those pictures,' he paused, and Dan sensed he was hesitating, unsure of how far he would go, 'those pictures weren't supposed to be for evidence. God, I don't know what they were for. All they've been are anchors to the past, keeping you back there, stopping you from moving on from it. That's why I paired you with John. To remind you what it was like before that night, to have someone on your team; John would have backed you then and I knew he'd still back you now.'

Dan bowed her head and looked at the ground.

'I need to go, Danny.' Blackett dropped his cigarette and stubbed it out.

'There's something there, Roger. I know there is. If I could get down to check out the machinery space, No.2 AMS, then I know I could find something.'

He turned and looked at her. 'It's done. It's checked. We had a team down there and there was nothing. Some old papers, some books and a half empty safe.'

He watched her, an almost pitying look on his face.

Dan thought quickly, knowing she must have looked desperate.

The Old Man had said to her that the boat had been crawling with people for weeks. If she was right, then whatever was on there that Ben wanted to show her, must still be on board now.

She licked her lips, thinking, aware that Roger's face was changing from pity to impatience.

'I need one thing, Roger,' she said, reaching out and touching his arm to stop him from turning away. 'Just one thing and I'll go home; I'll talk to people and help in any way I can, I promise. I just need Ryan Taylor's home address. That's all I need. Please, Roger?'

Blackett shook his head and placed his hand on hers, slowly removing it from his arm, and walked back to his car.

Chapter 36

Saturday Evening – 4th October 2014

She'd already found Ryan Taylor's address when a text came through from an unrecognised number, gifting it to her. It had to have been from Roger, late, but receiving it made her feel good anyway, like he was still on her side, as much as he was able. She saw another missed call from Felicity and mentally promised she would return it later, then typed the postcode and house number into her satnav and followed the commands towards the Waterfront.

The destination, a long, narrow street, was deserted. It was gone eleven o'clock and there wasn't a single gap in the rows of parked cars that ran the length of the road. Everyone who lived here, it seemed, was home and tucked up inside with their loved ones.

Finding a small parking space two or three streets away, Dan lifted the collar of her thin jacket against the wind and hunched forward as she made her way between the interconnected pools of light cast by the streetlights. She was heading towards Ryan Taylor's flat, which she now knew he had shared with Ben Roach.

341

The door buzzer at the entrance to the block wasn't working, but neither was the lock, and the heavy door made a long, loud groaning sound as it rubbed against the concrete floor when Dan pushed it open just wide enough for her to slip inside.

A faint smell of urine hung in the air and she looked around and listened for a moment, sure that she was alone.

Ryan's flat was on the second floor.

There was no longer any number mounted on the wooden door, but the clean shadow where the number had once protected the paintwork showed that she had found it.

Dan knocked.

The landing was eerily silent around her, even for the late hour, and the lights were dim enough that she worried at a small torch attached to her key chain. She couldn't hear any sounds of life from this, or any other apartments. Not a radio or television. No people talking or laughing, or voices raised too loud with somebody shushing them back into a respectable silence. There was only the wind outside and, in the odd times when that stopped to draw breath, the long, lonely silence inside.

Dan knocked, three quick raps, and waited.

The door opened a few inches and she saw half of Ryan's face look suspiciously at her through the gap. A thick chain ran just below his eye level and prevented the door from opening any further.

'I ain't allowed to talk to you,' he said.

'And I'm not allowed to talk to you,' replied Dan. 'But I really think we should.'

He didn't move, making no attempt to remove the chain and open the door, or to shut it.

'I can help you, Ryan. I want to help you.'

A snuffle, maybe a half-laugh, sounded from behind the door and she thought she saw a tear roll down the part of his cheek that was visible. It touched the metal door-chain and then gathered there, growing fat before it finally dropped onto the dusty floor.

'The Old Man said you'd try this shit if you found me. He said you'd chat about takin' the heat and gettin' me off.'

'I will, Ryan. I promise I will.'

'He also said it'd be total bullshit, 'cos I'm so deep in it that no fucker can do anything. He said you're proper obsessed with getting what you think you want and you'll trample any poor bastard into the deck to get it.'

'And he can help you?' Dan leaned her head forward as she said it, raising an eyebrow and waiting.

'I ain't saying nothing else,' he said again, and slowly pushed the door closed.

Dan felt a rage take her. She lunged forward at the door, but it was already shut-tight. She kicked it, hard, and then regretted it as pain shot up through her toes. She limped onto one foot and then lowered herself to her knees with her eyes scrunched shut in pain. Turning, she sat down, leaning her back against the door. Desperation had brought her here, and it was a mistake.

There was a sound.

It was faint, but enough to make Dan cock her head back up, forget the pain in her foot, and listen intently.

He was there, on the other side of the door, sitting with his back against it in the same way she was.

The sound again.

Maybe his clothes rubbing against the door, or maybe a sniff, a stifled sob.

She turned quickly and knelt up. There was a letter box, white, cheap and plastic; she pulled it open.

'Ryan,' she said quietly. 'I know you're hurting. I know I used you to get that signal off the boat, but everything I told you was true. I really think they killed Ben, murdered him. The Old Man was right, Ryan, I can't stop and I won't stop, no matter what I have to do, until they pay for what they did, and they can't pay until I know why they did it. If that means getting myself into trouble, then so be it. It also meant getting you into trouble, but I really think Ben was worth it. Whether you speak to me or not, I promise I'll try to help you. I'll tell them the truth about what I did and I'll tell them you had no part in it. I'll tell them I intimidated and coerced you into sending that signal. But Ryan, the thing I promise the most, is that I will not stop, regardless of any consequence, until I find the person who murdered Ben. I'll find out why they did it, and I'll see them rotting in prison for it.'

She waited, hopeful, listening for any further sound.

There was none.

She lowered the letter box down carefully and turned around again, leaning back against the door.

Without warning she fell a few inches backward. Looking up she saw Ryan again.

He was looking down at her now, his eye below the level of the security chain.

'Who knows you're here?' he asked.

'No one.'

She waited.

Then she was thrust forward as the door was firmly closed.

Her head dropped, her hopes crushed until she heard the familiar sound of metal scraping metal as the chain was removed from its housing. She leaned forward just in time to prevent herself from rolling backward into Ryan's hallway as the door was fully opened.

He didn't wait for her, didn't offer to help her at all. He just opened the door and left it that way as he walked along a short corridor, deeper into his home.

Dan clambered to her feet, leaning her shoulder through

the door immediately, as if it might blow closed at any moment and rob her of her chance. So delighted was she to have made it this far, that she had closed the door behind her and walked halfway down the corridor before the contrast hit her.

The drab grey outside, the dirty stairwells and peeling door were as far as the dilapidation went.

Inside the apartment, she was walking on solid oak flooring with a tasteful rug running down the centre of the hallway. There were paintings on the wall, a modern style that Dan didn't recognise, but permanent light fixtures illuminated them all. Four large LED screens acted as changing photo frames, wired into the walls and slowly meandering through story after story of Ryan and Ben's time together.

As she stepped into the living room the opulence increased further.

Ryan was seated on a leather couch; the light brown surface was the type of expensive leather that only looks better with age and use. The television and sound system were the centrepieces of the room, the television itself taking up what seemed like an entire wall.

Music was playing quietly from a large speaker in the corner.

'Oh, Ryan,' she said, turning to the young man on the couch.

He was seated on the edge of it, his knees together and his head resting in his hands. He didn't look up and his shoulders began to vibrate slowly as another tear made its way through his fingers and dropped onto his light-denim jeans.

'Ryan, you have to tell me how you paid for all this.'

He didn't move, didn't answer.

'Tell me the truth. I'll help you.'

He looked up, fresh tears on his face, but the look in his

eye was defiant, as though these were the very last tears that he had left and there was no more grief or pain that he could take.

'The truth?' he said. 'Tell the truth?'

'The truth, Ryan,' said Dan, nodding in a way she hoped was reassuring.

She moved across from the doorway to a single armchair in matching leather and perched on the edge of it, facing Ryan.

'The truth,' he paused. 'The truth is, I don't know.' He shrugged, turning his palms upwards as if offering her all that he had. 'Ben paid, he always did.'

'You must have questioned it, Ryan. Some part of you must have known that he couldn't be paying for this out of his wages. Some armed forces guys at Ben's grade are drawing income support. There's no way he was paying for this from his salary.'

Ryan nodded; he knew.

'Does he have a lot of debt?'

'He did. But it all got cleared off a while back.'

Dan looked around the room. She shook her head, she couldn't help herself.

'When did he come into the money?' she asked, already knowing the answer.

Ryan just nodded at her; he knew that she knew.

'The Old Man, he got Ben drafted to *Tenacity*, right?' asked Dan.

Ryan nodded again.

'And that was when Ben's debt cleared up and the spending started?'

Ryan nodded.

'And Ben never said a word to you about it? Nothing, not pillow talk or a drunken slur, nothing?'

Ryan looked her square in the eye, unflinching. 'He never told me nothing and I didn't ask.'

Dan stood up and took a deep breath.

'Why did the Old Man draft Ben to *Tenacity*? Do you know?'

Ryan nodded. He looked as though he was pleased that he could answer the question. 'The Old Man gets what he wants. Everyone knows it. He wants someone, he gets them, he wants to do a run ashore in Amsterdam, he gets it. That's why the lads love him, ain't it? *Tenacity*'s the luckiest boat in the flotilla.'

'But why Ben?'

Ryan stared at her; his cheeks seemed to flush. 'He always liked Ben.'

Dan shivered and wasn't sure why. Something in the way Ryan had said that made her uneasy, something in the way his eyes had become hardened and bright.

'What do you mean?'

He shrugged and looked away. He seemed agitated, like he didn't want to talk about this any more. 'They met on the boxing team.'

'Right,' said Dan, a little too enthusiastically.

Ryan looked at her and frowned.

'Sorry,' she said quickly. 'I still can't see the Old Man as a boxer.'

Ryan nodded and smiled. 'Yeah, he's piled on the pounds, right, but Ben said back in the day the Old Man was a proper, serious fighter; amateur international at light-welter.' He paused and Dan could see his face redden again. 'They was friends when the Old Man was the officer in charge of the navy boxing team, before he got his third ring.'

'That was years ago,' said Dan. 'How old was Ben?'

'Sixteen,' said Ryan. 'He joined the team straight from basic, he was handy as fuck.'

'Sixteen?'

'Yeah, he was a minor, so him and the Old Man spent a lot of time together.'

Dan was pausing now, thinking carefully about how to ask the question. She knew she needed to ask, but was unsure as to how he would deal with it.

'Ryan,' she began.

'I don't know,' he said.

'Don't know what?' asked Dan.

'I might sound thick, but I'm not. You want to know if the Old Man was fucking Ben and I don't know.'

His tone was changed, angry now, and the fact that he was hurting when he talked about this answered Dan's question.

'OK,' she said, adding no more.

'There's a load of them boxers on *Tenacity*,' Ryan said, seeming to forget his previous upset. 'Known each other for years. Ben used to say, right, if *Tenacity* put a team out, and they was all at their best, you know, in their primes, they could beat all the rest of the armed forces' boxing teams put together.'

Dan wasn't listening properly. Her mind was churning as she thought about Ben and the Old Man: a pair? Maybe. She thought about what might have been in No.2 AMS and then she thought about the Chief Stoker threatening Ben. Dan saw Aaron's face when she had spotted the chief back aft, before the exercise, down in the engine room lower levels, looking around where Aaron thought he didn't need to be, where Ben would have gone to act as the casualty for the exercise.

'Ryan, how well do you know the engine rooms?'

'All right, I suppose. We all have to learn the whole boat to get our dolphins.'

'When you look down from the lower level ladder and then out to your left as far as it goes, there's a little space . . .'

'Dog kennels,' he said. 'Yeah?'

'What's in there?' she asked.

He shrugged. 'Some kit, dosing pumps for the boilers, stores, an old safe and some other stuff. Crap we don't have anywhere else to put, really.'

'Who could access that safe? Could the Old Man access it?'

'Old Man can access anything he likes though, the whole boat's his. I guess the Coxswain could give access to anyone too, but that safe back there, I think that's one of the Chief Stoker's safes.'

Dan was silent for a long time, thinking about Ben Roach, the Chief Stoker and the Old Man, before she finally spoke. 'Ryan, I need you to get me back on board *Tenacity*, tonight.'

Chapter 37

Sunday Morning (Early Hours) – 5th October 2014

Dan's hands were shaking as she drove Ryan's car towards the dockyard gate. There was no traffic, but she still felt as though it was taking too long.

'Have you called anyone?' asked Ryan, from the seat beside her. He looked pointedly at her phone clutched in her hand as she drove.

Dan put the phone down in the centre console. 'Not yet,' she said quietly. 'I doubt anyone would come anyway, except maybe to arrest us.' She saw Ryan's shoulders slump. 'Me, Ryan, I really mean me. You'll be fine, I promise.'

He snorted and shook his head. 'If I'm in the shit now, how deep d'you think I'll be in it after I've robbed the combo for a safe?'

'Are you sure they'll let you on at all?' she asked, trying not to dwell on the possible answers to Ryan's question.

He nodded. 'The trots'll have been briefed about me at the boat, but at this time there'll be no one up to escort me, and they know I got kit on there to get. They'll let me on.'

Dan faced the road and drove on towards the dockyard skyline, the glow of lights from the ships and services silhouetting the cranes and buildings against the night-time backdrop.

She approached the gate slowly, dipping her main beam to avoid irritating the guards and drawing attention to herself. She looked ahead, her eyes grainy and sore from lack of sleep, and prayed that on a cold night like this the guards would only carry out the briefest of inspections.

She recognised his silhouette immediately, the guard who had stopped her the previous morning.

He was wrapped up in a warm coat, a black scarf around his neck, and was pacing in the wind, his hands clasped behind his back.

'What kinda dickhead walks that way?' said Ryan, his voice sounding like it might break with nerves.

Dan brought the car to a halt and held her ID up to the window.

He walked over slowly, leaned down and looked at their cards and then at them.

Dan looked down at the wheel, not sure if he had bothered to look her in the face the last time, certain she wouldn't give him the chance now.

He paused and then stood up and waved them through.

Dan exhaled as she turned the main beam back on and headed down towards *Tenacity*.

Submarines are manned by a duty watch at all times, twenty-four hours a day and three hundred and sixty-five days a year. Tonight, though, there was no one around on the jetty, as the security surrounding *Tenacity* was finally relaxed and the investigation wound up.

Dan still felt herself glance nervously up at the squadron building, checking that all the lights were out as they passed.

'Park in there,' said Ryan, pointing.

She pulled into a parking spot next to a Portakabin that sat just outside the perimeter of the exclusion zone. It was the temporary galley, where the duty submariners would come to eat when their galley on board was down for maintenance.

'So what's your plan?' she asked, turning towards Ryan. 'Are you sure you can get me on board?'

He almost smiled.

'First, I gotta go see who's on trot. Once I get them to let me go inside, I'll go get the combo and bring it here. After, I'll go back again and distract the trots and you're on your own.'

Dan knew the route she would take to get into the engine rooms. She had used the aft gangway the first time she had visited *Tenacity*: as had Walker, on the last time that he did.

'You sure you want into that safe? I bet it ain't even used; it's a pain in the tits to get in there, and if we're caught . . .'

'I'm sure,' Dan replied.

'OK,' he said, resigned. 'I'll be back in a while, wait here.'

He climbed out of the car and disappeared into the night.

The while seemed like an eternity as Dan sat alone and watched the dockyard around her. Her eyes were desperate to close, the past days seeming devoid of sleep, but the adrenaline of what she was doing, was about to do, was enough to keep her alert.

A security wagon trundled past, its lights causing her to jump as they suddenly illuminated the car from behind, but the driver and his passenger didn't even look at Dan as they drove past.

From where she was parked, she couldn't see the submarine's casing and so had no idea at all where Ryan had gone. She fingered her phone again, touching the key so that the screen lit up, and cycled between missed calls from Felicity and a single word text message from John, *'sorry'*. She read it again and waited.

Ryan was back suddenly, his hand grasping for the door and pulling it open.

Dan started, quickly putting her phone back down and turning to look at him. He smiled, seemed more relaxed.

'All OK?' she asked.

'Yeah.' He handed over a sheet of paper. 'Combo for the safe.'

Dan took it and read the numbers. 'And there are no other safes back there?'

'Well, yeah, there's loads, but not down where you're going.'

'OK, so I just sneak across the aft gangway, right?'

'Yeah. The engine room hatch is open with some services running through it. Wait a minute, 'til the trots change over. There'll be more of 'em there, but they'll be chatting and stuff. I'll go talk to 'em, you shoot over onto the casing. The Two Fatties are on watch in the engine rooms.'

Dan raised her eyebrows, even though she knew he couldn't have seen it, and turned her palms upwards in a shrug.

Ryan caught the second gesture.

'Two of the afties, both fat, both lazy, too much time scoffing middle watch spuds. They do this watch 'cos they get to do nothing but sit and fill their fat faces with biscuits and pizza. So you should get down to the lower level no bother.'

'OK,' she said, feeling anything but.

She looked at the clock; they had a few minutes left before she would need to go. She picked up her phone again and looked at the screen.

'No signal down there,' said Ryan.

'Yeah, I know. No one can hear you scream, eh?' she said, with a very nervous smile. 'Ryan, if anything goes wrong, would you call this number?' She showed him John Granger's number. 'Call him and tell him what's going on, please. He'll know what to do.'

'We didn't think you were the sort to call for help?' said Ryan.

'We?'

Ryan smiled. 'Me and Ben.'

He looked sad, as though the mention of Ben's name had brought back all the troubles that being focused on this task had removed. 'We talked about you sometimes. He liked you, you know. I think he'd have helped you.'

Dan smiled. 'I hope so. We'll get these guys; I swear it. I just need to confirm something.'

'Well, now's the time,' said Ryan, pointing at the clock. He took the phone and looked at the number. 'I'll call if it all goes to shit.'

'Thank you.'

She stepped out of the car and watched as Ryan got out of the passenger door and dropped the phone into his pocket.

Ryan went first and Dan followed him past the exclusion zone monitor's box, the monitor's boots the only thing she could see as she crouched below the level of the window.

'He's kipping anyway,' whispered Ryan. 'Go.'

Dan peeled off to her right as Ryan continued towards the main gangway.

On the casing she could see a small cluster of sailors talking among themselves.

She darted across to a large piece of equipment and crouched behind it. It wasn't running and although Dan had no idea what it was, she knew that she would have welcomed the continuous hum of a motor as she looked at the six feet of open space ahead of her. Beyond that followed the twenty feet of bridge-like gangway that would leave her further exposed as she stepped onto the black casing, aft of the submarine's conning tower.

There were lights all around, and their beams seemed only to accentuate the darkness that they pierced.

Glancing across, she saw Ryan step onto the forward casing and call out to the other submariners.

They turned as one and their greetings were almost audible above the freezing wind.

It was now; never was simply not an option.

She crouched low and scuttled across to the gangway. She'd forgotten about the large tarpaulins that ran down either side of it, proudly displaying the submarine's name and crest. A spark of relief ignited inside her and she kept low, hidden by the side screens. In seconds, she stepped down onto the aft casing, stumbling as she miscalculated the height of the drop.

The submarine groaned and she heard the roller, which allowed the gangway to move across the casing as the tide ebbed and flowed, grind against the metal surface.

She could still hear the men talking, but the dark shape of the conning tower blocked them from her view. To her immediate right rose a soft glow of light and she was able to see several heavy-duty black hoses running towards it, and down into the engine room hatch. She followed them and then lay down on her belly, dropping her head slowly into the hatch as the sea lapped like oil against *Tenacity*'s hull. The rim was so deep that she wasn't able to see a thing and she listened intently instead. The sound of the waves and the gangway groaning with the subtle movements of the water all seemed to grow louder. It was as though the submarine and the elements were working together to prevent any confidence of a safe and undetected descent.

'Do it, Danny,' she whispered to herself under her breath.

In a single movement, and trying to ooze confidence, she stood up and quickly climbed down the ladder onto the aft platform, the very spot where she had watched Ben Roach draw his final breath. Her hand went to her pocket, ready to pull out her warrant card and act in a superior manner the second she was challenged. The Milgram experiment was running through her mind, obedience in the face of perceived authority, and that was all her authority would be now: perceived. She clutched her card as she landed gently on the deck plates.

There was no one there.

Glancing through the large, watertight bulkhead door she could see the ankles and black pusser's socks of one of the watchkeepers resting on a seat.

She listened. The engine room was never completely quiet or free from the hum of some machinery and she finally heard a voice from the manoeuvring room and then, after a pause, the reply. They were both in there.

She turned quickly to her left and looked down the short ladder onto the starting platform, the same entranceway that she had seen Ben's suffocating body being dragged up while she watched, helpless. She took the short ladder and turned back on herself down onto the second level. As she rounded and descended again, she could see the long drop down into the engine room lower level, the lights dim, the shadows weak, the spectre of Walker's lifeless body flirting with her imagination. The near vertical ladder disappeared fifteen feet into the depths of the engine rooms, the drop that Walker would have faced before his end. She took a deep breath, faced the ladder and began to descend.

It seemed to take a long time, her forearms and hands tight by the time she had descended all the way. The men, used to these ladders, flew up and down them without a thought, but looking up Dan couldn't help feeling pleased she'd made it down at all.

She was facing aft, towards the back of *Tenacity*, and needed to go to the port side 'dog kennel', a storage area that was outboard on the left side of the submarine.

Ryan had scoffed at the idea of drawing her a map. It was too simple, he had said. 'Down the ladder, turn towards port and you can't miss it.'

'Come on, Dan, basic stuff,' she whispered, her throat dry and her stomach churning. She turned so that she was facing forward, towards the bow of the boat. Then she turned left and headed along the walkway past the equipment. When she could go no further, she looked down to her left and instantly recognised why this crawl space would be called the dog kennel.

Her knees felt sore against the metal deck-plates as she knelt down to look inside. It was dark and the lights around her failed to penetrate the space far enough for her to see the back bulkhead. She hesitated for a few moments before drawing out her small torch, gritting her teeth and crawling in. The safe, long, thin and antiquated, was halfway into the space; its chunky black dial looked worn and loose.

Dan pulled the paper that Ryan had given her out of her pocket, rested it on the floor, and began to turn the dial and input the combination to open the safe. Five turns clockwise to clear it, stopping at twenty-six, then four turns back anti-clockwise to number six, then three turns clockwise to the number five, and finally two turns to zero. When she had done that, she turned the dial sharply to the right and pulled. Nothing.

'Shit,' she whispered, instantly wondering if Ryan had given her the wrong numbers.

She took a deep breath and spun the dial five times again.

It opened on her third attempt and she smiled. She pulled

the door open, and then lifted the whole door off as it easily disengaged from its slot hinges. She placed it down beside her and looked inside.

'Holy shit,' she said.

The safe was probably a metre long and maybe half that in depth and height. Stacked in there, taking up almost ninety per cent of the space alongside some thick technical reference books and a short coil of EBS hose, were neatly stacked bricks, each wrapped in brown paper.

Dan had hoped to find some pictures, maybe a trophy or anything else that would link Ben Roach, the Old Man or the Chief Stoker to Walker's suicide, Cheryl Walker's assault and murder, or any crime at all. As she looked at the bricks now, she felt breathless. Leaning in, she pulled one out and ripped the brown paper. The brilliant white powder packed tight into the polythene bag seemed to cast off its own light in the gloom.

She had found a motive for murder.

Chapter 38

Sunday Morning (Early Hours) – 5th October 2014

'You'll be wanting to come out of there please, ma'am.'

Dan spun towards the voice, startled. She was hunched forward in the cramped confines and lost her balance, over correcting and falling onto her rump as she looked up.

The Coxswain was squatting down at the entrance to the dog kennel. He smiled at her, his arms folded across his chest.

Dan looked at him, then back to the open safe and the packages of drugs now in plain sight.

'The Special Investigation Branch are on their way. You're done, Jago,' she said, hearing the waver in her own voice.

She watched him smile, tried to read his friendly face and calm manner.

He must have watched her expression change and laughed, actually laughed out loud at her. 'I don't think anyone's coming, Dan, can I be calling you that now? I think it's Danny for your close friends, isn't it? Well, we did a lot of checking on you before you came here, Danny, and we're thinking you don't know how to be asking for help. So I'm going to be feeling pretty confident that no one's on their way. I bet no one even knows you're here. Hell, Johnny-boy Granger was telling me that charging on into places all on your own is something of a trait of yours.'

Dan stared at him, refusing to break eye contact.

He stepped forward and offered her his hand.

'Come on,' he said, as though he were talking to a small child. 'Let's be having you out of there.'

Dan jerked away, shuffling on her bum further into the dead end of the dog kennel and further away from him. She dropped her torch, instinctively scrabbling to find it again. The sound of it rattling off metal as it dropped down into the bilge below mimicked her diminishing hopes as she shuffled backwards further into the dark.

'Don't make this hard, Danny. You'll only go making me hard,' he said, smiling. 'You didn't get to feel me hard on our date, only my fingers. But you might not remember that.'

Dan's stomach tightened and she felt a sense of nausea grow in her gut. 'Fuck off,' she said, looking around her. She had crawled back further into the space now and the long, reinforced safe door lay on the deck between her and the exit where the Coxswain, Jago Maddock, was waiting.

'People know I'm here. They're on their way. Don't make it any worse, Jago,' she shouted, hoping she might be heard.

He smiled again. He seemed to be in no hurry at all.

'Ryan Taylor has already called the dockyard police too,' she shouted. 'You're done. Now back away.'

He laughed again. 'Ryan, eh? We've been a bit worried about him. He's not been liking me much since the whole "Ben Roach" incident; you could say he hasn't been talking to me, feels like we should have dealt with Ben differently. But it turned out that our Ben was loving the money, didn't mind beating up women, but bottled it when you turned up the heat. He thought he might get caught and was thinking he could hang us out to dry, snitch on all of us, show you some of this stuff and hope to get off for being a grass.'

The Coxswain shook his head and managed to look genuinely disappointed.

'Now old Ryan, he's a really complicated one. That boy loves the money. He was pissed about Ben, all right, but he was even more pissed that we were going to have to sit on this lot for another patrol. I think he nearly wet himself when you gave him the opportunity to get us back into Devonport.'

Dan looked at him, looked at his relaxed face and patient smile as he spoke.

'You really thought you managed to trick a submarine communicator into sending a signal without the Old Man knowing?' said the Coxswain, looking incredulous and shaking his head. 'I'd been thinking better of you, truth be known. Anyway, Ryan's forward of the Tunnel now, waiting to come and help unload this little lot.'

He leaned forward and looked around as though he was going to confide in her. 'I think he's forgiven us for killing his precious Ben; seems love does have a price.'

'Cheryl Walker?' said Dan, looking around, frantically trying to think of a way out. 'What was the price for her life?'

He looked perplexed by that, so much so that Dan focused on him for a moment, watching as the cogs turned. 'She was alive and breathing when I left her,' he said after a moment, shrugging as if it were one of life's little mysteries that might never be solved.

'You mean you raped her and killed her, and when Ben found out, he wouldn't go along with it,' Dan shouted, hoping someone might hear her as she reached down into the bilge and tried to feel for her keys and torch. 'You'll go down for her murder. You and anyone who helped you.'

'I won't.' He shrugged, so calm that it seemed he really couldn't have cared less whether Dan believed him or not. 'Now out you come, now.'

He reached forward into the tunnel and Dan kicked out at his hand the instant it came near.

'You'll not be wanting to do that again, Danny. I'm not one who's known for my patience.'

He reached for her again, having to turn his body and extend his arm to full stretch to even come close without entering the dog kennel himself.

Dan waited a bit longer this time, until she could see his hand and forearm within range, then she kicked out hard, aiming her toecap at his forearm and hitting it clean.

'Fuck. You stupid bitch.'

She could see his face as he checked his arm, his teeth gritted and his breathing starting to get heavier.

'Now come out of there,' he said, his voice rising now and his lips curling into a snarl.

He leaned forward into the entrance and Dan shuffled back again; this time she hit the cold, hard surface that marked the end of the space.

'You're going to jail for murder,' she shouted.

The metal around her reverberated as her foot slipped and kicked against the side as she pushed herself backwards. The noise was loud and sustained and she kicked again, fumbling around in the dark for something else to use to hit against the hull that would make more noise.

She could see him starting to shake; his face looked different, contorted.

'Stop that and come out of there,' he shouted. 'Do as you're fucking told.'

Even in the dim light, she was sure she saw some spittle running down his chin as his rage seemed to grow with every shallow breath.

She grabbed at the safe door, wielding it in front of her, and smashed it against the side of the submarine. The clang of metal against metal rang out, carrying easily in the silent spaces. She lifted it again.

He leaned further forward and began to lunge quickly into the kennel, his arms outstretched towards her.

Dan panicked. Instinctively, she hefted the long safe door in front of her; using all her strength, she drove it towards him. From a seated position she couldn't get much power behind it, but her effort, combined with the speed at which he was approaching, meant that the metal-reinforced wood struck him hard in the face, right across the bridge of his nose.

He stopped, stunned for a second, and Dan, seizing her only chance, spun onto her knees and drove the door into him again.

This time she pushed herself up to a standing crouch and charged towards the Coxswain.

He fell backwards, clutching his face, and toppled onto the platform outside.

As soon as she was clear of the restrictive confines of the dog kennel, Dan raised the door again and brought it down with all her might onto the Coxswain's head. She was sure that it had landed solidly, but she did it again anyway. Then she threw the door down onto him and ran towards the long ladder that would take her back up towards the platform and out of the submarine.

She grasped the first rung of the ladder and began to climb. Her hands were shaking and she felt as though she had no strength left anywhere within her. Her feet missed the unfamiliar rungs, slipping off, but she began to climb as quickly as she was able.

Her hand had grasped the final rung when she heard him mount the ladder below her.

His heavy breathing was distorted by muttering and swearing that Dan couldn't fully make out and his feet rattled on the rungs in quick succession as he climbed up behind her.

Dan knew, before it had happened, that he was on her, his hand reaching for her ankle.

An infusion of adrenaline burst into her as she gripped tight to a single rung with both hands and pushed her feet off the ladder below her. Her body dropped to arm's length and she kicked out hard in all directions, flailing her legs as though she were drowning and was fighting to keep afloat.

He couldn't have expected her to drop back towards him with such a violent response and one of her boots caught him cleanly in the face, forcing him to release her ankle.

Scrambling to get her feet back on the rungs, she hauled herself up. The adrenaline masked the pain as she scraped and banged herself against the metal surface of the submarine deck.

She didn't look back. As soon as she felt the hard corrugated metal floor, she was up and running.

But the Coxswain was there too; he had climbed the ladder and moved expertly around, cutting her off by another route that Dan couldn't see.

He was there now, standing across the walkway, blocking her approach to the next level.

She would have to pass him, or go near to him, to get to the aft escape platform, the place she needed to get to for help and to get off *Tenacity*. Behind her, the bulk of the main engines and gearbox sat centrally, the squared walkway running all the way around them in an unbroken loop. She headed away from him and then stopped and waited, looking back.

He realised his dilemma, she could see it dawn on him.

He would have to chase her if he wanted to catch her, but if she made it around the walkway ahead of him, she could escape; they were like children playing a deadly game of tag, facing off around a huge kitchen table.

Dan thought for a second and then screamed.

That made the Coxswain smile. His face was already swelling and blood was dripping down from a deep cut above his nose. His mouth looked cavernous as he opened it to speak and Dan wondered if she had knocked out some teeth during the fight.

'Scream away,' he snarled, the words mumbled and thick, obviously difficult to enunciate through the swelling and blood. 'Seventy-six bulkhead's been shut down. No one'll be listening.'

Dan's eyes flitted past him and through the gaps in machinery towards the bulkhead; he was right. She was locked in here with him; her only possible exit was the ladder she'd entered by.

From behind the Coxswain came a sound.

Someone was descending the ladder from the casing down onto the aft escape platform, the same one that Dan had used. She knew if it was Ryan Taylor, then she was done for. They'd simply cover both escape paths and have her.

From where she stood, she could see the legs and then the body, and finally the shoulders and head of someone descending.

Dan shouted again. 'Help me!'

The Coxswain spun around and together they saw Aaron Coles as he turned, his mouth dropping open as he saw the two of them. His eyes were wide as he took a few paces towards the platform, taking in Dan and the Coxswain, his expression one of complete confusion.

'What the fuck?' he said, looking around at them both.

'Aaron,' she shouted. 'Stay away from him.'

Aaron looked at her, his face still a mask of shock and horror.

'Jesus,' he said slowly, looking at the Coxswain. 'What the fuck has she done to your face?'

In that instant Dan knew how wrong she'd been, how far from the truth her intuition had led her. She felt like she lacked the strength to even stand, and she sank slowly onto the deck. The hard metal met her knees and hands in turn, and she flinched as she felt her ribs begin to ache. Her hands were scraped and bruised from running through this colander-like environment and she became aware of other pains too. One hand was bleeding from a cut between her fingers where the skin had ripped a good few centimetres deep without her even noticing. She looked up at the two men and saw the shapes and colours that made up the picture slowly move into focus. This wasn't the work of a pair, any pair – moving the quantity of drugs that she had seen in the lower levels required more than two. She had been so concerned at seeing another pairing, at seeing another Hamilton, that she'd failed to see what was in front of her. The words Ryan had said to her the night before came back slowly, 'There's a load of them boxers on *Tenacity*. Known each other for years.' And she saw the pictures from Walker's house, the boxing trophies and awards; the ones in the Old Man's cabin, the faces of the boxing team younger but recognisable; the ones mounted in the hallway at Ben and Ryan's house. Everywhere she looked they were there, the faces of a group within the group.

'You get Ryan?' she heard the Coxswain ask, his speech still distorted.

'Yeah, little bastard served his purpose,' said Aaron. 'Sneaking her in here wasn't his worst idea. We'll sort him out later.'

'He know what's going to happen?'

'Nah, he's happy.'

The Coxswain nodded. 'Can you get her?' He pointed over towards Dan. 'I'm in a bad way.'

He touched his nose and then brought his hand down, covered in fresh blood. 'I'm going to pull her apart with fucking pliers when we get there.'

Aaron looked over towards Dan and nodded, almost sighing. 'Yeah, I'll get her.'

He started towards her, the Coxswain behind him, leaning over now, using the top of the engine room ladder to steady himself.

'Come on, Dan,' Aaron said.

He spoke as though he was a buddy, helping an old friend to her feet after a long day-hike somewhere pleasant.

Dan watched him and shook her head. She couldn't even ask 'Why?' There was no answer that would work for her.

He offered to help her to her feet.

'You know, you're a tough nut to crack, Dan,' he said, reaching down when she didn't accept his hand and pulling her to her feet by the scruff of her jacket. 'I lost a few hundred quid on Bag the Gremlin because you wouldn't spread your legs for me.'

She looked up at him, tall and handsome, chatting to her as though they were discussing some loose change that they had lost on a good night out together. She slumped; too exhausted to fight when the odds seemed insurmountable.

'How we going to get her out of here?' asked the Coxswain, still gently dabbing at his face.

Aaron looked down at her and pursed his lips. 'I guess we're going to have to walk her out.'

He leaned down towards Dan, his lips close to her ear.

'Can you be quiet? Or will I have to cut your fucking tongue out?' he asked. 'I'm being very serious, Dan.'

'I think we should. She'll only want to be starting shouting when we get up top, and my face is going to be needing some explaining too; we need her to be silent,' said the Coxswain.

'Can you be silent, Dan?' asked Aaron. 'Is that something you can do?'

Dan ignored him, looking away.

She didn't see the punches coming as Aaron threw two powerful shots into the left side of her mid-section, expertly aimed from the much bigger man.

Dan felt as though she'd been cut in half, her feet actually clearing the floor before she dropped straight to her knees and then to her stomach on the metal deck. She was coughing and wheezing, struggling again to get air in or out of her lungs.

'You know the difference between Hamilton and me?' asked Aaron. 'See, if he'd beat the shit out of you before he did the talking, then he'd be free and you'd be in the ground somewhere. Not a mistake I'll be making.'

He reached down and used her jacket to turn Dan over onto her back. He drew back his hand to punch her in the face, when the Coxswain, Jago Maddock, stepped forward.

'Let me,' he said. 'Fuck knows I'm deserving of it.'

Aaron shrugged and stepped aside.

'I'll start bringing up the stuff, then; you can ensure our lovely Danielle is consciously compliant before we leave.' He looked at Jago until he was sure that the Coxswain was paying attention. 'Remember, she has to walk.'

The Coxswain nodded and turned back to Dan as Aaron started to walk away, moving down towards the safe in the engine rooms below.

The Coxswain raised his hand.

Dan saw Aaron look back at her, smile and wave as though they were neighbours passing on the way to their cars, and then his head dropped out of sight as he took the ladder down into the engine rooms.

'I'll walk,' said Dan, still gasping for breath, the pain in her side so intense that she couldn't move her arm away from it. 'You don't need to do it, I'll walk.'

The Coxswain paused, seemed to think for a moment, and then punched her anyway.

In the stars and numbness that followed, Dan wondered whether she was conscious or unconscious. She remembered lying in the woods on a hill near Portsmouth. She'd been beaten then too, but she'd survived. She thought about her sabbatical year, alone, running away from those that loved her as she clung on to the memories given to her by someone who'd hated her.

In her crappy cabin in Devonport Wardroom, only a few hundred metres from where she was now, she'd had the files showing what these men had done to Cheryl Walker, had done to Cheryl for money. Two children would now live with their grandparents, would never feel love from their mum and dad again, for money.

As the Coxswain raised his hand again, Dan thought of her dad, Taz Lewis, and imagined the look on his face if he saw her lying here now, defeated and beaten. She thought about the letter from him, still unopened on the desk in her cabin, and about the year she'd been without him, the very year she needed him the most.

'Jago,' Dan said. 'Wait, Jago. I'll tell you what Ryan told me, what he'll tell the police when they get him. Just don't hit me again.'

The Coxswain paused.

Dan was watching him out of one eye, the other starting to swell closed. She was sure that her depth perception would be way off as she watched him lean forward.

'I'm listening,' he said, his voice thick.

Dan waited and watched, gathering her breath to speak, knowing she had to have one last burst of fight inside her.

As his face came down towards her, within arm's length, she reached out, the pain excruciating on her left side, and grabbed at his shirt with both hands.

He over-balanced for a second, leaning further down, and Dan smashed her forehead onto the bridge of his already broken nose as hard as she was able to.

He grunted and sagged down further towards her, and Dan butted him again, hearing a sickening thud, crack and squelch as she inflicted more damage onto his face.

She pulled him down as he slumped towards her, rolling him over, and letting go with one hand so that she could force her thumb into his eye.

He squealed, scrabbling to roll away from her, the sound sending a shiver down Dan's spine, piercing the adrenaline and focus of her attack.

Then, she was up and running, heading for the ladder that would take her out of the submarine.

Metallic echoes sounded around her, sounds that could only have been Aaron hurrying back up from the lower level.

The Coxswain was shouting, his words jumbled and indistinguishable.

Dan stumbled, her legs heavy, her vision blurred. She looked up towards the submarine's engine room hatch and the darkness outside. The black night was something that had for so long meant only fear to Dan and now meant life and freedom; she climbed one-handed, her left arm clutched by her side, not able to raise it above shoulder level, and pulled herself up onto the hard, cold casing.

The metal ladder shook behind her as boots rattled against the rungs.

Dan stood up, stumbling and trying to orientate herself.

The aft gangway was only a few paces away and she moved towards it, only looking up as she heard someone speak.

'What the fuck?'

She looked up and focused on the speaker.

A few feet away from her, the Chief Stoker was crossing the gangway towards her.

Dan screamed. A loud cry for help that she was sure would be heard, but she was taking no chances, had come this far and couldn't quit now. She turned away from the gangway and headed forward, towards the large conning tower that rose from the top of the submarine.

There was a narrow path around it, one she'd seen the Old Man skirt round the first time she had visited *Tenacity*.

Dan knew it could be done and knew there were sailors on the other side of it, that all of them couldn't possibly be involved.

She rushed forward, not glancing back as she was sure she was joined on the casing by one of her attackers from the engine room. She heard an exchange of words, men shouting, but she focused on moving forward.

The conning tower was there and she touched the slippery metal surface with her right hand, running it along the slick black paint. The path narrowed as she followed it out towards the sloping side of the submarine.

A handrail ran around it at waist height, thick and cold, and Dan found it and gripped it in her good hand. She began to use it to hold herself tight against the conning tower as she edged around it in the dark, the footway narrowing further as she went.

He was there, a shape pursuing her that had now moved within grabbing distance. It was Jago Maddock, his face awash with blood and twisted in rage as he lunged for her. His fingers grazed her shoulder, missing their grip but sending a message; this chase was almost over.

As she felt him move closer, Dan inhaled deeply and pushed off the conning tower, driving herself backwards into space and falling away from the sloping hull.

'Man overboard!' she shouted, with what was left of her energy.

She seemed to float in the air for a few moments, before the black, freezing water of the Hamoaze swallowed her up.

The cold hit her harder than the water, pushing the air out of her body and numbing every one of her muscles. She heard shouting, more voices, and briefly saw two men fighting on the casing, before they too disappeared, a loud splash telling Dan that they had now followed her in to the dark, cold water.

She heard the general alarm being sounded; three loud blasts from the klaxon.

'MAN OVERBOARD – MAN OVERBOARD. MAN OVERBOARD STARBOARD SIDE. DUTY WATCH, DUTY FIRST AIDER CLOSE UP.'

There was a commotion in the water near to her, voices in the heat of a fight, and the cold was spreading in to Dan's body and muscles, her head starting to lie lower in the water as she struggled to keep afloat.

The water was lapping around her mouth, nose and eyes now and her head was lolling back. Dan knew she needed to get her boots off, to shed some clothes, but the cold was everywhere, and in her mind, she started to wonder if it wouldn't be such a bad thing to go to sleep now, to relax and breathe deeply.

Another splash, smaller, controlled; someone had entered the water and was swimming towards her.

Dan looked, forcing her good eye to open when it so badly wanted to close, and saw the Chief Stoker swimming in her direction.

How could she fight against these odds? She felt no terror now, just resignation. Her dad could be proud that she'd done her best, given it her all, hadn't quit until she'd had absolutely nothing left; she had pushed forward, maintaining momentum, until there was nowhere else to go.

The Chief Stoker was talking to her, but as her face began to drop below the surface, she couldn't make out what he was saying.

Then he had her and Dan waited to be pushed under, to be held there until she could finally sleep.

'Crazy bitch,' she heard him say, her face breaking the surface. 'Fuck.'

He was dragging her up, holding her in the air.

'Fucking kick,' he shouted. 'Come on, kick your legs.'

Dan's eye opened and she felt herself being turned onto her back.

'Here!' he was shouting. 'Over here!'

Dan winced as a bright light shone on her.

Then another light caught her eye. A first glimpse of flashing blue, the distinctive colour bouncing off every surface, penetrating the night. Then she felt her consciousness drain away.

Chapter 39

Friday Morning – 17th October 2014

'Still no sign of Ryan Taylor?' asked Dan.

She was standing in Roger Blackett's office looking out of the window. *Tenacity* was still alongside, visible through the other window off to her left, but now she was looking out along the main drag, watching John Granger walking along it with her father beside him. Dan couldn't help but notice how small John looked next to her dad's hulking frame, and John was a big man. She thought how if she were there too, she would be like the last of the Russian dolls, the little one with nothing else inside it that comes right at the end.

Her dad had driven down from Scotland as soon as Roger had called him, dressing quickly, grabbing his keys and leaving the house while he was still on the phone. He hadn't packed and, according to Roger, had phoned Dan's stepmother, Jean, who was still asleep in bed, to let her know he'd left the house and would be gone for a few days. Dan's sister, who'd also received a call after the fact, was unequivocal that he would pay for this upon his return; both women were angry that they weren't able to join him on the drive down south.

His arrival had caused a short, semi-kerfuffle in Dan's hospital room. He had met Roger, the two friends embracing, and then he'd met John, who'd stayed all through the previous night with Dan, even as she'd slept.

Felicity had ushered everyone else out of the room and for the first time in her life, Dan had seen tears in her dad's eyes as he'd looked down at her.

Dan thought she remembered saying 'please don't hug me; everything hurts' to him, but couldn't be sure she hadn't dreamt it.

Since then her dad had been with her constantly. He'd stayed at the hospital with her until she was discharged and had driven her home, opting to sleep on the sofa in her sitting room downstairs. In the last week he'd cooked dinner every night, painted three rooms, unpacked most of her belongings from their storage boxes and rebuilt the majority of her furniture. Next he was planning on laying new laminate flooring throughout the downstairs for her; he was driving her crazy.

Today he'd accompanied her into the base, handing her over to Roger like a delicate baton in a smothering relay race, and been persuaded to go for a walk around the dockyard with John while Dan dealt with some work.

'The big man testing your patience?' asked Blackett, ignoring her question about Ryan Taylor.

Dan smiled at him and it hurt. She could see out of both eyes now and although her face was still swollen, it was her ribs that caused her the most discomfort.

'He means well, Danny. I think he's just glad to have you back,' said Roger.

Dan nodded. 'I'm glad too.'

'He told me you never opened his letter?' Roger said, his eyebrows raised as though Dan had better have a good reason.

She watched him for a moment and then raised her eyebrows, mimicking him, and reminding Roger that, on some topics, she didn't have to answer to him. She waited for him to get down to business and answer her question, but he continued to wait.

'For goodness' sake,' she said, rolling her eyes. 'He's here now, we've spoken, I don't need to read it. Anyway, he said to me this morning that I should keep it and open it when he's gone. I'll do that.'

Roger seemed to accept her answer, relaxing and leaning back in his chair.

'No,' he said, returning to Dan's original question. 'No sign of Ryan Taylor, but he can't stay on the run for long. He's no money, or if he has it'll only be whatever cash he had, and the police are watching for him. I think we'll have him in custody before long.'

'They're going to walk, aren't they? Aaron Coles and Melvin Bradshaw?'

Blackett sat down behind his large desk and opened his drawer.

Dan knew he was looking at the flagon of expensive whisky that he kept there, but he must have decided against it.

'Dan, we haven't a single shred of evidence, aside from your word, that Aaron Coles was involved in this.'

'He broke two of my ribs.'

Blackett raised his hands in surrender. 'He says he didn't. He says he tried to save you from Jago Maddock, and the statement from the Chief Stoker – Ashley Campbell if you'll believe that name – states that he saw Coles trying to stop Maddock from getting you. He says he saw Coles fighting with the Coxswain to protect you.'

'It was dark,' said Dan. 'And then they both conveniently fell into the water, and Maddock drowned.'

'Again, Danny, Chief Campbell, who by the way almost certainly saved your life, says that he believes that Coles tried to save the Coxswain.'

'It was dark,' said Dan.

'It was,' agreed Blackett. 'And the Chief Stoker entered the water to drag you out; that must give his testimony some credibility.'

Dan walked across to the large leather chairs and slowly lowered herself into one.

'I don't deny what the Chief Stoker did for me then, but that doesn't undo his actions before that; it doesn't wipe the slate clean.'

'I agree. I agree completely,' said Blackett. 'And if you make a complaint against him for his previous actions, then there'll be an investigation and I'm sure that, on balance of probability, your complaint will be upheld. But using your same logic, what he did to you before shouldn't wipe away the fact that he put his life on the line to save yours when he didn't have to; the Hamoaze at night is no place to be swimming.'

Dan leaned back, silent for a moment, wondering whether Roger might spot her some of that whisky in his drawer, a drink she hated, but which might feel good now if it numbed some of her pain.

'You know the Chief Stoker's wife left him only a few days before you met him? Left him for another woman. Took the kids and is taking him to the cleaners; their house, his pension . . .'

'That doesn't excuse—'

'I know, Danny,' Blackett interrupted. 'I know it doesn't excuse his actions. But it is context. If your actions during the investigation had been looked at cold, without any context, then you could be facing criminal charges and discharge from the naval service; context isn't an excuse, but it always needs to be considered.'

Dan looked away. As was so often the case, Blackett was right.

'As for the other two, Aaron Coles and the Old Man, we've

been through everything, every detail of their lives, and there is nothing, not one single scrap of evidence, to support your accusations that they were involved in this. The drugs were recovered and there were no fingerprints or evidence on any of that packaging; they'd all been very careful.'

Roger pursed his lips apologetically.

'But other evidence shows that Jago Maddock, Ryan Taylor, Ben Roach and Stewart Walker were importing significant quantities of narcotic into the United Kingdom to fund their lifestyles. Things got out of hand.' Blackett looked out of the window. 'Money, power, love and revenge,' he said. 'I've never known a crime that wasn't connected with one of them.'

'There's more to this,' said Dan. 'More people involved.'

'Dan, we have nothing that even circumstantially links Aaron Coles or Melvin Bradshaw to any wrongdoing. Nor that other officer who was in your sights – McCrae, was it?'

'My word?'

'Your word against theirs, when your actions in the preceding weeks bring your word into doubt.'

Blackett wasn't agitated, but Dan could tell that he was getting fed up of going over this ground with her.

'People died, Roger. Cheryl Walker, who had no part in smuggling drugs, was killed over this.'

'And by your own hand, we know who did it. Searches at Ben Roach and Jago Maddock's homes uncovered evidence on clothing, blood and hair. They were there when Cheryl Walker was attacked. They killed her. We may never know which one actually did it, but we know one of them did. The length of air-hose that Cheryl Walker was beaten with was recovered, hidden beneath Maddock's mattress on board *Tenacity*.'

Dan shook her head.

'What? Danny, honestly, what? We know who killed Cheryl Walker and we know broadly why. You broke a drug smuggling ring that was using UK government assets to smuggle drugs into the country. How can you be unhappy with this? How can you still be shaking your head?'

Blackett's voice was rising, his frustration starting to grow. He looked into his drawer again, eyed up the whisky even as he was speaking.

'Just four sailors, all on their own, were able to get hold of that quantity and quality of narcotic?' Dan asked, not expecting or waiting for a reply. 'They were able to get it sold on and manage the huge sums of cash that would be involved in that type of transaction . . .'

Roger raised his hands; he didn't know any more than he'd told her the past dozen times.

'Danny, we don't know everything, we may never know. Maybe this one isn't a big conspiracy, maybe it's just exactly what it looks like. Every case isn't Hamilton.'

Dan was silent.

'Sorry,' said Roger. 'I didn't mean it that way.'

'And no one's interested in looking into it any further? No one's wondering—'

'Jesus, Danny, will you stop? We've looked. There's nothing to find, nothing. There's no conspiracy, no cover-up, no evidence. The civil police looked too, Branok Cornish and his team, and while he's no fan of yours, he's as straight as they come.'

She looked away, turning from him to look out of the window.

They sat in silence for what seemed like a long time, Dan looking out of the window, aware that Blackett was watching her.

The nuclear exclusion zone around *Tenacity* had made way again for a security zone, which had eventually been relaxed as evidence was gathered and the details of the incident became clear.

'So why did Aaron Coles attack the Coxswain? Explain that,' said Dan.

Blackett must have finally broken. He pulled open his drawer and lifted out his crystal whisky glass and flagon. He poured himself a long measure without offering any to Dan and then placed the bottle carefully back in its place. He raised the half-full glass. 'A willing foe and sea-room,' he toasted, swirling it, sniffing it, and taking a sip.

'Well?' prompted Dan.

'To protect you,' he finally answered.

'I didn't need protecting.'

'No? When I got to the hospital you looked as though you'd been doing just great,' said Blackett. 'I really wasn't sure when, or if, you'd wake up. That's why I called Taz.'

She ignored him.

'It still doesn't explain why Walker contacted me. Why *Tenacity* also asked for me by name. Why me, the only female investigator in the Special Investigation Branch.'

There was a knock at the door.

Blackett opened his drawer and carefully placed his quarter-full glass inside, sliding it carefully closed to prevent any possible spills. He stood, tucked in his shirt and wiped a hand around his mouth.

'Roger, look at *Tenacity*'s running, look how much power the Old Man had over the ship's programme and its crew. There had to be involvement at a level above the bloody Coxswain, there had to be involvement above the *Commanding Officer*, there's no other way this could happen.'

He turned and looked at her, his face stern. 'I went in to bat for you, Danny. You broke a big case, drug smuggling using nuclear submarines and a horrible murder, but you're still in the shit. You broke rules, showed a disregard for military and personal security, and you could easily have had your ass thrown out the service to face criminal charges. I arranged this and I saved your job, which, frankly, is all you have while you rebuild the shipwreck that is your life. So you do me a favour now and shut up while they're here.'

He'd rarely looked so angry and tense. Maybe once, a long time ago when she'd turned up on his doorstep in ripped clothing and covered in blood asking for his help. He was a friend and mentor, had looked out for her for years, and she accepted his message and stood up too.

Dan nodded once, gratitude almost on her lips as they looked at each other, then she turned away.

Another knock sounded at the door, this one louder than the last.

'Come,' Blackett shouted, and the door opened immediately.

Roger's assistant peered around it. 'Sir, Lieutenant Lewis, it's Captain David Harrow-Brown, part of the Joint-Chiefs Investigative and Intelligence at GCHQ?'

Dan nodded, returning the hawkish stare of the Captain as he entered the room before the assistant had finished speaking. She immediately felt cold and a shiver forced its way up her back and out across her shoulders. She couldn't hide or disguise it, and she was certain that her reaction brought a thin smile to the Captain's pallid face.

She didn't look at Aaron Coles and Melvin Bradshaw as they followed the Captain into the room.

Even without looking she could see that they were both smiling warmly as they shook hands with Blackett and took their seats, ignoring Dan entirely.

'I hope Lieutenant Lewis is recovering well?' said the Captain to Blackett.

'I'm over here, sir,' said Dan, unable to help herself. 'But I'm doing very well, thank you for asking.'

'I see this investigation has cost you none of your winning personality, Lieutenant Lewis,' said the Captain, still without looking at her.

The room was silent for a few moments.

Then the Captain spoke again. 'This investigation has been costly in many, many ways, for the Submarine Service, the Royal Navy and the armed forces as a whole,' he began. 'However, both the civil police and the Chief of the Defence Staff are content that the investigation is now complete and that those who are required to will answer properly for the part they played.'

Dan shifted in her seat. She finally felt able to glance over to where Aaron was sitting. To her surprise he was looking right at her, as was the Old Man; both were smiling, as though they'd been waiting for her.

The Captain continued. 'Elements of Lieutenant Lewis's complaint and allegations have been upheld, although her actions brought all of her assertions into question. As such, and henceforth, further Equality and Diversity training will now be routinely given to submariners as we move closer to females joining submarines in the coming year.'

Dan's jaw dropped open.

Aaron and Melvin Bradshaw smiled broadly and nodded agreement.

'After what happened, they'll receive *E and D* training?' said Dan, outrage clear in her voice.

The Captain stopped, but didn't turn towards Dan. He paused before addressing Blackett. 'Commander Blackett, have you not fully briefed Lieutenant Lewis on the precariousness of her position?'

Dan watched as Roger nodded, but said nothing.

'In that case, I'll continue. As you are all aware, Commander Bradshaw has resigned his command of HMS *Tenacity*, accepting full responsibility for what occurred under his command.' The Captain nodded towards the Old Man as if to ensure everyone knew whom it was they were talking about. 'Lieutenant Commander Aaron Coles has been commended for his part in attempting to apprehend Chief Petty Officer Jago Maddock and in rescuing Lieutenant Lewis—'

'What?' said Dan, eyes and mouth as wide as each other.

'He will be reassigned to HMS *Tenacity* at the earliest opportunity, with all of our thanks, I'm sure.' He turned to look at Dan this time, that thin-lipped half smile, half smirk, clear across his face.

Dan met his stare, refusing to back down even though the way he looked at her made her skin crawl. She fought back another shiver, this time keeping herself in check.

'Which brings me to Lieutenant Lewis,' he said, spitting her name as though it were a swear word he was being forced to repeat in church. 'She may maintain her position as an investigator in the Special Investigation Branch's Crimes Involving Loss of Life division, provided that she undergoes a full psychological assessment. No investigations are to be undertaken by her until such time as she is deemed fit for duty by the armed forces psychiatric team at Catterick.'

Dan turned towards Blackett, her eyes wide; he had not fully briefed her at all.

'Additionally, she will not be permitted to discuss or profit from any aspects of this investigation, nor to publish papers or reports with anyone not directly involved in it. She will sign a legal agreement to this effect. These are the terms on offer and they are only on offer for the next five minutes.'

He shuffled forward on his chair and reached a bony hand inside his briefcase, retrieving a folder from which he removed a sheet of paper then passed it to Blackett.

Blackett scanned it quickly and then passed it on to Dan with a pen from his desk.

She read it slowly, considered ripping it up and trying to force it down the Captain's throat, and then clicked the pen as though ready to sign.

'Quickly please, Lieutenant Lewis,' said the Captain. 'You've wasted more than enough of my valuable time already and I have a four-star briefing to deliver in just a few moments.'

Dan smiled her best fake smile and nodded. 'Sure, thank you,' she said. 'But I do still have more than four minutes of your allotted time remaining.'

The Captain drew in a deep breath, making no attempt to hide that his patience was growing thinner.

'I have an idea,' she said, turning slowly to look at the Captain and the two men behind him.

'You know, Lieutenant Lewis,' the Captain said slowly, over-pronouncing her name for effect. 'You have had time for ideas, now sign, or do not sign. I really do not care.'

'But this is a good idea,' she said. 'You'll want to hear it.'

She could feel the fury radiating from Roger Blackett, could almost hear telepathic messages from him as his eyes told her to stop talking and sign the agreement.

'See, my idea is this. I won't sign this, because it's illegal, unfair and immoral. But I will accept your terms of keeping my job and status within the Special Investigation Branch. In return, I won't write any papers that could be leaked, with horrible consequences, I'm sure, about this investigation and the misogynistic attitudes that have prevailed, not only during my treatment on board *Tenacity*, but afterwards and even now. I will also not write in my paper about how I don't believe for one second that four sailors alone managed to set up a complex supply chain, something that the Royal Navy is excellent at, to procure, transport and dispense significant quantities of high-quality, high-value narcotic into the United Kingdom. I won't pontificate about how far up the command chain this type of conspiracy would need to go, for the programme of a British nuclear asset to be altered in order to allow this business to operate effectively. I won't do any of those things.'

Dan paused and looked at the Captain.

Their eyes locked together for at least ten seconds, neither flinching, until Dan felt her fingers contract together and screw the piece of paper into a ball.

'So, in summary, you can shove this up your arse,' she said, enunciating every word slowly and carefully.

Then, without taking her eyes away from his, Dan tossed the balled paper at him and watched as it hit his waxy forehead, bouncing onto his lap and coming to rest at his feet, before she stood up, nodded at Roger Blackett, and walked out of the room.

John was leaning against the wall further along the corridor as she exited Roger's outer office. His arms were folded across his chest.

'How did it go?' he asked.

Dan shrugged. 'Hard to tell, really.' She smiled and it felt genuine enough. 'Where's my dad?'

'I got him a tour of HMS *Torbay*. She's back alongside for a few weeks. Buddy of mine's bringing him back up here when they're done. Shouldn't be long.'

'Coles is in there,' said Dan. 'Maybe my dad shouldn't come up here.'

John nodded and pulled out his mobile. 'I'll tell them to keep him down the boat. We can collect him from there. He's invited me to join you guys for dinner tonight.'

She looked at him. She'd known he would come that night when she'd texted him from Ryan Taylor's car. Known he would believe her. Known, or maybe suspected, that Ryan wouldn't make the call.

'I'd like to do that,' she said. 'But not tonight. Is that OK? I'm exhausted.'

He nodded. 'That's totally OK. That's why I mentioned it now.'

'I still don't get this,' said Dan, standing beside him and looking down towards Blackett's office. 'I still don't understand why everyone, independently, chose me.'

'I don't either,' he said, as though that might make Dan feel better. 'Maybe that lot'll come up with something?' He nodded to a procession of officers that was starting to gather outside Roger Blackett's outer office. 'Apparently the Chief of the Defence Staff is coming today, along with a whole host of other bigwigs: Second Sea Lord and more. This is getting scrutiny from the right people, Danny. Most of the authority figures in the Royal Navy will be in that conference room today.'

'Maybe they're all in on it?' joked Dan.

John laughed politely.

She turned to look at the officers who were beginning to arrive. She watched as Captain Harrow-Brown waited to greet them.

He stood at the door that led through Blackett's office to the conference room and reached out to shake hands with an officer that she didn't recognise.

Beside her John moved, suddenly standing up straight, posturing as he looked over her shoulder.

Dan saw Aaron Coles striding towards her, his wide frame now blocking her view.

'I'd like to speak with Lieutenant Lewis, please, Master at Arms,' Aaron asked, speaking to John as though he needed his permission.

'Well, I'm here,' said Dan.

'Alone,' added Aaron.

John eyed him, the menace obvious in his body language.

'It's fine, John, really,' said Dan. 'Could you wait for me, though, down by my car?'

He looked down at her and nodded. 'I'll just wait right there,' he said, pointing at a bench further along the corridor, but still in view.

Dan knew he was really speaking to Aaron, who shrugged as though he couldn't possibly care any less.

'What do you want?' Dan asked.

'I thought we might make peace?'

Dan reached into her pocket, pulled out a broken, luminous friendship bracelet and held it out, offering it to Aaron.

He looked down at it and smiled. 'My friendship bracelet,' he said. 'Thanks, I was in trouble for losing this.'

Dan just looked at him, weighing him up before she spoke. 'It must have fallen off your wrist and into my bag while you were choking me in the bomb-shop,' she said, as matter-of-factly as she was able. Her breathing was quickening and she cast an eye off to the side, turning so that she could see where John was sitting, watching. 'I assume it was Maddock that did the talking. You were just there for support.'

'Come on, Dan. Don't be sore,' he said, smiling. 'If I hadn't been there then things would have been much, much worse for you. Jago was out of control. To be honest, we were all a little worried about him and what he might do. We don't really like the attention that someone like that brings, but he served a purpose.'

Aaron stepped forward a pace and Dan, despite herself, retreated one.

'I just wanted to say, though, that I will answer a question for you, one I know's been bothering you,' he said, not trying to approach any further. 'Why you? Why did you get this case?'

Dan watched him closely.

'You were selected for this because we needed an investigation that would fail. We needed an investigator who was so damaged and discredited that they couldn't help but hit a brick wall everywhere they went. One that would have the credentials, such that the investigation couldn't later be called foul, but who simply couldn't succeed in the environment in which they were working.'

He stepped forward again.

This time Dan stood her ground.

'Of all the investigators available to us, you were the one, unique in your own way, that we felt certain couldn't succeed. Strangely, this was the very same reason that Walker contacted you. He knew that, as a woman, you were the only investigator in the SIB that couldn't possibly be part of our little club. He took a chance on you and it turned out he was right, didn't it? To an extent, I mean.'

'Couldn't be part of your brotherhood, you mean?' she asked.

He seemed to consider her words, a wry smile building on his lips. Then, emphatically, 'Yes, you were the one investigator who could never be part of the brotherhood, if you wish to call it that.'

He laughed.

'I'm telling you as a friend, Danny, you'd be doing the right thing to keep quiet and forget about this.'

Dan's mouth opened and closed, but no words came out.

'I tell you this, because I hope that having had this conversation, and with you knowing what happens to those who've tried to disrupt us, you'll be convinced not to pursue this any further.'

'And Whisky tried to disrupt you?' asked Dan. 'Didn't he? He killed himself on board *Tenacity* deliberately to bring me here.'

Aaron laughed. 'You think a lot of yourself; maybe you're right to,' he said.

He paused and seemed to think about whether to go any further.

'Whisky knew he had to die because he tried to leave and didn't heed the warnings until it was far too late, though it does seem his final act managed to attract you to *Tenacity*, doesn't it? But I don't think he stepped off that platform just for you. I think he stepped out into space with a rope tied tight around his neck, because we couldn't trust him any longer, and if he'd lived, he knows we'd have come for him next, and if he'd run, it would've been his kids after that. So he died for them, really, which is kind of romantic and beautiful when you think about it.'

'What?'

Aaron looked at her, his face suddenly serious. 'This is an honest, me to you, get-out-of-jail-free card, Danny. Now you know what you need to know to take this very seriously, and it's a special, one-time offer of a warning; there won't be another.'

He leaned in close to her and goose pimples chased each other up and down her spine.

'We'll be watching you, Dan Lewis.'

Dan raised her fingers into a pistol-like shape and fired at him. 'Gotcha,' she said.

Aaron laughed again.

'It's on you, Dan,' he said. 'It's all on you now.'

He turned to leave, then looked back. 'May I ask a question?' he said and waited.

'Sure.'

He held up the bracelet. 'Why didn't you submit this as evidence?'

Dan shrugged. 'It wouldn't have helped. I could have picked it up anywhere.'

He nodded. 'Of course.' He turned away again and began to walk back towards the conference room.

'Aaron,' Dan raised her voice so he could hear her.

He turned back.

'I'm coming after you,' she said.

Aaron Coles smiled and turned away. 'Sounds like I'll see you 'round then, Danny.'

TENACITY

J.S. LAW

Bonus Material

Reading Group Questions

How does Lieutenant Danielle Lewis's past case, which involved the killer Hamilton, affect her approach to the new case in *Tenacity*?

How does J. S. Law bring out the claustrophobic feeling of the submarine?

How does this claustrophobia affect Dan and the case?

J. S. Law has a background in the Navy – how is this shown in the detail of the novel?

Lieutenant Danielle Lewis finds herself in a heavily male dominated area: what challenges does this provide Dan? And how does she overcome them?

Patricia Cornwell said of Dan that she is 'fearless and doesn't quit in the faces of all odds'. What other characteristics make Dan an admirable protagonist?

The idea of healing is an important focus in this novel. To what extent, and through what methods, does Dan attempt to heal old wounds?

Is Dan a team player or a lone wolf in her investigation? And does this help or hinder her approach?

If you were to sum up Dan's character in three words, what would they be?

What are you looking forward to seeing more of in the next Lieutenant Danielle Lewis novel?

Q&A with J.S. Law

What inspired you to write *Tenacity*?

I was coming to the end of my service in the Royal Navy and I had previously written several novels, but after speaking to a literary agent, I realised that not everyone knew about submarines and the wider Navy and armed forces. This will seem obvious, I know, but it'd been my life for years and was commonplace to me, so understanding that I had a new and unusual setting for a story really got me thinking.

Then there was Dan Lewis, my lead; I started with what I didn't want – I didn't want a token female lead and I didn't want a female lead who was part ninja, kicking men's butts in 6-inch platform heels. I wanted a really smart, savvy, resourceful and intelligent woman, you know, like the women you actually meet in real life. I wanted her to have to fall back on her intellect and grit to get herself out of trouble, and I think I achieved that with Dan Lewis. After that, it was just a case of dropping her into a very hostile environment and seeing what happened.

Which authors or books influenced you?

I'm a big crime thriller reader, but there are some that probably helped me in specific areas. *American Psycho* by Bret Easton-Ellis, for instance, really instills a sense of detail and small things combine to form a big picture. I tried so hard to remember this in *Tenacity*, making sure the book wasn't *about* submarines – and it isn't! It's a straight up crime thriller, but it uses small details to build a credible environment in the reader's mind. Another would need to be *The Road* by Cormac McCarthy – the simplicity of language in that book is just phenomenal and the complicated situation and environment is expertly described using language anyone can understand and enjoy – again, I tried to utilize this in *Tenacity* to put over a fairly alien environment, without drowning people with techno-babble and I hope I achieved that and made *Tenacity* accessible to all.

What's the most challenging thing when writing your debut novel?

The uncertainty. I think there's always a point at around thirty-thousand words(ish) where every novel seems like utter rubbish; ill-conceived and ridiculous. When you're pushing through on your debut, it's just having the confidence that this novel is worth finishing, that it is relevant and interesting, that if the idea seemed good thirty thousand words ago, then it's probably still good now. The second hardest thing is getting your first editorial with a publishing professional. I mean, I didn't cry or anything...

And what was the best part of the process?

For me, it was plotting out the storyline. I love the part when the story could go in any direction and the characters could be anyone or do anything, and even when this plot is down, it isn't set in stone. When I started writing *Tenacity* it was actually very different, but I got halfway through and decided to change the storyline. I didn't start again though; I just carried on from around the fifty thousand-word mark and then went back and changed the first bit to match the second half afterwards. So as much as I don't always stick to it, I do love working out the plot.

Which novels have you been reading and what are you looking forward to?

There are so many great books around at the moment that it is really difficult to narrow this list down. So, in no order at all . . .

Eva Dolan is back with *After You Die* and her books always go to the top of my TBR pile! This will be the second in the Zigic & Ferreira series, focusing on a Peterborough Hate Crimes unit. It left me with goose pimples.

Clare Mackintosh hit the bestseller lists with *I Let You Go*, and with good reason too – that twist!! I'll say no more . . .

I really enjoyed *I Am Pilgrim* by Terry Hayes and I'd recommend it to anyone who likes their thrillers big.

Two others are *The Martian*, not my usual crime and thriller fayre, but I really loved it and one that I stumbled across called *A Pleasure and a Calling* by Phil Hogan. I don't remember how I came across that book, but by God it's good, and by good, I mean really, really creepy!!

For the future there are a few releases that I'm hanging out for:

Adam Hamdy releases *Pendulum* this year and I really, really want to read that. A twisting journey through a digital under-world, what's not to like?

I'll also be looking at Luca Veste's latest offering, *Blood Stream*, which is looking to be even better than his previous books, which really says something.

And Mason Cross is back with *The Samaritan*. *The Killing Season* was one of my top reads for 2015, so that's a must.

Finally, after the sad loss of William MacIlvanney, I'll be re-visiting the Laidlaw novels. If you haven't yet read those, then do.

And finally, can you sum up *Tenacity* in three words?

Pacey, Challenging and Tenacious (you saw that last one coming, right?)

Keep reading for an explosive extract from
the next spectacular novel featuring
Lieutenant Danielle Lewis

DEFIANCE

J.S. LAW

Available Autumn 2016

headline

Dan closed the door behind her and sat down on her bed.

The list of dates that Felicity had given her, the name of a dead woman marked against most of them, was hanging loosely between her fingers.

Her phone rang and she fumbled in her pocket to shut off the noise. She ignored the call and turned the phone to silent before tossing it behind her onto the bed.

She looked at the piece of paper again, examining the dates, before lowering herself onto the floor, turning slightly so that she could reach under the bed and pull out the lock box that she kept there.

It took her a moment to realise that her hands were now shaking. Memories of Hamilton jostled to the front of her mind. The image of the bodies she'd found in his garage, the snapshot that regularly visited her dreams, was now intensified by hindsight; her mind filling in the gaps and enhancing the detail, so that all that she knew of their injuries and the horror of their deaths was displayed in high definition: a perfectly presented study of torture and death.

Her breathing deepened and then quickened. She placed

a hand to her chest as she remembered fighting with him in that garage, remembered his eyes, his smile, the strength of his hand, the sound his blood made as it seeped across the floor and soaked into the dry concrete.

Dan looked away from the lock box, tipped her head back against the bed and blew out a long breath through rounded lips. She ran her hand through her hair, closed her eyes tight, and then pinched the bridge of her nose, trying to squeeze the memories away.

Then she remembered the car park, a year after Hamilton had been jailed for life. She remembered the men who'd been waiting there and their ruthless attack. As she did, the scars on her back, long since faded, seemed to burn, painful again. The agony only abating as she clenched her teeth and counted slowly to ten.

The hunt for Hamilton had been one of the longest and most uncertain manhunts in British history and Dan had ended it when she'd found three women stacked like firewood underneath a tarpaulin in the corner of Christopher Hamilton's garage, their bodies broken and their skin mottled.

But even though Hamilton was now locked away, there was so much that she still didn't know about him.

He'd been convicted of the murders of the three women, but was widely considered to be the most prolific, non-medical serial killer in British history. The number of victims reckoned to have suffered and died by Hamilton's hand, over his relentless thirty-year massacre, reached over one hundred, with some estimates at twice that. But what confounded police, and Dan, to this day was the absence of his victims' bodies.

Dan knew that everywhere Hamilton had ever lived, or spent any serious amount of time, had been searched, X-rayed and excavated, but no trace of the bodies of his victims had been found.

Theories raged that he carried them onboard naval warships and disposed of them at sea, but Dan knew that the risks involved with this undertaking were simply too high. She also knew that there were long periods when he wouldn't have had access to sea-going vessels, and so she had ruled this method out.

Dan had never come up with a satisfactory answer to this question. Where does a killer hide so many bodies so that they can never be found?

She'd assumed Hamilton would take this secret to hell with him, or that one day someone would discover a collection of bones whilst walking on a moor, and the mystery, or at least part of it, would be solved, the families gifted some modicum of peace and closure.

But what Felicity had just told Dan changed everything.

That some unknown person was now sending well preserved body parts to the police. That the body parts were arriving on the date of the victim's disappearance. That each of these victims was firmly believed to have been abducted and murdered by Christopher Hamilton. These things made Dan's head spin.

Dan rested her head in her hands and opened her eyes, now looking down at the lock box.

Could there have been a completely unconnected killer all along? A second killer working in parallel with Hamilton?

The idea seemed unlikely.

Flashing light caught Dan's eye, and she heard the noise of her phone vibrating. She ignored it at first, then reached out onto the bed, fumbling around until she found it.

The call was from Charlie again, her big sister, but Dan couldn't talk to her now.

She pulled the lock box towards her and set the combination to open it. She steeled herself for the first picture, the one she always kept on top, but she managed to set it aside without lingering on it; there was no time for self-flagellation now.

The other files and papers were there, including her notes and the laptop that she kept solely for her research into Hamilton's slow, relentless slaughter.

She reached for the computer and stopped. She didn't need it. She recognised all of the dates on the piece of paper and the names that would go with them too. She could have recited them from memory.

Felicity knew this.

Dan leaned back against her bed and looked at the picture of her family beside it

Felicity and the National Crime Agency didn't need help with theories or identification. Felicity would be in no doubt at all about the identity of these girls or the date they were abducted. Nor would she have any doubt that Hamilton was responsible for their disappearance.

No, Felicity needed something else, something that she hadn't been able to ask for, something that she'd needed to let Dan work round to herself. She wanted Dan to go and face him again. Felicity wanted Dan to go and speak with Hamilton.

THRILLINGLY GOOD BOOKS
FROM CRIMINALLY
GOOD WRITERS

CRIME FILES BRINGS YOU THE LATEST RELEASES FROM TOP CRIME AND THRILLER AUTHORS.

SIGN UP ONLINE FOR OUR MONTHLY NEWSLETTER AND BE THE FIRST TO KNOW ABOUT OUR COMPETITIONS, NEW BOOKS AND MORE.